Readers love the BJ Vinson Mysteries
by DON TRAVIS

The Zozobra Incident

"There are many likable secondary characters who play significant roles in the story. Combine that with the setting, beautifully detailed writing and a solid mystery makes this novel a must read for any mystery lover."

—Gay Book Reviews

The Bisti Business

"All the essential elements that made the first story so engrossing are there, with a fresh new mystery and more interesting characters."

—Michael Joseph Book Reviews

"BJ Vinson is one of my new favorite sleuths…"

—B. A. Brock Books

The City of Rocks

"Hands down, this is my favorite mystery series in a long time. Five stars!"

—The Novel Approach

By DON TRAVIS

BJ VINSON MYSTERIES
The Zozobra Incident
The Bisti Business
The City of Rocks
The Lovely Pines

Published by DSP PUBLICATIONS
www.dsppublications.com

THE
LOVELY
PINES

A BJ VINSON MYSTERY

DON TRAVIS

DSP PUBLICATIONS

Published by
DSP PUBLICATIONS

5032 Capital Circle SW, Suite 2, PMB# 279, Tallahassee, FL 32305-7886 USA
www.dsppublications.com

The Lovely Pines
© 2018 Don Travis.

Cover Art
© 2018 Maria Fanning.
Cover content is for illustrative purposes only and any person depicted on the cover is a model.

Trade Paperback ISBN: 978-1-64108-120-7
Digital ISBN: 978-1-64080-122-6
Library of Congress Control Number: 2017913247
Trade Paperback published August 2018
v. 1.0

Printed in the United States of America
∞
This paper meets the requirements of
ANSI/NISO Z39.48-1992 (Permanence of Paper).

To my late wife, Betty, and my sons, Clai and Grant.

Acknowledgments

MANY THANKS to members of my Wordwrights Writing Class.

THE
LOVELY
PINES

Prologue

A FIGURE watched from the edge of the forest as blustery night winds raced through undulating boughs to brush evergreens with feckless lovers' kisses and oppress the grove with ozone raised by a rainstorm to the west. Ground litter, heavy with fallen pine needles, trembled before gusts—as if the Earth itself were restless.

Advantaging a cloudbank obscuring the half moon, the intruder picked up a heavy duffel bag and breached a four-foot rock wall. The prowler crossed the broad lawn, pausing briefly before a brick-and-stone edifice to scan a white sign with spidery black letters by the light of a small electric fixture trembling in the breeze.

THE LOVELY PINES VINEYARD AND WINERY
Valle Plácido, New Mexico – Ariel Gonda, Vintner
Established in 1964 – Fine New Mexico Reds

Prompted by the rumble of distant thunder, the wraith made its cautious way to a large building at the rear of the stone house and removed a crowbar from the bag to pry a hasp from the heavy door. Unconcerned over triggering an alarm, the black shadow vanished into the depths of the deserted winery.

Chapter 1

Thursday, June 11, 2009, Albuquerque, New Mexico

I WAS reading an *Albuquerque Journal* article about the recent assassination of Dr. George Tiller, one of the few doctors in the US still performing late-term abortions, when my secretary, Hazel Harris Weeks, tapped on my office door before ushering a dapper gentleman inside.

He held out his free hand—the other clutched a small bag—and spoke with a slight European accent. *"Grüezi*, Mr. Vinson, I am Ariel Gonda. It is good to finally meet you."

Taking grüezi to be a German word for "hello" or "howdy," I stood to accept the proffered handshake as my mind grappled to place him. Then a memory dropped. Ariel Gonda was the corporate treasurer of Alfano Vineyards in Napa Valley. I had run across his name during what I mentally referred to as the Bisti business, but I'd never actually met the man before. If I recalled correctly, he was a Swiss national, so the word in question was likely Swiss German.

"Mr. Gonda, how are Aggie and Lando doing?" I referred to the Alfano brothers to let him know I'd made the connection.

"They are well, thank you. At least, they were when last I spoke to Aggie. I am no longer with the organization. I am now one of you. That is to say, a bona fide citizen of New Mexico."

I smiled inwardly as he neatly covered his tracks. It's best to be precise when drawing comparisons to a gay confidential investigator. "Welcome to our world, Mr. Gonda."

"Please call me Ariel. As you can see, I have become Americanized. In my native Switzerland, we would never have arrived at first names so swiftly. I find the informality refreshing."

"With pleasure—if you'll call me BJ. Please have a seat and tell me what I can do for you. Unless this is a social call."

"Would that it were. Unfortunately it is your services as an investigator I require at the moment."

He settled into the comfortable chair directly opposite my old-fashioned walnut desk and glanced around the wainscoted room. I detected a gleam of approval in his pale blue eyes as he studied pieces of my late father's cowboy and western art collection adorning the light beige walls. He brought his attention back to me, a clue he was ready to discuss business.

I took a small digital voice recorder from a drawer and placed it on the desk. "Do you mind if I record the conversation?" With his consent, I turned on the device and entered today's date and noted the time as 10:15 a.m. "This interview with Mr. Ariel Gonda is done with his knowledge and consent."

I lifted my eyes to meet his and asked him to identify the name and location of his business. He limited his response to "The Lovely Pines Vineyard and Winery, Valle Plácido, New Mexico." After that was properly recorded, I asked the purpose of his visit.

He cleared his throat. "The matter that brings me here is a break-in at my winery precisely two weeks ago today."

I consulted my desk calendar. "That would be May 28. What time?"

"Sometime during the night before. I learned of it when I went to work that morning."

"How was entry gained?"

"The hasp was forced, rendering the padlock useless."

"What was taken?"

"Nothing that I can determine."

"Vandalism?"

"Merely some papers in my office and lab disturbed. But nothing was destroyed or taken, and there are some quite valuable instruments in the laboratory."

"Tell me a little about your business."

I examined Gonda as he spoke. During my involvement in the Bisti affair, I'd built up an image of a rotund, stodgy European bean counter, but the man sitting across from me was rather tall—probably my height, an even six feet—solid but not fat, and darker than I pictured Europeans from the Swiss Alpine regions. His striking aristocratic face ended in a high forehead. Light brown hair brushed the collar of his powder blue cotton shirt. He might consider himself Americanized, but his pleasing baritone hadn't yet mastered the art of speaking in contractions.

"The Lovely Pines is located northeast of here just outside the village of Valle Plácido. Do you know it?"

I nodded. "The area, not the winery."

"I began negotiations to purchase the business from Mr. Ernesto C de Baca last summer. However, he passed away before we arrived at an agreement. In January of this year, I completed the transaction with his heirs."

Gonda lifted the small bag he'd placed on the floor beside his chair. The two glass containers he extracted looked to be green, hippy Bordeaux bottles often used for reds. The gold seal covering the cork was quite elegantly done.

"I brought samples. Please enjoy them with my compliments," he said before continuing his narration.

I listened patiently as he described the operation in his pedantic manner. The winery was located on ten acres fronting the north side of State Road 165 running out of Valle Plácido east toward Sandia Peak. A three-story stone-and-brick edifice housed the public rooms, offices, and family living quarters. The winery and the cellar sat some distance behind that building. A hundred-acre vineyard lay to the east, bordered on the south by a fifteen-acre lake or pond. Roughly one-fifth of a square mile in total land area.

I tapped my desk blotter with the point of a gold-and-onyx letter opener fashioned like a Toledo blade. "Valle Plácido doesn't have a police force, so I assume you reported the break-in to the Sandoval County Sheriff's Office."

"I did. However, since nothing was taken, the county officials decided it was a case of adolescent mischief and closed the investigation— such as it was."

"Apparently you disagree with that conclusion. Have there been other incidents?"

"Certain small things have occurred. Things I would not have noticed were it not for the earlier break-in." He leaned back in the chair and crossed his legs in a less formal manner. Covering the lower portion of his face with a palm, he pulled his hand down over his chin and neck as though smoothing a nonexistent beard. "I suppose I can best explain by telling you that two days following the actual burglary, if that is the proper terminology, I noticed some of my tools and equipment had been moved."

"How many employees have access to the area?"

"We have a viticulturist and two field hands working the vineyard. I am the vintner and have three assistants in the winery. Marc, my nephew, acts as my outside salesman and assistant manager. My wife, Margot, is responsible for the operation of the office. Then there is our chocolatier, Maurice Benoir, who is invaluable in making our chocolate-flavored wines. His wife assists him in running a kiosk in the entry hall. She acts as cashier for all the various profit centers and sells handmade sweets she and Maurice concoct. And, of course, we have a cook and waitress for the Bistro."

"A total of thirteen people if I counted correctly. And all of them have access to the winery?"

"Most of them. Our viticulturist's wife is also on the premises since they live at the vineyard. She does not work for us but has the run of the place."

"So the total is actually fourteen individuals. Let's be clear. All of them have access to the winery?"

"Throughout the day, anyone other than the cook and the girl who waits our tables will be in and out of the winery numerous times. But I refuse to believe any of them were involved in what occurred."

"I see. I must tell you in all candor, there is probably little I can do for you except to conduct background checks on your people. Chances are that a search might reveal something, but there's no guarantee. You might end up spending a lot of money for nothing."

He performed the palm-over-lip-and-chin maneuver again as he thought over what I'd said. "At least I would be assured of their honesty and would not walk around harboring dark suspicions about the people with whom I work."

Did he recognize his own inconsistency? He was apparently prepared to spend some money to reassure him of what he professed to believe. "Mr. Gonda... Ariel, anytime you do a thorough background check on that many people, any number of moles and wens and warts are going to surface. They might have nothing to do with your problem, but be warned. You will likely not look at some of your employees in the same light as before. All of us have secrets."

"True. But I would appreciate your undertaking this task for me. I will gladly pay your going fee. It will be worth it to clear any lingering doubts from my mind."

"Any exceptions? Your nephew, for example?"

"Please look into the history of everyone. Except my wife and me, of course."

"Very well. I'll need a complete list of employees with as much information as possible. Anything you give me will be held confidential. By the way, you didn't mention your own children."

"Margot and I have only one. A son. Auguste Philippe came rather late in our lives. He was born here, actually. He entered this world in Las Cruces in August of 1990 while I was working with the European Wine Consortium. He is presently a freshman at UC Berkeley pursuing a degree in chemical engineering."

"Are there individuals from your former life—either here or in Europe—who would cause such problems for you?"

"I have made my share of mistakes with people during my career. But I cannot conceive of anyone so aggrieved he would come like a thief in the night." Gonda gave a very European shrug. "Anyone who leaps to mind would certainly be more aggressive. The place would have burned down, for example." He pursed his lips before honing in on precise details, which I suspected was his nature. "Of course the building is brick and stone. But there are ample flammable materials on the inside."

So there was someone. But was he willing to reveal enough of himself to name him or her? Or them? "You could be making a mountain out of a molehill."

That comment brought a brief smile. "A charming analogy. I have worried over this for fourteen days before coming to see you. Deep down inside, something tells me not to ignore this. To get to the bottom of it quickly. And there have been two other incidents."

"Tell me about them."

"I am experimenting with a sparkling wine—what is commonly referred to as a champagne—using an imported grape, of course. My cabernet sauvignon varietal produces reds, not whites. At any rate, I have a small, temperature-controlled room adjacent to my laboratory with a special wine rack used in the *remuage*, what you here call riddling. Are you familiar with the procedure?"

"You'll have to forgive me. I am not a wine connoisseur. I enjoy a glass with my meals occasionally, but that's about it."

He nodded acceptance of my words. "After the second fermentation, champagnes or sparkling wines are racked upside down at a forty-five-degree angle so that sediments—mostly dead yeasts—settle in the neck.

At regular intervals, usually every three days, the bottles are given hard twists so the sediment doesn't solidify. At the proper time, the bottle necks are frozen, the offending plugs removed, and the wine is corked. That procedure is not, of course, limited to sparkling wines."

He must have recognized he was lecturing, because he got back to the point. "I do the riddling in that room myself. The last time I performed the chore, I noticed a disturbance in the slight film of dust on the base of one of the bottles."

"Did the sheriff's deputies take fingerprints?"

"I noticed the disturbance only after they closed their investigation. But it bothered me enough to pay you a visit."

"Has anyone handled the bottle since?"

"I picked it up before I understood the significance of the dust."

"You mentioned two incidents."

"At least one bottle of our chocolate-flavored wine has gone missing. And a bit of food stored in the place, as well."

"I'd guess several of your bottles go—"

He held up his hand and straightened in his chair. His posture and body language became formal again. "It is not what you are thinking. I have a very liberal attitude with my employees. I like them to enjoy the fruits of their labors. Each receives a ration of wine, and he or she is free to make special requests. I seldom refuse any reasonable petition."

After submitting to another half hour of questions, Gonda executed my standard contract, handed over a check for the retainer, and made arrangements for me to visit the Lovely Pines. Then he took his leave.

"Such a distinguished gentleman," Hazel observed when she came to collect the contract and the check. And the two bottles.

"You're just a sucker for an accent." I handed over the digital recorder for transcription, as well. Earlier this year, Hazel had threatened rebellion if I didn't do away with the tape recorder I'd used for years. I'd probably have ignored her except the thing was virtually worn out. Might as well join the twenty-first century, right?

My formerly dowdy office manager scoffed. "I can take them, or I can leave them."

She had blossomed since she and Charlie Weeks were married in a civil ceremony held in my living room last New Year's Eve. Like me, Charlie was a retired cop. But he'd put in his time at the Albuquerque Police Department, whereas I was medically retired by a gunshot wound to the thigh. Last year he earned his way into a partnership as the only other full-time investigator in the firm. After the legal documents formalizing this were signed, I made a big deal out of having the gold lettering on the outer office door redone to read "Vinson and Weeks, Confidential Investigations," but Hazel insisted I'd only done it because someone scratched a hole in the paint on the letter *C*.

"There will be a lot of background investigations on this one," I told her.

"Deep?"

"Record checking for the most part, I imagine. Unless that turns up something that needs to be pursued."

"Hmm." She left for the outer office.

I swiveled my chair to the window and took in the view that anchored me to my third-floor suite of offices in a renovated, downtown historic building on the southwest corner of Copper and Fifth NW. I enjoyed looking out the north-facing window and imagining I could look down on my home at 5229 Post Oak Drive NW. By craning my neck to the west, I could almost see Old Town where the twelve original families settled the new Villa de Alburquerque in 1706. Day or night, the scene outside that pane of glass always grabbed me.

Like a lot of confidential investigators, I preferred working for attorneys. They understood the limitations of my profession. We were fact collectors, not sleuths in the popular sense of the word. Movies and TV programs and novels had skewed the public perception of my trade to the point that private citizens often suffered an unrealistic expectation of what our job really was. I worried that the dramatic outcome of that nasty Bisti business might have led Ariel Gonda to the same misconception.

Turning back to the desk, I picked up the file I was currently working. Local attorney Del Dahlman—who was my significant other before I was shot while serving with the Albuquerque police—had hired me to look over the shoulder of the city's fire department as they conducted an arson investigation. One of his client's warehouses burned to the ground in a spectacularly stubborn blaze a few days ago. Del was concerned about where the inquiry might lead. I was beginning to think the case was heading precisely where he did not want it to go.

After phoning the lieutenant heading the arson investigation, I drove out to meet him at the scene of the fire for another walk-through.

Like most cops—and ex-cops—I wanted to see the scene of the crime up close and personal. More than once.

That walk-through took the remainder of the day, so I headed straight home from the South Broadway site to clean off the soot and mud. With any luck, the cleaners could salvage my suit pants. If not, I'd add the cost of a new pair to Del's bill.

I was surprised to find Paul home when I arrived. In his second year of a UNM graduate program in journalism and holding down a job as a swim instructor and lifeguard at the North Valley Country Club, Paul Barton carried a lot on his plate. Although we'd been together for almost three years now, I sometimes felt we were ships passing in the night. The nights were perfect, of course, but our schedules didn't allow us much time in between.

I'd offered him a job at the office, but he was an independent cuss and turned me down. He was still driving his ancient, purple Plymouth coupe even though he could have afforded a newer model. But he was determined to finish his education without any debt hanging over his head.

I returned his smile as he stood up from the kitchen table where he'd been studying. After a gentle but stimulating kiss, a pot of his very special stew percolating on the stove captured my attention. The savory aroma of green chili and chicken and potatoes sent my sudden hunger wandering back and forth between the gastronomic and the carnal.

"With warm flour tortillas?" I asked.

"And butter." He grinned. "After dinner, I'll expect a reward for my culinary efforts."

I beamed like a smitten teenager. "Abso-fucking-lutely."

Chapter 2

I DROVE to Valle Plácido directly from the house the next morning, saving myself a trip downtown and then a run back north. In a bucolic mood, I took the old Highway 85 to Bernalillo about fifteen miles north of Albuquerque.

Bernalillo was an interesting town, at least to history buffs like me. The area had been more or less continuously inhabited for probably close to 1,000 years, first as an indigenous Anasazi town and later by the Spaniards when they arrived in the late sixteenth century to claim it as a trading center and military outpost. In one of those odd coincidences, Albuquerque became the governmental center of Bernalillo County, while Bernalillo was the seat of Sandoval County. Go figure. The present day town fathers liked to say their community was the gateway to the Jemez Mountain Range to the west and the Sandias to the east.

At the north end of town, I hung a right on Highway 550 and crossed over I-25, climbing steadily toward the mountains on what was now a gravel state road. Before long, I passed through another former Anasazi settlement renamed Placitas, which meant Little Town. With its large adobe homes tucked into folds in the foothills or hanging on the slopes, Placitas managed to bring some of the famed Santa Fe style south.

Shortly after leaving the town limits, I entered an even smaller settlement about whose history I had no knowledge—Valle Plácido. All I knew of the place was that people had grown grapes and made wine here for centuries. New Mexico was one of the earliest wine-making centers in North America.

As instructed by Ariel Gonda, I turned north on a well-graded gravel driveway and saw the winery about 200 yards ahead of me. My first impression was of a French chateau plopped down in the middle of New Mexico. As I grew nearer, the image was reinforced. I passed over a cattle guard between an impressive black wrought iron gate anchored to solid four-foot stone walls stretching off in both directions. I assumed it enclosed the entire place, or at least the ten acres of the winery. The wall would probably have stopped a tank but provided little protection from stealthy intruders afoot. The vineyard lay to the east.

Up close the stately house did not seem so forbidding, less of a mysterious manor harboring psychopaths and star-crossed lovers. *House*, of course, was a misnomer. It was truly a chateau, even though small by European standards. I judged it to be three floors of around 1,500 square feet each. The gray stone of those tall walls wasn't native rock. A cloudy green patina stained the copper mansard roof. Brown brick framed doors, windows, and the roofline beneath the gables.

As I swung around to park beside a few other vehicles, some with out-of-state license plates, I caught sight of another solid-looking stone building about a hundred yards behind the chateau. Probably the winery.

A sign with black lettering mounted on a field of white to the right of the main entryway confirmed this as The Lovely Pines Vineyard and Winery. The placard mirrored a larger billboard I'd seen out on the highway. The effect of the whole layout was stiff and formal. A bit off-putting for my tastes.

That changed as soon as I walked into the front hallway. High ceilings gave the place an airy feeling, and windows that seemed rather small from the outside admitted bright light to play off eggshell and pale gold walls tastefully hung with good art. I couldn't be certain from this distance, but some seemed to be old masters. Reproductions, probably. The chocolatier's kiosk was modern without being jarring. The word *Schoggi* was prominently displayed, leading me to believe this was Swiss German for chocolate. An attractive woman of about fifty lifted her head from a notepad and smiled as I entered. I clicked the REC button on the small digital voice recorder on my belt as she spoke.

"Welcome to the Lovely Pines. Please feel free to make yourself at home. Our wine tasting won't begin for another half hour or so. The entire first floor is given over to our public rooms—the Bistro, a salon for lounging, our gift shop, and, of course, our tasting room."

I thanked her for the sales pitch and let her know that Mr. Gonda was expecting me.

She gave a real smile this time, one that dimpled both her powdered cheeks, and excused herself. Almost immediately she returned with Gonda through the double doors to the left. He held out a hand in welcome.

"BJ, I see you have met Mrs. Benoir. Heléne, this is Mr. B. J. Vinson. He's a private investigator who will get to the bottom of our little problem. He is to be given free rein of the property. Nothing is off limits."

"*Mol*, Ariel. Nice to meet you, Mr. Vinson. Please let me know if I can help in any way."

I had no clue as to what "mol" meant, and no one saw fit to translate. "Thank you, Mrs. Benoir."

"Heléne, please."

I turned to face her boss. "Ariel, may we speak privately before we inspect the property?"

"Certainly." He turned up the staircase as I paused to express my thanks to Heléne. A few individuals—mostly couples—stood or claimed seats in upholstered chairs or couches. Customers waiting for the wine tasting, I assumed.

If the first floor was somewhat formal, the second looked and sounded like a typical business operation. Ariel explained this level was totally given over to offices, except for a guest suite, currently the residence of his nephew, Marc Juisson.

An attractive blonde woman typed on a keyboard as she spoke into a telephone cradled between her head and shoulder. When she noticed us, she promptly terminated the conversation and stood.

"This is my wife, Margot. My dear, this is B. J. Vinson, the man I told you about."

My mouth must have been ajar, because Gonda laughed. "*Nein*, you are not seeing ghosts. Margot and Heléne are cousins. But they could be sisters, eh? Twins, even."

Margot, a striking woman probably slightly younger than Gonda's fifty years, had gray highlights in her long blonde hair, but she possessed the vivacity of a much younger woman while exuding sagacity and sophistication. I liked her immediately.

"I do hope you can help us," she said as she offered a manicured hand. "We are probably worried over nothing, but it is a mystery. And a mystery demands to be solved."

"Apparently so."

Gonda chuckled. "She is just making excuses for me. I am the worrier in this family. She is quite willing to shrug off the matter. Now, you wanted a word in private. Feel free to speak in front of Margot. We harbor no secrets between us."

"Does everyone here know who I am and what I'm doing? I ask because of what you said to Mrs. Benoir."

Gonda frowned. "Yes, the entire staff knows. Was that an impropriety on my part?"

"Not necessarily. I would have cautioned against it, but everyone will figure out what's going on within minutes of my arrival, anyway."

"My thoughts precisely. I must also admit I wanted to make clear that I took the intrusion seriously, just in the unlikely event one of my people was involved. Let me show you the rest of the operation."

For the next hour, Gonda walked me through the property, starting with the chateau. He took me to their living quarters on the top floor and prompted me to stick my head in every room. This tier had a distinctly European flair, from the eclectic blending of Louis XIV and Queen Anne furnishings to the heavy, somber Renaissance paintings on the wall. It was tastefully done.

From the chateau, we went to the large stone building behind the house, which was indeed the winery. On the way I met Maurice Benoir, the master of chocolates, who better fit my image of a Swiss merchant than did his boss. Solid, even stocky. Thinning sandy hair cut short. A fair but florid complexion. His accented voice rumbled up out of a deep chest as he greeted me amiably.

Gonda paused at the doorway of the winery to show me where the hasp that had been ripped away was now replaced with a new one firmly affixed to a reinforcing steel plate. Entry by the same means would be more difficult now. He led me straight to his lab—as sterile as any hospital facility—which also served as his winery office, Ariel told me this was the room where the mischief occurred. Then he opened a file cabinet drawer and handed me a gallon-sized clear plastic bag containing a bottle.

"This is the one that was disturbed. I thought you might wish to see if there are fingerprints on it."

"I can give it a try. I assume your prints are on record because of your alcohol license, but since we're going to have to take elimination prints from all of the family and staff, it would be better for your people to see you being printed as well."

"Certainly. Whatever you think best."

We toured the winery, and although I am not a wine aficionado, I had visited other such facilities in the area occasionally and was able to make mental comparisons. The big surprise was the aging or storage facility—the cellar. Until Gonda opened a heavy double door and ushered me inside, I hadn't realized the building backed up to a cavern. The cellar was actually a natural cave.

"This is one of the reasons I was attracted to C de Baca's operation," he explained. "This underground storage is ideal. The temperature seldom varies, and the humidity is easily controlled. I age my wines at fifty-five degrees Fahrenheit and keep the humidity rather high. I prefer to mature the product slowly. Rapid aging caused by elevated temperatures gives the product a questionable taste."

I stared at what appeared to be oak barrels stacked in rows that disappeared into the gloom of the large hollow in the earth. The darkness was only partially broken by low-watt bulbs placed at regular intervals.

"I bulk age in split-oak barrels for a period of time and then bottle age until the wine reaches maturity," he said.

"How long does that take?"

"Cabernet sauvignon has a fairly long aging period. Anywhere from four to twenty years, depending upon the product you are striving for."

That was when I realized the bottles he'd given us at the office were part of the former owner's wines. None of Gonda's had yet matured. I also snapped to the "Founded" date on the sign outside. C de Baca likely started the winery in 1964.

He confirmed my reasoning. "Most of what you see is inventory I purchased from C de Baca. Fortunately my practices mirror his closely."

I glanced around. "Is the only access to the cellar through the winery?"

"Yes. This door is the only way in and the only way out."

I pointed up. "Is the ground over the cavern on your property?"

He nodded. "Yes, but the end of this tunnel means you are within fifteen feet of the northernmost boundary of the ten acres the winery occupies."

Without waiting for an invitation, I walked the length of the long corridor. The cavern probably spanned around one square acre. Part of it was given over to barrels and part was lined with row after row of racked wine completing the aging process in bottles. Gonda explained that early aging was done in wood to give the wine the flavor of the oak, and then the product was siphoned off the lees by means of a racking hose attached to a racking cane. Thereafter it was bottled and placed in another portion of the cellar to mature.

At the far end, behind the oldest wine barrels, I found an area with a battered sofa, a few chairs, some cabinets, and other indications of human occupancy.

"What's this?"

"I suppose you could say this is our preparation against the—how do you say?—vagaries of both man and nature. Our own little shelter against disaster. We store water and canned and packaged foods in case our people need to take shelter for any reason. The prior management set this up, and I have continued it, although I cannot really think of a reason it would ever be required." He opened a cabinet. "Here is where some of the food disappeared. Chips. Cookies. Things like that."

"No one lives down here?"

"Oh no. It is a little too cool for my tastes, and I was raised in Switzerland. It is merely a precaution."

"I noticed no supports for the roof of the cavern. Do you have the occasional debris to contend with?"

"No. Never. A little settling dust, but nothing beyond that. The roof is solid stone, and as you can see, slightly domed."

As we exited the winery and walked toward the vineyard, Gonda kept up a running commentary. "As I say, there are one hundred acres to the growing field, although C de Baca planted only around fifty. I am placing the remainder under cultivation. This vineyard is another of the reasons I wanted the property. Despite the fact we are virtually on the side of Sandia Mountain lying directly to our east, the entire property slopes slightly to the south. This gives us good drainage and long hours of sunlight without too much exposure to the hot afternoon sun. This and the composition of the soil makes it ideal for my grapes. In a state full of caliche clay, Mr. C de Baca managed to find a fairly sizable tract without much on it. I cultivate the cabernet sauvignon. The berries are small with a very tough skin, so it is fairly resistant to disease."

Gonda was off and running on a discourse about his favorite subject. I allowed him to proceed as I took in every aspect of the field, including what appeared to be a cottage and a smaller workshop with a covered shed attached. Both were made of the same gray stone as the chateau and the winery.

He indicated the lake to the south between the vineyard and the highway. "C de Baca bought enough water rights to install a fairly sizable lake in the belief it would help offset the effects of cold weather. The theory is the heat stored in the water dissipates and helps to ameliorate extreme temperatures. I am not certain a body of water this small serves the purpose, but it is a nice addition to the property, is it not?"

A tall, slender man about my age, introduced as viticulturist James Bledsong, interrupted us. Actually, he was both vigneron, the one responsible for cultivating the vineyard, and viticulturist in charge of the health and well-being of the fields. Since the entire staff was aware of who I was and the assignment I'd been given, Gonda excused himself and left me with Bledsong, a man as eager to explain the vineyard as his employer had been to go on about the winery.

"We're pretty proud of our vines," Bledsong said in a voice that called up images of sun and surf. Gonda probably brought the man with him from California. "The fella who owned it before only cultivated about half of it. We're planting out the rest."

"High-quality grapes?"

His voice held a trace of pride. "The best cabernets in the country."

"Is that the only grape you grow?"

"Yes, sir. We don't do any field blending here. We use some other local terroir varietals in a few of our wines, but those berries are bought from other vineyards and blended in the winery."

"How many vines do you have?"

"Old man C de Baca was a pretty good viticulturist. He didn't overplant. He used an eight-foot by five-foot spacing, and that yields around 1,000 vines per acre. We're stepping it down a little, so the newly planted acreage will average around 1,500 plants. We get about four or five tons of grapes to the acre. We could produce more, but the lower harvest gives us a sweeter fruit. So we do some green harvesting."

I raised an eyebrow. "Green harvesting?"

"That's what we call removing some of the immature grape clusters. When these new plants mature, Mr. Gonda will be able to cork eighty thousand bottles a year or more."

"That much?"

"Oh yeah. And a high percentage of it'll be good quality wine too."

"Do you have any ideas about what happened a couple of weeks ago?"

"You mean the break-in? That happened at night, and I'm too far from the winery to have heard anything." He pointed over his shoulder to the larger of the two buildings at the east end of the field. "That's my house over there. It's just me and my wife, Margaret. Maggie, I call her."

"No children?"

A look of pain crossed his pleasant features. "Late-term miscarriage. Maggie can't have any more. Sometimes it weighs her down."

"I'm sorry. But she'll compensate. You both will."

"She already has. She's active in the Healthy Nation. It's a group of families in the area that works with local children to keep them out of trouble."

"Sounds like a good organization. How about your people? What's the scuttlebutt among them?"

"The guys who work for me, you mean? There are only two of them, Claudio Garcia and Winfield Tso." He pointed to two men working among the plants some distance away. One figure towered over the other, putting me in mind of the old Mutt and Jeff cartoons. "I guess they figure the deputies were right. Kids, most likely," Bledsong added.

"I don't know many kids who'd go to the trouble of prying a hasp off a door to a winery without doing damage beyond throwing some papers around and making off with a single bottle of wine."

"Yeah, that bothers me too. It's a puzzler."

"Any problems like that in the vineyard?"

"The lake's outside the fence, so kids come swim sometimes. We don't have a wall like they do around the winery, but our cyclone fence keeps wildlife—including kids—out of the field better than four feet of rock. Anybody and anything can get over the wall over yonder."

I asked a few more questions before returning to the chateau. On the way I started to change tapes in my little machine before remembering I'd joined the modern world and now used a digital recorder.

Gonda was still at the winery, but Margot showed me the tasting room—which was empty at the moment—where I learned I'd been drinking wine the wrong way for lo these many years. It wasn't a soda and shouldn't be imbibed in the same manner. Then she insisted we have a cup of espresso in the Bistro, where I met the cook, a plump lady with an angel face named Nellie Bright. A local girl introduced as Katie served us at a small, intimate table in the corner.

"Are you on board with this?" I asked as soon as we were situated.

"On board? Ah, you mean do I approve? After all these years, your colloquialisms still throw me on occasion."

I had assumed she was native-born. She spoke with no appreciable accent. "You're Swiss?"

"Oh yes. I come from Bern. Ariel and I met at the University of Zurich, where I was reading finance and he was taking a degree in oenology." She noticed my frown and came to the rescue. "That's the science of winemaking.

He also holds a second read… what you call a minor… in finance. We were wed in Valois in June of 1988, shortly before he came to the United States. I followed later. But to answer your question, yes, I am on board, as you say. If the incident worries Ariel, then it worries me as well."

"Do you have any idea what might be going on? Sometimes wives see things husbands don't."

She spread her hands, palms up. "I am at a loss. I can find no explanation for anyone breaking into the winery. Perhaps the sheriff's office is correct. It was children."

I asked Margot the same question I put to Bledsong earlier about children breaking in without at least stealing a lot of wine.

She frowned. "Then what could it be?" At that moment I believe the incident became as serious to her as it was to her husband.

Shortly thereafter, I excused myself and wandered back to the winery. Gonda was in his lab, but I didn't bother him. I merely walked around the place seeing what I could figure out on my own. I found the press and what I was pretty sure was the primary fermentation equipment. I also figured out the secondary fermentation setup, but beyond that I was lost.

The cellar beckoned, and I wandered down the long, silent rows of barrels. The temperature and the high humidity raised chill bumps on my arms. When I reached the area against the rear wall that looked like a campout spot, I paused to consider things.

The two wine bottles—the one disturbed in the rack and the one taken—argued someone gained access to the winery when they were not supposed to. There had been no additional break-ins, and Gonda kept tight control of the keys. That suggested the intruder laid his hands on a duplicate set.

Whoa, now, Vinson. Don't get ahead of yourself. Do the background checks and see if anything turns up that suggests skullduggery on the part of an employee. After all, they wander in and out of the place all day long. Gonda wasn't constantly in his lab, so someone could have entered and fussed with the champagne bottle. Likewise, it wouldn't be too hard to smuggle a bottle from the cellar during work hours.

The only way in and out of the cellar was through the winery, and thence to the outside by means of any one of three exits: the main entry at the front, a smaller portal opening to the east, and a large roll-up door giving out onto a loading dock on the west side. All three doors were sturdy and showed no evidence of damage, no appearance of having been picked. Of course, an expert thief would probably leave no such evidence. Gonda assured me all the locks had been changed after he acquired the business from the C de Bacas.

No, the break-in was not the work of a professional. Professionals did not rip a hasp from the door unless they were doing a smash-and-grab job. And this had not been one of those operations. Stealth. Except for the hasp.

I made a point of shaking hands with each of the three winery workers. Parson Jones was a black man in his early forties. Bascomb Zuniga looked to be a Hispanic barely old enough to work around alcohol. John Hakamora, a Japanese American, said he came out of the south-central New Mexico lettuce fields. Marc Juisson, the nephew, was away on a business trip, so I would meet him later.

It was midafternoon before I collected the payroll records from Margot and promised to have Charlie Weeks contact her to come out to fingerprint everyone. Then, with the champagne bottle still in its protective wrapper, I climbed into my white Impala and headed for Albuquerque. I'd tackle the two vineyard workers later.

Chapter 3

IN VIEW of my absence from the office the entire previous day, I made a point of arriving early the next morning even though it was Saturday. We do not formally open on weekends, but investigators investigate whenever we can, and that included weekends and holidays. Chances were Hazel and Charlie would stop by sometime as well.

After dropping the digital recorder containing my interviews and the Lovely Pines payroll records on Hazel's desk, I left the champagne bottle with a note for Charlie to get it to K-Y Labs on Monday for dusting. I also asked him to go take fingerprints of all the Lovely Pines staff. Our office didn't do enough fingerprinting to invest in high-tech equipment, but we kept a supply of inexpensive inkless pads. Once finished at the winery, Charlie would run by APD and ask my old partner Lt. Gene Enriquez to send them through the system for us.

By the time I'd finished reading the transcript of yesterday's initial interview with Ariel Gonda, both Hazel and Charlie arrived. I was fully invested in their marriage, because now Hazel didn't expend as much energy on trying to run my life. Apparently tending to Charlie satisfied her mothering gene. Perversely I missed the attention at times.

Paul was working this weekend at the country club, so I spent the rest of the morning making phone calls on Del Dahlman's arson case. Firefighters apparently work as much as cops and confidential investigators do. By noon everything was wrapped as tight as it was going to get. My job was to collect and verify facts, not to interpret them. Nonetheless, the data I'd gathered pretty clearly indicated Del's client was going to end up defending himself in a criminal trial. I dictated my report, brought my time and expense vouchers up-to-date, and dumped them all on Hazel's desk, instructing her to mail them to Del.

"It's that bad, is it?" She knew I would drop it off at Del's office in the Plaza Tower a couple of blocks away if it weren't bad news.

"At least he'll know what he's facing when they go to trial. If you'll give me the Lovely Pines payroll records, I'll start the background checks."

"Gladly."

Background checks are a staple for any confidential investigations operation. They are laborious and time-consuming, but not nearly as much so as before the internet came along. Licensed firms like ours have several databases available that private citizens can't touch. I generally start with social security numbers. If something really sneaky is going on, it usually shows up there first… except for criminal records, of course. But Charlie would check for those jackets after he fingerprinted the Pines staff.

Hazel got us corned beef on rye at the courthouse restaurant, so I continued working through lunch. My keyboard tends to get messy, but I get a lot of work done during the noon hour—especially weekend noon hours—when the phone doesn't ring so much. Motor vehicle department records filled my screen by the time Charlie returned from the winery.

"Man, don't send me out there very often," he said as he came through the door. "All that wine tasting can be hazardous to your health. Not to mention your DWI record. They've got a bunch of different wines, and they insisted I try them all."

"I think you're supposed to savor the taste and then spit it out."

"I don't spit in polite company."

"I thought you'd wait until Monday when everyone would be there."

"I called Gonda, and he rounded everyone up. I get the feeling the winery is those guys' second home."

"How did it go? Anyone balk?" I asked.

"Nope. Gonda and his wife went first, and everybody else followed along behind."

"Anybody seem nervous?"

"No more than usual."

"Did you print them before or after the wine tasting?"

Charlie chuckled. "Before, thank God. Not sure what they'd have looked like if it was after."

"Snoop around the grounds any?"

"Went over the whole place. I'm happy to take the man's money, but I can't honestly see how we're going to help him."

I spread my hands over the payroll papers littering my desk. "Me either, unless this reveals something."

"Anything so far?"

"Little stuff. You know, the usual. Gaps in employment records. A neighbor didn't like this or that. Petty stuff. But I'm not finished checking everything yet. I'd like you to do the criminal records checks."

"Start on it first thing Monday. But you know it's hard to see this as anything serious. No vandalism, no real stealing. Nothing like that."

"Even so, someone went to the trouble of prying a hasp off the door."

"You have any theories?"

"Nope. You?"

"Nope."

I resumed my task before the computer screen and spent most of the rest of the day checking out the staff of the winery. By the time I got home, Paul was standing at the door waiting for me, looking expectant.

"What?" I asked. Whatever it was, he could have it. His special brand of combining his juvenile side with the adult man could charm me out of just about anything. Anytime. Anywhere.

"I have tomorrow off."

"No studying?"

"Got home early today and did it already. Can we do something special?"

"What, go to the C&W and line dance?"

He grinned broadly. "No, really special. You know what I want to do?"

"What?"

"Drive up to Los Alamos and spend the night in a motel. And then get up early the next morning and play the municipal golf course."

"Okay. It's an easy drive. Let's do it."

"Second request?"

"I'm in a generous mood."

"Can we come back through Jemez Springs Sunday? I want to spend a little while at Valles Caldera."

That was a request easy to grant. The Valles Caldera is an almost fourteen-mile-wide volcanic caldera in the Jemez Mountains between Jemez Springs and Los Alamos. The broad grasslands and rugged volcanic peaks made up one of the most beautiful landscapes I have ever seen. The almost 100,000 acres comprising the National Preserve formerly known as Baca Location Number 1 have a fascinating history.

"Done. Let me throw some duds in a bag. I assume you've already packed yours."

He flashed that devastating grin again. "Yours too. If you go relieve your bladder, we can get started. Maybe they'll serve us a late dinner at the North Road Inn." I knew the B and B was one of his favorite spots to rest his head for the night.

I slipped into more comfortable traveling clothes while he loaded the Impala with our bags and gear. My pulse quickened at the thought of having him to myself for the next twenty-four hours. He crawled behind the wheel without asking. That was all right. I was content to watch him rather than the roads.

WE GOT into the Atomic City—or as it was otherwise known, The Town That Never Was—perched on the Pajarito Plateau too late for dinner at the North Road, but we stopped at the Blue Window Bistro, where Paul convinced me to join him for a duck BLT. Dubious at first, I soon found breast of duck went well with bacon.

Later in our comfortable room at North Road, he headed straight for the shower, saying he wanted to make an early night of it so we could hit the golf course at first light the next morning. Yeah, right. I no sooner joined him in bed after my own bath than he launched his assault on my body. And a long and vigorous and loving onslaught it was too. I knew well before it was over that getting up early was going to be difficult.

Paul beat me on the broad fairways of the front nine at the Los Alamos County Golf Course and literally trounced me on the narrow tee boxes built right into the evergreen forest surrounding the back nine. As I usually took him by a stroke or two, I blamed the bedroom calisthenics of the night before for the rout.

Sunday afternoon found us sitting in the tall grass beside the tiny Jemez River staring out over a great spread of grassland, listening to water trickle by and the flutter of wings and call of wild birds. Small creatures stirred in the nearby weeds. The odd volcanic bubble known as Cerro la Jara—or more fondly, Little la Jara—sat at our left, rising off the vast meadow like a miniature mountain with trees crowning the top. The vast hulk of Redondo Peak loomed in the distance. Paul leaned against me comfortably, adding the final ingredient to total peace and contentment. His touch and the aroma of gramma grass and weeds and wildflowers even quelled my urge to recite the colored history of our environment.

HAZEL, CHARLIE, and I huddled at the conference table in my office early Monday morning. Charlie opened the meeting. "Got the public record information back from APD. The Navajo, Winfield Tso, has an old disturbing the peace charge. He got probation and hasn't been in trouble since. The cook, uh… that's Nellie Bright, filed a domestic violence complaint against her husband a few years back. He spent the night in jail."

"They divorced in 2008," Hazel said. She'd spent Saturday afternoon checking the Sandoval County clerk's records. "That must be the reason why."

Charlie consulted his list. "Parson Jones, one of the winery workers—that's his real name, by the way—let alcohol trip him up a few years back. Has a record of petty misdemeanors. You know, public drinking, bar fights, and the like. But nothing in the past two years. I've not finished checking the records down in Las Cruces and Socorro. Probably be able to complete those today. The California records on the Gondas and the Bledsongs will be touchier, but I should have those results in a day or two."

I leaned back in my chair and ran a hand through my hair. "Nothing funny in the social security files. All the numbers appear to be legitimate. So far as I can tell, Zuniga is native-born, as is Hakamora. Garcia was born in Mexico but has been here for a few years. Legally, so far as I know at this point. The Gondas, the Benoirs, and the nephew—" I paused to consult my notes. "—uh, Juisson, are here legally."

"What about the son, Auguste?" Charlie asked.

"Found his birth certificate in Doña Ana County," Hazel said.

"He doesn't have a criminal or civil record in this state, but I still don't have results out of California," Charlie said.

"New Mexico motor vehicle records show they all have automobiles commensurate with their company salaries," I said. "Zuniga doesn't own a car but has a motorcycle. An older model Kawasaki. He's racked up some traffic violations on it, but nothing serious. No DWIs in the bunch, and that includes Jones, who is or used to be a drinker, according to what Charlie learned. We're coming up with zilch, folks. We're going to have to cast a wider net."

"Like what?" Charlie asked.

"Look outside the immediate corporate family. Take a look at the C de Bacas. The old man died before Gonda completed the purchase. Charlie, look into the death and see if there's anything suspicious there. Call in Tim or Alan for help if you need them." Tim Fuller and Alan Mendoza were retired cops we called on for help on occasion. "Hazel, check out the rest of the family. Call Gonda and see who he negotiated the purchase with. In fact, get a list of all the immediate members of the C de Baca family, okay?"

Charlie spoke up. "I knew one of the sons. Diego. Think he's the same family. At least, he comes from Plácido."

"Knew him professionally or personally?"

"Professionally. He was a hell-raiser and did most of it around here in Albuquerque. Drank. Played around with drugs. Got in trouble with a couple of girls. Some breaking and entering."

"He do time?"

"Just some community service. Paid some fines. Might have spent a night or two in jail to sober up, but as I remember, he didn't do any serious time. Think he went into the military to get out of his last jam."

"When would this have been?"

"Shortly before I retired, I think. Maybe '05 or '06."

"He have siblings?"

"An older brother and sister showed up a couple of times to bail him out."

"Okay, get on them, will you?"

I HOOKED up with Paul at the house after work. With a rare second free night in a row, we decided to go to the C&W Palace. Monday nights weren't the best time for the club, but you take what you can get, right? There would be enough stray cowgirls to help Paul indulge his passion for line dancing.

I donned a Stetson and cowboy boots, but Paul went the extra mile in stonewashed jeans, a pale blue slipover body shirt, and a mustard-colored leather vest with short fringes. When he plopped his black hat on his dark curls, he looked ready to take on the world... and handsome enough to do it.

The C&W on Central east of Expo New Mexico—more commonly called the State Fairgrounds—was a huge nightclub dedicated to attracting genuine cowboys and cowgirls, as well as cowboy and cowgirl wannabees like us. We no sooner found a small table near the dance floor than Paul was off and running looking for a partner. The C&W was a hetero place, so we never danced with each other here. There were a couple of gay spots for that.

My eye automatically went across the cavernous place to the spot where the *Santos Morenos*, a violent local gang, once held court on the east side of the room. Three years ago I had a hand in taking them down in the case I called the Zozobra Incident. So far as I could tell, nobody missed them.

My attention snapped back to the present when a couple swept by the table keeping time to a lively country-and-western tune I didn't recognize. That wasn't unusual, I didn't recognize many of them... except for Patsy Cline's tunes. Strange how that woman's warbling soulful tones grabbed a devoted classical music lover, but they had. I would stop in the middle of a busy freeway to listen to that powerful voice.

I wasn't certain why the couple snared my attention until they danced back in this direction again. The Pines' vineyard supervisor, James Bledsong and a woman… his wife, I presumed. Margaret. Or Maggie, as he'd called her. I caught his eye, and he nodded.

"Okay," Paul said, setting a couple of drinks on the table before claiming a chair. "Got a couple of dances lined up, but the band's about to go on a break. So I'm all yours for the next half hour." He blinded me with a smile.

I nodded over his shoulder. "Maybe not."

He turned as the Bledsongs walked up to us. James stuck out his hand as we exchanged introductions.

"Join you for a couple of minutes?" he asked.

"Sure. Need anything?"

"What're you having?"

"Long Island iced tea."

He shook his head. "Too strong for me. What's yours, Paul?"

"Plain old bourbon and water."

"That's more my taste. Honey?" he asked Maggie.

"Same, please."

I signaled a waitress and delivered the order before turning back to the Bledsongs. "You guys come here often?"

"Once a month. Whether we need to get out of the house or not," Maggie answered.

James laughed. "Don't exaggerate, honey. Well, I guess it's not much of one. We're on a limited budget."

"We're saving to invest in a winery of our own one day," she said.

Bledsong looked stricken. "Uh… that's a long way down the road."

I grinned at him. "Don't worry. Your boss didn't hire me to spy on you, just to find out about the break-in." I got serious. "That's not to say I won't tell him anything that's relevant, but I don't carry gossip."

Maggie gave a nervous laugh. "Thank goodness. I forgot about you being a PI and all that."

"Confidential investigator," Paul corrected. "He's too high-hat to be a PI."

She seemed to think that was funny. Their drinks arrived, allowing time for her tension to dissipate.

"As I understand it, Gonda brought you with him from Napa Valley," I said.

Bledsong nodded. "Yep. He stole me from Alfano Wineries. Not that I was a loss to them or anything."

"Don't say that," his wife protested.

"It's true. I wasn't anywhere near their top viticulturist, but I know my business. Ariel saw that and offered me a deal."

"You like it out here?"

He gave me the expected reply. "Except for the ocean. There isn't one. And that pond out at Lovely Pines doesn't raise much surf."

We talked for a few minutes about life in California versus life in New Mexico until the band returned with a rattle of drums and a strum of an electric guitar. The lead singer announced a line dance.

"May I borrow your wife?" Paul asked, rising and holding out a hand.

"Be my guest, but return her without dings, dents, or scratches, please."

"Ma'am?" Paul said in his best southwestern drawl.

"I'm not sure how good I am at this, but I'll give it a try."

We watched the tall attractive young man lead the much shorter attractive woman out onto the dance floor and take up positions opposite each other.

"This should be interesting. She hasn't line danced in a long time," Bledsong said. Then he shifted his gaze to me. "You and him... together?"

I met his eyes and nodded. "For almost three years now."

"You cover it well."

I'd engaged in this exact conversation with a dozen people over the years, so I gave him my stock answer. "Not covering anything. Just me being me and Paul being Paul. Fair enough?"

He took a sip of his drink and put it back on the table. "Sure. Have you met Zuniga yet?"

"Just to shake his hand. Why that question at this time? Is he gay?"

Bledsong shrugged. "Nobody's sure. But I've lived around the Bay Area most of my life, and sometimes I can tell."

"Would it bother you if he is?"

"Naw. Like I say, I've lived around Frisco too long."

"Zuniga's not married?"

He shook his head. "And doesn't go out much. He and Claudio Garcia, one of my guys, rent a house at the edge of Plácido."

"You think Garcia's gay too?"

"Naw. Claudio's obsessed with his wife. He's lonely, you know. He saves every spare dime to go visit them in Juarez as much as he can. He has no social life."

"If he's legal, why doesn't he bring his family up here?"

"Ariel's offered to help him do that. But she takes care of her elderly parents and won't leave."

I grimaced. A case of economics at work, pure and simple. Claudio could make a better living for them up here than back home. These days Ciudad Juarez was about the most dangerous city on the planet, especially for young males. I knew from the payroll records Garcia was twenty-four.

I leaned back in my seat and took a tiny sip of the Long Island. One of those was my limit for the night. "That provides a nice segue into the next question. Is it possible Garcia's so desperate for money for his family he would break into the winery?"

"For what?" Bledsong asked. "There wasn't anything missing. Except for one bottle of wine. And it was the chocolate-flavored wine. Claudio doesn't like that. He's a purist when it comes to the grape."

"One bottle that we know of. That place has so many bottles, who's sure of what's missing?"

"Don't let that fool you. Ariel riddles the place every three days, you know… giving each bottle a twist to break loose the sediment. So he knows what's there, and probably Zuniga, Jones, and Hakamora do too. Besides, Ariel took a fresh inventory as soon as he discovered that bottle missing."

I watched Paul and Maggie dance while I thought. She seemed to be keeping up just fine. "Gonda brought all of the top management with him, right? And that includes you."

"Right. The cook—Ms. Bright—Parson Jones, Garcia, and Tso were all hired by old man C de Baca. Ariel brought in the rest."

"Including the waitress?" I asked.

"That's a turnover position. You know, kids graduate from college or their schedules change, and we have to replace them."

"Katie… that's right, isn't it…? Katie?"

"Yeah. Katie Henderson. She works full time during the summer and during the holiday break. Otherwise she works only on weekends and holidays while she goes to school at UNM here in Albuquerque. She's a psych major."

"She's not married?"

He shook his head. "Got a boyfriend named Miles. Miles Lotharson, I think. She brought him along once when Ariel gave a little party for the staff. So far as I can tell, he's a loser. Decent enough looking, but she's way above him. That's the way I figure it, anyway."

The band ended the number with a bang and a twang, and the twin line of dancers broke up. Paul escorted Maggie back to the table. The Bledsongs took their leave shortly thereafter.

Paul emptied what little was still in his glass. "Learn anything?"

"Bits and pieces."

"Any good bits and great pieces?"

"Enough to make our trip up here to the Heights a business expense, not a personal one."

Paul fixed me with his brown-eyed stare. "Let's go home and indulge in some personal business."

Line dancing always charged his batteries.

Chapter 4

THE NEXT morning I drove straight up I-25 and exited at the north Bernalillo ramp east to the Lovely Pines. The drive, even obeying the speed limit, was no more than forty minutes. Gonda walked around from behind the chateau to greet me as I parked and got out of the Impala.

"Good morning, BJ. You have come to tell me my mystery is solved, I hope."

"No such luck. We've started the background searches, and so far it's just the usual. You know, traffic tickets. Minor stuff. Of course, the checks aren't completed yet. We're also expanding the search and looking into the C de Baca family's background."

His eyebrows climbed. "Why so?"

"Ariel, I could feed you some baloney, but to be honest, I'm casting around for demons. You've owned the winery for fewer than six months, so it's possible whatever is going on traces back to the prior owners. Can you tell me anything about the family?"

"Very little. The old man enjoyed a solid reputation as a vintner. He did not have much of a variety, but the wine he sold was good. Those bottles I presented you were his product."

"What do you know about his death?"

"Just that it was sudden and unexpected. At least, it seemed so to me."

"Did you see any evidence of illness during the time you were negotiating with him?"

"He was a spare man, but that's just the way he was built. He wasn't emaciated or frail."

"How small was he?"

Gonda dry washed the lower part of his face with his left hand in a gesture that was becoming familiar. "Let's see, I would judge him to have been about five seven. He weighed in at maybe a hundred and thirty or thirty-five pounds. He carried no fat, and the evidence of long years of hard labor still showed in his muscles. He looked entirely healthy to me. They said a heart attack took him."

"How did his family react?"

"Quite distressed over it, I would say. German—they spell it like 'German,' you know, but say it like Herman. Something about the *G*s. At any rate, he was the eldest child and took his father's death hard. He worked with Ernesto for his entire life. Consuela, the daughter, is a little harder to read. She is a tough one, that lady."

"Tough how?"

He squinted as he considered the question. "Grasping, I would say. She was the one who wanted to sell, but German held the power by right of his position in the company. During my months of talking with Ernesto, German never indicated one way or the other how he felt about selling out. But I had the distinct impression he preferred to keep it in the family."

"So why did he agree to sell after his father died?"

"Consuela's influence, in my judgment. She convinced him of it."

"Why were the negotiations taking so long with Mr. C de Baca?"

"The asking price. The old gentleman wanted two and three-quarter million dollars for the business. That included a total of 125 acres, made up of the winery property, the vineyard, and the lake. The buildings were quite substantial, and his equipment and inventory were good, to say nothing of the grapes, but there were too many intangibles—how do you say it?— too much blue sky in the price. With only fifty planted acres, the capacity was too small without buying other terroirs from neighboring vineyards. The investment in planting the additional fifty acres would be considerable. Therefore the return on investment would be insufficient."

"Wasn't he willing to come down on the price?"

"Modestly. But after an appropriate amount of time following his death, his heirs met my price of two million two."

"Is the daughter married?"

"Yes, and I have met her husband, Braxton Simpson, several times. He is a retired banker and seems a pleasant fellow."

"If Mrs. Simpson is so grasping, why did she agree to more than a half-million-dollar reduction?"

He shrugged. "Presumably because she wanted her share of the money more than she wanted a going business."

"Do you have any idea why?"

"I am afraid not."

"I believe there is a younger son. Was he involved?"

"You are speaking of Diego. He is serving in the Army, or at least one of the services. I was given to understand he did a stint in Afghanistan—or maybe it was Iraq—but may have come back stateside. He wasn't involved in our negotiations, and my lawyers assured me that since German was president of the company, the younger son's consent was not required. You see, the entire property was owned by a corporation, C de Baca Enterprises, Inc. Technically, I merely purchased assets from an existing corporation."

"That explains why it wasn't tied up in probate following his death."

"The shares of the corporation are subject to that procedure, but not the assets. Management was free to sell them."

"May I ask how you financed the purchase?"

"Certainly. Margot and I put in upwards of a million dollars of our own money into the venture. My father, Philippe, and my younger brother, Jean, each invested five hundred thousand. Something like six hundred thousand was financed by a private Swiss banking establishment, which was sufficient to complete the purchase as well as provide funds to plant out the vineyard and give us adequate working capital."

He took a breath, did his invisible beard brush, and continued without my having to ask for more. "C de Baca was producing around 35,000 gallons of wine annually. When the new vines mature, we will improve on that considerably. Our business plan calls for $300,000 in gross income during our first year. That is income from all sources— the winery, the Bistro, the gift shop, educational classes we conduct for various wine clubs, and the like. Next year we expect to double that. When we are at our peak, we should be able to gross around a million two."

"And that will be profitable?"

"Oh, yes. Our breakeven should be around nine hundred thousand."

"Thank you for sharing that information. You will notice I have not recorded it, nor will it appear in any of our reports, but I will share this conversation with my associates because it helps to understand your operation." I changed subjects. "Have you thought about getting some security? Cameras or dogs, for instance?"

"I would have to fence the place for dogs. The wall is not high enough to prevent animals of that size from entering or exiting at will. And there are the wild creatures to consider. Deer in the woods and such. The vineyard is adequately fenced for protection against them, but I would not like a similar wire fence around the chateau. And I fear the presence of such large beasts would defeat the purpose of alarms or cameras."

"I strongly suggest you consider the cameras, at least. And dogs can be trained to patrol within a given perimeter."

"Perhaps I will consider it."

"I'd like to visit the cellar again, if you don't mind."

"Certainly."

I wanted another look at the racks upon racks of bottled wines. According to Bledsong, Gonda kept them under a tight inventory. I wanted to see for myself. Gonda obligingly led me through that part of the cavern, explaining the various types of wines aging in the bottles as we passed. Suddenly he stopped short.

"*Das Schwein!*" he exclaimed. "Here is another one."

"Another what?" I moved up beside him.

He indicated an empty slot in the rack. "He has taken another bottle. One of our most expensive table wines."

"Could it have happened at the same time the other bottle went missing and you failed notice it?"

"Nein. We turned the bottles in this section yesterday. We have them on a very strict schedule."

We completed the circuit without finding anything else missing. But the discovery unsettled Gonda. It was clear evidence someone still had unauthorized access to the winery, lock or no lock on the door.

"Would you consider interrupting your schedule to assemble everyone in the reception area in the chateau for a few minutes?"

"If it will help us to determine what is going on, then the interruption will be trouble worthy."

"It may reveal nothing," I cautioned. "Still, I would like to do it."

THE GATHERING turned up no helpful information, but it gave me an opportunity to observe the body language of Gonda and his crew. Either the entire bunch was genuinely puzzled, or else someone among them was an accomplished actor. I read concern, even worry, but no overt nervousness. Parson Jones seemed the most affected.

I caught up with him right outside the back door of the chateau after the meeting broke up.

"You're taking this more seriously than anyone else except the Gondas. Why?"

He met my eyes squarely. "Mr. Vinson, what do you see standing in front of you?"

"I see a man who's worried."

"That ain't right. You see a *black* man who's worried."

I decided to get right to the heart of the matter. "Mr. Jones, I'm a gay man, so I don't wallow around in prejudice. I've had too much of it thrown at me over the years. I said what I meant. I see a man who's worried."

He nodded his head. I knew from his payroll record he was only thirty-seven, but a good bit of gray already sprinkled his close-cropped hair. During my Marine years, I'd had a Nubian in my MP squad. At least he claimed to be a Nubian despite the fact the old Nubian kingdoms disappeared long ago, absorbed into Egypt and Ethiopia. He'd been the blackest man I'd ever seen, but he had a high sheen to his flesh. Jones was just as dark, but his skin appeared to absorb light, not reflect it.

The obsidian eyes were hard with no evasiveness in them. Stringy, corded arms and torso suggested he was physically stronger than he looked. When I finished the background check on this man, I'd probably find an African American born somewhere in the south who'd worked the cotton fields and vegetable patches across the southern reaches of the United States.

"Fair enough," he said. "You might not hold no prejudices, but that don't mean nobody else don't. Mr. Gonda, he been fair to me. But them cops who come after the break-in, they give me an extra look. Course I'm worried."

"Do you have any ideas about the break-in?"

He puckered his lips together so hard, I thought for a moment he was going to whistle. "Blacks and gays ain't the only ones that run into that bigoted shit."

"You mean because the Gondas are European?"

He nodded. "That too. But mostly just because he ain't one of them. You know, a native of these parts. They kind of clannish around here. And an outfit with Swiss fellas and a crew with a black man, an Indian, a Jap, one from the other side of the border, and a California-surfer type... well, that makes for a pretty big target."

"Clannish? Not—"

He flashed a smile. "Not the white sheet kind."

"The problem with that theory is that nothing was taken—except two bottles of wine—and there was no mischief. People motivated by what you're talking about destroy things."

"There's that. So I don't rightly know." He screwed up his face. "Two bottles?"

I nodded. "Mr. Gonda just discovered another one."

"Be damned."

"Do you get hassled?"

Jones looked at me sideways. "Outside the gates, you mean? Uh-uh. I keep to myself and don't give them no reason to."

"Where do you live?"

"Rent a garage apartment at the edge of Plácido." The word came out Pla-ci-DO rather than PLA-ci-do. "Walk to work ever morning. Only mixing I do is right here on the job."

"You know I'm conducting background checks. What am I going to find on you?"

"Back in my drinking days, I boosted some stuff to buy hooch. They never made it stick, but it's on the record. A fight or two. Mostly in bars. Hauled me in for public drunkenness. That kinda stuff. Told Mr. Gonda all about it when he took me on."

"You don't claim any dependents. You're not married?"

The deep laugh lines framing the man's mouth tightened. "That ain't got nothing to do with any of this. That's my business." He flicked the brim of a floppy canvas hat he used to keep the sun off his neck and walked away.

Funny reaction. He answered every question I asked except about his family. Didn't he know that would only make me more curious? As he disappeared into the building, I followed along behind to see if I could corner the other two workers.

Zuniga was busy unpacking crates, each holding twelve empty 750-milliliter bottles. He stood with his back to me, and although the V shape from shoulders to waist was that of a man, when he turned to face me, the image of an adult shattered. The fine-featured face with its sensitive nostrils, broad expressive mouth, and big brown eyes reinforced my original impression that he was too young to work in a winery. I recalled my conversation with Bledsong at the C&W. I have pretty good gaydar, but I couldn't quite tell about this young man. His diffident manner and habit of not meeting your eyes as he spoke threw me off.

He was "pretty boy" handsome, but when he greeted me in a pleasing baritone, there was nothing effeminate in his voice or inflections.

I held out my hand. "Hi, Bascomb. May I call you Bascomb?"

"Bas. They call me Bas." He grasped my hand in a firm grip.

"Bas, I wondered if you have any ideas about what's going on around here?"

He shook his head. "No, sir. I don't have any idea at all. But I didn't—"

I held up my hand and smiled. "This isn't an interrogation. Nobody believes you had anything to do with the break-in or the missing wine, but I'd be a pretty stupid investigator if I didn't ask around to see if anyone knew something, wouldn't I?"

His lips peeled back in a grin, revealing good teeth. "I guess you would."

He sat on an unopened case of bottles and leaned forward with elbows on thighs. His gaze was fixed on a spot on the concrete floor. I propped up the nearest wall and crossed my arms.

"What was the most unusual thing you noticed yesterday or last night?"

"Yesterday or last night?"

"Another bottle of wine disappeared after the riddling yesterday."

Zuniga rolled his shoulders as if trying to relax. Being questioned by an investigator wasn't an everyday occurrence for most people. Was this natural nervousness or nervous guilt? He didn't answer my question right away, which was good. It meant either something was coming or he was giving it serious thought.

"Nothing. Not really."

"Not really means there's a question in your mind about it."

"Well, it wasn't yesterday or last night. What I mean is, a couple of times last week when I've been working in the cellar, I've heard things. Or thought I did, anyway."

"What kind of things? Voices? Movement? What?"

"No, not voices." He leaned back and met my eyes briefly before looking away. "That cellar's a noisy place for a big underground room. There's always a groan from a keg or a clink from a bottle. You know, something settling. I hear it all the time and don't pay any attention. But the other day—" He licked his lips and swallowed. "The other day I thought there was somebody in there with me. A somebody or… a presence."

"Did you tell Mr. Gonda?"

He shook his head, dislodging a shock of dark hair to curl over his forehead. "Uh-uh."

"Why not?"

"Because he'd just think I was getting spooked by nothing. Like you did."

"You're wrong. That's not what I thought at all. And in view of the fact Mr. Gonda's going to a lot of expense to get to the bottom of things, he would have taken you seriously too. Most of what he's doing is trying to make certain he, his family, and his staff are safe."

"I guess. He's a great boss. He's been good to us."

"You weren't here under the previous owners, were you?"

"No, sir. Mr. Gonda hired me."

"You have a history with him?"

"My mom was a secretary at the European Wine Consortium in Las Cruces. You know... where Mr. Gonda worked. While I was at NMSU, he offered her a position up here with him. She had a pretty good deal down there, so she didn't take him up on his offer. But when I left New Mexico State, she called him, and he gave me a job." Zuniga's features brightened. "He's going to teach me all about the business. I'd like to be a vintner one day."

I wished him well on achieving his goal and prodded him about his "left New Mexico State" comment, confirming that he abandoned his education before graduating. He was deliberately vague about why, but I didn't press him. It wouldn't be hard to get to the bottom of the matter.

I thanked him for his time and went in search of the other winery worker, John Hakamora. He was cleaning the primary fertilization chamber. I took a good look at him as I approached. Small, standing only about five six and weighing in at around one forty. With his large, round eyeglasses and an ever-present beige Panama helmet, he reminded me of a sinister Japanese spy in one of the old Humphrey Bogart/Sidney Greenstreet war movies. He acknowledged my greeting with a pleasant demeanor and open body language.

I went through the same routine with him as with Zuniga. He was also a Gonda hire, having worked at the Consortium with his boss. His parents, immigrants from Yokohama, Japan, owned and operated a lettuce farm south of Socorro. In view of the fact his older brother would inherit the business, Hakamora decided to learn about grapes. He was hired by the European Consortium shortly before Gonda left for the Alfano Wineries in Napa Valley. Apparently he made an impression, because Gonda phoned from the Lovely Pines with a better offer that Hakamora snatched up in a hurry. Gonda went to Napa Valley in 1990, so Hakamora must be older than the thirty years I'd pegged him at. I'd have to check the payroll records.

His reaction to my questions was straightforward. He'd noticed nothing unusual, but without prompting, admitted he'd sometimes heard unexplained noises while working in the wine cellar.

"What kind of noises?"

"Nothing I can explain. All I can say is that you get used to the atmosphere in a place. You know how it feels. And when it's different, it catches your attention."

"Have you always heard these noises?"

He shook his head. "Just the last few days."

"Since the break-in?"

His eyes widened. "Yes. Yes, it's just been these past two weeks."

"Did you feel someone was in the cellar who didn't belong there?"

He frowned in concentration, absently twisting a simple gold band on the ring finger of his left hand. "Not really. Just some noises that didn't fit." He held both hands out in a strange way: one palm up, one palm down. "I don't know how to explain it more'n that."

"Did you tell Mr. Gonda about what you heard?"

"There wasn't anything to tell. Just noises I couldn't explain."

"How many times did you feel that way?"

"More than one. I recall at least two different times."

I pushed the issue. "Morning? Afternoon? When?"

"I'm not sure. Afternoons, I think."

"Did you share this with anyone? Zuniga, for instance? Or Jones?"

"No, sir. I told nobody."

"Has either of those two said anything about hearing unexplained noises in the cellar? Or anywhere else, for that matter?"

He shook his head. Shortly thereafter, I thanked him for his time and walked away. It was getting late, so I decided to return to the office, once again delaying my questioning of the two vineyard workers, Garcia and Tso. I wanted to review the transcript of the conversations with the three winery workers before tackling the field hands. Besides, Gonda told me his nephew, Marc Juisson, was returning from his business trip tomorrow morning, so by waiting I could catch him as well.

I got into my Impala and headed back to Albuquerque, hoping Hazel and Charlie learned more than I had. That reminded me of something, so I dictated a note to Charlie to take another look at Parson Jones. His reaction to my question about a marriage elevated my curiosity level.

Chapter 5

THE PHONE rang at five thirty the next morning. Paul groaned and turned over. I swore for the thousandth time to delist my home number from the directory.

"Vinson," I mumbled into the pesky instrument.

"BJ, this is Ray Yardley."

I sat up, suddenly wide-awake. "Why is the state police calling me at this ungodly hour?"

Ray and I met back when we were both APD cops. We'd worked together on a couple of cases before I got shot and he went over to the state boys. He was a good man. Must be. He was a lieutenant now.

"Your client insisted I call you."

"Bless my client. Which one should I thank?"

"Fellow by the name of Gonda out at the Lovely Pines Winery. There's been a homicide involving one of his employees, and he said you were working on something that could tie in."

"Who got killed?"

"A fellow by the name of Zuniga. Bascomb Zuniga. Know him?"

"Talked to him yesterday for the first time. He seemed like a decent kid. When did it happen?"

"Sometime last night. Fill me in on your involvement, will you?"

I took Ray through the situation and asked if I could walk the scene of the crime.

"Not right now. The crime-scene boys still have it. Hell, I don't even have access yet."

"Who has jurisdiction?"

"When the call came to central dispatch, it was routed to us. We'll probably retain control, but Sandoval County has a deputy out here. An officer named Roma Muñoz. Know her?"

"No. She have any experience?"

"Been a member of the department for ten years now. I've worked with her before. Prickly but competent. I'll put in a good word for you. Why don't you drive on up and wait for us at the house? Your client's pretty broken up. We had to physically remove him from the crime scene and forbid him to return. And we could use some help making sense of things. His English deserts him, and he shifts into a foreign language now and then. Sometimes it sounds like French and sometimes it sounds like German."

"He's a naturalized citizen from Switzerland, so it's probably a little of both. It'll take me better than an hour to clean up and get up there. Will you still be around?"

"Oh yeah. I'll meet you at the Lovely Pines. That's a hell of a name, isn't it?"

"But appropriate. It's a pretty place."

I hung up and found Paul staring at me through sleep-filled brown eyes. "What's up?"

"I am, I guess. One of Ariel Gonda's people got himself killed last night. You catch some more z's. I'll try to be quiet."

"Naw, I've got to get moving anyway. I'll fix breakfast while you shower."

AFTER FEEDING my face on one of Paul's excellent cheese-and-chili omelets, I hit the road and pushed the speed limit. As I blew through Placitas, I was still wondering at Ray's description of Gonda's behavior. It was a tragedy when *anyone* was killed, and I could understand how he would be concerned by Zuniga's death. But it was difficult to see him broken up and incoherent.

Fewer than 100 yards from the turnoff to the winery, I encountered a state police mobile lab and several cruisers from both the NMSP and Sandoval County. A meat wagon from the Office of Medical Investigations was already on site. Crime-scene markers poking up from weeds and grass beside the road indicated the location of possible evidence. Even though it was not yet seven, several lookie-loos lurked in the distance. At times they presented a problem.

A Sandoval County deputy motioned me on up the road, but after I pulled over and identified myself, he directed me onto the Pines property. Ray came out of the chateau and walked down the steps as I parked. The deputy had apparently warned him of my arrival.

"BJ." He held out a hand.

Ray was about two years older than I was, which put him something shy of forty. He was a couple of inches shorter than my six feet, but at one eighty-five, had me by fifteen pounds. It wasn't fat, though; he simply carried a heavier bone structure. His sandy blond hair contrasted with the vaguely orange, bristly mustache on his upper lip. It always reminded me of carrot gratings my mom sprinkled over green salads.

"Okay, what can you tell me?" he said.

"Not much more than what I said on the phone. But you ask, and I'll try to answer. Do you mind if I tape this conversation?" I started for the chateau.

He stopped me with a hand on my arm. "No, but let's get comfortable out here. How about your Impala?"

"Why not inside? They have overstuffed chairs in the reception room."

"I want to talk to you before Gonda unloads on you. He's really taking this hard, and I get the feeling he expects you to figure out who did this to his employee."

"I hope you straightened him out."

"He didn't want to be straightened out."

We ended up leaning against the trunk of the car and watching daylight filter through the pines and the lights of the working criminologists near the highway. I got my question in first.

"Who found Zuniga?"

"Neighbor to the east of here was coming home about three this morning and spotted the body lying in the ditch beside the road. He called it in, but we didn't make the connection to the winery until somebody in Plácido tumbled to who he was."

"How was he killed?"

"OMI will tell us that. My guess is he was shot in the back. Probably when he tried to run away."

"And nobody heard the shot?"

"Look around. The closest neighbor is right in front of the turnoff to the winery, but the entrance wounds look like a small caliber. Hell, it could even be stab wounds with something like an ice pick. But if they turn out to be bullet holes, a gun like that wouldn't make much more than a pop."

"How many times was he shot?"

"I counted three wounds."

"A robbery?"

"If so, they didn't get much. Billfold still in his pocket with a few bucks in it. A Timex on his wrist."

"Three in the morning? What was the kid doing out that time of night? He was a loner. Didn't party. At least, that's the impression I had. How was Zuniga's body lying?"

"On his back, but I'll bet my bottom dollar he fell facedown. Neighbor who found him claims he didn't turn him over. Found him that way."

"You think the killer turned him over? Looking for something, maybe," I said.

"Wasn't that wallet or the two dollars in the kid's pocket. Okay, I satisfied your curiosity. Now it's my turn."

For half an hour, Ray plied me with questions. There wasn't much I could add to what he already knew, but he was a careful cop and covered the situation thoroughly. Finally he released me to go inside.

"Can I have a look at what you find?" I asked as we walked toward the front door.

"You know better than that. As long as the investigation's ongoing, nobody but law enforcement is privy to that. But I'll make you a deal. I'll share what I can if you promise to pass along what you learn." He cocked an eyebrow at me. "And don't give me that bullshit about leaving everything to us. I know you're going to poke around. Just don't become a thorn in my side. Deal?"

"Are you lead investigator?"

"That's the way it looks right now."

"Deal."

Ariel Gonda was a different man from the debonair winemaker I last saw. He rose with difficulty from an overstuffed chair in the salon of the chateau and stumbled forward, hair awry. Pale whiskers caught the lamplight and glistened like pewter. He seemed to have aged ten years overnight.

"*Danke Gott*, you're here, BJ."

I took his outstretched hand. "I'm sorry about Zuniga, Ariel."

He actually gulped. "Bascomb. His name was Bascomb. But he liked to be called Bas."

"Yes," I said as if dealing with a child, "Bas. He seemed like a fine young man."

"The best." Gonda made an effort to rally. He straightened his spine "One of the very best. He would have been my vintner one of these days." His face seemed to collapse. "Oh God. What have I done?"

Ray and I exchanged glances. "What do you mean, Mr. Gonda?" he asked quickly.

I interrupted him. "Ariel, do you have an attorney? You might want to speak to him before you—"

A bit of intelligence surfaced in the man's eyes. "What? No, no. I did not mean anything like that. But I may have placed the boy in jeopardy. May have?" His voice climbed. "I *did* place him in danger."

"Maybe you should explain," I said.

Margot moved up beside her husband and took his arm. "Let's sit over here, Ariel. We should make these gentlemen comfortable. Maggie Bledsong is preparing *Koffi* for everyone."

He allowed himself to be led into the reception room and obediently sat in the chair she indicated. We took seats around him.

When Gonda failed to speak up, Margot took over, explaining that her husband decided to accept my recommendation to get some sort of security for the facility. As usual, he made his plans known to everyone, and the staff volunteered to mount an around-the-clock watch until the surveillance equipment was up and operating. There were six volunteers who rotated on two-hour shifts after the winery was closed. Bascomb was on duty from midnight until two this morning.

"Who spelled him?" Ray asked when she finished.

"Spelled?"

"He means who relieved Bas?" I said.

She looked at her husband, who roused enough to answer. "Tso. Winfield Tso. He lives in Bernalillo and drove in a few minutes before two."

"Did you supervise the shift change?" I asked.

"No. I was sleeping in my bed while that child was being murdered." His voice broke. Tears moistened his eyes.

I glanced at Margot, who avoided my gaze.

Ray and I weren't getting much from Gonda, so we went in search of Tso. We found him talking with Hakamora, who was now standing guard at the door to the winery. They watched us approach without moving a muscle. Tso was thirty, towered considerably over six feet, and weighed in at around two ten. I knew from the search we'd done that he was a Navajo from Crownpoint, but the moon face hinted at Pueblo blood as well. In his earlier days, he'd built a record for public drinking and bar fights, but there was nothing on his sheet for the past three years. He was a C de Baca employee before Gonda bought the business.

Ray introduced himself and started asking questions. Tso's facial muscles gave nothing away, but his eyes shifted to me as if he expected me to run interference for him. When I didn't speak, he started answering Ray's questions. He wasn't hostile, but his distaste for talking to the law surfaced from time to time.

"I came in coupla minutes before two, parked my wheels, and found Bas standing right here where we are now," he said.

"I understand some of the employees live in Valle Plácido. Where do you live?" Ray brought out his recorder and flicked it on. Mine was already running.

"Bernalillo. Rent a house there."

"You live alone?"

"With a coupla other guys that work in the area."

"You have a family?"

"Wife. Three kids. Why?"

"They don't live with you."

"When they come to town, they stay with me. Mostly they stay with her mother on the rez."

"Did you notice anything unusual when you relieved Zuniga? Did he seem okay?"

"Didn't notice nothing. Bas was cool. Joked around a minute before he started hiking back to Plácido."

"He didn't ride his cycle?" I asked.

"Nah. Bas always hiked. Ain't far, and he saved on gas money."

Ray took over the questioning again. "You didn't hear anything after he left?"

Tso shook his head. "Didn't hear nothing except crickets and a couple of frogs over in the pond."

"No shots?"

A slight frown tugged at Tso's smooth, red-brown face. "Nope. Maybe a couple of pops, but didn't sound like no gunshots. I didn't think nothing of it. The pine trees pop now and then, you know." He squinted down at us from his greater height. "Was Bas shot?"

"Don't know yet. You get along with Zuniga okay?" Ray asked.

A smile erased the frown. "Yeah, Bas was okay. We didn't work together. I'm over in the vineyard. He worked here. But I seen him every day, and he was cool."

"How'd he get along with the other guys?"

"Ever'body liked him so far as I know. He wasn't no troublemaker. Minded his own business, but wasn't… you know, wasn't stuck up about it. He was okay for a college boy."

Ray addressed Hakamora. "How about you? What time did you get here?"

"I relieved Tso at four. Saw all the police cars and drove on up to the winery. Been talking to Tso ever since."

"Did you know what was going on?"

"Not till I saw lights in the chateau and went for coffee. Then I heard Bas got killed."

Ray questioned both Hakamora and Tso about relationships among the crew, but we learned little. According to both, it was an amiable bunch of men…. Everybody got along well enough, although there were the usual personal peculiarities that rubbed someone the wrong way once in a while.

Tso ended up by stating the obvious. "You oughta talk to Claudio Garcia. They roomed together in a house they rented over in Plácido."

We said our thanks to the two men and departed, leaving them in front of the winery building. Since another SP officer was in Valle Plácido handling the questioning of both Garcia and Parson Jones, I offered to accompany Ray to the scene of the crime. He waved me off, leaving me with nothing to do but return to the chateau.

Gonda was right where I'd left him earlier, still seated in one of the chairs in the salon. Margot poured coffee from what appeared to be an antique porcelain set and lifted the cup in my direction.

I accepted the black, unsweetened coffee and sat in a chair facing Gonda. He was still pale. His eyes were swollen but dry.

"I am sorry, BJ," he said softly. "I was not of much value to you or the policeman. How can I help?"

"By telling me why you're taking this so hard."

"A fine young man lost his life last night. He died a violent, untimely death while defending my property against intruders."

"You have no reason to believe that. He was on his way home when he was attacked. And even if that were true, you are no more responsible than if an act of nature took Zuniga while he was on the premises."

"I cannot accept that. Were it not for me, he would have been home in bed asleep and safe."

"Or he would have been out drinking and gotten into a bar fight. Ariel, if there is something you're not telling me, I need to know it. Now."

"There is nothing. I swear this. At least, there is nothing pertinent to this… this murder. I cannot help my sense of responsibility, nor do I apologize for it. Perhaps I am merely a foolish old man."

I took him over the events of yesterday and last night again before walking down to the highway. The OMI wagon had taken Zuniga away, but the crime-scene criminalists were still doing their thing.

Careful to remain outside the police-scene tape barriers, I strolled up and down the length of the cordoned-off area a couple of times. I always walk the scene of a crime. I did it when I was a Marine MP, an Albuquerque police officer, and now as a confidential investigator. Crime scenes, no matter how thoroughly searched by others, sometimes spoke to a man with a different perspective. This one didn't. At least not until I could walk the actual ground, and that wouldn't happen for a few days yet.

An essential task remained to be performed before heading back to Albuquerque, so I went back to the chateau. By this time Gonda had recovered a bit and taken refuge in his lab at the winery. He gave me a sheepish look when I entered. The man was hiding something from me.

"*Entschuldigung*, BJ. I apologize again for going off the deep end, as I believe you say."

I waved it away. "No need. We all react to tragedy in our own way. But I need to know if you wish me to continue."

He blinked. "Of course I do. Why would I not?"

"For one thing, the police are going to be all over your property for quite a while. I'm not certain you need my services any longer."

"More than ever. I expect you to find out who killed this boy."

Boy, not man.

I shook my head. "That's the police's job, not mine. I collect information and turn it over to you. They investigate crimes."

"Like they investigated my break-in? No, that will not do. I need a professional."

"They are professionals, Ariel. Ray Yardley is a good cop."

"So were you. And you are a fine investigator. Please continue with your investigation. I am relying on you."

Dammit, that's why I preferred working for lawyers. They knew the limitations of my job. I excused myself to go find Claudio Garcia. Apparently the NMSP and SCSO interrogators were finished with him, because I found him hard at work in the vineyard. After clearing it with Bledsong, his boss, I walked through rows of lush grape vines burgeoning with developing fruit to confront him. He stood five ten and carried around 150 pounds. Slender but with ropy muscles corded by long hours in the field. I noticed he walked with a slight limp, which I knew from our background check was the result of a childhood bout of infantile paralysis. He was twenty-four and a holdover from the C de Bacas.

He heard me approach and turned to meet me with a slightly wary look in brown eyes that wandered over my chest or my shoulder… anywhere to keep from meeting my gaze. "Señor…. Mr. Vinson. What can Claudio do for you?"

"Just wanted to talk to you a minute. Did the cops give you any trouble?"

"No, sir. They just asked… you know, questions. Made Claudio show them green card. Mostly they ask about Bas."

"What did you tell them?"

"He was a good guy." He looked at me frankly. "Why anybody wanna kill him? Bas wouldn't hurt nobody."

"Tell me about him."

He and Zuniga shared a small house they rented at the eastern edge of Valle Plácido ever since Zuniga came to work shortly after the Gondas bought the winery. They walked to and from work together, even though Zuniga owned an old Kawasaki motorcycle. He was a loner, which suited Garcia fine since that description fit him as well.

"After work we go home, pick up around house." He gave a shrug. "You know, clean up and just relax."

"Relax how?"

Another shrug. "Play dominoes. Watch TV. That kinda thing."

"You didn't go out? Bars, clubs, movies?"

"Sometime we get on Bas's *motocicleta*—" Garcia's voice caught. He cleared his throat. "We get on his hog… that's what he called his bike. 'Course it wasn't no Harley, just an old Kawasaki, but that's what he called it. Anyways, 'bout once ever month we go to the two-dollar movie off San Mateo down in Albuquerque. Sometimes we go to Bernalillo to Blake's for a Lotaburger. Most nights we just stay home."

"You talk to him much?"

Garcia thumbed his upper lip, making me suspect he recently wore a mustache. "Claudio talk. Bas listen. He like to hear about *mi familia*."

"He tell you much about his family or his history?"

He shook his head. "Not much. I know he come from around Cruces. Went to school at the big university there. Papa dead. Mama still down there. That's all."

"Any girlfriends?" I asked when he ran down.

Startled, he met my eyes briefly. "No, no. Claudio married. His wife in Juarez. He don't run around."

His reference to himself in the third person threw me for a minute. "No, I mean, Zuniga…. Bas. He was a good-looking guy. The ladies shoulda chased him all over the place."

Garcia's look went dark. "I know what they say about Bas, but it ain't so. He wasn't no queer."

"How do you know? Just because he didn't make a move on you didn't mean—"

"Claudio been around enough *maricónes*. He know one when he see him."

I questioned that statement since he hadn't seemed to grasp that I was one of those maricónes myself. Nonetheless, I was interested in his reasoning.

"Some people can fool you."

"*Sí*, but Bas like women."

"Did he ever connect with one while you were in town?"

He frowned and shook his head. "No. But…." He looked frustrated. Maybe his English wasn't good enough to express himself adequately, but if that were the case, my limited command of Spanish damned sure wasn't going to help.

Apparently he figured out what he wanted to say because he continued. "Bas and me, we rent some a them movies sometimes. You know from *adulto* places. Bas, he watch them, and he get excited. But he get sad too. When it over, he go in his room and close *la puerta*, you know… door. Stay there rest of night."

"Maybe he was giving himself some relief."

Garcia shook his head. "Claudio think so too. Sometimes he sneak over to door and listen. Know what he hear?"

I shook my head.

"*Llorando*. Crying."

My eyebrows shot up. "Crying?"

Garcia gave me an angry look. "Not like no girl. He cry like a man hurting. Hurting real bad. You understand, no?"

I agreed, but I didn't understand. Not at all.

I ARRIVED at the office around ten. I'd left a message telling Hazel and Charlie what happened, so we went into a huddle as soon as I arrived. We sat at the small conference table in the corner of my office to update one another. I handed over my voice recorder and wished for a few more hours of sleep before launching into a detailed report of the events of the night and morning.

"What do you think Gonda's hiding?" Charlie asked when I finished.

"I don't know, but I intend to find out. Hazel, dig into Zuniga's background. Go deep. Check out his parents. He told Garcia, his roommate, that his father was dead, but his mother lives in Las Cruces. Look for gang connections. Drug running. Anything that might explain why he was killed. It certainly wasn't a robbery."

"It could be a random shooting. A drive-by," she said.

"Possibly. But that's a remote area for a drive-by. And Gonda's reaction to his death has me scratching my head."

"You want me to head down to Cruces and snoop around?" Charlie asked.

"Not until we see what Hazel comes up with. Right now, I'd like you to take another look at Jones and see if you can determine why he's reluctant to talk about his marital status. Then concentrate on learning all you can about the C de Bacas." I sagged back in my chair and ran a hand through my hair. "Is there anything going on you need my help with?"

"Nothing we can't handle. Why?"

"I'm going to focus on Ariel Gonda and the Lovely Pines case for the next few days."

"Don't get your tit in a wringer," Charlie warned. "Yardley might feel like you're interfering with an ongoing investigation. The state boys frown on that."

"I don't think Yardley's going to be my problem." A Sandoval County deputy by the name of Roma Muñoz might fill that bill.

Chapter 6

MY NEXT task was to develop a relationship—be it cordial or adversarial—with Roma Muñoz, a sergeant in the Sandoval County Sheriff's Office Criminal Bureau of Investigations. When I caught up with her in the sleek, modern Thirteenth Judicial Court Complex at Hwy 528 and Idalia Road in Bernalillo on Thursday morning, she turned out to be an attractive woman of about thirty-five, diminutive in size but not in personality. Even from across the room, she exuded a sense of power and determination. This relationship would have to be earned.

"Nice to meet you, Mr. Vinson," she said as my escort from the front desk deposited me in her office. "I've heard a lot about you. Some good and some…." Her voice trailed off as she held up a hand, palm down, and wiggled it back and forth a couple of times.

"That's too bad. All I've heard about you is good."

She breezed right past the bullshit. "Am I going to have trouble with you? I warn you right up front, I'll haul your ass to jail if you interfere with my investigation."

I took a seat, uninvited, and smiled at her. "Has something changed? I understood this was Ray Yardley's case."

"It's a joint investigation, and you know it. So don't play games with me."

"I don't play games, Sergeant. I put in my time with the police—both military and city. Probably would still be if—"

"Yeah, yeah. I know all about your heroism. Shooting a murderer dead at the same time he shot you in the groin."

"It was the thigh, and that's the first time I've heard the word 'heroism' connected to it. I don't expect that to buy me anything except some respect. Ray and I have an understanding, and I wanted to do you the courtesy of offering the same to you. He won't give me access to your investigation records. Until they become public record, that is. But he has asked me to keep him abreast of anything I learn on my client's behalf and promised to apprise me of anything he feels he can share."

"So that means you intend to stick your nose in."

"It means I will continue to do what I was hired to do. Look into the break-in at the Lovely Pines Winery. That's not interfering in your investigation, but it does run parallel since last night's victim was returning from the winery after pulling a shift guarding against that intruder."

Her manner eased. She leaned back in her chair and tapped the eraser end of a lead pencil against her cheek. Her big brown eyes watched me closely. "Okay, I'll buy that. I want you to give me whatever you share with Ray. In return, I'll go easy on you."

I shook my head. "Uh-uh. I'm fulfilling my civic responsibilities by reporting whatever I learn to the state police. If you want simultaneous information, it has to be a two-way street. I want access to you and the freedom to ask questions. You'll have the right to decide which ones to answer. But I want your word you won't withhold out of cussedness. Just out of necessity."

She grinned, revealing large white teeth with a mouth generous enough to accommodate them. "I think we might get along after all. Deal."

As I shook the hand she offered, I asked, "What was the so-so info you heard about me? I thought my reputation as an investigator was spotless."

She laughed aloud, a good sound. "It's not that you're gay, if that's what you're thinking. I don't give a rat's ass about that... well, except it's a shame when a good-looking guy is out of the game. You don't act gay, Vinson. Are you sure?" Devilment sparkled in those eyes now.

"Pretty sure. There's a guy by the name of Paul Barton in Albuquerque. You can ask him, if you want. But you can call me BJ. That's how most of the world addresses me."

"Great. You can call me Sergeant Muñoz."

I left the SCSO and headed for Valle Plácido relatively certain the relationship with the Sandoval County deputy contained some shoals but was navigable.

Ariel Gonda had recovered some of his aplomb by the time I joined him on the patio of the Bistro where he was having an espresso. Margot was with him. I accepted the offer of a vanilla coffee and took a seat.

"You seem a little better centered now. Have you thought of anything my office ought to know about Zuniga?"

He shook his head. His brow creased. "No. I have nothing to add. And his name was Bascomb... Bas."

"Yes, it was. And that leads me to the next matter at hand. You're not leveling with me about something, Ariel." I deliberately used his name to make certain he knew what was coming was specifically addressed to him. "And when a client lies to me, I walk away."

He started, his fear evident. "But I have not lied to you, BJ."

"Holding out on me is the same as lying." I met his stare. "And you are holding out on me. How did you come to hire Zuniga, anyway? You must have known him in Las Cruces. Nothing else makes sense."

"There are a lot of people in Las Cruces. Why do you say I must have known him?"

"Because Zuniga—Bas—told me his mother called you about a job for him. Zuniga was born January 24, 1989, to a widowed mother named Barbara Cortez Zuniga. She named the father as her then deceased husband, Arnoldo. Frankly, given your reaction to Bas's death, I would suspect a blood relationship between you and the boy, except you didn't arrive in the US until that year... 1989."

Ignoring his stricken look, I continued. "The kid lived with his mother and grew up in Las Cruces. He enrolled in New Mexico State in 2007 on some sort of anonymous scholarship—we're looking into that right now—but he dropped out of school the following year. There was some sort of trouble. Something about a series of fights with some locals. After that, he seemed to wander around the area working for various pecan farms, vineyards, and lettuce fields. He was a virtual migrant worker until you hired him."

I glanced at Margot before putting the final nail into Gonda's coffin. "I'm gay, Ariel, so my suspicions are preprogrammed. Were you having a relationship with the man? Your reaction to his death this morning went far beyond the pale."

I expected him to become angry, but he fooled me. His shoulders slumped. He hand-brushed the beard that wasn't there and then put a knuckle to his lips.

Margot stood abruptly. "I'll leave you two alone."

He caught her hand. "No. Do not go, my dear. I—I want you here. By my side." He turned to me. "Are our conversations confidential? Legally, I mean? Are they the same as discussions with one's attorney?"

I watched the man as his body language opened. The tenseness left him as he made what was apparently a difficult decision for him. Everything now depended upon my answer to his question.

"My situation is not the same as an attorney. My records can be subpoenaed. Now, if I were working for a lawyer and not a private individual, that would change. As his agent, I could not be forced to reveal information gathered in his behalf. I know a good attorney you can call if that protection is needed."

He was silent for an entire minute as he considered my offer. "That will not be necessary." Gonda sighed and patted Margot's hand. "I was withholding not only from you but also from my wife... my family. It has nothing to do with what you are investigating, but it is time I set the record straight. Margot, my dear, I must confess something to you. Bas was my son."

She touched his cheek fondly. "You old fool. I've known that for years."

His eyes widened. Then he smiled at her lovingly. "That should not surprise me, but it does." He turned to me. "Let me explain. I came to Las Cruces in the spring of 1988 to meet the local management of the European Wine Consortium prior to joining the firm as comptroller at the beginning of the following year. While I was there, I met a young recently widowed secretary at the firm who was helpful in showing me how things were done on this side of the pond. I asked her to dinner in return. I—I swear I did not intend it to happen, but we ended up spending the night together."

Gonda returned to Switzerland with his guilty secret. He considered sharing it with his wife but did not. When they moved to New Mexico in early 1989, Gonda got a shock when he found he had a new heir. Fighting an even greater guilt now, he agreed to provide for his unacknowledged son.

"Barbara quit the firm," he said, "and stayed home to raise her... our child, supported by funds provided by one of the Gonda family trusts in Europe. She and the boy wanted for nothing." He paused to look at his wife. "I saw Bas occasionally when Barbara was invited to company picnics and the like, usually as an invited guest of one of the other employees. That same family trust provided the scholarship funds for Bas to attend NMSU."

Gonda reached tentatively across the table and took one of Margot's hands, looking as if he expected her to reject his touch. He sighed gently when she did not. "I was bitterly disappointed when the boy dropped out of university. The cause was not scholastics, but rather Bas's adverse reaction to a fraternity hazing that flared into minor violence. The boy was not expelled, but he was no longer comfortable at the school."

Both Gonda and Zuniga's mother lost contact with him for a period while he bummed around New Mexico and Arizona working the vegetable fields. The young man returned to Las Cruces about the time Gonda was hiring for the Lovely Pines. Barbara contacted him, and he hired Zuniga.

"Part of your story doesn't work," I said when he finished. "According to the birth certificate on file with the state, her husband had been dead for a year and a half by the time he was born."

"Ah, that." He stole a glance at Margot. "It was a bit of subterfuge. Barbara and I created a phony birth certificate for her records that altered the year of birth to read 1988. This fit her claim that her dead husband was the father. Frankly, that worked to my benefit as well. We couldn't alter the *official* record, but we had an altered certificate to present upon demand. Most people accept that little piece of paper without ever bothering to check the state's archives." He gave Margot a pained look. "I am sorry, dear."

"No wonder Bascomb looked younger than his age," I said. "He was."

"When did you learn about him?" Gonda asked his wife.

"When he was about six. Barbara brought him to one of the company functions, a picnic, I think. She was Bill Burham's date, do you remember? The child was obviously younger than she claimed. Or so it seemed to me, at any rate. I casually remarked how much his eyes reminded me of you, and she looked absolutely stricken. She tried to cover it, but at that moment, I knew in my heart Bascomb was your child. Later, I asked someone to look up the real birth certificate—the one on file with the state—and simply put two and two together."

Gonda shook his head. "You never said a word. Why?"

"Because I know you. You have never allowed other women to come between us. So I knew this was a one-time thing. Barbara had lost her husband, and you are a compassionate man. It went further than you intended. Barbara is a fine person. She never tried to insinuate herself in our lives, and the child was innocent. Why should I make things uncomfortable for all of us?"

"You are a wonder, my dear." He patted her arm again before turning back to me. "So now you know. What will you do with the information?"

"Nothing publicly. It gives me another place to look with respect to the break-in, but I suspect nothing will come of it. Were there any Zuniga brothers and sisters?"

"Bas is… was an only child."

"Did the boy know the truth? That you were his father?"

"Both Barbara and I decided he should continue to be comfortable believing his father was dead."

I mentally reviewed my interview with Zuniga and agreed the young man hadn't known about his true parentage. "Did you intend to tell him at some point?"

"I had not made my mind up about that. I liked the boy. Immensely. As he grew and became more important to the winery…? I don't know."

"You need to inform Lieutenant Yardley."

"Is it really necessary?" Margot asked.

"Yes. Withholding the information from him will merely raise his suspicions. I've learned enough to know the Gonda family fortune is quite impressive. He'll have to consider the inheritance angle."

"So I must now cast suspicion on my own family." Not a question—a lament.

"I'm afraid so. I can do it for you if you wish."

"Please. I would appreciate it."

I made the call to Ray on my cell phone while both of them were still at the table. The state cop listened carefully and then requested an appointment with the Gondas. I arranged it and told him to bring Sergeant Muñoz with him.

They arrived an hour later while we were having an excellent corned beef on rye with hot mustard, german potato salad, and kosher dill pickle spears. The wine was red, of course.

The interview was thorough but not as rough as it could have been because neither of the Gondas had ever shared the secret of Bascomb's birth with anyone else. Most of the questions were directed at determining how funds had been channeled to Barbara Zuniga over the years and how the scholarship was set up. Darkness approached before the two officers took their leave.

Gonda gave a big sigh. "I am relieved everything is finally out in the open. How are you handling it, my dear?" he asked his wife. "Barbara will be here tomorrow, you know."

"Yes. And I shall act toward her as I always do. I am fond of her."
She paused. "But there is another step to take, you know."

"Yes. We must inform Auguste he has… had an older brother."

"He will take it well, I think," she said. "He always got along with
Bas, although they did not have a great deal of contact."

As they talked back and forth, I decided to revisit a question already
asked and answered. "Ariel, are you absolutely certain Bascomb did not
know you were his father?"

"Barbara and I agreed from the beginning to tell no one. Frankly,
after my exposure to Bas here at the winery, I suspect I would have
confessed to him at some point. But first I wanted him to have more
exposure to me. And to Margot." He looked around the cozy room with
an abstract look on his face. "He would have run this place someday.
Auguste has little interest in it, so I was counting on my older son to step
into my shoes."

"Good. We'll have to confirm with Mrs. Zuniga that she shared
your secret with no one. But if she does, that means Bas couldn't have
told anyone. I'd hate to think someone out there we don't know about
was aware of your blood relationship."

Ariel avoided looking at Margot. Were his thoughts mirroring mine?
Was Margot concerned over sharing an estate between the two boys?
One legitimate and the other born on the wrong side of the blanket? Had
she tumbled to the fact that our inheritance laws and practices were quite
different from the aristocratic European system of primogeniture? Despite
myself, I frowned. Did Switzerland even have such a concept?

Chapter 7

PAUL LEFT for a seven thirty class the next morning, so I arrived at the office earlier than usual. I spent the time before Hazel and Charlie arrived by bringing my time and expense tickets up-to-date, dictating a few thoughts on the events of yesterday, and dumping all of it on Hazel's desk. Then I read reports of their efforts so far.

It hadn't taken long for Charlie to determine what was at the bottom of Parson Jones's reluctance to talk about his family. The man had been married and sired a child—a boy—by his wife, Zerise. He took his little family with him across the Southern states working as an itinerant farmer—cotton this season, lettuce another, beans yet another. They had been in Georgia picking cotton when he lost his family to a fire. The farmer he'd been working for provided a few tumbledown shacks for workers, and everyone fought hard to rent one because lodgings in town were more expensive—in time as well as money.

Zerise usually worked alongside her husband, but on this day the boy, Willie, was ailing, so she stayed behind to take care of him. A fire of unknown origin originated in the shanty next door, and before anyone was aware of what was happening, swept through two more cabins. One had been Parson's temporary home. His entire family burned alive that day and kicked off the young black man's battle with alcohol. Alcohol to forget and perhaps as a way of joining his wife and son.

Charlie also gathered a good deal of biographical information on the C de Baca family and laid it out in a written summary in his usual clear, concise way.

Ernesto C de Baca, born in Palomas, Mexico, came to El Norte as a migrant worker in 1951 at the age of fifteen. A physically small man who was nonetheless a good worker, he married Esmerelda Vasquez in 1955. His new wife's family had deep New Mexico roots and a share in a large Spanish land grant long since confirmed by the Treaty of Guadalupe Hidalgo. The couple produced two children: German and Consuela. When Esmerelda died of breast cancer in 1960, Ernesto inherited her share of the land grant and promptly sold it to other members of the Vasquez family. That was the source of the funds to build the Lovely Pines.

That was as far as I got before Hazel and Charlie arrived, full of questions about what went on at the chateau yesterday.

"I was just starting to read your data on Ernesto C de Baca," I said to Charlie after finishing my verbal update. "I got to the part where he started the winery. Give me the rest in a nutshell."

Charlie took a breath. "Things were difficult the first few years, but he survived, mostly because the business was virtually debt-free. His dead wife's land-grant share financed almost all of it. Of course, it wasn't so grand as it is now. No chateau, just an old adobe house. But he owned the entire 125-acre tract free and clear. Ernesto's immediate family was involved in the business with him. His older brother, Arnoldo, was viticulturist. The brother died in 2002. Both Ernesto's son and daughter were also active. The old man was a widower for twenty-six years. Then in 1986 he married Maria Candelaria. It was a May-December thing. He was fifty, and she was thirty-three. She gave birth to a son, Diego, and shortly thereafter died in a boating accident."

"Did the boy survive?"

"Yes. His mother was the only casualty. Diego was raised at Lovely Pines."

"What about the rest of the family?"

"Ernesto's daughter married a banker named Braxton Simpson and left the business. Shortly thereafter, Diego entered the Army. But German stayed with his father right to the end. Ernesto died suddenly in November 2008. The death certificate gives the cause of death as SCD—that's sudden cardiac death. It's often unexpected and is the largest cause of natural death in the US. And in Ernesto's case, it came on suddenly and unexpectedly, I'm told."

"Suspiciously sudden?"

He shrugged. "He was seventy-two but was in good health as far as anyone knew. I'll do some more checking."

"Is the younger son still in the Army?"

"I'll have to check."

"Hazel, what did you find out about our victim… Zuniga?"

"I know why he dropped out of NMSU. And it wasn't because of grades. It was because of a woman. He got his high school girlfriend, Lucia Dayton, pregnant in their senior year. He went to college, and she went into labor. It was long and hard. After the birth, the girl suffered serious health problems and committed suicide."

"Was it a live birth?"

"Apparently so," she said. "A boy."

"Uh-oh. Is there a Gonda grandchild out there somewhere? I don't believe Gonda's aware of that fact. He told me Zuniga dropped out of school because of fraternity hazing."

"Maybe that's true, but maybe he wasn't being straight with you." She grimaced. "Most of our clients start lying at some point in our investigation."

"You might be right, Hazel, but I'll bet you a dime he's ignorant about a child. Where is the boy?"

"That's something of a mystery. He doesn't seem to be around anywhere. The Daytons still live in Las Cruces, but there's no evidence of a two-year-old child living with them," Hazel said.

"We need to find that boy. Now tell me about Zuniga?"

"I talked to some of his professors who said he took it hard as well. But he seemed to rally and was getting better. Until Lucia's brothers started harassing him. One of the brothers… uh, Patrick, was at NMSU at the same time Bas was. Two other brothers lived in town."

From what Hazel learned, the brothers apparently held Zuniga responsible for their sister's death and started exacting retribution. Zuniga showed up at the dorm and in class with cuts and bruises a couple of times, but he refused to explain what happened. Then one day he must have figured he'd paid enough, because he fought back when all three brothers came for him at the same time. He used a baseball bat to defend himself.

"Two of the brothers ended up in the hospital," Hazel said. "Zuniga ended up in hot water. But the judge ultimately decided his use of force was justified. After that he quit school and worked as a migrant worker until he showed up back in Las Cruces. After that our client hired him to work at Lovely Pines."

"That explains a few things," I said, recalling what Claudio Garcia told me about Bas going into his room and sobbing on occasion. "But where is the child? Did Zuniga assert his claim as the father?"

"No evidence of that," Hazel said. "The birth certificate didn't list a father, so he'd have trouble claiming parentage if the Daytons wanted to keep the child. Of course, blood tests should clear that up. But that would take the cooperation of the Dayton family or a court order."

"We need to find that boy. What name was he given?"

She consulted her notes. "David James Dayton."

HARD ON the heels of our early morning meeting, Ray phoned to let me know his people were finished at the crime scene and I was free to examine the area on my own. Although the autopsy wasn't yet performed, the ME had expressed the opinion Zuniga died of gunshot wounds, probably a .22 or .25 caliber. There were three such insults to the body. It was possible other shots were fired and went wild, but no other projectiles had been located.

As soon as Ray terminated the call, I drove to Valle Plácido to examine the crime-scene area. The evidence markers were gone, but when I walked the outer perimeter of the area yesterday, I'd taken photos of the markers, allowing me to recreate the scene. The state boys used an alphanumeric evidence indicator system I was familiar with. The letters represented different types of evidence such as blood, clothing, glass, and the like, while the numbering system pinpointed location, progressing outward from the body.

Ray's observation about Zuniga possibly being shot in the back while running away was a plausible theory. I found scuffmarks well short of where the body was found, indicating he had been accosted and then killed, possibly while trying to escape his assailant.

A house sat directly across the road from the entrance to the Lovely Pines—no more than a tenth of a mile from the murder scene, yet Ray said no one heard the shots that killed the man. Why? A silenced pistol would indicate a professional killer and a premeditated murder. More likely, the report of a weapon that small might have gone unnoticed. This was a rural area, so locals probably shot at varmints fairly often. The neighbors wouldn't necessarily pay attention to a shot unless there was something unusual about it, such as being close by or extremely loud. In addition to that, the house across the road was a solid adobe with thick walls.

The neighbor returning home found the body around three. Zuniga left the winery at two. That meant the kill was fresh. The police cast a number of vehicle treads, but Highway 165, although dirt, was well traveled as a way into the Sandias, so the odds of that effort bearing fruit were remote. No strangers had been reported in the area, but again, the human mind is a funny thing. Strangers passed this way all the time heading up into the mountain or to the Huerfano picnic area just up the road, but if they hadn't been "lurking," they wouldn't have been noticed. The killer could have been seen without being *seen*.

Finished with my examination, I drove the short distance to the winery to talk to the staff again. As I entered the chateau, Gonda and another man met me in the foyer.

"BJ, your timing is perfect. My nephew Marc has just returned from his trip."

I examined Juisson as we went through the introductions. He was tanned, extremely good-looking, something shy of thirty, and almost my height. The brown hair was so dark it looked black at times. He tended to hold his head back so that his piercing green eyes appeared to be gazing down his aristocratic nose. Even before he acknowledged the introduction in a pleasant baritone with hardly an accent, I'd formed the impression he was not as generous a man as Gonda. This guy would be keenly aware of the family's wealth and position. And his place in it. I do not ordinarily rush to judgment about a new acquaintance, but I reached this one in a short mental footrace.

Gonda pled pressing business in the winery and asked Marc to provide whatever I needed. What I needed was a conversation with this nephew. As we took a seat in the salon, I clicked on the recorder attached to my belt.

"I understand you've been on a business trip," I said. "When did you get back?"

"Last night. It was combination business and pleasure. Although Uncle Ariel always introduces me as manager-in-training, I'm actually the firm's sales force. Of course, he and Aunt Margot do their share of schmoozing customers who show up on the premises, but I'm the outside salesman. I was in Los Angeles making the rounds of a couple of distributors, but I found time to visit the beaches. With Uncle Ariel's knowledge and approval, of course."

"Was it a successful trip? From a business standpoint, I mean."

"Very." He grinned. "From a commercial *and* a personal standpoint."

I smiled back at him. "I gather you're not tied down by a wife tucked away somewhere."

"Not a single one. Someday, maybe, but not right now."

"Is there a target in your crosshairs?"

"Several. But I haven't settled on one yet." He ran a hand through his thick hair. "I assume you want a bio."

I nodded. "Sure. That would be helpful."

The picture that emerged was that of a young man born in Vétroz, Switzerland, of the union of Count Konrad de Juisson, a Belgian living in Antwerp, and Countess Candice Gonda de Juisson, Ariel's sister. Did this entitle him to an honorific or title? I suspected not, because he represented himself as Juisson rather than de Juisson. Or else he chose to derogate or disavow titles in order to pursue a commercial venture. At this point I was merely rambling around in my own head, as I had no idea if such strictures were still placed on noble families, although historically I believed that to be true.

Marc was a natural athlete as well as a born flirt. I suspected he was firmly planted in the heterosexual side of the male universe, but that did not prevent him from flashing those green eyes at me. It could have been from a desire to experiment but was more likely to try to exert control over the situation. Or perhaps disrupt it. An interesting thought.

Juisson came to the US to attend college at Texas A&M in College Station, graduating in 2003 with a degree in agriculture and going to work for the European Wine Consortium where his uncle was the comptroller. He came north to the Lovely Pines with Gonda in January of this year.

What Juisson didn't say, but what Hazel had turned up in her background check, was that he owned a modest rap sheet for drinking and fighting and a more serious charge of attempted rape. Although the charge was later dropped when the young lady refused to cooperate, it almost cost him his student visa.

That raised a couple of interesting possibilities. Perhaps he was aware of Bascomb Zuniga's parentage, which placed another heir—and an outsider, at that—between him and the family fortune. I wasn't certain that held water because Ariel's sister, Marc's mother, likely had an equal claim to that same fortune.

Or he could have gone for a macho fling with the handsome young Zuniga and been rebuffed. It was hard to see this self-confident man killing out of rage over rejection, but indulging in violence to keep a gay pitch to another man from becoming public knowledge wasn't out of the question. Likewise, violence against gays was often a method of denying such tendencies. Juisson was once accused of attempting to rape a woman. Why not a man?

Why was I assigning such malevolent traits to Marc Juisson? Why did it matter, anyway? Zuniga's murder was a police problem, not mine. I'd been hired to get to the bottom of an unknown trespasser. But maybe they were connected somehow. At any rate, I knew Gonda expected me to look into the matter. Look into, hell. He expected me to solve the damned thing.

"Marc, this is a matter of form—" I paused and rephrased. "No, it's something you'll be asked to do by the police when they interview you, so please put together your trip itinerary, along with your receipts, places you stayed, and people you contacted. Give them to me so I can look them over before Lieutenant Yardley or Sergeant Muñoz requests them. Okay?"

"Sure. I'll start putting things together. Will copies of receipts be okay for you? You know, so I can give the originals to the cops."

I agreed and then asked another question. "Do you own a firearm?"

He shook his head. "There's no need. There are weapons in the chateau. Any time I go hunting, I use one of them."

"Do you hunt often?"

"Not often but regularly. I've bagged my share of deer, black bear, elk, and antelope. But I prefer the birds. I've taken pheasant, partridge, quail… the usual."

I thanked him for his time and watched him rise and walk away. Deliberate, studied, polished, and perfected. He moved as if on display, like a peacock before his hens. It was a confident, arrogant, and yet somehow provocative manner. He likely did everything that way.

I FOUND Gonda in the winery preparing to leave for Cutter Flying Service at the Albuquerque Sunport, where he was to pick up Bas's mother. Barbara Zuniga was flying in on a chartered plane from Las Cruces. From there they planned to go to a funeral home to make arrangements for their son's services, which couldn't take place until OMI released the body.

Now wasn't the time to brace the man over an unacknowledged grandson, so I once again gave my condolences and asked if his people were still standing guard over the winery.

"After what happened to Bas, I refused to allow them to pursue the venture any longer. The security people will be here early next week to install their devices. Until then we will just take our chances."

"Good. I need a key. I'm going to spend the night inside the winery."

"Are you sure that is wise? I mean, after what happened to Bas."

"We don't know that your son's death had anything to do with the intruder. Besides, I'm a little better prepared for such things than he was. I need the key to the side door. I want everyone to see the padlock on the front door is securely fastened. And I don't want anyone except you and Margot to know what I'm planning to do. Anyone, understood?"

"If you think that best."

He led me upstairs to his office, where duplicates of all his keys rested in a securely locked gunmetal-gray case. He looked through them, selected one, and handed it over.

"This is a master key. It opens all of the locks except the padlock on the front door. This will give you free run of the place."

I thanked him and took my leave for Albuquerque to clear my desk and get ready for a long Friday night. Stakeouts are boring as hell—until something happens. And then they are not. I'd much rather spend this night with Paul, but there was a job to be done.

Chapter 8

I SELDOM walk around armed, but I brought my new Ruger .357 Magnum revolver with a 2.25-inch barrel along on the stakeout of the winery. A deadly shooting in the vicinity tended to make me err on the side of caution. I also packed a small but powerful, rechargeable halogen flashlight, a lined lightweight jacket, and a big thermos of black coffee.

The forest was quiet as I parked the Impala in a turnoff beside the road directly west of the Lovely Pines property and struck out through the woods. I'd waited until dusk to arrive, gambling no intruder would do what I was doing... walking around while it was still light. I sat on the stone wall surrounding the place, swung my legs over the top, and as simple as that, I was on Gonda property.

At that time of year, twilight didn't start falling until nearly eight o'clock, so the place had a deserted appearance. Gonda and his wife kept their cars in a garage at the chateau, but there were still two other vehicles in the parking lot. The front gates to the property were closed, so the odds were those vehicles belonged to employees. Several lived on the premises. Juisson, for one, and the Bledsongs. The red Mazda Miata MX-5 was probably Juisson's. The Ford Fusion might be a rental for Barbara Zuniga.

So far as I could tell, I hadn't been observed as I walked to the winery's small door on the east side and let myself in with Gonda's skeleton key. The first thing I did was to make sure no one else was in the building. I knew Gonda sometimes worked late in the lab, but I'd asked him not to do so tonight.

I checked out the cellar next, which was a more difficult task. The place was huge and dimly lit, with rows and rows of barrels and racked bottles. As I went down one aisle, half a dozen people could have been sneaking up the other side. Nonetheless, after an hour of steadily prowling the chilly place, I was reasonably satisfied I was alone.

I made myself comfortable in the odd little employee lounge area at the far north end of the cavern behind the wine casks and laid the small recorder I carry on my belt on the arm of the sofa. I snapped it on before pouring a mug of coffee, all the while wishing I'd brought a heavier coat. What I was trying to accomplish wasn't clear in my own mind. Furthermore, it was probably counterproductive. If Zuniga's murder was connected to the intruder in the winery, then the heavy police presence yesterday and today should cause the intruder to ease off. That made perfectly logical sense. Yet here I was.

I chose to remain in the semidarkness of the cellar because that's where Zuniga and Hakamora heard the unexplained noises. Nonetheless, I took occasional jaunts into the winery, since some of the mischief was done there. I'd brought my old tape recorder since I had no idea how long the newfangled digital ones would record continuously. I changed tapes in the recorder three times during the night, carefully marking the time span on each, even though they'd only recorded noises I'd been making. The barely luminous dials on my father's old Elgin wristwatch read 3:00 a.m. before I decided to give it up as an exercise in futility.

I was screwing the cap back on my coffee thermos when I froze. A distinct noise came from off to my right. It sounded like a low rumble. I tried to orient myself. I was sitting on the broken-down couch shoved against the far north end of the cavern. That meant the noise came from the west side of the room. I waited but heard nothing else. I slowly got to my feet and began to edge along the wall. Every few steps I paused to listen, but the place was silent except for sounds I caused.

Then I heard a scurrying. Rats? Did the cellar have rats? Awfully big ones, if that was a rat. The inside of my right thigh began to pulse. The old gunshot wound was acting up. It usually waited until I faced danger to give me problems. Did my scar know more about this situation than I did?

Then all doubt vanished. A bottle rolled across the concrete floor somewhere in the distance. Had he heard me and dropped the bottle in surprise? I abandoned stealth and raced down the row of wine racks, trying to cut the intruder off from the exit. Within seconds I reached the south end of the cave without seeing anyone. I paused to listen again. Nothing. I pulled out my flashlight and flicked it on briefly… just long enough to check out the dark recesses at the western end of the wall. Still nothing. I turned the light off before my night vision was completely spoiled, pulled the Ruger from the belt at my back, and started walking. As I passed each row of racks, I quickly raked it with the halogen beam.

One row short of reaching the west wall, my light picked up a gleam on the floor. A bottle of wine.

I spun on my heel and raced back to the door to the winery. It was firmly closed. Could the trespasser have made it past me and out the door? Possible. I'd been faked out of position by the rolling wine bottle. I rushed through the door and out into the winery. The place was empty.

I stood at the locked door I'd used to enter the building and considered my options. I wanted to rouse Charlie out of bed and have him join me, but that would take too long. I pulled out my cell and dialed the private number Gonda had given me. When his sleepy voice answered, I quickly told him what happened. He woke up in a hurry and said he'd be right there.

"Bring your nephew and a couple of flashlights to the side door," I said.

I unlocked the door and then stepped to a spot where I could keep watch on both the entrance to the winery and the door to the cellar. While I waited, I dialed central dispatch and informed the officer on duty of what happened and asked him to contact Lt. Ray Yardley of the SP and Sgt. Roma Muñoz at the SCSO, stressing this might have something to do with their homicide case outside the same place two nights earlier. Those two would appreciate my disturbing their Saturday morning, I'm sure.

Within five minutes, Gonda and Juisson showed up, both of them armed. Gonda, dressed in faded denim, toted a shotgun. Juisson, although tousled-headed, looked as if he were dressed to go partying: dark slacks, light-colored open-weave shirt, and loafers. He held what looked to be a genuine German Luger pistol in his right hand.

I touched Gonda's arm and nodded toward the shotgun. "You know how to handle that?"

"Since I was a boy of ten."

"You?" I asked Juisson.

"Don't worry about me. I know how to use it."

I hesitated. I'd feel much better about entering an unknown situation without armed men I didn't know very well guarding my flanks. But if they left their weapons in the winery, I might be inadvertently arming our intruder. I filled them in on what happened.

After they were briefed, I led them into the dank wine cellar. The scar on my thigh burned fiercely. It didn't like having two armed men behind me any more than I did.

The wine racks ran in neat north-south oriented rows, so I put Gonda at the entrance to the cellar to block anyone's escape. Then Juisson and I started walking from the west end of the cellar to the east, one of us at either end of the rows of barrels and wine racks.

When we reached the area where the barrels were stacked, our task became a little more difficult, both because of the bulk of the containers and because someone could have lain prone on the top of a stack and not be visible. Even so, by the time we finished our sweep, I was convinced we were the only three people in the cavern.

We moved out of the chill of the wine cellar into the more comfortable atmosphere of the winery to assess the situation. Before we had a chance, the sound of footsteps and the darting beam of flashlights announced the presence of the police. I opened the side door to admit Ray and Roma and a couple of other officers. Ray looked like he'd been yanked out of bed; Roma didn't seem to have been in one. I thought of Juisson and wondered if it was a generational thing.

"You coulda opened the gate so we didn't have to hike up here" were Roma's first words.

"I marshalled my manpower where they'd be most efficient." Might as well be as sarcastic as she was.

The officers heard us out, but it was obvious Roma thought I was jumping at shadows. Before taking them to the wine bottle, I backed up the tape in my recorder until I picked up the first noise I'd heard. The rumble.

Gonda spoke up. "I do not recognize that sound. Someone dragging something across the floor, perhaps? But did you hear that faint clink? That is someone brushing a wine rack. I've done it a thousand times myself. No matter how careful he is, everyone does it from time to time."

Then there was the noise of me getting up, but as I moved away and became less intrusive, we heard the sound of a bottle of wine rolling across concrete.

"Is that enough for you?" I asked Roma.

"Okay. It wasn't shadows. But if the place is empty, maybe it was a shade."

I appreciated the difference. "Ghosts don't roll wine bottles."

"No," Ray agreed, "but people do. And you were faked out, my friend. Whoever it was figured you'd hear the bottle and try to get between him and the door. When you didn't see him, you hunted for the bottle. In the meantime he skirted around the other way and went out the door." He turned to Gonda. "You say there's only one way in and one way out of that cellar?"

Gonda nodded to the double doors behind us. "That one right there."

"It probably happened the way you say," I agreed. "But he moved fast to get through those doors, unlock the outside exit, lock it behind him, and get out of sight before I came out."

"Well, let's go see if I'm wrong." He walked to the cellar and opened the door. "Damn, it's cold in here."

"Try spending three or four hours in it," I said.

Ray sent Roma and one of the other officers to check out the place again while the fourth, a Sandoval County deputy, guarded the door. Juisson went to help search the place, probably because that's where Roma was. Gonda and I led Ray to the wine bottle. After assuring him we'd stayed out of that particular aisle and hadn't touched the bottle on the floor, we squatted down and directed the light from our flashlights across the bare concrete. We could see where the bottle had rolled in the dust. There were also a few indistinct footprints.

"This is our sweet dessert wine," Gonda said when we located where the bottle rested before it was disturbed. There were two empty places in the rack.

"He took two. One for himself and the one he left for you," Ray said.

Despite the police's more thorough search, we found no one in either the wine cellar or the winery.

Chapter 9

THE STATE and county people searched the entire area in and around the winery without turning up a single clue to where the mysterious intruder went. Gonda brought in locksmiths to change the hardware on all the doors, including the chateau and other buildings. So many people marched through the wine cellar in search of a trespasser or evidence of an intruder, the temperature actually went up to the point where Gonda became alarmed and ordered everyone out. I didn't blame him. In addition to the temperature and changes in humidity, the cops had knocked against racks holding bottles of aging wine. The entire season's production was probably in jeopardy.

Ray sent most of the officers away, but he and Roma remained behind to talk to the Gondas and Juisson. I heard enough to believe there was nothing new to be learned before walking out to take a tour of the grounds. The police and sheriff's people covered the premises pretty well, prompting me to eye the forest. Those thick pine woods would be my preferred way of ingress and egress if I didn't want to be seen.

Sandia Peak still shielded the early morning sun and everything was in shadow when I crossed the Lovely Pines' west boundary. As I walked deeper into the forest, I grew curious over who owned the acreage north of the winery. So I called the office and left a voicemail asking Hazel to do a title search using the metes and bounds legal description for the Lovely Pines.

Gonda had told me the wall surrounding the ten acres of the winery ended at the northwest corner of the property, where it was replaced by an ordinary four-strand barbed-wire fence closing off the north side. I cut through the forest to locate that juncture and was surprised to see a small tumbledown log building that people around here called a homesteaders' cabin—whether it was or not. The ruined, roofless building sat just outside the Pines' wall within a few feet of the north boundary. The south and back walls still stood, but the front of the cabin was virtually gone, and the north wall was only half-standing. Most of the roof lay on the planked floor of the structure.

After checking the small building thoroughly and finding no sign of recent intrusion, I walked south along the stone wall toward the highway. About halfway to the road, a wallow caught my attention. This was where local mule deer or some such large animals often chose to bed down for the night. Curious, I paused for a better look and spied a couple of tracks. I couldn't say they were human footprints because they had no real shape, but they certainly weren't made by any cloven-hoofed creature. While puzzling over them, some broken twigs on nearby bushes snagged my attention. Someone had made an effort to conceal the fresh breaks. The twigs had been straightened and made to lean at an angle to make the damage less obvious. Only one animal was capable of that... a human. A human who didn't want his presence to be noticed. I glanced over the wall and noted I was almost directly opposite the chateau, with a good view of the winery and the parking lot.

The indistinct trail leading to the west, deeper into the forest, proved difficult to track. I went blindly for distances before finding another place where the dirt and leaves and fallen pine needles had been disturbed. Half by guesswork, I kept going until a scrap of something caught in a thorn bush drew me. Small tufts of thread moved gently in the morning breeze. Burlap. It looked like burlap.

Now I knew why the footprints were so indistinct. Someone had covered his boots with burlap to obscure his trail. A particularly good hunter might do that. But one kind of hunter existed who did it as a part of his trade. A sniper.

The trail led to a narrow, rutted road cut into the forest years ago and then abandoned. It was half-grown with weeds and young saplings. Nobody used it anymore, except perhaps the occasional hunter or kids looking for a place to drink beer and party. At the side of a pair of deep ruts, the footprint impressions disappeared. The intruder had parked his vehicle there. He was long gone by now.

Walking on the verge to avoid destroying any vehicle tracks, although there was little sign of any, I followed the road back to the highway. To my surprise, I came across my own Impala blocking access to the road running beside the winery. That meant the spoor I'd been tracking was made prior to around eight o'clock last night. Unless the vehicle headed north and found another way out, that is. If not, then the watcher in the woods must have been delivered by a second individual already in the winery by the time I arrived.

Unless, of course, he walked in. Somehow I doubted that. The hiding place had been used several times, judging from the way the grass and weeds were crushed. That meant the intruder held to a pattern. Perhaps the sniper—and that's the way I thought of him now—and the intruder in the wine cellar were *not* the same. I mentally shook my head. Two skulkers? That required believing in one hell of a coincidence or accepting them as somehow related.

A state police cruiser and an SCSO unit were still in the parking lot by the time I made it back to Gonda's property. Good. Ray and Roma were still on the premises.

RAY, ROMA, Gonda, and I stood at the property line and peeked over the wall at the wallow area, even though the span of the stone prevented us from seeing much. Neither cop wanted anyone tramping over the area until some technicians could make it back to the site. They were more inclined to view this as evidence in Zuniga's murder than anything to do with the break-in. They could be right.

"If the perp went out after you parked here last night, he must have gone north." Ray stated the obvious as he turned to Gonda. "Where does that road go?"

Gonda lifted his hands helplessly. "I do not know. I have never set foot outside my own property line. Perhaps Marc or James or one of the others know."

"I'll check it out," Roma volunteered. "I'll walk up the wall for apiece before going over. I don't think the forensics team's going to find anything, but we might as well keep from contaminating the area. Vinson, you want to come along?"

I shrugged. "Sure."

The underbrush where she elected to enter the forest was heavy, which made me realize the area where the intruder came and went was a natural trail. Maybe a game trail or an old firebreak. After finally fighting our way through the foliage to the logging road, Roma knelt beside the ruts.

"I don't see any sign of a vehicle passing recently," she said.

"I don't either, but I merely assumed a vehicle waited for him. It's possible he walked in and out."

"Possible but not likely. Let's see where this road goes."

We walked for thirty minutes before the ruts simply petered out. It was obvious that at one time they proceeded on up the hill, but weeds and brush and immature trees clogged it to the point it was impassible, except for someone afoot.

Roma stood with her hands on her hips. "Well, he didn't go out this way. Let's hike back to your car."

"Okay, but you'll have to explain to the crime-scene boys why we tromped all over their territory."

"Screw the crime-scene boys." She seemed to reconsider. "We'll keep to the west side of the ruts."

Our inspection of the lower end of the road revealed exactly what I'd found earlier—nothing. No vehicle had gone up or down that rough, overgrown track last night or this morning.

We found Ray in the salon at the chateau talking to Gonda and Maurice Benoir, the chocolatier. Benoir told us what we'd learned for ourselves. The road dead-ended two miles north of the Lovely Pines property line.

Barbara Zuniga joined us at that point. My reaction to her was unsettling. She was an attractive, older, female version of her slain son. Somehow that highlighted the androgyny some of the others had seen in Bas. As soon as the introductions were over, she turned to Ray.

"Lieutenant, have you apprehended the Dayton brothers yet?"

"No, ma'am. It's a little early for that. Our people have questioned them and the rest of the family."

"They should be in jail. They murdered my boy. Killed him in cold blood."

"Why do you say that?" Roma asked bluntly. I think she liked pushing people's buttons.

Barbara sniffed and fixed the sergeant with a defiant stare. "Don't tell me you don't know about their assault on Bascomb after their sister's suicide."

"Yes, ma'am, we do. But that doesn't mean they shot your son."

Ray spoke up. "Troopers in Las Cruces say they're alibiing up, but we're checking things out right now. If they need to be apprehended, we'll see to it."

"Talk to the police in Las Cruces," she said. "Willie Dayton, the eldest boy, threatened to kill Bascomb. Said he would shoot him down like a dog the next time he laid eyes on him. That's a matter of public record."

"Was that because Bascomb was contesting the Daytons for custody of his child?" Ray asked.

Barbara Zuniga's eyebrows shot up. The Gondas both looked as if they'd been struck.

"His what?" they all said in unison.

Chapter 10

Lt. Ray Yardley had blundered right into a hornet's nest. It was almost comical the way he found himself fending off three individuals aggressively pelting him with questions. It became less humorous when Gonda turned to me for answers.

"I just found out yesterday, Ariel. And I didn't want to mention anything about a possible grandson until I confirmed it and learned more about him." That didn't earn me much compassion.

"You should have informed me immediately that I have a grandson. You did not think it important that I know?"

"I wasn't aware you didn't know."

"I assure you that I did not. Did you, Barbara?"

"Absolutely not!" she exclaimed sharply. "Where is the child?"

"With the Daytons in Las Cruces. How is it that you know of the Dayton brothers harassing your son without knowing he fathered a child by their sister? After all, you knew of her suicide."

"I know because a neighbor whose daughter attended NMSU told me Bas had come to class several times with obvious injuries. But she certainly never said anything about a pregnancy."

"Didn't you ask your son about his injuries?" Roma asked.

"Of course I did." Those two were fast building some enmity between them. "But Bascomb said it was the result of bullying during some fraternity initiation." She lowered her eyes. They appeared damp to me. "Bascomb and I weren't in regular contact at that point. I was trying to allow him to spread his own wings."

"So you didn't know he and the Dayton girl had been going together since high school?" I asked.

"Well, yes, I was aware of it. But from my son's deportment, it seemed like a casual thing. Something to fill a social expectation, I suppose you could say."

Had she seen something in her son that others hinted at? Had Barbara Zuniga considered Lucia Dayton as a "beard" for her possibly gay son? "You live in Las Cruces. You never heard any talk of a child?"

She blinked her large eyes at me. "Never! Nothing at all. Of course, the Dayton family and I do not socialize. I didn't even know they existed until Bas became involved with the girl in high school."

"You didn't meet the family then?" I asked.

"No, I never met them. Tell me what happened to the girl. Does anyone know why she killed herself? *That* much I learned from the paper."

"Apparently it was a difficult birth, and the young lady never recovered from the delivery."

I needed some alone time with Mrs. Zuniga, but my opportunity didn't come until after Yardley and Muñoz left. Ariel hesitated when I asked to speak to her privately, but Margot took him by the arm. I watched as they mounted the staircase and then switched on my recorder as I laid it on the coffee table between us.

"Do you know who I am, Mrs. Zuniga?"

"I understand you are the private investigator hired by Ariel to find the intruder he had at the winery. He speaks highly of you and expects you to find out who killed our son."

"You are right about the job he hired me to do. But the authorities are more likely to learn who killed your son than I am. They have more resources and the power of the subpoena. However, I will do my best to assist the police in the matter. May I ask you some questions?"

"Certainly." She leaned back in the chair and crossed her long, shapely legs. She was a statuesque woman of somewhere around forty-five. She could have been looking at me through her son's eyes, but her hair was lighter, almost ash blonde. With a little help from her hair stylist, I suspected.

I entered the appropriate data into the digital voice recorder with her permission and then led her over material we had already covered so it would be a part of the formal record. She willingly went over private details without seeming to withhold anything. She painted a picture of a typical single-parent household. Bas had a happy but male-free upbringing, since she had no relatives in the Las Cruces area. Although she occasionally attended parties or company functions at the European Wine Consortium, she purposely avoided social contact with Ariel and Margot. She felt that her son should live the lie she had concocted for him and believe that his father was dead. On one point she was steadfast:

she never revealed the secret of his true parentage. No one, not even members of her own family who lived in south Texas, knew Ariel Gonda was the boy's father.

"I find your description of your relationship with the Daytons—or rather the lack of one—to be curious. Bas was friendly with one of the Dayton sons. I have to assume he brought his friends home from time to time."

"That's true. And I did know Patrick. Found him very likeable but a little...."

I waited, but she didn't pick up the thought. "But a little what, Mrs. Zuniga?"

"He wasn't very masculine."

"Did you object to their friendship?"

"No, but I felt I had to warn Bas about—" She brushed her lips with a forefinger. "—well, about inappropriate behavior."

"Homosexual behavior, you mean?"

Her complexion darkened. "Yes. Precisely."

"How old was Bas when this happened?"

"Senior in high school. Almost eighteen. I didn't know of Patrick except as a casual acquaintance until then."

"So I assume you were relieved when Bas started dating Patrick's sister."

She looked flustered, leading me to believe my assumption that she considered the girl as cover was correct. "Yes, I guess I was."

"So you suspected your son of being gay?"

"No!" The exclamation was a little too forceful. "But I was keenly aware he grew up without a male role model in the home. So it naturally concerned me. But my concerns were pointless. After all, he fathered a child, didn't he?"

I didn't bother to point out that many gay men have fathered children over the centuries. Besides, I was beginning to think Bascomb Zuniga had handled his maturity into adulthood pretty well.

After another fifteen minutes of questioning, I thanked her and left, convinced that while she likely did the best she could in raising her son alone, there was something missing in the relationship. She lived an insular life and had been overly protective of Bascomb. That was probably why Zuniga kept his private affairs private. Not many sons withhold knowledge of a grandchild from their mothers. Nor did they become itinerant farm workers when overwhelmed by problems at school. Zuniga, who seemed like a pretty squared-away young man, had done both. The pity was that a ready and able masculine influence was foreclosed to him because of a conspiracy of silence between his parents.

MY COMPANION, Paul Barton, was a pretty sharp interviewer thanks to his journalism training, so I often shared details of cases with him. To cover him with the admittedly skimpy confidentiality protection New Mexico law provided, I insisted he accept a modest check each month as a consultant to the firm. That protection didn't mean much of anything, except when my client was an attorney, which provided Vinson and Weeks coverage under the lawyer's umbrella. A consultant to the consultant? Iffy. Following a dinner of shrimp and stir-fry vegetables that evening, we settled on a couch. After a few soul- and libido-stirring kisses, I brought him up-to-date on the Lovely Pines affair.

"So it looks like it's two different cases," he said after hearing me out. "The intruder is one thing, and Zuniga's murder is another."

"Zuniga having a son, another potential Gonda heir, gives that second option a new twist. I'm convinced Gonda didn't know of his grandchild, and Zuniga's mother certainly seemed caught off guard by the news."

"That doesn't seem right. I don't know how, but my mom would have known."

"That was in the South Valley. Everyone knows everything down there. I think Barbara Zuniga lived differently. Either she was deeply ashamed of having Gonda's baby, or else that was the deal she made with him."

"How do you know they weren't simply acting surprised at news of the baby?"

"They're damned good thespians to fake that surprise. Gonda gave me hell when he found out I knew about the child."

"Why hadn't you mentioned the boy? Asked Gonda about him?"

"I assumed he knew and hadn't had the chance to discuss it with him. Other things kept getting in the way," I said. "And what I told him was true. I wanted more information before I went off half-cocked and told him things I hadn't verified."

"Why do you think Zuniga didn't tell anyone?"

I shook my head. "Who knows? Shame, maybe. Having a child out of wedlock is not such a big deal these days, but he was seventeen years old when he got her pregnant and eighteen when the baby came. Then the trauma of his girlfriend's suicide on top of all that."

"How did she die?"

"Overdosed on prescription meds."

"Why?" he asked.

"That's what everyone wants to know. Supposedly she was in ill health after the birth, but Hazel suspects the family kept her away from Zuniga, and that, on top of her health problems, sent her over the edge."

"So the Daytons blamed him for their sister's death. Crazy."

We were in the den of our home the house my father built in the north valley. It was a 1950s contemporary with a stone foundation and redbrick walls in a settled neighborhood. I'd managed to keep my mother's treasured roses alive and prospering since I inherited the place— along with around $12,000,000 in other assets—upon their death in a car accident on I-40 in January of '03. How a couple of schoolteachers came to amass a fortune like that is a whole other story.

Paul scratched his chin. "If that brother… uh, Willie Dayton… made a threat on Zuniga's life, that ought to make him a pretty good suspect in the guy's murder. But I can't see that having anything to do with breaking into the winery at night when neither Zuniga nor anybody else is around."

"At this point there's no real evidence Willie Dayton, or any of his brothers, killed Zuniga. But you're right. Breaking into a deserted building at night doesn't seem to have anything to do with Zuniga's murder. Still, I don't like—"

"Coincidences," Paul finished my familiar refrain. "If you don't like coincidences, you're not going to buy the theory there were two different intruders, are you? So explain this to me. If the guy needed to break a lock off the door to get in the place once, how has he gotten in after that without doing the same thing? How many times has he been in the building, anyway?"

"Four or five times, at least. The first time—when he broke the lock and threw some papers around as a diversion, in my opinion—the time some of Gonda's instruments were moved. After that, a bottle of wine was disturbed in the lab. Another bottle went missing from the cellar. And then last night while I was there. In addition to that, both Zuniga and Hakamora told me they thought they'd heard someone in the cellar."

"Seems like things happen mostly at night."

"Except Zuniga and Hakamora didn't work at night. Not usually, at any rate. Hakamora said he thought it was afternoon but didn't specify a time."

Paul frowned in thought before continuing. "The guy forced the lock the first time because he needed to gain access. He didn't after that. So he obviously laid his hands on a key during the first break-in."

"Gonda swears there were no keys inside the winery. He keeps all of them locked in a steel box in his office at the chateau."

Paul gave me a lazy grin—which was almost as sexy as his last kiss. "Chateau. Tell me, what's the difference in a chateau and a big-assed house?"

I shrugged. "It just looks like a chateau. You know, a tall stone building with a continental air."

"Are you sure the guy didn't get past you and slip out the door after he faked you out by rolling a bottle across the floor?"

"It's possible, but the outside door to the winery was locked, and he'd have to be pretty quick to stop and key it. It's a deadbolt, not one of those where you press a bar and step outside."

"Maybe he was hiding in the winery somewhere?"

"Possible, but I searched the place pretty thoroughly."

"Then it's simple, isn't it?" he asked.

"Yeah. There's another means of entering and leaving the building."

"One he couldn't use until he got inside the first time."

"Right."

"So where does that lead you?" Paul asked.

"More than likely back to the C de Baca family. But even if we're right, that still doesn't tell us why the intruder keeps coming back or what he's after."

Later, as Paul reached up to snap off the light at the head of the bed, not even the tiny black dragon tattoo on his left pec lured me away from my thoughts of the Lovely Pines affair. That's how engrossed in the mystery I'd become.

THE NEXT day—a Sunday—I sat in my home office rereading my notes on the Gonda case and deciding it was time to determine if something in my client's background had reached out and touched him. During our first interview in my office, he indicated there might be someone, acknowledging they'd be more likely to burn down his building than to break into the winery. I called Charles Bosco, an old Marine buddy now enmeshed in the State Department swamp in Washington, DC. He was home enjoying a hot June day with his wife when I reached him. We reminisced about our leatherneck days before I laid my problem on him. He agreed to see what he could find out about my client, both here and in Europe. In addition to his own contacts, he had a friend in Homeland Security who would likely help out.

Next I ran down Ray Yardley, who gave me the results of the interviews with the Dayton brothers. The older two, Willie and Bart, were certified neighborhood bullies who'd butted heads with the local police several times. Mostly over busted noses, black eyes, and the like.

"Unfortunately they have alibis for the time of Zuniga's murder," Ray said. "Willie worked swing shift at a produce-packing plant and hit a bar afterward until it closed down at two the next morning. Bart's was even better. He'd been an overnight guest of Las Cruces PD for his specialty—busted noses and black eyes."

"What about the youngest boy?"

"Patrick? He was a friend of Bas Zuniga's and was closest to his sister. He doesn't have a sheet. But then he doesn't have an alibi, either."

"You told me all three of the Dayton brothers ganged up on Zuniga. That doesn't sound like Patrick was a friend."

"Turns out that wasn't entirely accurate. Patrick was trying to discourage his brothers from beating his friend to a pulp. Still, he's the Dayton who was out-of-pocket the night Zuniga died. Up in Albuquerque with two friends to catch some comedian at The Stage at the Santa Ana Star."

"Whoa," I said. "That's not Albuquerque. That's Bernalillo. Not far from Plácido, as a matter of fact…."

"Ten, maybe fifteen minutes. Anyway, no one at the club was able to identify any of them. His two traveling companions are old schoolmates and back up Patrick's story, but if they'd been along when their buddy shot a man in the back, they'd be unlikely to expose themselves as accomplices."

"Any evidence at all? Ticket stubs to the show, for instance?"

"Looking for them. I'll let you know how that comes out," Ray said. "Why are you interested, anyway? You were hired to catch a break-in artist."

"Like you, I'm not convinced they're two separate cases. I'm not convinced they are related either. But I've got to keep my options open."

MONDAY MORNING, Charlie and Hazel plopped down at my conference table for our daily huddle. Hazel had accepted a new case, a background investigation on a prominent local realtor suspected of engaging in a Ponzi scheme. There was no known involvement by the authorities, but rumors were rife. The attorneys felt it was merely a matter of time before someone—probably the feds—became involved. Our client wanted as much information as possible before the hammer fell.

By rights that should have been my top priority, but I hated to let go of the Lovely Pines problem. Once I started something, I liked to see it through to the end. There were enough records for Hazel to check before Charlie and I needed to begin interviewing. We could bring in Fuller and Mendoza to help out if things got to rushed. Providing, of course, APD or the FBI didn't move in first. But knowing our client, a large Albuquerque law firm who represented some prominent citizens who thought they were often on the butt-end of unfair tactics from the authorities, they'd want us to stay with it regardless of what occurred.

When we got around to Gonda's problem, I briefed my two associates on the latest developments as I knew them. Afterward, Charlie brought me up-to-date on the C de Bacas.

"Diego—you know, the youngest son—isn't in the Army anymore. He received an honorable discharge, showed up briefly in Albuquerque, and then fell off the proverbial map."

"Okay, Hazel," I said. "Perform your magic." She was a pro at finding missing people.

"You want me to do that before or after I perform my magic on the real-estate case?"

"Okay, I'll look for C de Baca the younger."

"Youngest," Hazel said. She was always a stickler for what was proper. Which made her soft spot for Paul strange. In her book, our relationship was anything but proper.

"Is it worth your time?" That was Charlie's subtle way of asking me to prioritize.

"Yeah. It's a loose end. I've got to gather all of those up before I know which one to pull and magically unravel the plot."

Hazel pushed her glasses up on her nose and leveled a look at me. "Are you reading whodunits again?"

THE OBVIOUS place to start my search for Diego was with the C de Baca family. German, the eldest son, now ran a consulting business for vintners, specializing in enzymes and hydrology. His office was on Wyoming NE near Paseo del Norte. Before I tackled him, Hazel let me know a quick records search in Albuquerque and Bernalillo for Diego C de Baca turned up nothing but minor stuff. I asked her to dig deeper.

Few people can absolutely disappear off the grid, but Diego did as good a job as anyone. He didn't own a car or have insurance, and the only address she'd found was an RFD Route in Valle Plácido, which turned out to be Lovely Pines. The Visa and a MasterCard he carried when he entered the military didn't seem to be active now. I located a couple of people he served with, but they claimed no contact with him since his discharge. They told me he'd bummed around with a Spec 3 by the name of James K. Natander—gifted with the nickname of Spider—and Staff Sergeant Hugo Pastis. He worked with both in a motor pool in the US Division-South at Basra. Both of those two would require a little work to locate.

By the time I headed north to C de Baca Consulting LLC, all I'd learned so far that day was something I already knew but forgot—and had nothing to do with the case. C de Baca was the shortened form of Cabeza de Baca, which meant Head of the Cow.

German was in his office and agreed to see me. As I stepped over the threshold, I mentally reviewed what Charlie learned about the eldest child of Ernesto and Esmerelda. He'd been born in Doña Ana County fifty-one years ago and was married to Yolanda. They had no children. He worked alongside his father all his life except for the four years he spent at NM State, where he took a degree in management. In the final years of the family's tenure at the Pines, German ran the business end while his father confined himself to the lab.

As we shook hands, I noted he was shorter than I was, probably around five nine, but he outweighed me by twenty-five pounds. Graying black hair, brown eyes. He would have been distinguished had there not been a cast to one eye that made him turn his head away slightly when he looked at you. Wall-eyed, we used to call it.

I flicked on the recorder on my belt as I took the seat he offered.

"Why are you looking for Diego?" he asked after I put the question to him.

I didn't want to mention a murder at this point, but I needed to come up with some sort of story. "Process of elimination, really."

"You can't possibly think he had anything to do with that shooting out there the other night."

So much for not talking about murder.

"Like I said, process of elimination. Have the authorities been in touch with you?"

He shook his head. "No. And I don't expect them to be. Diego isn't around. Hasn't been for several months."

"I understood he returned after he received a discharge from the Army in September 2008."

"He did briefly. Stayed for a week or so. He was changed. He went into the Army a boy and returned a man. But it wasn't the man I expected him to become."

"In what way?"

I could see from German's expression he considered terminating the interview, but he didn't. "Diego went into the Army in 2005, after he graduated high school, because he got into a little trouble."

I nodded, encouraging him to continue. He grimaced, probably realizing he was getting in deeper. "He got caught with some drugs. Not heavy stuff, just marijuana."

"That's interesting, because there's no record of any arrests. No record at all except for public drinking and a suspected DWI."

"Yeah, the kid was sorta wild there at the end. Drank pretty heavily, but he wasn't a hopeless case. So when he got caught with more weed than would fit in one pocket, the old man used his influence with a friend to stave off an arrest. But Diego had to agree to join the Army."

"He was dealing?"

"Using. Experimenting, really. Anyway, Dad and… this deputy… believed the military made men out of boys. You know, straightened them up. So Diego agreed and ended up in the infantry. He did a tour in Iraq."

Might as well check the facts as I knew them. "Where?"

"Basra. He was with the First Infantry Division down in Southern Command."

"Doing what?"

"Started in transportation, ended up in a motor pool."

"Transportation?"

"You know, trucking ammo and supplies to the more remote outposts."

"When was that?"

"Went over in '07 and came back in August of '08. Transferred around a couple of times after he got back and mustered out at Fort Bliss down in El Paso."

"Did you see any evidence of drug use when he got back? Was that what you meant when you said he was changed?"

"At first I thought that's exactly what I was seeing. But no, it wasn't that. He was settled down. I didn't see any wild streak in him anymore. He was nervous as hell. Never relaxed. Always looking over his shoulder." German shook his head, remembering, "But I guess a lot of people who go through a shooting war act that way. At any rate, I didn't see any sign of drugs. Hell, he'd even quit smoking. He looked healthy. But he was so damned nervous. I wondered what kind of horrors he'd seen over there. What do they call that? PTSD? There was still some pretty nasty fighting over there before he came back."

"Did you ask him about it?"

"Yeah, but he wouldn't talk about it. I understand that's not unusual either. A lot of vets don't talk about their experiences with people who haven't been through it."

"When did he leave Lovely Pines?"

"He wasn't home more than a week."

"He give any reason before he left?"

"He got a couple of phone calls before he took off. In fact, he left right after the second one. I got the feeling he talked to Dad before he disappeared, but I didn't have an opportunity to ask, because my father got sick rather suddenly and died."

"From what?"

"Heart attack. I say suddenly, but he'd been complaining for a month before. Wouldn't go see a doctor until it was too late. He wouldn't even talk about going until he fainted on the stairway one night and broke a hip. When we got him to the hospital, the doctor gave him hell for not getting in earlier. They did everything they could, but he was dead within two days."

"Did Diego come back during the illness?"

"He didn't even show up for the funeral."

"And you have no idea how to get in touch with him?"

"Not a clue."

"Pardon me for being blunt, Mr. C de Baca, but Ariel Gonda paid a pretty hefty price for the Lovely Pines, and as an heir, Diego presumably received a share of that."

"Everything was put into a trust. He, my sister, and I are beneficiaries under the trust and are entitled to certain funds, but the corpus is intact."

"I understood Lovely Pines was a corporation."

"It was, but the shares were owned by the trust. Dad transferred everything to the C de Baca Family Trust about five years before he died."

"Then the trust must have some way of conveying the funds to him."

"He hasn't touched a penny. I checked. It's still sitting in the trust's disbursement account."

"How was the relationship between you and your brother? Actually half brother, if I'm correct."

"My brother was so much younger than I was, we were more like cousins. When he was first born, I was a little resentful. But he was such a great kid, I got over it. I liked being around him." He frowned. "Until the last couple of years before he went into the Army."

"What happened?"

"He turned into a different guy."

"Why?"

He spent five minutes *not* answering the question, but when I asked about his sister's relationship with Diego, I thought I understood. She wasn't quite as forgiving as German. Although he didn't come right out and say it, she resented another heir, especially one from a different wife.

When German started showing signs of impatience, I thanked him for his time and asked for a photo of Diego. He declined but showed me a family photo made after his younger brother's brief return last September. A handsome, serious, almost dour-looking young man standing at German's left peered into the camera's lens. He stood slightly apart from the other two, as if acknowledging the age, blood, and emotional gaps between them. Somehow he seemed familiar to me.

German provided the phone numbers for Lovely Pines while the C de Bacas owned the business, although he wasn't certain if the calls Diego took came in over the landline or the cell phone his brother carried. He did not have the number or the cellular carrier but seemed to recall it was one of those pay-as-you-go services. If Ray Yardley wasn't interested in trying to track down the source of those calls that may have lured Diego away, then perhaps my old APD partner, Lt. Gene Enriquez, would check them out.

SINCE I was already halfway there, I hightailed it to Plácido before the light failed in order to have another look around. If I was right that no one got past me and escaped out the door the other night, then Paul's conclusion was correct. There was an unknown entrance into the winery.

I parked beside Juisson's red Miata and walked the exterior of the winery building looking for cracks that could have signaled a hidden door. After that revealed nothing useful, I bummed a couple of cigarettes from Parson Jones and spent an hour walking the interior of the building, blowing smoke all over the walls in the hope a draft would suck smoke and reveal an opening. All I accomplished was to rekindle a hunger for tobacco I thought I'd killed eight years ago.

Before it got too dark, I hiked the woods north of the winery, trying to imagine the cavern holding the wine cellar beneath my feet. Unfortunately I lost the light before I finished that search.

The intruder would be too skittish after the close shave the other night to show himself so soon, so I decided to find a spot where I could observe the winery from the outside. The best one seemed to be the place where someone kept watch just on the west side of the wall. I made myself comfortable a few feet south of the wallow I'd found. I didn't want to be discovered if the sniper returned. That thought rolled off my mind so effortlessly, there was no question I'd accepted that was who utilized the spot.

What was the significance of that? Could it have anything to do with Zuniga's shooting? He certainly wasn't the victim of a sniper shooting from concealment. The caliber of bullet was wrong; the pattern of the wounds wasn't right. And judging from what I'd seen at the crime scene, Bas was confronted before he was shot.

Satisfied no one was concealed in the wallow, or for that matter in the general area, I used my cell phone to let Paul know I wouldn't be home until tomorrow. He offered to drive up and protect my rear while I kept guard. The idea of him snuggling up against me from behind was attractive, but I discouraged him. A call to Gonda informed him of my plans and asked him to go ahead and shut the front gates even though my car was still in the parking lot. I took my stubby Ruger from the belt at my back and checked that all five chambers were loaded. Satisfied, I transferred it to a front pocket in my windbreaker for easier access. After that, there was nothing to do except to wish I'd brought a heavier jacket and a thermos of hot coffee or tea. The days might get hot, but the evenings cooled off considerably, especially up here on the haunches of Sandia Peak.

Years of investigative work had taught me patience, but a long stakeout gets boring for even the most experienced of us. The Lovely Pines community shut down relatively early. I watched one car leave, presumably Zuniga's mother going back to her hotel either in Bernalillo or Albuquerque. Reason told me that no matter how generous and accepting Margot Gonda was, neither woman would be comfortable with Barbara sleeping in the same house.

Nothing moved across the silent landscape for hours. The place was well lit with external lights on two corners of the winery, over the door to the chateau, and a couple of lights in the vineyard area. By using a small pair of binoculars I habitually keep in my car, I located the security cameras Gonda had installed at both the winery and at the chateau. The most distant visible light was the bulb at the door of the Bledsong cottage. Another illuminated the open work shed directly adjacent to it.

That meant whoever was entering the winery probably approached through the forest to the west. I was reluctant to leave the spot near where someone obviously spent a good deal of time watching the winery, but logic determined that I should shift my position to have more of a view of the northern fence line. As I was about to rise, movement caught my eye. Wishing my glasses had night vision, I put them to my eyes and scanned the fence area between the lake and the vineyard. Tension flowed out of me as two mule deer strolled up to the tall cyclone wire looking for a way to get to the grapevines. As I watched, they came to the end of the tall fence and nimbly hopped the four-foot stone wall to resume looking for an entry point. When they didn't find one, they lowered their graceful heads and began munching on Gonda's lawn.

I smiled to myself as I dropped the glasses back onto their leather strap around my neck. I was ready to make my move toward the forest when the sound of a motor vehicle moving up the road behind me reached my ears. I sank down into the grass again and waited. The driver killed the engine. There had been no glow of headlamps, so he must have used parking lights to maneuver the road.

As soon as the motor went off, the night went so quiet I realized I'd grown accustomed to hearing: animals in the bush, night birds calling, the flutter of unseen wings. Now everything waited and watched.

Ten minutes elapsed with no sign of the prowler. Had he walked on up the road? I was about to go check when I heard a faint rustle, as if a large serpent slithered through the grass and weeds. After a moment of panic—

snakes and I aren't compatible—I realized it was the intruder. He was crawling on his belly. Alarm bells went off again. This man was a pro. He moved like a couple of people I knew back in the Marines. Snipers. Men who could appear behind you without warning. Men who knew how to kill.

The old gunshot wound in my inner right thigh began throbbing. I pressed my hand down on it as if afraid he would hear the blood rushing, but otherwise I didn't move a muscle. Another seemingly endless ten minutes elapsed while my body cried out for movement—any kind of movement—to relieve cramping. But I held still. Finally I saw the tall stalks of grass nearby twitch. The wily son of a bitch hadn't returned to his former watching place. He'd picked another spot a few yards to the south... and closer to me than I liked.

The moonlight feebly penetrated a thin layer of clouds, giving me only a hazy view. Objects began to swim before my eyes, so I switched to my peripheral vision. That was a little better. Very slowly, a dark figure rose up no more than five feet to my left. He was concentrating on the winery, so he didn't notice my presence. He placed his elbows on the wall and put a set of large binoculars to his eyes. I waited in silence to see what he would do.

While my companion of the night moved like a sniper, he did not appear to have a rifle of any sort with him, unless it was lying at his feet in the grass. As I watched, he scanned the lawn and parking lot, probably with night-vision equipment. He paused as he scanned my car. This guy was familiar with the routine at Lovely Pines and recognized the Impala did not belong. Cautious. And careful.

He transferred his attention to the winery building, turning away from me slightly so that his features were in silhouette briefly. My view was imperfect; my eyesight strained in the darkness, but this did not appear to be Diego C de Baca... or at least, the image of Diego I'd built up in my mind. It was more of an Anglo face, although I couldn't have described him adequately because of the darkness.

I expected him to complete his surveillance of the area and head for the winery, but he surprised me. He slipped down behind the wall so only a portion of his head appeared above the top. He was waiting and watching for something... or someone.

Moving slowly, I pulled a small camera from my jacket pocket and pointed it in his direction. I closed my eyes before triggering the flash to protect my night vision. I heard a suppressed grunt when the light flashed, but when I opened my eyes, he was gone. This time he didn't even try to keep quiet. He blundered through the underbrush, heading west toward the forest road. I took off after him. His night vision should be destroyed, so there was a chance I could catch him. Even so, I had trouble seeing once I reached the dark forest, smacking into a sapling or a bush now and then.

I fumbled for my flashlight and snapped it on. That allowed me to move faster, but it also painted me for the intruder. If he moved like a trained sniper, he probably *was* a sniper. Once I reached the road, I turned the light off and made the best time I could over the rough ruts in the darkness. Almost immediately, I twisted my ankle, which slowed me considerably.

A motor fired in the distance ahead of me. He'd reached his vehicle. I saw a glint of metal a moment before bright headlights blinded me. As I tried to cover my eyes, the vehicle backed down the road and out of sight, leaving me struggling to see anything other than the bright afterglow of his headlamps painted on the underside of my eyelids. I would never catch him now.

I grabbed my cell and dialed 911, explaining the situation to the operator and asking that a county deputy be dispatched from Bernalillo to stop any vehicle on the road and detain anyone until Lt. Ray Yardley or Sgt. Roma Muñoz could reach the area. The intruder headed west toward I-40, but that didn't mean he couldn't reverse course and head into the mountains. So I limped on down the road until I reached the highway. There was no traffic moving in either direction.

As I stood in the middle of the road looking toward Valle Plácido, I reached a couple of conclusions. The intruder was military… or at least, military-trained. My overwhelming impression was of a sniper. His stealth tactics had been impeccable. I knew he was coming from the time the car motor died, yet I hadn't heard him until he was within feet of me. His reflexes were lightning fast. Yes, military. But not Diego C de Baca.

I pulled out my digital camera and checked the photograph I'd taken. The flash dimly illuminated an indistinct figure screened by tall weeds and grasses. The shape of the head was distorted by a dark woolen cap, but it nonetheless reaffirmed my belief the mysterious man was not Diego. Did that mean the sniper was *looking* for the ex-infantryman?

Chapter 11

NEITHER THE New Mexico State Police nor the Sandoval County Sheriff's Office caught anyone fleeing toward I-40. After alerting the authorities, I used Gonda's master key to free the Impala from the parking lot and make my way down the road toward Bernalillo, checking each turnoff into a yard or into the forest, looking for signs a car had recently passed. It was more difficult to determine recent traffic in the small commercial areas of Plácido and Placitas, but in any event, I didn't locate a vehicle that did not appear to belong.

I stopped at SCSO in Bernalillo to download a copy of the photo of the intruder for Sergeant Muñoz and to fill out a detailed report while it was fresh in my mind. Then I went home. Paul threw an arm over my chest as I slipped into bed, but he didn't really wake up. I soon joined him in slumber.

THE NEXT morning, a fine late June Tuesday, I settled down at the office to learn more about Diego C de Baca and his two missing Army buddies, Spider Natander and Hugo Pastis. I managed to locate the former commander of their headquarters company, a captain named Donald D. Delfonso who remembered the trio vividly.

"Why are you interested?" Triple-D asked.

I explained the break-in at Lovely Pines and the intruder I'd flushed there the night before. He listened carefully as I revealed everything except the murder of Bas Zuniga. No need to spring that on him unless I needed leverage. But he was cooperative.

"You're right. Spider Natander was a trained sniper. He went a little rogue, so they changed his MOS and made him into a motor pool mechanic. He didn't take it too well. If your intruder was one of those three, it was Natander."

"What do you mean 'a little rogue'?"

"During one mission, he took out the target okay, but he also shot the man's wife and father. Since the old man was rumored to be a bad guy too, nothing came of it. Officially, that is. But he was reassigned to my motor pool."

I played a hunch. "What was Pastis before he came to your command?"

"A demolition expert. He located and disarmed IEDs until it got to him. I understood he was a good one before he cracked."

"Cracked?"

"Wrong choice of words. He just got so nervous the rest of his team were afraid to work with him any longer. So my motor pool inherited him. He was a decent worker. Night dispatcher, as I recall."

"Sounds like they dumped their misfits into your motor pool. What was C de Baca's story?"

"Basically a decent kid but dependent. Easily led. I think the other two recognized him as an easy mark. At any rate, they bummed around together after hours."

"Any trouble?"

"Yeah. Drank too much. Went out and shot up the desert a few times. Pastis blew up a couple of boulders. Pain in the ass stuff. Almost got them dishonorables, but C de Baca managed to muster out clean."

"And that's it?"

"Criminal Intelligence came around once asking questions, but that wasn't too unusual. The locals were always filing complaints, and the brass just needed to show they were listening."

"Do you know what they were looking for?"

There was a pause, and I heard a noise like he was shifting the phone receiver from one hand to the other. "There were rumors, but if I paid attention to all the rumors, I wouldn't have time to do my job."

"What was the nature of the rumors?"

"Usually women. Petty theft. Sometimes it got heavier. More than one of our men took out his frustration on the locals. There have been a few murder and manslaughter charges. Plus the Criminal Investigation guys were always looking for stolen artifacts."

"Artifacts? You mean like those looted from the Iraqi National Museum?"

"A lot of them's been recovered, but there are plenty still missing. The locals have made an industry out of offering some of the loot to our guys. At least, that's what they claim. Of course, our people get taken. You know, offered priceless relics from antiquity that turn out to have been carved last week by the local stonecutter. I never paid much attention when they came around."

The captain offered little else, so I hung up with the firm conviction Diego had fallen in with two adventurous types, to put it politely. Was he hiding out in the winery to get away from those two? If so, why? That would have been a drastic step, but maybe his situation was drastic. The winery was where he grew up, and if a secret door to the building existed, he would probably know about it. I considered asking German about such an entrance but didn't want to expose my hand yet.

If I followed the theory of a military connection to the end, the guy I'd flushed last night was probably Spider Natander. Was Hugo Pastis hanging around too? Why would they be looking for C de Baca so doggedly?

I phoned Diego's half sister, Consuela C de Baca de Simpson. Apparently she was a liberated woman who didn't change her name when she married. Instead, she fell back on the old Spanish custom of adding her husband's name at the end. A female voice answered the Simpsons's home telephone and then agreed to get "the señora" on the line.

"I'm afraid I can't help you, Mr. Vinson." She got right down to business. "I talked to German and can add nothing to whatever he's told you about Diego."

"You haven't heard from him?"

"Not a word. He didn't even bother to come to our father's funeral."

"He knew about it?"

"Of course."

"How? Did you notify him?"

"Well, no. But my father's passing was well covered in the newspapers and TV. How could he not know?"

"By not reading a newspaper or watching TV." This woman wasn't willing to cut her brother any slack at all, which probably meant she resented his existence.

She brushed it off. "Unlikely. He just didn't care."

"I understood he was close to your father."

"At one time. You know how he ended up in the Army, don't you? And this is the thanks my father got for keeping him out of jail."

"So you have no idea where he might go?"

"I have no idea where he would run to. He's probably snookered some poor girl into hiding him."

I bit my tongue to keep from getting sharp with her. "Hiding him from what?"

"I haven't the foggiest. But if I know him, he's hiding from the law for some reason."

"Do you know what poor girl he'd run to?"

"I know nothing about Diego's friends. I have guests, and I have to go now. If you have further questions, I suggest you contact German."

The phone clicked in my ear.

With a sister like that, I'd probably hide out too. But the kid was an heir. There was money waiting for him anytime he chose to come pick it up. Hell, he probably didn't even have to come in. He could do it through bank transfers. Why had he disappeared? Was he lying dead somewhere? Injured? In the Bisti case I'd worked last year, a guy went missing after suffering a head wound and went half out of his mind. Could that have happened to this young man? When I got back to the office, I asked Hazel to search the hospitals and police jurisdictions around the state to see if she could pick up a trace of Diego C de Baca.

While Hazel and Charlie worked their ends of the case, I turned to what I knew was uppermost in my client's mind at the moment: Bas Zuniga and his two-year-old child, David James Dayton. Gonda's grandson.

I tried to save myself a trip to Las Cruces and interviewed the Dayton patriarch by telephone. I didn't manage to reach James Dayton until after five that afternoon. He was still a working man. His rough voice and abrupt manner went hostile when I finally reached him and revealed the subject of my interest.

"How come you asking about the baby? Who're you again?"

So I went over my credentials a second time and spun a story about Zuniga's family wanting to make sure the child was all right and hinted at the possibility of support, all without revealing Bas Zuniga was dead.

"Don't want no support and don't need none, neither. The baby's taken care of, so don't go sticking your nose in my business."

"You may feel the child's adequately taken care of, Mr. Dayton, but a court might want to be reassured."

"That little shit's gonna involve a court? That baby's coming on two years old, and we never heard a word from Zuniga. My poor girl barely gets over there to that school before he knocks her up."

"It could be that Mr. Zuniga was discouraged from contacting you when your sons beat on him every time they saw him. That's something the court would take into consideration. Where is the child, Mr. Dayton? No one's seen him in quite some time."

"Where you can't get your hands on him. He didn't have no mother, and his daddy's worthless, so we put him out for adoption."

"To whom?"

"Ain't got no idea. They don't tell you that."

"What adoption agency was involved?"

"That's none of your business." With that, James Dayton hung up on me.

I was accustomed to that sort of treatment, so it didn't cause any heartburn. I swiveled to my computer and began searching for adoption agencies in the area. Dayton was right about one thing: adoption agencies, private or public, were notoriously tight-lipped. But they were willing to share one thing. None of them found a record of handling an adoption for little David James Dayton.

On further reflection, Bascomb Zuniga fell a little in my estimation. If *I* had a child, I'd fight anyone I had to in order to get him. According to Dayton, he hadn't bothered to make contact. But then, what was Dayton's word worth on the matter?

Chapter 12

THE NEXT morning, Charlie phoned to say that his watch on the chateau last night had been quiet and uneventful. He stationed himself at the same place where I'd spotted the intruder, but the man hadn't showed.

I skipped going to the office and headed out to the winery. Gonda was still halfway ticked at me for not informing him about Zuniga's kid before Ray Yardley dumped it on him, but he was civil as he led me upstairs to his office.

"BJ," he said as soon as we were seated. "Give me your best assessment of our intruder. And how on earth does he keep eluding us?"

"Okay, let's take this step by step. First, I do not believe any of your staff or employees are involved in the break-in."

"Thank the good Lord. Then who?"

"It has to be someone familiar with the property, and that argues it is someone who was at the winery before you purchased it. I believe there is a secret entrance to the winery or cellar the intruder uses to come and go when he pleases."

"Then why break into the winery in the first place? The hasp was forced, you know." Gonda drew a sharp breath. "I see. The secret door was locked. The intruder needed to get into the winery in order to access it."

"Right. Then he simply left it unlocked... or there was a key inside he needed to obtain. That's the only thing that makes sense. The break-in wasn't really vandalism. All the intruder did was scatter some papers around in the office to throw us off track. There has only been a limited number of bottles of wine taken, which argues he likes a drink with his meals."

Gonda nodded. "And he takes only the very best, so he must be familiar with the grape."

"The disturbance you noted in your lab was a new product you're experimenting with. I'd say that raised his curiosity, and he couldn't resist looking at it closer. Which tells me he was intimate with the way the C de Bacas operated the winery."

"Were you able to identify the print on the bottle?"

I shook my head. "No, it was too smudged. I used K-Y Labs, and they're good. If it was identifiable, they'd have done it."

"Unfortunate. So you think it was a former C de Baca employee?"

"Or one of the C de Bacas. The younger son, Diego, is off the grid. He is out of the military, but he might have gotten mixed up in something over in Iraq and is laying low for some reason."

"And where better to lay low than where you are most familiar with the territory, especially if there is a secret room somewhere," Gonda said.

"Exactly."

"My staff and I will examine every inch of the place. If there's a hidden entrance, we'll find it."

"Won't that disturb the temperature in the cellar? Place your yield in jeopardy?"

Gonda did that beard-stroking thing where there was no beard, reaffirming my belief he once wore one. "Perhaps you're right."

"I took a preliminary look. I even lit a cigarette and blew smoke at the walls, hoping for a draft, but I found nothing. I pounded on them trying to find a hollow space. Nothing. Whoever constructed that door took a great deal of care with it."

He had no comment, so I spoke up again. "For the moment let's keep this just between the two of us. And Margot, of course. But caution her to mention it to no one. Otherwise, everyone will be tempted to go find the entrance, and you'll have the same problem. Let me and my associate, Charlie Weeks, look around."

His face sagged. "Agreed. We have already suffered one terrible loss. I see no value in placing anyone else in potential danger. Everyone is alerted against intruders as it is, and I trust that will be enough."

I watched the sadness cross his features and knew what was coming. "BJ, could... could this intruder, this Diego, if that's who it is, have murdered my son? He was on guard that night."

"Yes, but Bas was already through the gate and out on the road. It's possible he stumbled on the intruder—whoever it is—and challenged him. At this point, there is no evidence this happened."

"But is it not logical?"

"Possibly, but Bas left your property and was walking on the edge of the road toward Plácido. If I were your intruder, I'd have cut through the forest west of the winery, nowhere near where Bas was shot. And even if we had crossed paths, I'd simply run away."

"Do you believe he is a danger to my employees?"

"There is no way to judge until we know for sure who it is and why he keeps coming and going."

"You say this Diego person might be hiding from pursuers? Perhaps my son saw him and he didn't want to be identified."

I shook my head. "That makes no sense. Zuniga... uh, Bas was new to the area. He didn't know the C de Bacas."

"Then why?" It came out as a muted wail. "Why did he die?"

"I can't answer that, Ariel. The police will find the man who killed him."

"Perhaps, but I want you to investigate his death."

"I accepted the assignment of finding your intruder because the authorities closed their case. The death of your son is a joint investigation by the state police and the county sheriff. It's active and ongoing, and they'd take a dim view of me interfering."

"Then find my grandson. Make arrangements with the Daytons for me to see him."

"I don't believe they have the boy any longer. I think they put him up for adoption as soon as his mother died."

Gonda reacted as though he'd been slapped. "Why, for God's sake?"

"Any number of reasons. It's a household of men. James, the father, is widowed. None of his sons is married. Perhaps they didn't want to raise a child."

"Then why didn't they turn him over to Bas?"

"Because in their eyes, he was the source of the problem, not the solution."

"Then find him so Margot and I can raise him."

"That's not as simple as it sounds. Adoption information in this state is private. I've already contacted Dayton Sr., and he told me to go to hell. Then I checked all of the legitimate adoption agencies I could locate." I paused. "There might be one way. Take him to court. The judge might at least compel him to say what he did with the baby."

"Then by all means, we will file suit. Can you do it for me?"

"No, you'll need a lawyer. I work with one who's good. Del Dahlman. But before you contact him, let me have another try at Dayton."

"The quicker the better, BJ."

"Is Margot on board with this?"

"Absolutely. You can ask her yourself."

THAT WAS how I found myself headed south on I-25 for the 225-mile trip to Las Cruces on Friday afternoon. I didn't mind too much because Paul managed a rare weekend off and decided to accompany me. I'd met him while he was a senior at UNM and working part-time at the North Valley Country Club as a lifeguard. I'd been using swimming as therapy for the gunshot wound to my thigh, and when this handsome, hunky guy wasn't put off by the ugly purple scar, I began to look at him through new eyes. There hadn't been anyone in my life—not even casually—in the year since I'd broken up with Del Dahlman. I think Paul saw my hunger and was generous enough to sate it. We've been together ever since.

As we raced down the freeway, he casually threw an arm across the seat back and massaged my neck. His touch was magic… easing the tension there and raising it elsewhere.

"Damn, it's good to get away, Vince." He and Del were the only two who called me that. Probably because the rest of the world addressed me as BJ. Then he glanced at me and grinned impishly. "I'm not going to be shot at or hit in the head or trussed up again, am I?"

Ours had not been an uneventful relationship. Three years ago, he was first a suspect and then a kidnap victim in what I referred to as the Zozobra Incident. Then last year, he narrowly escaped being hit by a hail of bullets at the Lazy M Ranch down in the boot heel country while I was working the City of Rocks investigation.

"Don't worry. This is a simple domestic matter. Well, the domestic end of a murder case, at any rate."

"I hear those are the worst kind. Cops hate domestics."

"Then just stay in the car."

"No way. If my man's gonna walk into danger, I'm gonna be right beside him." He laughed. And some of Paul's laughs still sounded like giggles. "Well, behind him, anyway."

The road was long, but we got off I-25 to have an early dinner at the Owl Café and Bar at San Antonio, rumored to have the best hamburgers in the state. Served with a cold Dos Equis Ambar, it was all a man could ask for. Paul still looked young enough to be carded, even though he'd turned twenty-four last month.

Stomachs well padded, we got back in the Impala and headed south again. I'm a lifelong history buff, and by the time Del Dahlman and I broke up, we'd visited just about every town, village, and city in New Mexico, so I knew a little about the state's second-largest city.

Known as the City of Crosses, it was the center—both geographically and economically—of the Mesilla Valley agricultural flood plain. The area was originally the home of the Menso people, with the Mescalero Apaches nearby, until 1598 when Juan de Oñate brought the Spanish flag northward and declared everything on the high side of the Rio Grande as part of New Spain. After they threw off the yoke of the Spaniards, Mexico ruled the region until the Treaty of Guadalupe Hidalgo ceded it to the United States in 1848. At one time, the Republic of Texas claimed the area. Cruces was the home of New Mexico's only land-grant college, New Mexico State University, and serviced the nearby White Sands Test Facility and White Sands Missile Range.

Before long we spotted Picacho Peak northwest of the city, and soon thereafter the Organ Mountains hove into view. These strange, jagged peaks paralleled the city about ten miles to the east. We found a decent motel on Telshor Boulevard, the city's main north-south drag, and checked in. As soon as we freshened up, we piled back into the car and headed out to find the Dayton residence. Our timing was good... after normal work hours but early enough so most people wouldn't have gone out for the evening.

Dayton's house turned out to be in a lower-middle-class residential area not far from the renovated downtown area. The plain, once-white clapboard building could use some renovating itself, especially when measured against the late-model cinnamon Lincoln Continental sitting in the driveway. As good as his word, Paul walked up the sidewalk to the house with me.

I figured the man who answered our knock was Willie Dayton... or perhaps Bart, the second son. When I asked for his father, he backed away without either answering or opening the screen door. A few minutes later, a heavy man with scowling features took his place.

"Yeah?"

"You're James Dayton?"

He didn't bother to answer, so I continued. "Mr. Dayton, I'm B. J. Vinson, and this is my associate, Paul Barton. I spoke to you by phone a few days ago."

"Yeah, you that PI asking about the kid."

"That's right. I'd like to discuss the matter a little more."

"Don't have no interest in that. Ain't none of your business."

"Is there some reason you won't discuss the child with me?"

"Like I said, it ain't none of your business."

"It might be of interest to the children's welfare department. Where is the child, Mr. Dayton? Is he safe?"

"No business of the state. The baby's getting good care. I told you on the telephone, he's been adopted. All legal-like."

I put some steel in my voice. Enough so to draw the Dayton son forward. He stood right behind his father. "I've checked every legitimate adoption agency in the state, and no one's handled an adoption for David James Dayton."

"No law says it's gotta be in this state."

"Are you aware the baby's father is dead? Murdered. And we're having a hard time finding anyone who didn't like him except for your sons."

"Yeah, the state police already asked their questions. We got alibis. Ever' one of us."

"Except your youngest son, Patrick. I understand he was up in Albuquerque."

"Crap!" Dayton said with a sneer. "Pat was the only one who give Zuniga the time of day. Hung out with him even after the kid knocked up his sister. No pride, that one."

"Is he here?"

"No, and that's all I'm going to say about it." Dayton slammed the door in our faces.

"Not a very friendly fellow, is he?" Paul said.

I paused behind the Lincoln and wrote down the license plate number in my pocket notebook. If there was any justice, the Daytons were watching from inside and would worry about my action.

When we were in the Impala, I started the car and asked Paul if he noticed anything unusual about the Lincoln.

"Other than it doesn't fit in with the environment around here, no."

"You put your finger on it first try. I think David James Dayton financed that car."

Paul's fine dark eyebrows raised. "You think they sold the kid?"

"Interesting possibility, isn't it?"

"What do we do now?" Paul asked.

"Some old-time detective work."

We left the area but didn't go far. Working the neighborhood on foot, we knocked on doors. Lots of doors. It didn't take long to learn the Daytons were not popular. The two oldest brothers were local bullies while their father was abrupt and rude. Even so, we didn't come up with much information. Two months ago, one elderly woman saw a man and a woman carry a child out of the house and drive away in a green car. She could add little to that except to say the four-door sedan had New Mexico plates. Within days after that, James Dayton drove up in a new Lincoln.

After a good meal, we retired to the motel, where I watched Paul's small dragon tattoo dance for half an hour before we got a solid night's sleep. Then after an early breakfast, we headed back to the Dayton house, arriving just in time to see Dayton Sr. throw a bag in the back of the Lincoln and pull off down the street. An admission of guilt if I'd ever seen one. We followed discreetly until he picked up I-10 and headed south. He was fleeing the jurisdiction of the state by heading for Texas. There was no legitimate reason for detaining him, so I headed back into town. We tried the challenging NMSU golf course the next morning before driving back to Albuquerque Sunday night.

We'd no sooner unloaded the car than I caught a call from my former Marine buddy now with the Department of State. His contact in Homeland Security, plus some of his own State associates, had delivered. Ariel Gonda had a very clean record both in Switzerland and abroad. The long and the short of it was that Bosco said the family enjoyed a good relationship with their government, including law enforcement jurisdictions. To wit, Ariel had no sheet, but his family money could have cleaned up minor indiscretions.

However, Bosco declared, it had been a close thing. The fly in the ointment, and undoubtedly the matter Gonda had indirectly referred to, was a youthful competition for a fair hand. Margot's hand, as a matter of fact. While at the University of Zurich, Gonda vied with a fellow named Bernard Solis for the heart and soul of Margot. Solis was a member of a wealthy family and considered quite a catch. So when the fair lady in question selected his rival, Solis reacted badly. The story was, he challenged Ariel to a duel, but as these were outlawed at the time, wiser heads prevailed so the challenge simply ended up in a fistfight/wrestling match. The record didn't say who won, but the entire affair caused a rift between the two families.

Even so, as Gonda and Solis built their professional careers, the competition continued, contributing to some juicy gossip in the salons of Swiss society. For youthful passions to engender enmity that lasted a lifetime was not unheard of, but not common either. It was possible Gonda had not exaggerated when he mentioned that his place would have burned down if Solis were involved.

Bosco had gone to the additional trouble of determining that Mr. Solis was in Europe on the night of June 16 and the morning of June 17, when Bascomb Zuniga was murdered. Of course, had Solis really intended mischief, he could have hired it done. But why would he do so? He knew nothing of the young man's connection to the Gonda family. No, it wasn't logical. To my mind this was an issue that reached the end of its road. Gonda's past—unless it was something so deeply hidden as to be invisible—had not reached out and touched his present... and future.

Chapter 13

CHARLIE USED Tim Fuller and Alan Mendoza to keep a watch on the winery while Paul and I were in Las Cruces. Neither saw anything of interest, although Alan thought he heard someone or something in the forest behind him. Because it sounded like a deer or some other animal, he remained in hiding. So I had nothing to report to Gonda other than my abortive meeting with Dayton.

"You think he sold the baby!" Gonda exclaimed at the end of my report.

"That's what it looks like to me. Now we need to get a lawyer involved. A court can require Dayton to reveal the whereabouts of the child, especially if it wasn't a legal adoption."

He stroked his invisible beard. "But you said he fled to Texas."

"That's my supposition, but we'll find him. And the Dayton boys may have the information we need."

I handed him Del Dahlman's card and instructed him to call for an appointment. I agreed to accompany him to see the lawyer.

After that, I took a hard look around the grounds surrounding the cellar, including walking on top of the cavern and all around the edges. I saw nothing that even hinted at an opening to a tunnel or a door to a hidden room. Would ground-penetrating radar work here? I dug my toe into the earth. The vineyard was sandy soil, where such equipment might penetrate several meters, but the ground around the cavern was heavy with clay-covered stone. Sometimes the equipment wasn't so successful in that type of soil. The foliage on the hill might make ground-contact antennas impractical, though aerial ones might work. But what would they show? A cavern that we already knew was there? At the end of that reasoning process, I concluded the prospect was iffy, but I'd talk it over with Charlie before mentioning the possibility to Gonda.

Next, I walked the thick forest west of the winery. The road that Roma Muñoz and I explored the other day showed little signs of recent traffic. I did find a few footprints, but those could belong to locals out hiking or hunting

varmints. What was more interesting was a faintly worn trail that ran parallel
to the road on the west side. Who would wear a path through the forest when
there was a road within paces? Animals, perhaps, but I found an indistinct
footprint in one area. It was too faint to cast, so I took out my pocket notebook
and drew the design and noted the dimensions simply because it looked to be
deliberately smudged. Had the sniper made the track?

I'd not yet explored the area east of the Lovely Pines, so I walked
down to the welltraveled road in front of the winery and followed it
past the Pines' east property line without spotting anything but a faint
trail leading north. I trekked up it for a distance without finding any
footprints. This was likely a game trail.

After that I called it quits and headed back to the office to see if
Charlie or Hazel had better luck than I had. Hazel had completed all the
background checks on the Lovely Pines' staff without finding anything
other than minor things that threw no light on the subject. Of course, I
was pretty well convinced the break-in had nothing to do with Gonda's
employees. Zuniga's murder? Probably not, but Ray and Roma would
shake that tree, and hopefully they'd share information.

LATE THAT afternoon, I parked in the Lovely Pines parking lot, grabbed
my five-battery flashlight, and crawled over the wall on the west side of
the property. If Alan thought he heard someone in the forest last weekend,
I'd stake out a position alongside the logging road and see what happened.
But first I wanted a look around before the light failed. This time I found
something I'd missed before. Thin tire tracks running along the hump
between the two ruts in the forest road. Grass and weeds almost obscured
the impressions, but they were there. Likely several days old. Certainly not
fresh. Too small for a motorcycle. Probably a mountain bike.

The fact the rider took the trouble to hide his trail argued this was
either the intruder or the watcher I'd spooked the other day. Anyone else
would have ridden in one of the ruts… much easier going. I managed to
track it back down toward the highway and discovered the rider cut through
the forest in order to avoid riding straight up the logging road. That led me
to believe this track was left by the intruder who broke into the winery. He
was trying to avoid not only me but also the man watching for him… the
man hunting him. This wasn't proof of that, but I was willing to leap to that
conclusion. That meant I needed to go on the hunt for a bicycle.

Reversing course, I headed back up the rough track. Just before the light failed beneath the thick canopy, I found where the tracks stopped. And they did just that… halted. There was a smudged spot in the sandy dirt, and then nothing. The canny son of a bitch got off his wheels and simply picked the bike up and carried it from that point onward, his prints muffled once again. Were *two* snipers involved? Not necessarily. I wasn't a trained military sniper, but I knew about the use of burlap and other materials to distort and make tracks harder to find.

I searched diligently but unsuccessfully for signs of more footprints before the light failed. Then I walked east until hitting the winery property line and discovered I was some distance north of the small bluff where the winery backed up to the cavern. At this juncture, the four-foot wall ended, replaced by a six-foot wire fence. The falling-down cabin ruins called to me again, but I found no evidence of humans disturbing the premises.

I should have started this search earlier. By now the light was failing rapidly. I walked back to the spot where the tire tracks stopped and settled down to watch from a few feet away.

It was an uneventful watch, although I did hear some noises to the north of me. But I was willing to bet the intruder hadn't gotten past me on the road, so it must be some animal. Probably one of the mule deer in the area.

Before heading home for some much needed sleep the next morning, I walked all the way around the Lovely Pines. I found no hidden access to the property through the fences on the north end and found no secret entrances anywhere along the cliff face sheltering the cavern. Time to try out that GPR, I thought. As soon as I got some rest, I'd discuss it with Charlie.

MY BATTERIES were recharged enough to go to the office by midafternoon. As I walked through the door, Hazel handed me a message slip saying German C de Baca phoned this morning. I dialed, and after a few moments, he came on the line.

"I thought you should know that Diego withdrew a portion of his trust money. He transferred $10,000 to the SunTrust Bank branch on Fort Benning Road where he did his banking when he was taking training in Columbus, Georgia."

"He was able to do this without going into the Albuquerque bank?"

"Yes." He cleared his throat. "We made sure the funds were transferrable at his request because he was away in the Army."

"Did he ever draw on the funds while he was serving?"

"Small amounts on occasion. A hundred dollars here and a hundred dollars there."

"But never such a large amount?"

"No. But at least this lets us know he's okay, right?"

Did I detect a little fraternal feeling here? Certainly more than his sister expressed. So I chose not to tell him it meant nothing of the sort. Such a large, uncharacteristic withdrawal more likely signaled trouble. Someone was pressuring Diego for money or extorting it. Or perhaps he just needed it to flee.

"I certainly hope so, Mr. C de Baca."

After I took down the transfer data, I thanked him and hung up. The information was a bit disconcerting. I was willing to bet that Diego was the intruder in the winery. Nothing else made sense... unless old man C de Baca had come back from the dead to haunt the place.

I ran into a brick wall at SunTrust. They wouldn't even confirm an account in Diego's name, much less whether there was more than one signer on the account. I expected as much but had to try. Columbus was an Army town, so it was logical that Diego maintained his banking there throughout his service.

But I was willing to bet that Diego was nowhere near Columbus. He was here in the Albuquerque area. That meant he needed to have the funds transferred yet again to a local bank in order to lay his hands on the money. I reconsidered. Had he left the area after our near-encounter in the wine cellar? Not necessarily, but it was possible.

Charlie poked his head in the door at that moment, and I took the opportunity to apprise him of the latest development and discuss the GPR idea. We concurred that such a scan would only reveal a cavern we already knew was there. We'd wait before trying that expensive undertaking. Then I did something I'd been remiss in doing. I asked him to get photos of all the C de Bacas and of Diego's two buddies from US Division-South in Basra.

CHARLIE WAS scheduled to keep watch Tuesday night, but I decided to take his place. With an ample supply of coffee, I should be able to stay awake. The problem with that was, if I held a cup of hot coffee in my hand all night, any sniper worth his salt would smell it a mile away. Couldn't be helped. That was the only way I could remain halfway alert for the second night in a row. Jeez, was I already over the hill at thirty-seven? Sometimes my sessions with Paul raised that same question. Here was further proof.

Remembering how the sniper had scanned the parking lot the one time I'd caught a glimpse of him, I pulled off into the forest on the south side of the highway a hundred yards west of the logging road that paralleled the Pines property and hiked the rest of the way in. I located a likely spot with an oblique view of the winery doors near the wallow where I'd encountered the sniper. By turning my head, I could see the area where the bicycle tracks had ended. Satisfied, I pulled my backpack off and settled into a sheltered spot. This was not the perfect stakeout location, but since I was keeping an eye out for two separate individuals on two separate missions, it would do. Once comfortable, I hauled out the old Smith & Wesson M&P Shield 9mm semiautomatic I'd elected to carry and stuffed it in a jacket pocket. My new Ruger revolver rested in the trunk of my car.

We might just be heading into July, but twilight was coming up fast, and at this altitude the temperature would drop sharply once the soil lost the sun's warmth. I no sooner poured myself a lid of coffee than the odor of weeds and wildflowers and fallen pine needles surrendered to the pungent aroma of the hot liquid. I resolved to take my refreshment in smaller doses thereafter.

Hours passed. Despite the coffee and isometric exercises, I was rapidly losing ground to the need for sleep. I'm a trained stakeout artist and had done this a hundred times, but the gentle swish of the pine boughs all around me was as effective as a sleeping tonic. I'm sure I dozed at times but for the most part managed to remain on guard.

Somewhere around midnight, I grew aware of something. I hadn't actually heard a car, but there was one down on the highway. I glanced south but caught no glare of headlamps or parking lights. Then I heard a slight growl as a motor accelerated. The vehicle had stopped for some reason. To let someone out, perhaps? But there was no bang of a car door. Of course not. He was sneaking in.

Just as I was about to go check on the intruder, I caught movement down near the wallow. It wasn't much, just a slight swaying of brush.

In the darkness I wasn't even certain I'd actually seen anything, but something snared my attention.

Son of a bitch! The sniper! He'd snuck into place right under my nose. And movement told me he'd heard the car too. He was going to intercept whoever got out of the car. Sniper and intruder were about to meet.

I stood, making sure to create a racket while doing so. No reaction. Cautiously I worked my way, tree bole by tree bole, toward the wallow. He wasn't there. He'd slipped by me again. I turned and ran to the road and headed south. I caught a glimpse of a shadowy figure ahead of me. There was just enough moonlight piercing the overhanging canopy to determine the man carried a rifle. No doubt he'd use it if cornered. More troubling, would he use it if he met the intruder? I couldn't take the chance. I raised my S&W and fired three bullets into the trunk of the nearest pine. The flashes blinded me, but I stumbled left into the covering wood in case the fleeing man decided to return fire. There was nothing. Nothing but the roar of an approaching vehicle.

Before I reached the logging road again, I heard a car screech to a halt, a car door slam, and the vehicle roar away. The sniper likely phoned a buddy who'd been hanging around nearby to retrieve him. That settled things in my mind. Natander and Pastis, Diego's two buddies from Iraq, were hunting him down.

That was probably Diego in the other car. Someone dropped him off, and he was out there somewhere. I phoned the police dispatcher and gave a message for Yardley and Muñoz before starting my search for Diego. Voices caught my attention, so I returned to the wall near the deer wallow and saw two flashlights playing near the chateau. Lights blazed in the house's upper floor. Gonda and Juisson, likely.

I hailed them and brought them up-to-date. Both immediately insisted on helping me search despite my effort to dissuade them. I had no idea if Diego—and I was virtually certain he was our intruder—went to ground or fled. Or if he was armed and frightened enough to shoot without asking questions.

As long as they refused to be deterred, I decided to leave the field to those two and play a hunch. As I hustled back to my car, I replayed my logic in my head. The first car I heard had been someone dropping off Diego. That was probably the way he got into the area; then he rode the mountain bike he either brought with him or stashed somewhere in the woods nearby. Why a bike? Because if he didn't have a car, he'd at least be mobile on a conveyance that did not need to stick to the roads. He might not be able to outrun a car, but he could likely outmaneuver one. And he could certainly leave someone afoot behind very quickly.

If I were a fugitive who heard gunshots and figured they were aimed at me, what would I do? I'd take off on that bike as fast as possible, right down the road, with my ear cocked for the sound of a pursuing vehicle so I could leave the road and take cover in the woods. Which way would I go? Up the mountain into more isolation or toward town and civilization? If someone caught me in the mountains, they'd be more aggressive about doing me harm than if they found me in the midst of witnesses. Time to head to the biggest town nearby, and that would be Bernalillo. Upon reaching my Impala, I got in and raced down the mountainside toward town with one eye out for a bicycle.

I failed to spot any two-wheelers as I sped into the northern end of town, by which time the mountain road I'd been traveling crossed the I-25 overpass and became the busy State Highway 550. I cruised the main streets without locating a bicyclist, but that didn't bother me. He likely hadn't gotten here yet. That thought sent me back to the north end of town, where I ordered more hot coffee from one of the many fast-food places with a view of the road. After a while I decided he'd arrived by another route and started the next part of my planned search. I drove around looking for beer joints. Bernalillo had plenty of those, but I wanted exactly what I'd said... joints, not upscale places. There were plenty of those too, but not many of their patrons rode a lime-green $800 REI Cannondale mountain bike. Only one, as a matter of fact. At a place appropriately called Los Borrachos... the drunkards.

The joint was crowded. I was pretty sure Diego had never seen me, just as I'd never seen him, so I ordered a beer from the bartender—he searched through a variety of Mexican brews before locating a Coors— and looked around for a vacant table. A small one at the far end of the room beckoned. Halfway there, I found myself staring into the handsome brown eyes of Bas Zuniga.

Chapter 14

THE MAN wasn't Bas Zuniga, of course. In the dim light of the crowded bar, I couldn't even be certain those eyes were brown, but I was willing to bet they were. He was a bit older and slightly heavier than Zuniga, but he could have been the kid's doppelganger.

I had stopped dead still upon spotting the man, and my reaction brought him alert. Without pause he slung his beer at me and dashed past as I dodged the heavy mug but caught the splatter of the brew full in the face. By the time I cleared my eyes enough to see, he'd disappeared out the back way. I started to move after him and found myself hemmed in by several rough-looking customers. My false cry of "police business" didn't earn me much respect but allowed me to plow through the throng.

I burst through the back door with the beer dripping off my face turning cold in the night air. The bicycle was gone, and I had no idea which way the guy fled. Probably through back alleys and remote lanes. He'd go to ground in a ditch or an arroyo somewhere, unless he'd already called someone for help. With that thought in mind, I crawled into the Impala, dried myself off as well as I could, and settled down in the relative warmth of the car to see if anyone showed up.

Someone might have, but I'd never know. Several pickups pulled into the parking lot and discharged people, mostly men in worn Levis and cowboy boots. One Jeep Wagoneer slowed on the street and crept past the bar, but I couldn't make out the driver. Nonetheless, I wrote down the license plate number to check out later.

I returned home slightly before the joint closed down at 2:00 a.m. The stink of beer clinging to my clothing woke Paul and aroused his suspicions, so I invited him to join me in the shower so I could explain what happened and see if I could arouse anything else. It wasn't difficult.

LATER THAT morning, Hazel, Charlie, and I huddled at the small conference table in my office, where she told me the property to the north and west of the Lovely Pines was state-owned. In fact, the winery was surrounded on three sides by state or federal land. I couldn't find any significance in the fact, but it was another detail I'd had to check out.

Next, Hazel informed me that Gonda had already called this morning to ask for me. I'd deal with him later, but right now my team needed to know of last night's events. When I finished, Charlie took a photograph from a file and slid it over to me.

"Meet Diego C de Baca."

Had it not been for the uniform the man wore, I would have insisted this was a picture of Bas Zuniga. This was likely a photograph from a few years ago, which would put Diego at just about Bas's age. Army life had not yet filled out his frame.

"Uncanny," I said. "This is the guy in the bar last night."

Hazel took the photo and looked at it. "I've never laid eyes on either of them, but I've seen snaps of Zuniga. They could be twins."

"I guess this pretty well settles the question of who the intruder and his stalker are," I said.

Charlie dug around in his file and handed over another photo. "Diego's the Lovely Pines ghost, and his motor pool buddy from Iraq is the stalker. Spec-3 James K. Spider Natander is an Army sniper who went rogue and ended up in the division's motor pool."

The photo showed a spare, hawkish man with a stiff military spine who cast a cold eye at the camera. Scandinavian blond hair cut short. In other words, a sniper.

Charlie passed over a third photo. "And the guy driving the car that picked up Spider was probably Sgt. Hugo Pastis, the demo expert who got shaky and ended up tinkering with Jeeps and deuce-and-a-halves with the other two."

Pastis had a more human look to him than his buddy. The brown eyes had a soul behind them. Dark without being swarthy. Stocky.

"Those two are Army AWOLs," Charlie went on. "Their unit got shipped back to the States, where Diego was discharged. Natander and Pastis deserted shortly after he left."

"If you're right, that may explain why C de Baca hid out in the winery. He's being stalked by the other two," I said.

"I thought they were thick as thieves," Hazel said.

I nodded. "You may have just put your finger on the problem. A falling-out among thieves."

"What do you mean?"

I took out the pocket notebook I carried to jot down short, pithy facts and thoughts so I wouldn't have to go through transcriptions of my voice recordings and thumbed back until I found what I was looking for. "Back on June 22, I spoke with their company commander, a mustered-out former captain by the name of Donald Delfonso. He hinted at some trouble and a criminal investigation of some sort."

"I remember transcribing that," she said. "Something about drinking and assaulting civilians and stolen cultural artifacts."

"Exactly. What if they managed to get some things out of Iraq…?" I let my voice die away.

Charlie picked up my thought. "And then had a falling-out among themselves. Diego must have ended up with the loot—"

"And hid it at the winery," Hazel finished for him.

"Without letting the other two know where," Charlie said.

"If our assumptions are correct, they know where it is all right. They just don't know how to get to it."

Charlie thumped the table. "You need to get to Ray Yardley right away. You just solved the state police's murder for them. Natander and Pastis saw Zuniga and mistook him for Diego in the dark."

"Possible, but if that's the case, why kill the kid? They needed him to retrieve the loot."

"Hell, BJ, these aren't the most stable people on the side of Sandia Peak. Natander and Pastis got relegated to the motor pool because they were basket cases when it came to their professions. They got in an argument. Diego—or who they thought was Diego—ran, and in the passion of the moment, one or the other shot him down. Or maybe after they discovered their mistake, they killed Zuniga to cover their tracks."

"Possible," I repeated. "We've made some giant assumptions to reach this point, but I guess there's enough for us to give the information to the state and the county cops."

"Don't forget to call Gonda back," Hazel reminded me.

"I have to take care of a couple of things, and then I'm driving out to the Pines. I don't want to talk to him until then. If he calls again, let him know I'm on the way."

HAZEL FAXED the photos of the three former infantrymen to Yardley and Muñoz before I got them on a conference call. They both listened carefully as I detailed what my investigation turned up so far. They had been traveling down the same road but hadn't yet seen a photo of Diego C de Baca, which was what *possibly* tied the intrusion at the winery and the murder together. Before we wrapped up the conversation, I asked Yardley about fingerprints on the wine bottle the intruder had rolled on the floor of the cavern.

"We have a good palm print but not much in the way of fingerprints. Haven't learned anything from it so far."

After keeping my part of the bargain with the two cops, I turned to the New Mexico Motor Vehicle Division database available to licensed PIs and found a registration for the Wagoneer I'd spotted last night while checking out the parking lot of Los Borrachos. The vehicle belonged to a Nancy Hummerman, with an address of 3501 Holiday NE in the Heights area of Albuquerque. My cross-reference directory didn't confirm that address, but I decided to give it a try anyway.

Someone peeked out the window as I parked on the street in front of the redbrick house but stepped back quickly when I turned my gaze in her direction. Whoever it was took her time in answering the doorbell a minute or so later.

The woman who stood on the other side of the screen door was blonde and attractive rather than pretty. In my book, Diego was a lot prettier than she was... but I was getting ahead of myself. Perhaps there was no connection between the two. Even so, my comparison was apt.

"Ma'am, my name's B. J. Vinson, and I'm looking for Diego C de Baca. Is he here?"

She blinked and paused just a little too long. "I'm sorry, I don't know anyone by that name."

"Are you certain? I saw his green bike on the porch the other day."

She blinked twice at that lie. "No, this is my house, and I can assure you no one of that name lives here. And I don't have a mountain bike. Green or otherwise."

"Maybe not, but...." I was speaking to a blank front door. When she didn't respond to another ring, I returned to the Impala and took my time dictating what just happened. The lady was a little too abrupt in her denial. Better yet, she'd correctly identified Diego's wheels as a *mountain* bike. At this point, I wanted her as nervous as possible. Then I scribbled a note on the back of one of my cards, saying I knew Diego was in trouble and wanted to help. Understanding that my every movement was scrutinized, I got out of the car and walked back to the porch to wedge the business card between the screen door and the frame.

From the Heights, I headed straight for the Lovely Pines to update my client. I knew from experience he would insist that I put my own spin on the report, and that gave me some heartburn. Spinning was not my business. Collecting was.

There was little doubt that Diego C de Baca was Gonda's intruder. He was hiding from his two Army buddies and likely intended no harm to either Gonda or his employees. There was nothing in the background checks so far to indicate he was a violent man. The fact I'd not yet learned how to access his hiding place was frustrating but not an essential element of the case, at least in my opinion.

The temptation to take the second step and declare that Gonda's son was attacked and slain in a case of mistaken identity was strong, yet despite providing this information to the authorities, I wasn't secure in that belief. The method of death wasn't consistent with assassination by a military-trained sniper. And there were too many other factors involved, the largest of which was that Bas Zuniga was a potential heir to a very large family inheritance. And if I accepted the mistaken identity scenario, would I be ignoring the possibility that Bas's son might be in danger?

As I entered the chateau's lobby, Heléne Benoir greeted me with a broad smile from the chocolatier's kiosk. We barely had time to greet each other before Ariel Gonda rushed in to grasp my hand, hope hanging all over his face.

"BJ, do you have news for me? Shall we talk in the salon? Should I get Margot?"

"In a moment. But a private word first, okay?"

He led me to the large parlor filled with overstuffed furniture where his groups waited before tastings or wine classes began. At the moment it was deserted.

"Ariel, I believe I know who your intruder is and why he has chosen to honor you with his presence. I also believe I know his intent, which is benevolent, although not without some risk."

I had his full attention, so I told him what happened after I alerted the household with gunshots and left him and his nephew searching the place while I went looking for a bicycle. This necessitated sharing more than I wanted; nonetheless, I did so, short of showing him the photo of Diego.

Gonda's brow cleared a bit. "So this young man returned to his boyhood home to escape some unpleasant associates from his past? This certainly relieves my mind, but I must know where he is hiding and how he has access to the wine cellar."

"Understood. We must also be cognizant that his continued presence presents a bit of a threat because of the two men looking for him. The police are aware of their identities and have photographs of the two."

"Photographs?"

I opened my folio and extracted the pictures of Natander and Pastis. "Have you seen either of these two men here on the premises?"

Gonda frowned over the photos for a long minute and then glanced up, shaking his head. "To the best of my knowledge, I have never seen either of them. I cannot be positive, of course, because a number of people pass through here daily for our wine tastings. I can pass the photographs around and see if anyone else recognizes them. They are this Diego's pursuers, I take it."

I identified the two for him and then passed over the third picture. "How about this man?"

Gonda's eyes widened as he scanned the photograph. His hand shook. "What? Why, that's Bas! No… no. Yes. Oh good Lord, no. But it could be him." He lifted his head and stared into my eyes, the blood draining from his face. His jaw sagged. "Does this mean…?"

He made the connection. Should I leave it alone and continue the investigation on my own?

"Oh my God! They shot my son by mistake!" The words came out in an agonized groan. "Benevolent, you said? That man came back and claimed my son's life! That is benevolent?" He rose. "Margot. She must know."

I clutched his sleeve. "Yes, she must, but first we must discuss something else."

I wasn't certain how much he was comprehending, but he sank back down on the sofa.

I took a deep breath. "Ariel, is there anything else you aren't telling me?"

"No!" He dry washed his chin. "I learned my lesson when I failed to confide in you about Bas." He straightened. "Oh, I see. The resemblance. No, I can assure you this Diego is not another son. I-I have no explanation for why they resemble one another so strongly."

"Nor have I. One of nature's tricks, more than likely. But such a strong resemblance raises the easy… and perhaps the logical conclusion that Natander or Pastis shot your son in the mistaken belief he was Diego C de Baca. That certainly could have been the case, especially given the shooting took place in the middle of the night. But I'm having trouble with some aspects of that explanation of the shooting."

His pale blue eyes focused on me. He was back with me again. "Such as?"

"First, but perhaps the most easily explained anomaly, is that the method of killing isn't consistent with a military sniper."

"If they accosted Bas, there was no need for a powerful, noisy weapon."

"True, but if my theory is right, why would these men kill Bas believing he was the man they were looking for? Something set them on Diego's trail. Something they wanted from him."

"Such as the artifacts you mentioned?"

"Exactly. Was Bas carrying anything when he left the winery that night?"

"I wasn't there, of course, but he did not normally carry anything with him."

"Did he wear a backpack to and from work?"

Gonda paused to think over my question before shaking his head. "Not normally. And there was no backpack found on him the morning he… died."

"That argues they would have simply seized him to force him to hand over the artifacts or lead them to them. Had they done that, it wouldn't have taken long to discover they'd accosted the wrong man."

Doubt shadowed his features. "We are assuming these are rational men. Perhaps Bas fought back and they shot him without considering the consequences."

"Very possible. But in my experience, people who take this much time and trouble and risk to stalk a target are very goal oriented. They wanted whatever Diego took from them more than they wanted Diego. At least, that's my belief."

Gonda shook his head, denying my conclusion. "If this was truly a falling-out of thieves, Diego C de Baca might not have the artifacts or whatever it was they stole. Perhaps he was planning on… how do you say it? Oh yes, planning on ratting them out."

"That too is possible. And it would explain some things. But there are other, more painful explanations," I said.

"Family considerations, you mean?"

"Yes. And if you wish, we can allow the police to do their job and work up a case against these two former associates. But there is a further consideration, I think."

Ariel Gonda studied the pattern on the carpet for a full sixty seconds before lifting his eyes to me. "The infant."

"Exactly. The infant. Except he'd be around two now. Hardly an infant."

His pain-filled eyes met my gaze. "Spell it out for me, BJ. Please."

"Had Bas Zuniga lived, he would have likely worked here with you, ultimately becoming an integral part of your organization. The fact that he was your own blood would not only have played a role in his position in the company but also his position within the family. From what I understand, the Gonda family fortune overseas is considerably larger than your investments here. Someone may have wanted to protect those assets from a new, heretofore unknown heir."

He spread his hands. "But no one knew of the blood ties."

I held my tongue.

He turned red in the face. "Margot? You mean that Margot knew he was my son."

"Known for years. Surely she has confidants inside the family. Heléne, for example. I'm sure they share secrets. It's possible—"

"Preposterous!" he said sharply. "I will not tolerate such talk. It is not possible."

"That's your call, Ariel. So far as I am concerned, I have delivered what you asked. I've identified the intruder with reasonable certainty. And I've informed the state and county authorities of what I know, so they will pursue that line of reasoning in Bas's death. I'll have my office manager forward my report and my final bill."

"No, no, BJ. I apologize for my outburst. *Hilfe bitte!* Help me. Even though I have suffered some of the same thoughts, I could not bring myself to face them. Not until you gave them voice. I am afraid for this grandson I have never met. I feel an attachment. I feel family blood calling to me. Even though I cannot conceive of Margot, Heléne, Marc, or anyone else in my family being capable of such horror, I cannot leave a helpless babe to the mercy of whoever murdered his father, no matter how remote the possibility. Do not desert me now."

I gazed at the man caught between family loyalty and the need to protect another member he had never seen, hadn't even known about until days ago. That he might have to stand against the one to shield the other was a very real and painful possibility.

"Have you contacted the lawyer I recommended?"

"Yes. He cannot see me until Tuesday because of the upcoming Independence Day holiday. I am to be in his office at ten o'clock."

"Very well, I'll meet you there. We'll see what he has to say before deciding on my future role."

"Understood. And *merci vielmal.*"

Chapter 15

DESPITE WHAT I'd said to Ariel yesterday afternoon, I couldn't wait out the upcoming holiday weekend without making another stab at finding a nearly two-year-old boy named David James Dayton. As my client acknowledged, if someone deliberately killed his father because of his bloodline, the child might be targeted as well. The purpose of meeting with Del Dahlman was to explore legal means of forcing the Dayton family to reveal the whereabouts of the child, but a little more digging on my part might move us down the road, so to speak.

We are all products of a combination of things, including our past experiences. So it was not surprising that my mind reached back to where I first ran across Ariel Gonda. Alfano Vineyards. Remembering that two-year-old case raised my hackles in ways I didn't want. It had revolved around money as well. Lots and lots of it.

Was I preparing to deliver a helpless toddler into the arms of a loving grandfather or a cold, calculating man devoted to pruning errant offshoots from his family tree? Ariel Gonda was no Anthony P. Alfano—at least not outwardly. From my background checks, I actually knew quite a bit about him. He had a good, solid upbringing, a stellar educational background, and a history of stable employment and family ties. The affair with Barbara Zuniga was aberrant, but he'd done his best to do the right things.

I often say that paranoia is the constant companion of a good confidential investigator, and this line of reasoning was proof positive. I did not subscribe to the theory that just ran through my head. Nonetheless, I was grateful for the intellectual exercise. That meant my subconscious was aware of a potential danger. Now I needed to proceed carefully and allow my suspicions to guard against an ambush.

Turn that coin over and look at it from the other side. If Zuniga died because someone mistook him for Diego, then the danger to young Mr. C de Baca was real. Natander and Pastis—or someone—wanted him dead. True, I had turned that problem over to Yardley and Muñoz, but I'm cursed with this finely tuned sense of responsibility. I had to prevent that possibility as well.

Charlie was checking his contacts with the Cruces police to see if he could pick up a clue to the baby's whereabouts before I headed down there. While he pursued that avenue, I left the office Friday afternoon to see if I could cajole any information out of Nancy Hummerman. I parked a couple of houses down from 3501 Holiday and walked to Hummerman's brick home. Closed front drapes prevented me from glimpsing inside. No one answered the bell. I strolled around behind the house, noting that while Nancy's public front yard was moderately well-kept, her private backyard was a mess. There were almost as many weeds as there were stems of grass. No mountain bike. I tried to see inside the detached garage, but a curtain on the window to the side door blocked my view.

As I stepped away, I heard a motor approach. A second later the garage door began rising. Assuming Nancy Hummerman was returning home, I moved against the back side of the house where I couldn't be observed but had a good view of any vehicle entering the garage. Tires crunched on the two parallel strips of concrete of the driveway. The driver obligingly slowed to a crawl in order to steer the Jeep into the small building. As she passed I could clearly see Nancy was alone. Even so, the door was not yet closed behind her before I heard voices. More than one. I blocked access to the backyard gate and waited.

The woman emerged first with her back to me, still speaking to someone inside. Stuffed into short shorts and a tight halter top, she looked much more interesting than the other day. She held a bottle of milk in one hand and a small plastic bag of what appeared to be groceries in the other.

She turned around and spotted me just as Diego C de Baca emerged, loaded down with other bags. Nancy gave a short scream and dropped the milk. Diego froze where he was. Before either of them recovered, I barked in my best Marine Corps MP voice, "Stay right where you are, Specialist C de Baca. That's an order!"

Surprisingly he did as requested. His feet seemed frozen to the ground as he straightened and appeared to stand at attention, although he was so laden with grocery bags it was hard to tell.

"What are you doing in my yard!" Nancy shrieked. "You're trespassing."

"And you're harboring a fugitive. Let's see which one carries the heavier penalty."

Diego spoke in a pleasant baritone with a slight catch in it. "Fugitive? Who says I'm a fugitive?"

"For starters, the Sandoval County Sheriff's Office and the New Mexico State Police. I can probably take care of those for you, but I keep hearing about a Department of Defense investigation of you and your two buddies. Don't know if I can help there. But let's sit down and talk. My name is B. J. Vinson, and I'm a confidential investigator. I'm not a cop."

"Don't listen to this guy," Nancy said. "I'll just yell rape, and you'll have all the time you need to get away."

Diego looked confused.

"That might work," I said calmly, "if I wasn't gay. And every cop in Albuquerque knows it. Come on, Diego. Let's go inside and talk."

"How do I know you haven't already called the cops?" he asked.

"Why would I? I didn't even know you were here until the garage door opened. Do you always ride around crouched down on the floorboard?"

A sheepish look came over his features. "Pretty much... lately."

"Look, I think you need help. Maybe I can give you some."

"Why would you do that? I can't afford your rates."

"That $10,000 you transferred to Georgia would do a pretty good job of it, but I'm not looking for money. There's a situation I'm working that kicked off when you started hiding out at the Lovely Pines. Maybe you can help me with it."

Despite Nancy's stated objection, he marched past me into the house and held the door open for both of us. I took a seat at the table in the small, neat kitchen while they put away groceries.

He spoke into the refrigerator as he put away milk and eggs. "Why do you think I hid out at the Lovely Pines?"

"Didn't you think the owner would call for help when you broke into the winery?"

"Yeah, but I didn't steal nothing, so I thought they'd put it down to kids and forget about it."

"Too neat for kids. And you did take a couple of bottles of wine."

"Curiosity got to me. I wanted to see if this Gonda fella's wines were any good. Shoulda remembered he hadn't had the place long enough for his product to ripen." He paused in the act of putting coffee in a cabinet. "Pretty good stuff, but it was ours, not his."

They finished with the groceries and settled down with me at the old-fashioned oak table. If I had to guess, I'd say Nancy Hummerman rented the place furnished.

Both of them listened carefully as I sketched out the way I figured things were. Then Diego, who'd been leaning forward over his elbows on the table, settled back in his chair.

"You're the guy I threw my beer at the other night, aren't you? I guess you are a PI. You got it nailed pretty good. Except it's not exactly the way things went down."

"Okay, enlighten me."

He scowled, but I got the feeling he was just reliving some unpleasant memories. "Me'n Spider and Hugo went to this bombed-out monastery, I guess you'd call it. Like he always did, Spider went his own way. Pretty soon we heard shots from Natander's M16. Two bursts. When we found him, he was putting things in a sack he'd found somewhere. There was fresh kill lying nearby. Some guy in black that Spider claimed was an Ali Baba."

"Did you see a weapon of any kind?"

Diego shook his head. "Didn't really look. Spider had us scooping up shit and stuffing it in sacks. By the time we boogied for our Humvee, we each carried a load."

"What kind of stuff?"

He shrugged. "Souvenirs. Don't really know, but Spider seemed to. We hid it back at base, and for the next few months, he sold most of it off to the other guys. We only had a couple of things left by the time some OGAs showed up and started asking questions."

My military jargon was over a decade old, but I'd understood the reference to an Ali Baba. That was an insurgent, a bad guy. But OGAs, escaped me, so I asked about them.

"Other government agencies. Usually CIA or the FBI."

"And that's when you realized you were in trouble."

"Yeah, and I was getting to be a short-timer then. Since I was the only one with a permanent stateside address, I'm the one who mailed the one artifact we still had left back to the States. Spider claimed it was something special. Something that would make us all rich."

As Diego rose to get us cold sodas from the refrigerator, I told him that was a load of bull crap.

He passed around cans, sat down, and popped the lid on his drink. "That part about me having the only home address stateside was. But not that part about getting rich. I didn't know it at the time, but there was a lot of looting going on, and these OGAs were trying to put a stop to it. Spider and Pastis didn't want to be caught shipping it out, so they conned me into doing it. But by the time I figured out how serious things were, I'd already sent it through the APO. Man, I didn't get much sleep the next month, but the package sailed right on through."

He guzzled a swig and rubbed the cold can across his forehead. "When they shipped us back home, I got a scare. They questioned everybody who was getting on that plane, and I thought for sure I was toast."

"Why?"

"That was the first time I heard a priest in some monastery got murdered and something called Our Lady of the Euphrates got stole. I knew right off she was what I mailed home. A beat-up, ten-inch clay figure of a woman about a thousand years old with traces of faded paint clinging to her. Didn't look like anything special, but she was supposed to have cured diseases, made crazy people sane again."

"And sane men crazy, apparently. Why didn't you put a stop to it right then and let them know what happened?"

He stared at me with eyes the color of dark chocolate. "Man, you don't know those guys. If they get down on you, they're worse than the LNs. Local nationals," he added when he saw my frown. "Those two fuckers will kill you. At least, Spider will if you cross him."

"Okay, that explains that. But when did you start having trouble with Natander and Pastis?"

"Right then. Spider saw how shook I was, so he or Hugo stayed with me all the time. As soon as we hit the States, Spider wanted to take off and get the *Lady*, as he'd started calling the clay statue. He'd figured out it was worth real dough. A million bucks, he claimed. But I insisted I was going to finish my enlistment and get out with an honorable."

"But they deserted and came to New Mexico with you after you were discharged."

"One on either side of me. But I threw them a curve. I didn't send the package where they thought I did. I sent it to Nancy." He saw my look and explained they'd been going together before he left for his Army service and remained in touch. He gulped his soda. "And that's when things really started going sideways."

Diego went on to explain that his father was seriously ill, and he didn't want to bring strangers home. Natander insisted and reminded Diego he was complicit in the murder of the priest and an active participant in stealing valuable artifacts.

So he convinced the other two this was something he had to do alone and went back home. He knew they stayed close by to watch what was going on, so he didn't dare try to slip the statuette into the winery. That was probably the time German told me about. But before Diego could figure out what to do, he spotted Natander's car pulling into the parking lot at the Pines. Unwilling to introduce his companions to his father and brother, Diego panicked and took off through the woods and hitched a ride back to Albuquerque and to Nancy.

Before he figured out what to do, his father died, and he hadn't even dared attend the funeral. He and Nancy took a quick trip to Colorado to put some distance between Diego and the two AWOL GIs.

"I shoulda gone to the Pines and accessed the hidden room while everyone was at the funeral, but I was hiding out in Pueblo with Nancy, trying to figure out how to extricate myself from the situation."

"Why not just give them the artifact and say goodbye?" I asked.

"That's what I wanted him to do," Nancy said. A faint trace of her perfume reached me. She didn't spend a lot of money on her toiletries.

Diego squirmed in his chair. "That wouldn't solve the problem. By then, Spider figured out how squirrely I was about this whole thing. He believed I was going to turn over the artifact to the authorities and confess everything."

"Why haven't you?"

He spread his hands and lifted his shoulders. "Who to? What do the police know about stealing artifacts in foreign countries? They'd laugh me out of the station."

"The FBI wouldn't."

He sighed. "I know. And that's probably what I'll have to do."

"Not without a deal, you won't," Nancy said.

"And how do I get a deal?"

"You need legal help," I said. "I know a lawyer. He doesn't practice criminal law, but he can steer you to the right place. Where is the artifact now? Not here, I hope?"

Diego shook his head. "No. I took it to the Pines the night I broke in. But now Spider's got it staked out. He almost got me last time."

"That was me who fired the warning shots, by the way. I spotted someone with a rifle on your trail."

"Thanks."

"Does he want to kill you or does he want to recover the Lady?"

"Both. He doesn't trust me any longer. Not since I gave them the slip and disappeared."

"That would have been around the first of June."

"How'd you know? Oh yeah. The break-in at the Pines."

"I assume there's a hidden room behind the wine cellar, but you needed access to the winery in order to enter. But you haven't been going in or out through the winery since then."

"There's another way in, but before I left for the Army, I made sure it was barred."

"How'd you find the room in the first place?"

"My dad showed it to me back when I was getting into trouble in high school. Best hideout in the West, he always said. So far as I know, he never showed it to anyone else."

"Well, you're going to have to tell me about it. That's the only way I can see to get the artifact out of there."

I sat back and regarded the handsome young man seated opposite me. He was probably pretty decent, even if there were a few chinks in his moral code. But that was a quick judgment. I hadn't been plopped down in the middle of a foreign country and told to start killing people who were a little different from me before they killed me. After a while I imagined the killings became indiscriminate. Or was that writing him an excuse to give to the headmaster?

"Diego, if the artifact is safely hidden away at the winery, why did you keep going back to the place? That just increased the odds Natander or Pastis would catch you."

"I was afraid they'd tumble to Nancy and catch me here. That might put her in danger. I didn't dare stay any one place for long. So some nights I snuck back into the winery. It's worked so far. Spider's a trained sniper with more patience than me'n Hugo put together. But so far I've managed to fool him. Well, except for last time when you bailed me out."

"Did it ever occur to you that you were putting the people at the Pines in danger?" I asked.

He frowned over that one. "Spider wouldn't have any reason to hurt anybody at the Pines. He knows the place has been sold, and nobody there is family. That wouldn't gain him anything."

"I'm going to go out to the car and get my case. Are you going to run?"

He shook his head. "Think that lawyer you talked about might be what I need. I'm not going anywhere."

"Glad you recognize that. Be back in a minute."

Both of them were still seated at the kitchen table when I returned. I sat down and handed over a cheap cell phone, one of several I keep to hand out to confidential informants. "Diego, I assume you're a reasonable man and that we'll be able to help one another. Keep this phone on you at all times. My numbers—home, office, and cell—are already programmed into the phone."

He pushed it away. "I have a cell phone."

"Take it and use it exclusively for contacting me. And for me to contact you. Don't let it out of your possession, and don't give the number to anyone else. Understood?"

He nodded and picked up the little flip phone. "Not exactly a Samsung Galaxy."

"But it's what's needed at the moment. Now, take a look at this." I removed a photograph from my folio and slid it across the table to Diego.

Once he focused on it, he squinted. "Why, that's me! No. But it could be. Who is he?"

"He was a worker at the Pines who was ambushed and shot to death as he left the winery property about 2:30 a.m. exactly seventeen days after you first broke into the place."

"Oh my God! You think Spider and Hugo thought they were ambushing me?"

"Do you?"

"How was he killed? I mean, at a distance or up close."

"Close. Small caliber. Probably a .22 or .25."

He frowned. "That doesn't make sense. If they were that close, they'd have grabbed me and roughed me up until I told them where the artifact was. *Then* they might have killed me."

"Logical. But sometimes logic doesn't play into it. Does either Natander or Pastis have a hair trigger?"

Diego nodded. "Spider does. But he'd have shot me in the legs or something just to stop me. When he got what he wanted, well…."

"I understand. But you have to face the possibility that a young man named Bas Zuniga died because you broke into the winery."

Chapter 16

I DROVE back to the office squarely on the horns of a dilemma. My agreement with Yardley and Muñoz required me to share information with them. Yet I didn't want to confess all until I'd talked to Del. Diego would be far better off turning himself in to the authorities, but not until he was represented by counsel. As I parked in my spot in the office lot, I decided to walk the block and a half to Del's office and see if I couldn't squeeze in a meeting. He'd probably be busy as hell right before a three-day holiday, but he could damn well make time for me. After all, I'd saved his butt in that Zozobra foul-up three years ago. But I'd probably ridden that horse pretty well to death. I was no sooner out of the Impala when the phone rang.

It was Hazel. "Where are you?"

"Downstairs in the parking lot. I'm going to see if I can get a word with Del—"

"Come on up. We've got a problem."

I knew her well enough not to try to pull the facts out of her, so I took the back stairwell to the third floor and rushed into the office. She and Charlie were both waiting for me.

"Someone just tried to kill German C de Baca."

"Probably just trying to get information out of him," Charlie said in a more reasonable voice.

"Then why is he in the hospital?" Hazel asked.

We automatically gravitated to the small conference table in my office, where I made sense out of the situation. A few minutes earlier, Hazel took a call from a woman who identified herself as Consuela C de Baca de Simpson. She was calling because her brother German was attacked in his office and beaten badly. Although he was rushed to the UNM hospital, he'd managed to tell her to contact me to ask if I knew how to get in touch with Diego.

When I reached Consuela at the number she left with Hazel, she apparently remembered our aborted telephone conversation sometime back.

"Did you find him?" she asked as soon as I identified myself.

I hedged. "You mean Diego? I talked to him once, but I don't know where he is at the moment. Can you tell me what happened to your brother?"

As she told the story, German was accosted while alone in his office by two masked men demanding to know where Diego was. When her brother tried to reason with the intruders, they beat him ruthlessly. Even so, he could not give them information he did not have. Then they asked about access to the winery other than through the doors to the building. At this point I interrupted her.

"Did he give them that information?"

"Give it to them? He doesn't know anything about a secret way into the winery. And neither do I. Do you?"

"How would I know?"

I can equivocate with the best of them when necessary. So Ernesto didn't share the secret room with anyone but Diego, his favorite son... or a troubled one who might need a place to hide from the world.

Apparently after German lost consciousness, the two assailants— Natander and Pastis, most likely—left. I heard the rest of the story and then told her to get in touch with Lt. Raymond Yardley at the New Mexico State Police.

"Why?" she asked. "The Albuquerque police are handling the incident."

"Because Yardley has some knowledge the city cops don't. Who's handling it for APD?"

"I don't know who the detective was, but right now there's a Lt. Eugene Enriquez here."

"Here? Are you at the hospital?"

"I am."

"Let me speak to the lieutenant, please. I know him."

After a pause, my old APD partner's tired voice came across the line. "I mighta known you'd show up in this case somehow. What can you tell me?"

I filled him in on everything, withholding only that I was in contact with Diego. He listened silently, interrupting with pithy questions only occasionally.

"Okay. You gotta bring him in, you know that."

"Have to find him first."

"Don't gimme that shit. You found him, so you know his haunts. Go get him and bring him to my office."

"Yardley and Muñoz have a claim on him too."

"And probably the feds as well. But I'm the one's got a violent crime committed. I want him."

"Murder's pretty violent," I reminded him.

"You think he's involved in that?"

I shook my head even though he couldn't see me. "No, I don't. I'll see what I can do."

I hung up and dialed the cell phone I'd given Diego. He answered with a hesitant "Hello."

"Diego, your brother's been beaten by two men asking for you and about a hidden room at the winery. They put him in the hospital. My old APD partner's in charge of his case, and I told him I'd talked to you."

"Shit, man, I trusted you."

"And I honored that trust. But things have changed now. Members of your family have been harmed and threatened. You have to turn yourself in."

"What about that lawyer you talked about?"

"I can have him there when you do it."

"I gotta think this over."

"Does German know about Nancy?"

"Oh yeah. He's even met her a couple of times."

"Then we have to assume they questioned him about people you knew and might turn to when you're in trouble. They may know about her."

Diego indulged in some dark GI vulgarisms. "They might come after her?"

"Not if you turn yourself over to the cops. No point in it then."

His hesitation told me he was considering it. "I wanna talk to that lawyer first."

"So you don't mind putting her in danger?"

"I'll just have her tell them I headed out to turn myself in to the police as soon as I heard about German. That ought to take the heat off her."

"Speaking of the cops, they're probably already on the way to Nancy's house right now." Sensing I'd lose his trust completely if I insisted on turning him in, I changed tactics. "Have Nancy drive you to the winery. Go underground until you hear from me. I won't lead them to you until you've had a chance to think things over. Okay? But one thing's clear. You'll have to turn yourself in sooner or later. I'll call you after I talk to Del... uh, the lawyer."

"That's a problem. My cell phone doesn't work from inside the cave, so I'll bet this cheapie doesn't either. Tell you what. Go up the road east of the Pines just short of where it dead-ends. Off to the right, you'll see the remains of an old cabin."

"I know where it is. I've walked every inch of that ground."

He gave me instructions what to do when I reached the place and warned me to watch for a tail. "Hell, Spider might be out there already, just waiting. This is probably what he hoped I'd do when he got to German."

"Are you armed?" I asked.

"Naw, but I got a mean club with nails in it in the hideout."

"Don't use it on me."

"Depends."

"Depends? On what?"

"On whether I can trust you or not."

"Look, guy. Maybe you'd better find your own way to the authorities."

"I didn't mean it. You're the only hope I've got. I thought about just taking off to California or somewhere where nobody knows me. Maybe that's still what I ought to do."

"Your choice. But believe me, it's very hard to live anywhere without leaving a trail. Natander and Pastis might not have the contacts to find you, but the police do. Do I come to the Pines or not?"

"Yeah."

"Then you better get your ass out there right now."

I'M NOT certain why I didn't call Gene and have him accompany me to the Pines. Or for that matter, why I didn't alert Gonda to what was going on, but I didn't. I'd told Diego he could trust me, and I would keep my word for as long as possible.

It took me more time than usual to get to the winery because I parked in Plácido and walked through the forest. I also circled far to the north before approaching the ruins of the log cabin. The cabin remains had a pitiful, sad feeling about them. They told of a life in the past that no longer existed. Despite the lack of a roof, the sheltering pine trees left the interior in deep shadow.

I took concealment in the woods fifty feet from the wreckage and settled down to wait. I spotted movement, but my blood pressure dropped to nearly normal when Diego, still astride his bicycle, paused at the edge of the wood to observe the scene carefully. As he hid the mountain bike in some bushes, I resisted the urge to call to him. He darted to the front of the building's carcass, slowing to avoid a patch of sand at the threshold before slipping inside the building and disappearing into the gloom.

After another ten minutes to make certain he wasn't followed by Natander or Pastis, I slipped inside the collapsed structure and followed the instructions Diego gave me on the phone. Even though I knew what to do, I had trouble spotting the specific planking I was looking for. The cabin once had a wooden floor, but much of it was gone. I finally settled on a board roughly the size of the bottom half of a dutch door. But that couldn't be the right one. There were pine needles all over the wood, even though Diego entered just minutes ago. Nonetheless, I grasped the right edge of the plank and lifted. It came up relatively easy, but the debris atop it remained in place. I examined it more closely and found it covered by burlap, to which the needles and leaves and even small rocks were cemented.

Even then, I was confounded. There appeared to be solid earth beneath the raised planking. Then a stubby, rusted nail caught my attention. I grasped it and tugged upward. The bottom fell away with a click, revealing a ladder. I took my place a few rungs down and carefully restored the debris-covered plank. Then I crept blindly down a few more rungs before pushing the trapdoor back into place. Enveloped in total gloom, I fumbled my way to the bottom, rung after careful rung, and used the tiny beam of light from my cell phone to locate another ladder. As I climbed it, the faint glow of a lantern ushered me up into a spacious cavern.

When I cleared the tunnel, I was startled to see a figure brandishing a club like a Louisville slugger. Just as I grunted in surprise, Diego relaxed and dropped the business end of the club to the ground.

"You weren't expecting me?" Anger tinged my voice.

"Yeah, but what if it had been Spider? He coulda followed me. I don't usually come and go this time of day."

"He didn't."

"How do you know?"

"Because I watched you arrive and waited around to see if he showed. He didn't." I looked around at my surroundings. The place was probably twenty-by-twenty, with a head clearance of around eight feet at its apex. An old cot and ancient dresser sat at the far side of the cave, while a table with peeling white paint attended by two chairs took up this end. Two electric lanterns relieved the gloom. Diego's hideout wasn't as cold as the wine cellar on the other side of the wall, but a man would need a sweater if he stayed for long.

"Neat, huh?"

"How in the hell did you find this place?"

Diego leaned his nail-studded bat against a wall and walked to the table. After taking one of the chairs, he invited me to sit in the other. "The fellow my dad bought the land from showed him the big cavern. That's why he was interested in the place. That cave looked to be the right place for a wine cellar. The place was just about square except for this recess here."

"So it was open to the big cavern?"

"Yeah. Or so my dad said."

"He's the one who made a secret room out of it?"

"Him and my Uncle Juan. I never knew my uncle, but he was said to be a heller. That tumbled-down cabin where you entered the tunnel was where he lived. Wasn't ever married, but he sure liked other men's wives. Always in trouble. Sometimes he found himself needing a place to hang out while a storm or a mad husband passed. He's the one who dug the tunnel. Him and my dad rigged the door closing this off from the cellar."

I shook my head. "And they never told anyone about the place?"

"Not even after one of those husbands caught Uncle Juan in a bar over in Bernalillo and put a bullet through his head. Only one Dad shared the secret with was me."

"Why you?"

Diego managed to look rueful. "I was a handful when I was younger. Always in some scrape with the law or someone. He showed it to me one day when he hid me from the county sheriff until he could clear up the mess."

I got up and walked to the wall abutting the wine cellar. The outline of a door was clear from this side. I ran my hand down it. "Diego, I examined every inch of the other side of this wall. I couldn't find anything that looked like this."

He walked up beside me. "Uncle Juan was something of an engineer. He's the one who designed this." He grasped a small lever and pulled it down. Then he used it to pull the door to the right. It rolled easily and almost silently. Instantly the wine cellar came into view. The couch where I'd spent the night wasn't more than ten yards to the left. Now I knew what that rumbling sound I'd heard was.

He fingered the right side of the opening. "Here's why you couldn't find it."

The C de Baca who crafted this entrance years ago left the natural contour of a fold of rock and simply faced the door with matching rock. From the other side, there would be nothing to reveal the presence of the door. Just the normal, natural contours and crevices of the rock wall on both sides of the door. I stepped back into the hideout and took a closer look at the door. It was an actual slab of natural rock mounted on rollers. That was why thumping on the wall hadn't given off a sound different from any other place.

Diego closed the door and lifted the lever.

"Okay," I said. "There must be a way to open the door from the other side. How?"

He fished in his pocket and came out with a device that looked like a slender, tapered awl. "With this. I slide it into a certain place in the crevice and it triggers the release just like the lever does on this side."

I went back and sat down at the rickety table. "Let's see if I have this straight. When you returned from the Army and eluded your two minders, you needed a place to hide. So you came here. But you couldn't access this room from the cabin because you'd barred that entrance before leaving for the Army. That's why you broke into the winery."

"Right. I kept the awl with me all the time I was in the Army. Lugged it all over Iraq. Dad kept another one here in his toolbox. It looked just like all his other tools."

"But you planned the break-in right down to bringing a crowbar with you."

"Got it in a hardware store in Albuquerque and stowed it in my duffel bag."

"Duffel bag. That's where you carried the artifact too. Right?"

"Right. You wanna see her?"

"In a minute. I need to get the rest of this straight. While you were hiding out, why did you keep going into the wine cellar? It's not like you were stealing food or drink."

"In a way it was. Maybe you haven't noticed, but I don't have plumbing here. I needed to haul in my water, not to mention emptying the chamber pot. Where's the closest water and bathroom?"

"On the other side of that wall. But you could do that at night when the place was closed."

"And I did. Mostly. Once or twice I ventured out when I felt the need for some liquid refreshment. Never had a problem."

"Until I almost caught you."

"Yeah, and that was at night during the safe time. You really spooked me when I figured out somebody was in the cavern with me. You were too close to the door for me to just slip back out, so—"

"So you rolled a bottle on the floor to lure me away. Wonder how the hell we missed seeing one another? I was supposed to be on guard watching for just that sort of thing."

"You were tired by then, I guess."

WE SAT at the rickety table while I examined Our Lady of the Euphrates. She was as Diego described her, about ten or eleven inches high, the fired-clay effigy of a hippy woman. Bits of gold paint clung to a crude diadem. Smears of black above her eyes reminded me of kohl-eyed Egyptian pieces. Nothing special to look at, she nonetheless represented a cultural treasure... a Christian sculpture born in the midst of Islam. That she survived virtually unbroken represented a miracle. Few such intact clay pieces survived a 1,000-year history.

"Not much to look at, is she?" Diego said after a lengthy silence.

"Not unless you're a museum curator or clergy... or a collector. To them she looks beautiful."

"Or like money," he added.

I lifted my eyes to meet his. "I assume you're Catholic. Why doesn't she mean something to you?"

He lifted his shoulders and dropped them. "Lapsed. Long time ago. But I gotta admit, when I learned who she was, I got a shiver down my back."

"Was that when you decided not to go along with selling her?"

He grimaced. "I don't really know. Maybe. All I know is it didn't seem right selling her to somebody who'd hide her away for another thousand years."

I began to like Diego C de Baca a little better. "Who did your buddies intend to sell her to?"

"I don't know, but Spider said once we got her to the States, he knew somebody who'd pay a hundred grand for her."

"From the research I've done on the internet, more like a quarter mil. He was going to stiff you two guys. And that's after he put you in the spotlight by having you mail it home. Miracle you weren't caught then." I looked at him again as a thought struck me. "Why didn't you mail it to your father and have him put it in the room?"

"Are you kidding? If he'd have found out I was stealing a religious piece like that—you know, historical—he'd haul it straight down to the sheriff's office."

"Come on. He got you out of all kinds of scrapes."

"None of those had anything to do with his church. This one did."

"Okay, let's figure this thing out. I was headed to the attorney's office when I got word of the attack on your brother. I still have to get in touch with him. I'll do that next. You just have to hang tight until I can talk to him."

"What about Nancy? You sure she'll be all right?"

"You call her and make sure. Tell her I'm going to have someone keep an eye on the house until you turn yourself in. He'll be an ex-cop who'll ring the doorbell and introduce himself. Right now, it's time you met your host."

His eyebrows climbed. "He'll kick me outa here."

"Don't think so. I'll pave the way, but we'll have to let him in on how to access this secret room."

"I don't think that's a good idea."

"Okay, then you figure a way out of this. I'll give you time to clear out, and then tell the Gondas I've solved the mystery of their mysterious break-in."

"Wait a minute. Where am I going to go?"

"Don't have a clue. If you hadn't met me, what were you going to do?"

His head drooped. "Hadn't decided. Look, I'll go along with it, okay? But he can't tell anybody. Not till that lawyer can come up with something."

I left through the door that gave out onto the wine cellar, leaving it ajar. John Hakamora and Parson Jones were working with some equipment at the far end of the winery, but I managed to slip into Gonda's lab without being seen. Ariel was concentrating on something on his desk and almost jumped out of his skin when I spoke.

"*Verdammt*, BJ! You startled me. I didn't hear you come in."

"I didn't. In the way you mean it, at least."

"You have come to tell me you found who killed my son?"

"No, but I've solved your intruder problem. For the moment, however, I must ask you to keep what I reveal to you to yourself. You can't tell anyone." I hesitated, thinking about Zuniga's murder. I still didn't know how the two incidents tied in, so I added something that brought a frown to his face. "Not even Margot."

"I see. Very well. Tell me."

"I'll show you. Follow me, but try not to attract the attention of your winery workers."

He silently followed me into the depths of the wine cellar. The look on his face was something to see when I swung open the heavy stone facing that covered the hidden door. Diego's expression was similar… astonishment.

I ushered Ariel inside and made certain the door was securely latched before introducing the two and launching into a partial explanation.

"Ariel, Diego has a problem, which is the reason he invaded your premises in the first place. Because of something that happened when he was stationed in Iraq, two men are on his trail. He knew of only one place that was secure, but it required that he initially break into your winery. Thereafter, he could come and go as he saw fit without disturbing you or your property."

Gonda listened patiently, his features composed. I finished by posing a question to Diego.

"Will you trust me with the artifact until after we receive our instructions from Del Dahlman—from the lawyer?"

"She's all that's keeping Spider from killing me outright."

"Even more reason to trust me. If he catches you with the statuette, he's free to do just that."

"I don't carry her around. She stays here where she's safe."

"Do I need to point out that he's closing in on you? If he catches up with you, he'll sooner or later force you to give her up." I held up a hand as he started to protest. "Believe me he'd get it out of you. But if I have her, all you have to do is tell him you delivered her to me for safekeeping with instructions that if anything happens to you, I'm to turn her over to the authorities together with a signed statement naming Natander as the killer of that priest in Iraq. That should make him more interested in me and less interested in you."

"You'd take that risk?"

I nodded.

"How do I know I can trust *you*?"

"Think about it, Diego. If you can't trust me, you're in big trouble. I have access to your hideout and know who's been helping you. The question is, what do you do if you *can't* trust me?"

From his body language, Diego clearly hadn't thought that one through. In the end he agreed and handed over the Lady, as he called her.

That done, Ariel stepped up and faced Diego. "Tell me, son. Did you kill Bas Zuniga?"

"Who?"

"My son. Bascomb Zuniga."

"I don't even know who that is. But I can tell you one thing. I haven't killed anyone." He looked flustered before adding, "On this side of the pond, anyway. And over there, it was just holding up my end… you know, doing my duty."

"Do you know who did kill him?" Ariel persisted.

"Sir, I don't even know what you're talking about."

"I am talking about someone shooting my son in the back on the road out in front of this winery in the middle of the night when he was coming off… duty." Ariel almost choked on the last word.

Diego turned to me. "You told me he was killed with a small caliber pistol?"

I watched him closely. "In the back."

"No, sir," he said to Gonda. "I do not know who killed him."

I could see from his eyes he'd leapt to the same conclusion I had. The shooter wasn't Spider Natander. Could it have been Hugo Pastis?

Chapter 17

ANGST CLOUDED Diego's features when I exited the hidden chamber via the wine cellar with the Lady in my possession. Couldn't be helped. I wanted the artifact locked securely in my office floor safe.

No, wait. In Del's safe. That way we could argue Diego turned it over to his attorney in preparation for surrendering both himself and his swag to the authorities. Because I'd parked a considerable distance away in order to avoid surveillance, I accepted Ariel's offer of a ride to my Impala. We were no sooner in his big boat of a car, a blue 2008 Cadillac Escalade, than Ariel asked the question I knew was coming.

"Do you believe him, BJ?"

"Absolutely. Think about it a minute. Bas's murder called unwanted attention to the Pines. It wasn't in his interest to kill your son. Nor did Bas resemble either of the two men on Diego's tail."

"Those are the two photographs you showed me earlier, is that not right?"

"Yes. James Natander and Hugo Pastis. They were all in the service together, and if Diego is telling the story right, Natander stole the artifact and conned him into mailing it stateside. A big risk he didn't want to take himself. When Diego suffered second thoughts about the theft, the three Army buddies had a falling-out."

"Is that young man's life in danger?"

"Yes, although what he said is true. They want what he has more than they want him dead. Although I believe they'd end up killing him anyway. To keep him from talking."

"Then he is welcome to remain in hiding at the Pines for as long as he needs to."

"That's only until I can arrange to have him turn himself in."

No one seemed to be watching the Impala, but there were plenty of hiding places nearby. So I tucked the artifact, still wrapped in the cloth Diego used to protect it, as unobtrusively under my arm as possible and got directly into my car upon our arrival. As I sped back to Albuquerque, I couldn't spot a tail, but traffic was heavy on I-25, so I couldn't be sure.

I used the time to call Del's office on my cell and smooth the way to him. Fortunately he could squeeze me in.

DEL STARED at the figurine standing in the middle of his desk for one long minute before lifting his eyes to mine. "That mud ball is worth how much?"

"Several hundred thou."

He snorted. "I don't believe it."

"Remember Mildred Muldren's duck?" I referred to a case last year that was labeled the City of Rocks in my files. "I didn't believe she was worth two hundred fifty thousand either. But people got killed over her just the same."

He chuckled. "Quacky the Second."

"Quacky Quack the Second, if I remember correctly."

"Okay, so what do we do with this thing?" Del asked.

"Turn it over to the authorities, presumably so it can be returned to Iraq. At the same time, I want Diego C de Baca to surrender himself in order to get him out from under a death threat."

Del arched his left eyebrow. "For ratting out his confederates?" I'd already filled him in on the details. "I doubt that'll do the job."

"It will if they're in custody."

He sighed. "Hope they don't end up in the same prison block."

"You're going to keep that from happening."

"How do I do that?"

"You're going to get Diego off."

"Vince, I am not a criminal lawyer."

"Maybe not, but some people would disagree."

He raised both eyebrows at my play on words. "And what do you mean by that?"

"Forget it. I want to turn Diego over to Gene Enriquez. He wants to talk to Diego because of the attack on German C de Baca."

"Yeah, but Gene will just let him go. He didn't attack his brother, so there's no reason for APD to keep him. This is federal. Why not go straight to them?"

"Two reasons. Gene will have my ass if I don't give him first crack. He's had a felony committed in his jurisdiction, and he wants it cleaned up. So do I. If Gene gets Natander and Pastis, he'll hold on to them until the feds can act."

"That's one reason. What's the other?"

I scratched the bridge of my nose. "Because Gene will tell them Diego turned himself in voluntarily *with* the stolen artifact. And if another officer of the law attests to that fact, it's less likely to get lost in the paperwork. As a matter of fact, Roma's going to want to talk to him about breaking into the winery, so that gives us two jurisdictions attesting for him. Even better."

"You don't trust the feds?"

"I don't know the feds. I know Gene. Besides, do you trust them?"

Del didn't deign to answer. "All right. Bring him in, and we'll walk him over to APD."

"That won't work. There's a trained sniper out there looking for Diego. If he goes to the police, Natander might figure the artifact is lost to him anyway, but killing Diego will keep him from naming them as the perpetrators."

"How will they even know? If I understand you, they can't find him."

"They know he's somewhere in the vicinity of the Lovely Pines Winery. They'll be watching everyone who comes and goes."

"So how do you want to handle it?"

"There's a wine tasting at the Lovely Pines—"

"But you said that's where his two trackers are looking for him. Why pick him up there?"

"Because that's where he is. I'd rather take him out in a crowd than try to slip him past Natander and Pastis again."

"So when's the tasting?"

"In about an hour and a half. And I want us there. We'll buy a case of wine that someone from the winery will put in our trunk. A couple of someones. And Gonda will walk with us to the car too."

"I see. In all the confusion—"

"Diego, who'll be one of the someones, will slip into the back seat of the car and lie on the floorboard."

"And then we'll drive the artifact and the fugitive to APD."

"No, the artifact will be locked in your safe here at Sloan, Hedges, Blah, Blah, Blah."

Del snorted through his nose. "You've got to stop that. It's disrespectful."

"You didn't object before you became one of the partners."

"Well, I am, so I do. Don't turn my part of the name into Blah. Why do you want to leave the artifact here?"

"Gene doesn't need or want it. I'd rather have it in your safe than in the APD evidence room. Not because it might be stolen, but because it might get broken. You can turn it over to the feds when they're in the picture."

He sighed. "All right. If we're going to the wine tasting, we'd better get a move on. Your car or mine?"

"Yours. I don't want mine shot up if things go wrong."

"Typical," Del said dryly.

WE ARRIVED a few minutes early, so Del obviated the need for next Tuesday's appointment with Gonda by reviewing New Mexico's liberal grandparental visitation statutes with him. If either or both parents were dead, any grandparent of the child could petition for privileges, which should be enough to provide us the location of Zuniga's vanished son. Del agreed to start the legal proceedings to enforce the Gondas' rights as quickly as possible. They would consider whether or not to apply for visitation, custody, or adoption once we knew the circumstances.

Two couples, as well as some singles, joined Del and me at the six o'clock wine tasting at the Lovely Pines. Two of the singles were my old APD partner, Gene Enriquez, and his last riding partner before he made lieutenant, a tall blond detective named Don Carson. They drove up to be on hand in case of trouble. Del argued that made our presence superfluous, but I knew the deadly accuracy of a military sniper better than he did and shut him down.

Gene, however, voiced his own ideas when time came to depart the winery and insisted we make a change in plans. Carson would ride with us in Del's Volvo while Diego, wearing Carson's hat, sat beside Gene in his departmental Ford as we pulled out the front gates of the winery. I made the detective lie on the floorboard of the back seat so Natander and Pastis wouldn't see more people leaving than arrived. I was pretty sure they knew who I was and would be keeping a close eye on me. The fact that two of the other couples who'd been at the wine tasting left the property at the same time we did made me feel a bit easier.

Ninety seconds after turning out onto the main road, Carson popped up and slid onto the seat. "I'm too damned tall to crouch down on the floorboard. This is better."

"Get back down," I warned. "We're too close to the—"

Just as Del touched the brakes to avoid hitting a squirrel running across the road, both rear passenger windows shattered. Del almost lost control of the Volvo, slowing even more.

"Don't stop!" I yelled. "Get us the hell out of here!"

Del stomped on the accelerator, and the powerful automobile shot forward. Then the rear window exploded.

Chapter 18

GENE, WHO was in front of us, apparently saw us running up his tailpipe and goosed his Ford. Catching our urgency, he lowered the window and plopped a magnetic light onto the roof of his car and switched on the siren. I turned in my seat and found Don Carson flat on his back on the rear floorboard. He was covered by broken glass and bleeding a little because of it but otherwise appeared unharmed.

Traffic—light until we hit Bernalillo—opened up before Gene's siren as he led us straight to the Sandoval County Sheriff's Office. He'd apparently put out a call, because as soon as we pulled around behind the building, four deputies in vests and helmets surrounded our cars and escorted us to safety. Del and I stood with Diego in the corner while the law officers sorted out the incident. Sgt. Roma Muñoz, in all her diminutive authority, seemed to have taken charge. I heard her tell Gene that investigating officers and a forensics team had been dispatched to the ambush site.

Eight of us sat in a conference room at SCSO, although the sheriff soon excused himself and left Del, Diego, Gene, Carson, and me with Roma and Detective William Soto to sort through what happened. I started at the beginning and instructed Diego to lead us through how he got into the wine-tasting room in the chateau that afternoon.

GONDA HAD fetched Diego by opening the hidden door in the wine cellar and leading him into the winery, where John Hakamora and Parson Jones, the two surviving winery workers, waited. As a group they walked to the chateau, with Diego wearing a hat Gonda gave him. In a side room, I introduced Diego to both Del and Gene, whereupon Del started acting like a lawyer and formally surrendered his client to the APD.

After the wine tasting, in which we all participated, we adjourned to our vehicles, as did the others in attendance. According to plan, Gonda walked his guests to their cars with Diego—still masquerading as a winery employee—in tow, bearing a case of wine to be placed in the trunk of Del's car. Then, as Gonda went about engaging the other departing guests in conversation, Diego climbed into the front seat of Gene's Ford while Don Carson sneaked into Del's Volvo and lay on the back floorboard so any watcher would not see more people departing than arrived.

"Sounds copasetic to me," Gene said. "Then we took out of the winery in kind of a procession."

"In what order?" Roma asked.

"We let two cars leave ahead of us," Gene said. "Then I followed, trailed by Del's Volvo. There was one car behind him."

I picked it up again. "About a mile west of the winery, there's a deserted spot where the forest opens up south of the road. Natander picked that spot because he had a good field of fire for about forty seconds."

"But how did he know you were coming and which cars were which?" Detective Soto asked.

"I suspect his buddy, Pastis, was at the winery. Probably in the wallow at the west wall where I first found evidence of them," I said. "He contacted his buddy—"

"How?" Soto asked.

Roma answered her partner. "Cell or walkie-talkie. Probably the latter. You're sure invested in Natander and Pastis being the perps, BJ."

"Makes sense to me. Natander's a trained military sniper. He and Pastis accompanied Diego to New Mexico. I spotted Natander tracking Diego west of the winery—with a rifle, I might add."

Roma swiveled her chair to Diego. "So you're copping to a plea of theft of artifacts, right?"

"Well, I was there—"

Del interrupted him. "And that's all he'll say about the subject at this time."

He had made sure I was the one to explain about Our Lady of the Euphrates, so the information remained hearsay. When questioned about my source of information, I truthfully said it was from multiple inquiries.

"However," Del spoke up, "I do want it made a part of the record that at some point my client came in possession of the artifact in question and turned it over to me. I am holding it in safekeeping and am prepared to surrender it to the proper authorities when so asked." He looked pointedly at Roma Muñoz. "Do you want me to turn it over to you?"

"No way. That's a fed matter. Someone should contact the FBI." She leaned back in the chair and squared her definitely feminine shoulders. "Right now we have two separate incidents."

"Three," I corrected her. "Don't forget your murder case."

"Right. Bascomb Zuniga. All right, three incidents. Lieutenant Enriquez, you caught the case of physical assault of this man's brother by two men in Albuquerque. The state police and I have the murder of a local citizen, and now I have what is presumably a shooting, possibly an attempt on the life of Mr. C de Baca here." She looked at Diego again. "But if they want you alive in order to regain the… uh, Lady, why try to kill you now?"

I answered her question. "Sergeant, these are two highly trained men. As a sniper, Natander knows how to assess and process information. He notes details and draws conclusions. He saw the official plates on Gene's car. He saw me arrive and put two and two together. Diego was being turned over to the police. *At the Pines.* That meant the artifact was lost to him. Now his priority was to keep Diego from talking to the authorities."

Throughout the discussion, Roma Muñoz kept her eyes on Diego. I knew what was bugging her. I'd shown both Lieutenant Yardley of the state police and Roma photos of Diego and remarked on his resemblance to Bas Zuniga, but Diego in the flesh showed the resemblance even more starkly. Finally she could constrain herself no longer.

"Mr. C de Baca, did you know a man named Bascomb Zuniga?"

"No, ma'am. I heard about him, and I'm sure sorry what happened to him, but I didn't know him. Never laid eyes on him, unless he was one of the winery workers I saw when I was sneaking into my hideout."

Roma spent half an hour coming at Diego from all different directions but ended up with exactly the conclusion I reached. He knew nothing about the killing of Zuniga.

By the time she finished with that line of questioning, a tall, balding forensics man named Roscoe Hilger entered the room with a preliminary report.

"Not much to see," he opened. "Found the likely spot, but no brass. Policed. Have a tire print, possibly a pickup, but could be a local." He turned to a green board and quickly sketched the site. As I suspected, the forest retreated from the roadside in a large V shape. Hilger indicated the probable position of Del's Volvo at the time of the first shot and its more precise position at the time of the second. That was made easier by the calculation of the spot the vehicle needed to be for a bullet to take out the back window and pass through the already blown right passenger's window.

Hilger turned to face us. "As I understand it, Mr. Dahlman braked slightly to avoid a squirrel crossing the road. If he hadn't done that, whoever was sitting in the back seat of that car was toast."

"That would be me," Don Carson said. "By the time the second shot came, I was hugging the floorboard."

"Smart man," Hilger said in a dry tone. "I suspect the shooter was highly trained. Probably military training."

"Natander," Diego said. "Spider Natander. Spent years as an Army sniper before he got himself sent to the motor pool in Basra. That's where I met him."

Del repeated his earlier warning. "And that's all we'll say on the matter."

"Do you think he knows he missed?" Roma asked.

"He does if he had a spotter," Hilger said.

"He didn't," I replied. "His spotter was back at the winery, keeping him informed of when we left and what car we were in."

Hilger grunted. "Well, he knows the car slowed suddenly and spoiled his shot. That's evident because of the second shot before you passed from his view." He smiled and threw a thumb Carson's way. "Just think, you owe your life to a squirrel."

"I quit varmint hunting about an hour ago."

The county officers left the room as Gene started questioning Diego about his brother's violent beating at the hands of two men, likely Natander and Pastis. Del allowed him to answer most of the questions, except when they touched on how the Lady of the Euphrates came into his possession.

APD didn't have armored vehicles, so they sent a couple of closed vans at Gene's request to get Diego back to Albuquerque. In all likelihood, Natander and Pastis immediately went to ground somewhere, but my old partner wasn't willing to risk anyone's life on that theory. Del decided to ride in the van with Diego to discuss whether or not protective custody was a good idea at this time. That left me with the privilege of driving Del's drafty Volvo back to Albuquerque. Before I left, Roma lassoed me in the hallway.

"You found the intruder," she said. "You figure he ties into Zuniga's murder in any way?"

"Not directly. The verdict's still out on whether the two men on his tail mistook Zuniga for Diego, but I'm satisfied Diego had nothing to do with it. In fact, he's having trouble believing Natander is the killer. Not his style. A sniper prefers to kill from a distance. He's less sure of Pastis but can't see why they wouldn't have just grabbed Zuniga until they saw they had the wrong man and then let him go."

"I'm having trouble with the concept as well," she said. "Does Gonda intend to file charges against C de Baca for the break-in?"

I shook my head. "No. All it cost him was a hasp and a couple of bottles of wine, and Diego's good for that if he wants to recover his costs. Have you turned up any new information on the killing?"

She leveled her big brown eyes at me. "Not a thing. Forensics did find some tire tracks. We'll see if they match the ones the unit cast today at the ambush site. Did you ever see the vehicle Natander and Pastis are using?"

"It was always already out of sight by the time I reached the road. I've heard the motor. The engine has a throaty growl like one of those muscle cars." I paused. "Are you investigating any theories other than the two Army fugitives?"

Roma tugged at an earlobe. She didn't wear earrings or studs in either of them. "Just checked the alibis of the people at the winery, such as they are. Can't find any sign of infighting among the winery crew. Nothing serious, anyway. The Dayton family down in Cruces is a possibility, I guess. One of them was in the area at the time."

"Pat," I supplied the man's name. "He was attending a concert here in Bernalillo with two friends. But he was supposedly a friend of Zuniga's."

She shrugged. "That's what they say, but when you knock up a guy's sister…?"

As I herded Del's injured Volvo down I-25 on the fifteen-mile ride back to Albuquerque, I reviewed my recent conversation with Roma. There were only three obvious reasons for Zuniga's murder—four, if you included the drive-by shooting theory. Which I did not. The wound placements did not favor the idea of a passing car randomly shooting at a man walking at the side of the road. That left Natander and Pastis as the killers, the Dayton family in Las Cruces taking a pound of flesh for their daughter, or someone from the winery… either one or more of the people Bas Zuniga worked with or some of Gonda's family.

Claudio Garcia, the vineyard worker who roomed with Zuniga, was a loner, interested only in working and his family back in Juarez, Mexico. He'd forged a friendship with the dead man, not only according to Garcia but also confirmed by the other workers. It was unlikely Claudio engaged in a dispute that rose to that level of violence. The same was true of the rest of the winery workers. Regardless of how I looked at things, if Diego's former buddies weren't the killers, it looked like a family thing. But which family? The Gondas or the Daytons?

I was no closer to figuring things out by the time I left the Volvo at Whitesell's Auto Glass on Griego NW, but I *had* decided how I wanted to proceed.

Charlie responded to my call for help and picked me up to give me a lift back to the office parking lot, where my Impala awaited. By the time we arrived, I had dictated the events of the day.

After leaving the recorder with Charlie to give to Hazel and picking up an alternate—I couldn't function without a recorder within reach—I crawled into my car and headed straight to 5229 Post Oak Drive, where I hoped to find my significant other waiting. I needed him badly. It was my great good fortune that Paul was at home and suffered a similar desire, which we joyfully fulfilled… for both our sakes.

EARLY THE next morning when I staggered out of the bedroom after a shower and shave, Paul was reading the morning paper at the kitchen table while sipping black coffee and working on a bowl of oatmeal. He was perky and ready to go; I was barely functioning. That's what a thirteen-year difference between me and my lover did to me—Paul was twenty-four. I looked at him fondly. If this was the way I had to die, there were worse ways to go.

"What?" he demanded when he caught me staring.

"Just remembering last night. That dragon dancing."

He grinned but kept his mouth shut.

"Is that why you got the tattoo, so your bed partner could admire it prowling around while you demonstrated your athleticism?"

"You want the truth? I lost a bet, and the penalty was to get a tattoo. Didn't see anything I'd rather have than that dragon. The guy wanted to put it somewhere else, but I couldn't see Pedro peeking out from behind a bush."

"I've known you for three years, and that's the first time you've ever told me you named the dragon."

"Of course I named him. I gotta live with him from now till I die. A fellow oughta know who he's living with."

"Surprised you didn't go with something like 'Mom.'"

Paul snorted. "No, thank you. How'd you like to see 'Mom' staring you in the face every time we made love?"

"How old were you when you got Pedro?"

"Sixteen."

"And you were already thinking ahead back then. You're a wise man, Paul Barton."

"Thank you, sir." He rose, rinsed his dishes, and stowed them in the dishwasher. "Gonna head out. You wanna go to the C&W tonight?"

"I've got to go to Las Cruces. You wanna tag along? Tomorrow's the Fourth, and we can get in some golf at the U's course."

Dismay distorted his handsome features. "Can't. Like you say, tomorrow's the Fourth. That's a big day at the country club. Especially in the pool. Can't get time off. Is this on that missing baby thing we went down there on last month?"

"Yeah. Gonda's grandson."

"Too bad about his son. From his picture, he was a good-looking dude."

"And a good man from all accounts."

"Okay, if you're heading south to Cruces, then I'm going car shopping."

"You're finally going to give up the Barrio Bomb?"

"I got that Plymouth about the same time I got Pedro, and it was old then. I've pretty much got the last of my educational expenses behind me, so it's time for a new set of wheels. Besides, Niv's interested in buying it." He referred to Niven Pence, my across-the-street widowed neighbor's teenaged great-grandson.

"You need some help?"

"Naw. I can handle it. Just kinda like having you along when I go looking."

"Wait until next weekend, and I'm all yours." He took his leave without making a commitment, but I knew my man. He was an independent cuss and would likely be driving a new car by this evening. Well, a used car that was new to him, at least.

LAS CRUCES hadn't changed in the month since Paul and I confronted the family over little David James Dayton, Bas Zuniga's son. At the time, we decided the Daytons sold their dead daughter's baby for the Lincoln sitting in the family driveway. Later we watched James Dayton, the family patriarch, flee in the pricey auto headed for Texas. Had he returned yet?

No sign of the luxury car in the Dayton's driveway. I debated knocking on the door anyway but decided to do some snooping around first. My first stop was the elderly woman down the street who'd been willing to talk to Paul and me last month. She was home, and she was still talkative. My notes identified her as Mrs. Wilma Brandini, a widow.

"I remember you, sonny," she said when I tried to introduce myself. "Where's that handsome youngster who was with you last time?"

"Working back in Albuquerque."

"Well, next time you stay up to Albuquerque and send him down here." She gave a hen's cackle. "Handsome as my late husband in his salad days."

"Yes, ma'am. May I ask you some more questions?"

"About them Daytons? Come on inside." She turned and allowed me to follow her into a small living room covered with needlepoint. Crocheted doilies, embroidered afghans on both couch and chairs, fancy pillows. She'd even hand-stitched a pattern on her ottoman. No need to ask what kept her occupied. She plopped down on an overstuffed chair angled to give her the best view of the street outside the window. Busy eyes and busy fingers both, I suspected.

I switched on the recorder attached to my belt as I took a seat on the couch and watched her hands flutter. She needed some kind of needles in those fingers to keep them from twitching. "I'm interested in learning what happened to the Dayton infant after his mother died."

"Poor little thing. The mother, I mean. Lucia, her name was. Sweet thing. And her young man, likely looking. And nice too. Always took the time to speak when they saw me. But nature makes its call and takes its toll, I always say. I hope he's doing okay... the young man, I mean."

"He was killed the other day. That's why I'm trying to locate the baby. His relatives want to exercise their rights."

"As well they should. No child needs to grow up around Bart and Willie Dayton, I can tell you. Pat's not so bad. More like his sister. But the rest of them...." She left anything else unsaid.

"Do you know what happened to the baby? He doesn't seem to be a part of the household any longer."

"Gone. Not seen hide nor hair of the child since that car came and picked him up. Guess that means he's not growing up around the Daytons, don't it?"

"Can you tell me any more about the car or who picked the child up?"

"Green with New Mexico plates, like I told you last time you was here. That's all."

"Do you know what kind of car it was?"

"Just four wheels, four doors, and green. That's all I know."

"New? Old? Expensive? Beat-up?"

"Oh no. It wasn't beat-up. Clean and shiny. Wasn't old."

"Foreign or domestic?"

"Huh? Oh, foreign, I'd say." She motioned downward with her right palm. "Low. Sat low down on the ground?"

"And the driver?"

"A woman. Clean and shiny too. Not trashy. Course, can't always tell from looking. Dressed like she was going to church. And it wasn't Sunday, neither."

"Young, old? Blonde, brunette?"

"About James's age. Forty-five or thereabouts. Blonde hair. Likely bleached. Most of them do that these days. My time, we left our hair natural."

"Had you ever seen the green car before? Or again."

She shook her white-fringed head. "No. It was strange to me."

"Do you know of any relatives the Daytons might have, maybe over Texas way?"

She screwed up her left eye so that it almost disappeared. I understood she was thinking. "Seems to me I heard old man Dayton... that's James, you know. Well, seems to me I recollect he had a sister over in Carlsbad. Carlsbad's too hot for me. Couldn't stand living there."

"Do you know her name?"

"Don't believe I ever heard it. Wait a minute. Heard one of the kids talking about Aunt Jane once. If I recollect right, said she and her husband owned a car company over there."

"Car company?'

"You know, selling them and buying them."

"A dealership?"

"That's the thing. A dealership."

Fifteen minutes later, I escaped Mrs. Brandini's clutches—with no additional useful information—to retire to a nearby park for some research. During the City of Rocks case last year, I'd invested in a little "hotspot" device to provide Wi-Fi when I was on the road. It worked more or less well—more when I was in an urban area with strong signals. And Las Cruces was one of those, so I got my laptop working just fine.

I'm not as good at searching the internet as Hazel, but eventually I located a used car dealership in Carlsbad with registered owners named

Hadley and Jane Forsyth. Forsyth Motors was located in the 1100 block of North Canal, which seemed to be a popular street for used car dealers. The Forsyths had operated their business at that site for over ten years, so they likely had a decent reputation. There were no customer reviews, so I got no help in coming to that conclusion.

I sat back in the Impala's seat and considered my options. Carlsbad lay to the east of Las Cruces, which was toward Texas. When Paul and I trailed James Dayton in his new Lincoln, he'd taken the road to El Paso, which was one way to reach Carlsbad. Chances were decent that's where he was headed. That left me with two options: phone the dealership and speak to one of the owners about little David James Dayton, or spend three hours driving 200 miles to do the same in person. I'm a great believer in face-to-face interviewing, but a phone call might at least establish that Aunt Jane was in Carlsbad at the moment. I dialed the number provided by my search for the dealership and moments later was greeted by a pleasant contralto.

"May I speak to Mrs. Jane Dayton Forsyth?" I asked.

"I'm sorry, sir, but she's not in at the moment. May I ask who's calling?"

"Has she been in today?"

"Yes, sir. Earlier today, but she's left for the day. May I—"

"Thank you, I'll call later."

I ended the call. The receptionist hadn't reacted negatively to my request for Jane *Dayton* Forsyth. Of course, that might mean nothing. We often hear only what we're expecting to hear, but the call was enough to send me to a service station for a refill before heading down I-10, where I would eventually pick up US 62 E and breeze into Carlsbad. Would it prove to be a fool's errand? Tomorrow was the Fourth, a holiday. But what better day to car shop than Independence Day? Betting that the Forsyths would be tending to business tomorrow rather than taking a holiday, I reluctantly dialed Paul's cell phone and left a message, saying I wouldn't be home until sometime later tomorrow.

Chapter 19

THE CITY of Carlsbad straddled the Pecos River near the edge of the Guadalupe Mountains. Located in an ecoregion designated as the Chihuahuan Desert—which covered 140,000 to 200,000 square miles of west Texas, southeastern New Mexico, and northern Mexico—the town was born sometime in the 1880s. Originally named Eddy for a local cowman, the fledgling village was rechristened Carlsbad after the famous Bohemian Karlsbad Spa in the early 1900s. This renaming was presumably an effort to advertise mineral springs discovered near what is now the Pecos Flume. Eighteen miles southwest of the town lay Carlsbad Caverns National Park. As an inveterate history fan, facts like this clogged my brain... likely crowding out more useful things.

I arrived in the community Friday night after a nonstop drive from Las Cruces. Tired from what was essentially a day of driving, I took a room at the Holiday Inn Express on West Pierce, grabbed a bite to eat, cleaned up, and then reached Hazel at home. She had little new to tell me, so I closed the call and dialed my home phone, doubtful if I'd reach Paul. This morning he'd expressed interest in going dancing at the C&M, so I was gratified to hear his smoky baritone.

"Thought you'd be out dancing."

"Then why didn't you call my cell?"

"Didn't want to disturb you if you were shaking your thing."

"Disturb me, guy. Anywhere, anytime. Please."

My heart did the two-step. "Wish I was there right now."

"Wish you were too. We'd celebrate my new wheels by making love."

"Don't wanna slide over that 'making love' part too quickly, but you have a new car?"

"New to me, anyway. A 2006 Dodge Charger."

"Stayed with Chrysler Corp., did you? Is it purple like the Plymouth?"

"Coal black. Cuts through the air like shadowy seduction."

"Oh man, I wish I were there."

"Me too. We'd go up in the mountains and break it in."

"You stay out of the mountains until I get back. Hear me?"

His laugh was golden. "I hear you. When will that be?"

I brought him up-to-date on what I was doing and finished by saying I hoped to be back tomorrow night.

"I figured that," he said. "Someday next week we can drive up Sandia Peak and christen the Dodge."

I slept restlessly that night. Too many dreams about seductive pectoral dragons and black automobiles.

FORSYTH MOTORS looked to be a substantial operation for a used car dealership. From the look of the lot, they specialized in late-model mid-to-large-sized luxury models. Such as a certain cinnamon-colored 2008 Lincoln Continental.

I sat for a while observing the comings and goings—and recording them on my digital recorder—until a low-slung green Jaguar XJ-Series automobile pulled into the lot and took one of the reserved parking spots near the showroom doors. The fact a man got out of the Jag rather than a woman disconcerted me. Nonetheless, I was pretty certain I'd found Aunt Jane's green car. Was that enough to tie the Forsyths to Ariel's grandson? Enough to take the next step, anyway.

I pulled into the lot, parked in a convenient customer parking space, and got out, eluding two salesmen on my determined march into the showroom. The silver-haired, fiftyish-something gentleman who'd exited the Jag was talking to an attractive young receptionist at the front of the vast room. I walked up and interrupted their conversation.

"Excuse me, Mr. Forsyth, may I speak to you?"

A slight frown marred his distinguished features momentarily before the super salesman took over.

"Certainly, Mister…?"

I rushed through the introduction as I slowly walked toward a late-model Cadillac a few paces away from the receptionist's desk.

He smoothed the silver wing of hair over his left temple. "And what would a private detective want with me?"

"I was hoping to talk to you and your wife. I represent the child's paternal grandfather."

He was good, but the slight tightening around his eyes belied his next words. "And what child is that?"

"The two-year-old boy your wife took from the home of her brother, James Dayton, last month. The child called David James Dayton."

From the look on his face, he considered denying everything but relented. "You are speaking of my wife's dead niece's child. Our understanding was that she died without revealing the father of the child. We are in the process of legally adopting David."

"The father was a young man well-known to the Dayton family named Bascomb Zuniga. Mr. Zuniga was murdered about a month ago outside the place where he worked. There is, of course, a criminal investigation into his death, conducted jointly by the New Mexico State Police and the Sandoval County Sheriff's Office. Lt. Ray Yardley and Sgt. Roma Muñoz, respectively. As you can imagine, there is a possibility the murder revolves around the child, so I suspect the adoption will not be approved until this is cleared up. Then there is my client's interest to be considered."

"I think it best you speak to our attorney William Jenkins. You can find him in the book. Now, if you'll excuse me." Stiff-backed, Hadley Forsyth disappeared through a walnut-paneled door and out of my sight.

Locating William Jenkins's office wasn't difficult. Finding *William Jenkins* was another matter. Not only was it Saturday, it was also the Fourth of July, as attested by the groups of people lining the street, apparently in preparation for a parade. The only individual I found in Jenkins's two-story building was a custodian who had no interest in helping me find the attorney. I tried the home phone listing my database search provided, but it went unanswered except for the automated voicemail. When invited, I left a lengthy message. Then I did an even more detailed message to the email address it also provided.

Understanding that Ariel would want to know that I saw the child with my own eyes, I further intruded on the Forsyths' privacy and pulled up to the curb in front of their two-story, white brick residence of no particular style and walked up the sidewalk to their door. The green Jag sat in the driveway. Forsyth had rushed home to alert his wife to a possible hitch in their plans. He answered my ring with a scowl on his face. I snapped on the recorder at my waist.

"Told you to see—"

I put some steel in my voice. "It's a holiday, Forsyth. His office is closed, and I'm not about to leave until I can tell my client—whose name is Ariel Gonda, by the way—that I have seen with my own eyes that his grandchild is in good health." I eased up. "And judging from what I've learned about you and Mrs. Forsyth, I suspect that is the case."

After a moment's hesitation, he stood back from the door. "You might as well come in. William is here. I called him as soon as you left the lot. Maybe you can clear up a few things for us." He led me to a bright, spotlessly clean living room filled with Hepplewhite, some originals and some knockoffs. The man standing at the window turned and walked to meet us.

William Jenkins should have been anathema to people like the Forsyths. He wore a rumpled, disheveled, and rough demeanor, which I took to be habitual. He accepted my hand and examined me through shrewd gray eyes.

"I've heard of you, Mr. Vinson. Do some business with the Stone Hedges firm up in Albuquerque occasionally. Thought I needed a private investigator on a case once, and Del Dahlman picked your name out of the air. Turned out we didn't need nobody."

"Del and I go back a long way. Knew him when I was with APD."

He nodded and released my hand. "Hmm. What's your client's interest in this adoption?"

"The welfare of his grandchild is his first interest. His rights in the matter are his second."

"Hmm. Explain."

"He's only recently learned of his grandchild's existence when his son, a decent young man named Bascomb Zuniga, was shot down in the middle of the night as he left work at Mr. Gonda's Lovely Pines Winery. Naturally, he wants to make sure the child, his own blood, is provided for."

"He wants to take the child?" Jenkins shot back at me.

"He's not made that clear. Depends on circumstances, I imagine."

"Who's handling the murder?"

"It's a joint investigation by the state police and the county."

"Where are they on the murder investigation?"

"They don't confide in me. Right now I'm tasked with locating the missing child, making sure he's safe and being well taken care of."

"Child ain't missing, Vinson. He's here with his aunt and uncle, who intend on adopting him now that both his mother and father are dead. Nothing standing in the way of this adoption."

"That depends upon where the murder investigation leads."

"Meaning to the Daytons, I guess you're saying."

"I need to see the boy."

Jenkins eyed me speculatively. "The Daytons ain't murderers."

"Not for me to say. I'd like to see the boy," I said again.

When the attorney nodded, Forsyth called out, "Bring the boy in here, Jane."

My first glimpse of Jane Dayton Forsyth startled me. Tall, thin, she wasn't the suave, sophisticated woman I would have thought a man like Forsyth favored. Her voice redeemed her. It was a strong, determined contralto.

"Davy is not leaving my side."

"Not my intention, ma'am," I said. "I just want to see him and reassure his grandfather he's being well taken care of."

"Taken care of *and* loved," she said, a protective hand on the boy's dark hair. David James Dayton was a miniature Bas Zuniga. No doubt this was Ariel's grandson.

I knelt down in front of the child. Jane Forsyth bent over to place both hands on his shoulders, protecting him from the big, bad detective. "Hi. My name's BJ, what's yours?"

The boy popped a finger into his mouth for a second before removing it and stuttering, "D-David."

I coaxed a few more words out of the shy child before taking out my phone and snapping two pictures before anyone could object. "Just for proof the boy's healthy and happy," I said.

"Why ain't this client of yours, this Ariel Gonda, demonstrated no interest in the boy before this?" Jenkins asked.

I'd already admitted that Gonda wasn't aware of David until recently, but this was a matter that might well end up in court, and I didn't want to say any more than necessary. I detected a sharp mind behind Jenkins's homespun appearance and folksy manner.

"You'll have to ask his attorney," I said. "And that would be the Del Dahlman you mentioned earlier, Mr. Jenkins."

"Hmm" was all he said.

With that noncommittal comment ringing in my ear, I thanked them for their hospitality and took my leave. My business done in Carlsbad, I dodged the local Independence Day parade and headed up US 285 on the 300-mile trek to Albuquerque. If the holiday drunks didn't slow me down too much, I'd be home tonight to inspect Paul's 2006 Charger intimately... as well as its owner.

Chapter 20

As it turned out, I reached 5229 Post Oak Drive before either the Charger or my lover. I showered and shaved and started a couple of sirloins before I heard the growl of an unfamiliar motor outside on the driveway. A moment later, Paul burst through the back door with a huge grin on his face. After those strong, wiry arms closed about me and his face was buried in my neck, I truly felt at home.

"Sorry to be late," he said after a kiss. "Big doings at the country club. Swim team had its own party after that, so I got roped into staying."

"What was that noise I heard in the driveway?"

"That was the sound of brute power, my man. Come on."

He released me and rushed out the door. I rounded the corner from the backyard to the driveway and saw the familiar crossbar grille of the Charger. Black and beautiful and sleek.

"Low miles, two-owner, no body damage. It's a Hemi," he said, referring to a type of motor in Chrysler vehicles. "Puts out 340 hp and 525 torque. A muscle car."

"Hope they didn't burn you." The comment was teasing. Paul was too levelheaded to be taken financially.

"Decent price, decent down, decent interest. And I can afford it. If you ask nicely, I'll let you drive it… while I'm in the car."

"Tomorrow. I want to head for the hills and christen it tomorrow."

He leaned close and leered. "You can drive up, but you won't have the stamina to drive down. I'll take care of that."

Paul pretty well called it. After a wonderful romp Saturday night, I drove the Charger up Sandia Crest, where we found a secluded spot. I normally lock my semiautomatic S&W in the car trunk, but out of innate caution over driving into the mountains where we were isolated from the usual human traffic, I'd tucked it into the belt at my back. That proved a problem during the gymnastics that followed, so it ended up lying in the driver's seat as we gloried in nature and one another… in the car and on the car.

After a couple of wonderful hours, Paul handed me my S&W as he climbed—on shaky legs, I'm proud to say—into the driver's seat. Too exhausted to put the weapon in the Dodge's trunk, I restored it to the belt at my back. Then he drove down the back way so we could stop at the Pines to report the results of my Las Cruces and Carlsbad trips to Ariel. The parking lot held more cars than usual, so there must be a tasting underway.

Even so, I spotted Ariel sitting in the salon as soon as I walked through the front doors. He was talking to Margot and Marc Juisson. Upon spotting me, he bounced to his feet and called my name.

"Have you found the boy?" he asked.

"I have." After the trio acknowledged Paul, I gave them a full report on my recent trip. "The Forsyths' lawyer, Mr. Jenkins, asked me an interesting question," I said after finishing my narration. "He wanted to know if you intended to press for custody of the child."

He and Margot exchanged glances before he turned back to me. "At this point I do not know. Depends upon the circumstances, I suppose. Is he being well cared for in a good environment?"

I pulled out my phone. "You tell me."

Soon the Gondas were oohing and aahing over the two images I'd snapped of the handsome child. Marc seemed to take a more considered attitude but made appropriate remarks. "Cute little guy. Looks like he's being cared for okay."

"I'll have my report typed up tomorrow morning and get a copy of it to Del Dahlman, along with the photos."

"May we have prints of the photographs, as well?" Ariel asked.

"I'll see to it. Since I've located your grandchild, you interface with Del from now on."

"Have you learned any more about who killed Bas?" Gonda asked, tugging on that invisible beard again. I decided it was a sign of stress.

"The state and county police are on that, so I made it my priority to trace the child."

"But you will keep looking for the killer," Ariel said. "Please, BJ. I'm counting on you."

"The authorities are far more likely to solve this thing than I am."

Marc spoke up. "I thought it was those two AWOLs who were stalking Diego C de Baca. You know, mistaken identity."

"Possible."

"Or that family down in Las Cruces that has the baby," he went on. "Bad blood between Bas and the brothers, I heard. Over knock—" He stumbled over his tongue. "—over getting their sister pregnant."

"They're looking into Bas's murder from several different viewpoints," I said.

Gonda dropped a hand on my shoulder. "BJ, I saw what you did for the Alfano brothers when Lando went missing up in the Bisti Wilderness area. Stay on this for me, please."

"I'll monitor the police's progress. Save you some money that way."

Ariel's face went red. "Money be damned! Find my boy's killer."

"By the way," Marc said. "We had another intruder. Parson worked in the winery late the other night, and when he left the building, he saw someone step over the wall and walk into the woods. Is that Diego fellow still in custody?"

"Been out of town for a couple of days, so I'll have to check. Did Parson describe the man?"

"Too dark," Marc said. "Just caught movement out of the corner of his eye. But I checked the next morning and found some footsteps. Hugged the wall of the winery."

"Did you report it?" I asked.

Ariel answered for him. "I was afraid it was Diego and didn't want to cause him trouble."

I shook my head. "Wouldn't be him. If the trail went all around the winery building, it was someone else. Report it to Sgt. Roma Muñoz at SCSO. Paul and I will take a look around before we go."

The mountain breezes had pretty well scrubbed away the tracks Marc told us about, but in some sheltered places, we found a faint footprint or two.

"That's a military boot," Paul noted.

"Natander or Pastis, no doubt. They know Diego's in custody but hope he's hidden the statuette somewhere in the winery. Probably giving it one last try before they go on the lam."

On the other side of the wall, one visible bootprint seemed to indicate the intruder had escaped into the woods, just as Parson had reported. On impulse, I walked to the ruined cabin and noticed the same prints in the sandy spot before the collapsed front of the place. As I opened the trapdoor that gave access to the hidden chamber, Paul peered over my shoulder.

"So this is it, huh? The way to Diego's hideout."

"There's another entry through the wine cellar," I said, examining the underside of the trapdoor. "Diego said there's a way to bar access from the inside. I probably should lock it. You wanna see where Diego hid out?"

Paul backed away. "It's pitch-black down there, man."

"I've got a flashlight on my keyring."

"That dinky thing? That wouldn't light your way to the bathroom."

"You'd be surprised. Enough light to get to the lantern inside with no problem."

"Thanks, but no thanks. I'll meet you back at the car."

"Shouldn't take me long. Might even beat you there."

He held up the wooden slab as I felt my way down the ladder. After turning on the small but powerful flash, I caught a glimpse of his handsome face twisted into a worried frown as I reached up for the trapdoor.

"See you in a few minutes."

The tunnel got considerably darker as the trapdoor closed. I used the beam of the flash to locate the lever Diego said secured the hatch. The place did seem sort of creepy then. I felt my way to the bottom of the ladder step after careful step until I hit solid earth. The focused beam of my light shot straight ahead, stabbing the darkness but not defeating it.

I had no trouble with the second ladder that brought me back up to the floor of the chamber, which I judged to be on a level with the ruined cabin. Maneuvering the short tunnel, I emerged into the larger chamber of the hidden room. The chilled temperature now probably matched that of the wine cellar on the other side of the rock wall. A small, indistinct rosy glow caught my attention. After focusing the light on the area, I saw the wick on Diego's candle slowly dimming away.

I swept the area with my pitiful light and stopped as it fell on a pair of camo pants. As I started to move it up, a harsh voice broke the eerie silence.

"Turn it off, man. Now!"

I happily complied. Darkness might prove to be my savior now. But my light no sooner died than a larger, stronger beam blinded me. I resisted the urge to shield my eyes and steadied my voice.

"There's nothing to find here, Natander," I said, assuming it was the sniper and not his buddy. "Where's Pastis?"

"You right. There ain't nothing I want here." The light shifted so I was still illuminated but not blinded. "You the guy that turned Diego in to the cops. Vinson, right?"

"Surprised you know my name. Resourceful."

"Damned right. I'm trained for this stuff. Wasn't hard. Followed you back to Albuquerque once and let Pastis out of the car. He followed you into your building and watched to see what office you went into. Nice of them to leave the center of the building hollow like that."

My building was built around an atrium that soared up all five floors, with landings providing access to the offices lining the outside walls. All Pastis would have to do was stand in the middle of the ground floor and watch.

"I'm impressed."

"You not much of a private dick. You never tumbled to us following you."

"How did you find Diego's hiding place?"

"I've checked out every inch of this winery property. I've been in that falling-down cabin a dozen times. Today was the first time I put my hand to that big board out there."

"And found it was covered with camouflaged burlap," I said.

"After that, it was just poking and thumping around till I found the nail that tripped the false floor."

"So now that you found his hidey-hole and determined what you're looking for isn't here, you can leave."

"So you can tackle me, huh?"

"Why would I do that? I'll just let the police pick you up later."

"Ain't the way it's gonna work. You turned Diego in. You know where the statue is. So you're gonna take me to it."

"Be happy to. Like as not Diego's attorney has turned it over to the feds. So let's go. By the way, that lawyer's pissed at you for shooting out the windows of his car."

"The blond dude, huh? Tell him he oughta thank me. Woulda been easier to shoot him in the head and then pick off everyone that survived the wreck."

"Why didn't you?"

"Too messy. But that's probably what I oughta done."

"Glad we cleared that up. I'm going to leave now."

A raspy laugh froze me in place. "Wonder how long it'll take them to find your body down here? You think they'll ever—"

I relaxed my muscles and simply dropped to the ground. Natander's pistol roared and spit fire. The bullet whistled over my head. But his reaction time was good. The flashlight died as I rolled twice to my left. My S&W 9mm was out and ready when he fired blindly again. A projectile thunked into the earth right beside me before he swung the opposite direction. The next time he fired, I pulled the trigger twice. He grunted and fell.

I'd lost my keyring when Natander surprised me, so I fumbled my phone from my pocket and used the even smaller light to locate the keyring. Holding my flashlight off to my right, I clicked it on and swept the area. I saw his boots first. Military. Parallel to the ground. I traced the line of Natander's prone body until I reached his face. He was still alive, but from the blood leaking from his chest, at least one of my bullets had found him—probably fatally. I scrambled to his side and took a heavy semiautomatic from his limp fingers. By the feeble light, I saw him trying to focus on me.

I stripped off my shirt and stuffed it against his wound to staunch the flow of blood before clawing my digital voice recorder from my belt and holding it close. "Natander, you're dying. But you need to tell me one thing."

His eyes flickered, but there was still life in them. "Wha...."

"Did you or Pastis kill a man in front of the winery?"

"Naw...." He shuddered. "Killed priest... in Iraq."

"But did you kill Bascomb Zuniga thinking it was Diego?"

"Uh-uh. B-but... was there. Saw it. Somebody talking... to him. He walk... away. Shoot'm... in b-back."

"You didn't try to help the guy?"

He sighed heavily and then between labored breaths said they'd checked the victim because they thought it was Diego. Took a minute to figure out it wasn't the right man; the resemblance was so strong.

Tremors started in his legs and worked their way up to possess him. He groaned but was still there. Barely.

"Did you recognize the shooter? See where he came from or went afterward? Was there a car?"

He gave a peculiar whining sound for a moment. Then: "N-no car. Went... to p-pines."

Spider Natander's eyes lost their light. He stopped shivering. Stopped moving at all. He was gone.

"Pines?" I mumbled aloud. *Was that pines as in trees or Pines as in winery?*

After that, I clicked off the recorder.

Chapter 21

A NOISE behind me and a sudden light penetrating the darkness sent me whirling around. My heart almost stopped when I found myself pointing a pistol at Paul. I dropped it in the dirt.

"Vince! Are you all right?" Gonda stood behind Paul in the wine cellar, his eyes as round as Little Orphan Annie's.

I took a deep breath and dragged myself up out of the dirt, snagging my weapon as I did. Waving it vaguely behind me, I said, "Natander. He's dead. We need to call the cops."

"Sergeant Muñoz is already on her way. Marc called her as you suggested." Paul started to come inside, but I stopped him with a hand up. "This is a crime scene," I said. "Nobody can enter. But I'm coming out there to sit on that old couch."

Paul stepped forward and clutched my arm as if helping an old man to his chair, and I sort of felt that way. I'd killed the man who shot me in the thigh while I was an APD detective, but that didn't prepare me for killing another human being. At the thought, my old wound throbbed so hard I stumbled. But my man was right there to catch me.

As I settled on the sofa, Roma and two deputies hit the door and entered like a hurricane. Her rash approach caused a few minutes' delay, but she quickly settled down and asked questions like a seasoned pro— after she scanned my naked chest.

"You shot Natander, Vinson?"

"You can quit looking for him. He's in that room right over there." I glanced at Gonda. "He didn't kill your son, Ariel."

"How do you know?" Roma asked.

"He told me. Deathbed confession, I guess you'd call it."

Roma turned and ordered everyone out. Gonda was clearly relieved. This many people in the wine cellar was already disturbing the temperature. Once we were in the winery, she got on her cell to order the county crime-scene unit out to the site. Then she went over everything again while Parson Jones walked to the chateau to get a shirt for me.

She satisfied herself that Paul and Gonda had become concerned when I didn't reappear after entering the secret chamber to secure the outside entrance behind me. Gonda tripped the lever Diego had shown him inside the wine cellar, and they found me sitting beside Natander's body. She confiscated my weapon, ordered one deputy to remain on site, and hustled me to a county cruiser for a trip to the station. When Paul insisted on coming, she told him to provide his own transportation.

Sergeant Muñoz went up in my estimation over the next two hours. I already recognized her as a competent cop, but she put me on a figurative rack and pulled everything out of me. Even though I was 100 percent cooperative, she treated me like a hostile witness. Until we were finished.

"You were lucky, BJ," she said, addressing me by the name the rest of the world used. "That was an armed military sniper you faced down in there."

"I had one advantage."

"What's that?"

"He didn't want to kill me—until he lost control of the situation, that is. He was still looking for the artifact, and I was his last hope of finding it."

"But you said he—"

"That was a threat to make me cooperate with him. Once I helped him, he might have carried out the threat. What about Pastis? Any sign of him?"

"I've got people out scouring the countryside for him, but nobody's reported spotting the man."

"He was close by. Probably took off as soon as your patrol cars started showing up."

We exited the interview room to find Paul fit to be tied. He'd been corralled in another interview room, but it took only a few minutes to get his statement.

"Settle down, sonny," Roma said, "or I'll put that black Charger you drove up in on the watch list. You go one mile over the speed limit, and you'll get a ticket."

"Yes, Mommy, I'll be a good boy."

His retort took her by surprise and almost drew a laugh out of me, but it served its purpose and defused the issue. After that, we were free to leave. Roma held on to my Smith & Wesson until the case was properly disposed of.

MOST PLACES were closed on Monday because of the Fourth on the previous Saturday, but it was a big day at the country club, so Paul was scheduled to work. With nothing better to do, I trailed him to the club and put in an hour of swimming. That was partially so I could admire his nearly naked body as he sat in the lifeguard's chair and partially as therapy for the gunshot wound in my thigh. I'd become slack about that lately, and as a result, the right leg started to stiffen. After that, I wandered into the card room and got roped into a game of gin rummy.

Hazel and Charlie greeted me at the office Tuesday morning with stares. I'd called Hazel to let her know I was all right, since they'd probably read about the shooting in this morning's *Albuquerque Journal*. As we settled down at my conference table, Hazel led the verbal assault.

"You just had to have some fireworks of your own on the Fourth, didn't you?"

"Technically it was the fifth, Sunday."

Obviously they needed more, so I recounted the events of my last three days, even though the recorder I slid over to Hazel contained everything in detail, including Natander's dying statement.

"Hazel, I can't even count all the legal jurisdictions that are going to want Natander's confession, statement… whatever you want to call it. Better make some copies. Get Gene's to him first."

Charlie's methodical mind started the process of reordering our priorities. "Our contract with Gonda oughta be complete. Diego C de Baca was the intruder, and he's in custody."

"Ariel wants us to continue. Another contract, I suppose. He wants us to find his son's killer."

Hazel snorted in a ladylike manner. "The state police and the county deputies aren't enough for him?"

"Apparently not. I pointed that out to him and offered to monitor their progress, but he wants us to actively pursue the case." I tugged the slips I used to record time and expenses from my attaché case and handed them to Hazel. "These are for the Carlsbad trip. Include them in the final bill. Send it to him and include another contract for his signature on the murder case. Don't request a retainer. Specify that we are to assist the appropriate authorities in investigating the death of Bascomb Zuniga."

The admittance bell on the door to our suite of offices pealed, pulling Hazel out of the meeting. She appeared at the door a moment later with a disturbed look on her face.

"There's a man out here who wants to talk to you, BJ. He claims his name's Pastis."

Charlie and I came to our feet as one. I felt for the S&W that wasn't there, and I hadn't dug out my Ruger backup. Charlie understood my reaction and showed me the S&W .38 he'd carried since his days as an APD policeman. I nodded. He followed me out into the reception area, where we confronted a stocky brown man about five nine. When I said brown, I meant brown. Smooth brown skin, hair tending toward ebony, and chocolate eyes. He stood with his eyes flicking back and forth between Charlie and me. But he ultimately concentrated his stare on me.

"You Mr. Vinson?"

"And my guess is that you're Sgt. Hugo Pastis, presently AWOL from your unit in Fort Bliss, Texas."

"You got it. What happened to Spider? I saw all the cops and the ambulance."

Charlie's hand went to the pocket where he carried his .38 as I answered. "I'm afraid your buddy's gone. He objected to me walking in on him in Diego's hideaway. We exchanged gunfire. I defended myself."

"You shot him?"

"He had no choice in the matter," Charlie said.

Pastis sighed. "You don't need that weapon you're fingering in your pocket, mister. I ain't carrying. Besides, I got nothing to gain from taking you two on."

His face was clear, no frown, no tightening of the eyes. He seemed to accept his friend's death.

Pastis apparently read my mind. "It was gonna happen sooner or later. Spider didn't cut nobody no slack. Always pushing. But you're lucky. He was fast, and he was accurate."

"But in a pitch-black hole, you don't go shooting off rounds and giving away your position."

"He was smarter than that, but he was getting awful tired of all this bullshit. Maybe he was ready to go."

"Suicide by private investigator?" Charlie asked.

"Maybe."

"I just have one question for you," I said. "Why did you kill that young man in front of the winery? Did you mistake him for Diego?"

His head jerked back. "That kid that got whacked in the middle of the night?" I nodded. "Hell, we didn't kill him. We didn't kill nobody."

"Except the priest in Iraq you took the Lady of the Euphrates from."

"That was Natander. I was with Diego when that happened. That was on Spider's back."

"He admitted that to me before he died," I said. "Knew he was dying, so it was a deathbed confession."

Something cleared from Pastis's face. "You'll tell the feds that?"

"I will, just as soon as anyone asks me. You ready to turn yourself in?"

"I ain't gonna run for the rest of my life. I'm guessing you turned the statue over to the feds, so that takes some of the sting outta the situation." He shrugged. "If you'll take me to them, I'll surrender without no trouble."

"First there's a lady sergeant in the Sandoval County Sheriff's Office who wants a piece of you."

"The ambush, huh? Well, nobody got hurt."

"She's pretty stubborn, but I think I can get her to drop the charges if she turns you over to the feds."

"What about Enriquez?" Charlie asked.

"Oh yeah. There's an APD lieutenant who wants to discuss a beating two men gave one of our Albuquerque citizens. He's probably first in line."

"Shit. That was Spider's idea too."

"I had to guess, Sergeant, I'd say most of this problem you're facing started with him. You and Diego both would have been better off dropping him back in Iraq."

Pastis nodded. "You don't know Natander. Nobody dropped him."

"Hazel, please call Lieutenant Enriquez at APD. Sergeant Pastis and I will wait for him in my office."

Charlie joined us at my conference table in the office. Good. He'd be a witness. Never hurts to have one, even though I'd been recording our conversation since I'd turned on my recorder at my waist before speaking to Pastis. Once we were comfortable, I pulled if off my belt and laid it on the table.

"Do you mind if I record our conversation?" I asked.

He shook his head but mumbled "Okay" at Charlie's prompting. I went about identifying the parties as if I'd just turned the device on.

"Let's go back to the attack on Mr. German C de Baca. What was that all about?"

"Wanted to find Diego, man. We wasn't getting nowhere running him down, so Spider looked up the address of the brother Diego used to talk about. I didn't know he was gonna beat the shit outta the man until he started whopping on him."

I ignored the fact that German said both men had beaten him and moved on. "What information did you get from him?"

"Nothing. Claimed he didn't know where his brother was. But he give up your name. Said you was looking for Diego too."

"Let's go back to the night the young man was killed at the Pines. You're claiming you had nothing to do with that?"

"Not a damned thing. Neither did Spider. That's one thing he ain't guilty of."

"Did you see or hear anything?"

"Hell, yes. Saw it all."

"Why were you there at five in the morning?"

"Wasn't five. More like zero-two-hundred."

That was more in line with when the neighbor found Bas's body. "Then why were you there at two in the morning?"

"Usually wasn't nobody around that place at night. Not after the winery closed down. Then we cased the place one night and seen some guys moving around after dark. First time that happened. So we give up looking for Diego in the daytime and started staking out the place by night. We knew Diego was somewhere at that winery. We caught sight of him a couple of times, but he disappeared every time before we could catch him."

"What was your location that night?"

"Little grove of pines west of the house across the road from the winery. Took turns catching shut-eye and watching. I was asleep when Spider shook me awake. Said Diego was coming out the gate. I wasn't too sure. I peeked through my spotting scope. The guy looked like Diego, but he didn't walk like Diego."

Pastis pulled out a pair of military-style sunglasses and fiddled with the earpieces as he continued. "We was about ready to go face the guy when someone come outta the trees at the edge of the winery wall and stopped him."

"Then what happened?" Charlie asked.

"Diego—or who we thought was Diego—started walking on down the path. The guy pulled out a weapon and shot him. The Diego guy stumbled but started running. The shooter pulled off a bunch more rounds. Probably emptied his popgun. But it did the job."

He closed his thin lips firmly, but Charlie and I waited him out. After a moment he started talking again. "The shooter used a little penlight to police his casings. Then he disappeared back into the trees where he come from. Spider wanted to shoot him because he thought the guy offed Diego without us finding the Lady. But I told him his rifle would wake up the people in both houses... you know, the one to our east and at the winery. So after we waited some longer—"

"Why?" Charlie asked.

"Wanted to see if those little pops woke anyone and brought them running. Didn't wanna get caught standing over a dead guy, did we? And we wanted to make sure the shooter didn't come back. Anyway, we eased across the road and turned the dead guy over. And he was dead. We took a coupla quick looks with a flashlight and seen it wasn't Diego. You know, it was hard to be sure. That guy coulda been Diego's little brother." Pastis glanced up. "Was he?"

"No, he was a winery worker named Bascomb Zuniga," I said.

"Too bad." He shrugged. "Luck of the draw, I guess."

"Tell me as much as you remember about the killer. How big was he? How was he dressed?"

Pastis hadn't taken a look at the guy through his scope. Didn't even think of it, he claimed. But the guy wasn't particularly big. About the same size as Zuniga. All he could say about the clothing was that it was dark.

"How did Natander find Diego's hiding place?" I asked when he seemed drained of information about the murder.

"We already figured the general area where he disappeared but couldn't go the last mile. We been through that ruined cabin half a dozen times. We even tried lifting that slab of wood that covered the trapdoor, but it wouldn't budge."

Diego must have barred the trapdoor every time he entered his hiding place. Merely left it open when he left in order to give himself access later.

Pastis got up suddenly, startling both Charlie and me, but he just needed to work off some nervous energy. He took to pacing my office.

"We knew Diego got nabbed by the cops but thought maybe the Lady was still where he hid her. I wanted to take off for parts unknown, but Spider... uh, Natander insisted we take one more look around the winery. We waited until most of the workers was gone. I stayed off behind the wall with my walkie-talkie to watch his back. I clicked him once when he needed to evade somebody and twice when it was clear. I couldn't see too good from where I was, but he disappeared into that tumbledown cabin and didn't come back out.

"I was about to go look for him when you and that other guy come outta nowhere and started snooping around. When your buddy took off for the parking lot and you didn't come back, I knew we was in for it. Wasn't nothing I could do for Spider. Didn't know if he was picking up my walkie-talkie clicks in that cave, so I hoofed it to the car and fired up the engine in case I needed to pick him up. Then I heard the cops and saw an ambulance."

He stopped pacing and pointed at me. "I figured it was you the meat wagon was coming for. Anyhow, when I seen you come out of the winery with the cops, I knew Spider was a goner. I lit out of there and went up the mountain to where we bivouacked. Intended to break camp and hightail it, but I got so tired, I figured I'd end it. So I come here."

Pastis tensed as the outer door opened, but he sat back down and dropped his aviator glasses on the table. The sound of Hazel and Gene exchanging snatches of conversation preceded her opening the door to the office to admit my old APD partner and a uniformed officer I didn't know. Gene wasted no time. He marched to the table.

"Are you Sgt. Hugo Pastis?" The GI nodded. "Get up," Gene ordered. "I'm arresting you for criminal assault with intent to do bodily harm."

"You can relax, Gene," I said. "The sergeant has come here for the express intent of surrendering himself." I held up my digital voice recorder. "He's made a full confession and supplied some missing information on the murder of Bascomb Zuniga. He and Natander witnessed the whole thing."

"You don't buy that." He made it half a question and half a statement.

"You and Yardley and Muñoz will have to sort it out, but at the moment I'm inclined to believe him. Natander gave me a shorter version of it as he was dying, remember?"

"I need that recording," Gene said. "Both recordings."

"Hazel's making you copies."

"Not a transcript. I need the recording."

"And that's what you'll get." I sighed. "It was simpler when we used a tape recorder, but there's still a way. Hazel will have to use some translator software to make copies. Either Charlie or I will deliver them… today. I'll leave it up to you to notify the state and the county that you have Sergeant Pastis."

"Yeah, I'll do that. Tomorrow."

ONCE GENE and the uniform departed with Pastis in custody, Charlie, Hazel, and I huddled around the table. As usual, Charlie's clearheaded thinking framed the situation for us.

"For a simple breaking and entering, this turned into a mess. Breaking and entering, a couple of AWOL military guys pursuing Diego C de Baca, and a murder."

Hazel spoke up. "Don't forget a missing child. Well, you've caught the intruder, dealt with the AWOLs, and located the child. Looks like our end's pretty well done."

"Ariel's not going to let me off the hook so easily," I reminded them. "He wants us to find the murderer. I'm convinced it wasn't Natander and Pastis. Diego's a possibility, but damned if I can figure a reason he'd step out from some trees and accost one of the very people he's been avoiding."

"He could have mistaken Zuniga for Pastis or Natander."

I shook my head. "Makes no sense. If he saw one, he'd know the other wasn't far away."

"If you believe that, you don't have anyone left but the Daytons."

"They're alibied up down in Las Cruces except for the youngest brother, Patrick, who was up in Bernalillo. Besides, he was friends with Zuniga."

"Before Zuniga got his sister pregnant," Hazel said.

"True."

"Course, it could be someone from the winery. Some of them have alibis, but it's hard to get a handle on that many people," Charlie said.

"Hazel, you better get to duplicating those voice recordings. And I'd like a written transcript of them as well. I'm heading to the winery to bring Gonda up-to-date on things."

Charlie put his finger squarely on the dreadful feeling building up inside me. "He's not gonna like hearing Natander and Pastis aren't his son's killers."

Chapter 22

EVEN THOUGH he already knew of Natander's denial of the murder of his son, Ariel Gonda was not pleased with Pastis's corroboration. He'd hoped that as tragic as it was, his son had been killed in a case of mistaken identity. Once I finished my report, he sat opposite me in the sitting room and did that hand-brush of a missing beard.

Then he placed his hands on his knees and leaned forward. "So our killer is someone in the Dayton family." His voice held an air of finality about it that I pegged as denial. He was too intelligent a man to fail to comprehend that the killer might lie closer to home.

"According to the police, they all seem to have been in Las Cruces at the time, except for one son who is alibied by two companions. A young man Bas's age called Pat."

"I recall you telling me that he was a friend of my son."

"People I interviewed confirm that to be true. But even friends fall out at times." I drew a breath. "We can't overlook the possibility that the attack came from someone at the winery."

"Nein!" He leaned back in the chair. "All my people were exonerated, were they not? With—what do you call them?—alibis, no?"

"I merely established alibis for the time of the initial break-in. But I'm sure the police have questioned your people about the murder."

All of a sudden, he looked tired. "Will they share information with you?"

"To a point." I paused again and took a stab. "Have you learned anything that might be helpful?"

He shook his head. "Nothing."

"I'm not just talking about your hired hands, Ariel."

He stiffened. His face grew mottled. "My family? You are accusing my family!"

This was the first overt hostility I'd seen from the man, which told me he'd searched his soul in the dark of night about this very subject.

"It has to be considered. You know that. Bas was a potential heir to a considerable fortune."

170   Don Travis

"Bas *was* an heir. There was no question of that."

"So you'd made up your mind. Who else knew of your decision?"

"No one. Not even Margot. I was still weighing how she would take the news, but now I realize she would have done what she always does. The right thing. She would have accepted that the decision was mine to make."

"Did Marc know?"

"I have told no one."

ONCE I was back in the office, Hazel dumped a pile of reports and correspondence on me for signature. Charlie and Tim Fuller, the retired APD sergeant who helped with our overflow cases, had been busy. They'd cleared two missing person cases, located a lost relative for a Kansas City banker, and completed background checks on new hire candidates for two local businesses.

After my pen scratched enough signatures to satisfy Hazel, I invited Charlie and her into my office to rehash Bas Zuniga's murder. I opened the discussion.

"Let's go over things again. Why is it we don't believe Diego C de Baca is the killer?"

"No motive. They didn't know one another. Diego was avoiding contact with everyone," Hazel said.

"And I think we know from Natander's and Pastis's recount of the murder that if the killer who stepped out of the tree line and accosted Zuniga had been Diego, they'd have recognized him," Charlie added.

"Right. So we all agree he's not our man." The two nodded, so I moved on. "A drive-by is not on the table. The wound placements on the body weren't right. Wasn't a robbery of opportunity for someone passing in the night. Watch was still on his wrist and a few dollars in his pocket. And again, the two AWOL GIs' stories preclude that."

"Maybe we're giving their story of the murder too much weight."

I shook my head. "Natander was dying. He readily admitted killing a priest to steal the Lady of the Euphrates. Why would he deny another killing? I got the feeling he was confessing to cleanse his soul."

"Besides," Hazel said, "they support one another. In the telling, I mean."

We talked each of our theories to death, and by the time we finished, my belief was that the killer lay with the Daytons in Las Cruces or with someone at the Pines itself.

"We need to start all over on the people at the winery. Hazel, you dig deeper into the background of everyone. Everyone, including the Gondas. Charlie, take another look at alibis. I'm going to tackle Ray Yardley at the state police and see if I can learn anything new. Then I'm going to concentrate on the Daytons."

"There's an angle we haven't mentioned," Charlie said. "Gonda money's not all that's involved. There's C de Baca money as well. And I get the feeling the sister… what was her name—?"

"Consuela Simpson," Hazel said.

"—wasn't too fond of her daddy's youngest son."

"You're right. Charlie, you take another look at German. I'll take Consuela. And that reminds me, there was a boyfriend of the Pines' waitress. Her name is Katie. Katie Henderson. Someone mentioned the boyfriend was of doubtful character."

"Miles Lotharson," Hazel again provided the name. She transcribed everything I dictated and had a better memory than I did.

"We probably ought to check him out too. He and Zuniga are about the same age. Maybe there was some jealousy over a girl." I stood, ending the meeting. "My first task is to check in with Lieutenant Yardley."

RAY YARDLEY took my call but couldn't scrape together enough time for a meeting. So I settled for discussing the case by phone. He had taken a hard look at the Daytons as suspects in the Zuniga killing, and while he still wasn't willing to rule every one of them out, he was edging closer to doing so.

"If I remember right, Willie Dayton, the oldest brother, claimed he was working a swing shift and hit a bar after work, right?" I asked.

"The Mesilla Valley Produce Company," Ray came back at me. "Two-to-ten shift. Then he hit the Ocotillo Club until closing at 2:00 a.m."

"I assume you questioned witnesses."

"You telling me how to do my job, BJ? Of course, I talked to witnesses."

"And there were no holes in the story? He could have gone off shift at ten and easily made it to Valle Plácido by two."

"I should ignore the testimony of three witnesses who speak for him?"

"Who are the witnesses?"

"Two buddies and a cocktail waitress."

"Who could also be a pal. So you tell me. Is it airtight?"

"The middle brother's a cinch. Bart was locked up in the Doña Ana County Detention Center overnight for drunk and disorderly. He was released the next morning."

"Did you—"

"Talked to the jail administrator himself. Had him personally look up the records."

"That leaves Patrick, the youngest brother, and James, the old man," I said. "I remember that Patrick was in the Albuquerque area, in fact not all that far from the Pines."

"At Santa Ana Star with two buddies, watching a show. They claim they were together the whole time. Besides, Pat was the one brother who was friendly to Zuniga."

"The old man," I said. "I forget what his alibi was."

"Weakest of the bunch. In a bar with a lady. A married lady, he claims. So he won't give up her name. But he was seen in the place drinking by himself as late as ten thirty or eleven that night."

"He could have hauled ass and made it in time to catch Bas," I suggested. "Should I drive down and have a go at him?"

"Do what you like. I'm not through with him yet. But honestly, I can't quite make one of them fit into this killing."

I hung up a little unsettled. Two of the Daytons… maybe three were possibilities, but other than Patrick, they'd have a dickens of a time getting up to the winery in time to hide in the trees and wait. And why would they wait in the dark without some foreknowledge that Bas Zuniga was standing guard that night? The obvious answer was that they wouldn't.

Could Patrick Dayton have contacted his friend to let him know he was going to be in the neighborhood and learned Zuniga was slated for guard duty? Possible. But there was no evidence that either Zuniga or his roommate owned a cell phone. Was there a telephone in the room they rented? My gut told me I was wasting time concentrating on the workers at the winery, but every base needed to be covered.

YARDLEY HADN'T been able to add much to my store of information on the C de Bacas. Neither German nor Consuela had jackets. I found some unpaid speeding and parking tickets, mostly for the sister. Acquaintances who knew the Simpsons wouldn't say a cross word about Braxton Simpson, a respected retired banker, but there were plenty who expressed a dislike of his wife. Some of it could be placed at the feet of jealousy, but a pattern emerged that reaffirmed my initial opinion of a liberated, selfish woman, who cared little what others thought of her. Her husband's reputation and popularity were enough to gain her admittance to the right clubs and living rooms but were not strong enough to make her liked. When asked to describe her in one word, almost invariably, *greedy* was the answer.

Gene wasn't able to help me. Even he had to have some reason for hauling a respected banker's wife down to the station house for a grilling. So I tackled the lady on her own turf. The maid left me standing on the front porch while she carried my business card to the lady of the house. The señora appeared at the door shortly thereafter.

"What do you want?"

I considered asking how the twelve million dollars my parents left me stacked up against her inheritance but resisted the urge. It wasn't a fair comparison. My schoolteacher folks had advanced a little working capital to a garage business that turned into Microsoft. Hers labored the whole of their lives to build what they had. Of course, her mother's land-grant claim was a matter of chance too.

I expected to have to talk my way into the house, but she just leveled a look at me and said I was the fellow who'd turned Diego over to the police and invited me in. That wasn't enough, however, to earn me the offer of coffee. Merely a seat on the living room couch while she asked me what I wanted. Sweet-talking would gain me nothing with this woman, so I didn't try it.

"Tell me, Mrs. Simpson, did you attempt to kill your half brother, Diego?"

Her dark, expressive eyes widened, but I couldn't honestly tell if she was surprised by my question or by my manner of address. Her familiars all told me they were required to go through the whole "C de Baca de Simpson" bit.

With a great deal of dignity, she rose to her feet, making me notice that she wasn't appreciably taller when she stood than when she sat. "Mr. Vinson, I know of no such attempt. Nor would I be a part of it if I did."

"Why? If he died, he has no heirs. His portion of the family estate would revert to you and German. And he's left his share virtually untouched."

She made a point of glancing around the elegant room, heavy with expensive furniture, lace, and ormolu. "I assure you I am adequately cared for."

"That is obvious. You have a very good sense of style."

That earned me nothing but a fish eye. But my question had sparked her interest.

"When and where was this attempt made on his life?"

"I didn't say it was an attempt, but yes, it was over the night of June 16 into June 17 and again on Thursday, July 2. A daylight attempt."

She smiled faintly. "I see. Well, I am sorry to disappoint you, but Braxton and I were in Taos visiting friends that entire week in June. I don't recall the July date, although that was shortly before the holiday on the Fourth, so I assume we were preparing for guests."

"You could have hired someone."

"To do what? I still don't know what you're talking about."

"Have you been out to the Pines lately?"

She sniffed. "Not since those Swiss people bought it. Are you going to answer my question? What happened that night at the Pines?"

"Someone accosted a young man who looks enough like Diego to be his brother when he left the Pines at around two o'clock."

"Accosted him how?"

"By shooting him in the back three times."

"Killed him?" At my nod, she continued. "And why do you assume the murderer was looking for Diego instead of this other man?"

"Because Diego broke into the Pines a few weeks earlier and has been living there ever since."

"Living where?"

"Living someplace on the premises."

"I see. One of your people asked about some secret room in the winery. I told him that was nonsense, of course. It doesn't exist."

"Oh, it exists, all right. I know. I killed one of the men looking for Diego in that very chamber behind the wine cellar."

"I don't believe you."

"Your privilege. But you can ask Sergeant Muñoz of the Sandoval County Sheriff's Office or Lt. Ray Yardley of the state police."

That's pretty much the way the rest of the interview went... nowhere. She seemed to be more offended by her father not sharing the secret of a hidden room than the death of two men.

I left the house feeling as if I'd wasted my time. Sometimes I felt as if 75 percent of my time was wasted, but that's all right. This was something needing exploring in order to close one more avenue that led away from the killer.

HAZEL'S INTERNET search on Miles Lotharson turned up a driver's license showing a home address on Railroad Track Road, an MVD registration of a

2003 Custom Harley Davidson Hardtail motorcycle, and a mediocre credit report showing him working at a gas station with the name of Drive-By Gas. She located no jacket with any police jurisdiction in our vicinity.

A drive to Bernalillo revealed no one with the name Lotharson lived at the Railroad Track Road address, nor did the current occupant know of him. The attendant at Drive-By Gas, hiding behind her bulletproof pane of plexiglass, allowed as to how she knew Miles Lotharson, but he no longer worked there. She didn't know where he'd gone.

So I invaded Roma Muñoz's space at the Sandoval County Sheriff's Office. She was more closemouthed than Ray Yardley, but she'd likely not hold out on me on such a minor player in this little drama. I reconsidered. Why was he a minor player? He wasn't on site all the time, but I gathered from speaking to people at the Pines he was around occasionally.

Roma met me at the front desk at SCSO rather than have me escorted back to her office. While I don't have an outsized ego, I *do* have one and couldn't help but wonder if she was a bit afraid I'd identify the murderer before she did. She struck me as a woman with drive and ambition. I could easily see her petite form sitting in the sheriff's office one day in the future.

"Lotharson?" She looked a bit startled. "Why are you asking about him?"

"Well, he's Katie Henderson's boyfriend, isn't he? So he has a connection."

Her brown eyes looked vacant for a moment, making me realize she hadn't even turned up the kid's name as yet. She covered her lapse well. "So far as I can tell, he wasn't around much."

I couldn't help myself. "And when was the last time that happened?"

"Have to consult my notes. But Gonda can tell you that. Now is there anything else?"

I answered my own question. "After the tasting on the Fourth of July. They all gathered in the common room and drank a toast to the holiday."

"Including Lotharson?" she asked a little too quickly.

"Not at the tasting, but his bike was on the premises. Of course, that was after Bas Zuniga's murder. But back to my question. Will you share the information you have on Lotharson?"

"Have to check out what we have on him. Let you know."

That ended that. And probably our tenuous relationship. I'd embarrassed her by asking about a lead she hadn't pursued. At least that's the way it looked to me.

Since I was in the vicinity, I decided to go to the winery, where someone was bound to know something about this Lotharson kid. If I remembered right, it was James Bledsong who told me about him.

I FOUND the Pines' viticulturist, appropriately enough, in the vineyard, talking to Claudio Garcia and Winfield Tso. They broke off their discourse about the new planting—which looked to be about done—when I walked up to them and asked for a moment of Bledsong's time. Once we were in the shade of the shed near his cottage, I asked him what he knew about Katie's boyfriend.

"Like I told you at the C&W, the kid's a loser."

"What makes you say that?"

"I know for a fact he borrows money from her." He snorted. "Borrows. More likely takes money from her. And she's a college student working to make ends meet."

"How do you know this?"

"Walked in on them one day when she was handing over a twenty and heard him say it was just until Friday. Didn't say what Friday."

Okay, so that colored Bledsong's attitude. Might mean something, might not. "What else can you tell me about him? Does he hang around much?"

"Brings her to work and picks her up sometimes."

"Doesn't she have her own car?"

He nodded. "Maybe she likes to ride on that motorcycle of his."

Zuniga owned a motorcycle too. Did that mean anything? "Were he and Zuniga friendly?"

He shrugged. "Casual, so far as I could see. Whenever Miles showed up at a picnic or something, they spent a few minutes talking bikes."

"Did Zuniga show any interest in Katie?"

"I see where you're going. Yeah, he did. Until he found out she was taken. Then he backed off."

"Where does Lotharson live, work? That sort of thing?"

"Think he's a motorcycle mechanic. That reminds me, I know he worked on Bas's bike once. Does that help?"

"Know where to find him?"

"Katie can tell you for sure, but I think he works at a bike shop in Bernalillo. Don't know the name, but it's on the main drag. You know, Camino del Pueblo. But watch out. I get the feeling he's a mean one."

Chapter 23

KATIE HADN'T come in for her shift yet, but the cook, Nellie Bright, gave me the information I needed. She also managed to convey her disapproval of Lotharson without saying a word about him.

Childer's Motorcycle Repair was located a few blocks south of the Range Café, a well-known eatery in the older part of Bernalillo. The owners operated a restaurant under the same name in Albuquerque, but I preferred the original.

The cycle shop was unique in that it occupied a wood-frame building, whereas 99 percent of the structures in this town were adobe or at least stucco. The relatively grease-free middle-aged man laboring in the front of the building waved to the rear without evidencing the least bit of curiosity when I asked for Miles Lotharson.

Lotharson in the flesh—and I do mean in the flesh—was a handsome muscle boy. He would have been exceptionally good-looking had he not been shrouded in an air of desperation. He wore old-fashioned bib overalls without a shirt, and the tanned muscles that flexed as he knelt beside a Kawasaki bike were sexy as hell. I knew with a fair degree of certainty what was eating at his soul.

By virtue of his looks and spectacular build, he'd latched on to a bright, pretty girl. But now that girl was going to college, bringing to the fore a probably well-ingrained feeling of inferiority because he either had no inclination to climb higher on the socioeconomic totem pole or didn't have the chops to do so. He would forever remain a grease monkey while Katie Henderson graduated to bigger and better things. What he didn't realize was that he might have made it work if he could rein in the inevitable jealousy gnawing at him. Unfocused jealousy of anyone and anything that threatened his relationship.

"Miles Lotharson?" I asked.

"Yeah. That's me. What'chu want? You look like fuzz to me."

"Used to be. Now I'm private."

"Private fuzz. Public fuzz. What's the difference?"

That gave me more insight into the guy. Nice wasn't going to work. Logic wasn't in the cards. Go tough. "Not much, except that I can get away with a lot that the boys with badges can't."

He looked up from his work and regarded me through eyes so startlingly blue they disconcerted me momentarily. "Like what?"

Better watch myself with this one. Don't get lost in his looks. "Like beating the shit out of you without compromising your testimony."

He straightened his back and flexed his shoulders. "You can try it."

"Might be worth it. But on the other hand, I might bruise a knuckle. If we've spread enough machismo on the ground, let's get down to business."

"What business?" He remained knelt beside the bike.

"What did you have against Bascomb Zuniga?"

"Who? That kid that got waxed up at the winery? Didn't have nothing against him. Didn't even know him. Not really."

"You worked on his bike."

"I work on lotsa bikes. Okay, yeah, I did him a favor once and did some adjustments to his wheels. Ran a lot better too."

"Where were you on the night of June 16 and the early morning of June 17?"

"You know where you were three weeks ago? I sure as shit don't. Besides, why would I off the guy?"

"He was good-looking and made moves on your girl."

The blue eyes were a little duller now. "He was?"

"Don't play dumb. You were afraid he'd take Katie away from you. Pretty girl like Katie who's got the gumption to put herself through college was worth protecting, wasn't she?"

His cheeks blazed as he banged the wrench he was holding against the bike's seat, something I'm sure both the shop's owner and the bike's owner would disapprove. "Me'n Katie are solid, man."

"Me'n Katie? Is that the way you talk to a college girl?"

Cheeks still blazing—now joined by his fiery ears—he stood… all six two of him… and pointed the wrench at me. "Don't make fun of me, man. Nobody pokes fun at me."

I snaked my right hand behind me. "If you don't drop that wrench, I'm going to consider myself under threat. Then I'm going to pull my weapon. After that, who knows what'll happen?" It was all a bluff. Despite Bledsong's warning, my S&W was still with Roma, and the Ruger lay in the trunk of the car.

He didn't drop it, but he lowered the heavy tool to his side.

"Look, Lotharson, no need for this to go bad. Just tell me what you told the police about that night, and I'll go about my business."

"Police?"

Crap! Neither Roma nor Yardley had sent anyone to question this bozo. "If they haven't been here already, they'll be here soon. Just account for your time that night."

We sparred a few minutes longer before he set about trying to reconstruct his calendar. When I reminded him Zuniga died on a Tuesday night, he came up with a meeting of his bike club, the BBAs. I took that to stand for the Bernalillo Bad Asses.

"Did Katie go with you?"

He frowned, revealing more of his insecurity. "She don't... uh, doesn't go for that kind of thing. Katie and my club are two different things."

So far as I could see, he'd just condemned his relationship to ultimate failure. I poked at the guy for another fifteen minutes, getting information I could verify later. Then I got into the Impala and drove away convinced I had met a man capable of violence if he felt threatened, but unable to shake the feeling he hadn't even considered Zuniga a rival. Too soon for judgments. I needed to confirm the BBA meeting and dig a little deeper into Miles Lotharson.

BACK AT the office again, I turned the expanded search of the internet for Lotharson over to Hazel and settled at my desk to call Del for an update. He was handling both Diego's custody situation and pursuing Gonda's interest in his grandson, the Dayton child. Ever since I'd crossed swords with Del's executive secretary during the Zozobra trouble, Collette Brittain always put me through to her boss unless there was a good reason not to. Today she connected us without a hitch.

Del was more interested in hearing about my shootout with a trained military sniper and coming out unscathed than he was in talking about what I wanted. Nevertheless, after I gave him the gory details, he got serious.

"You said those exact words to him, 'You're dying'? And it's on the voice recorder?"

"Yep."

"Might hold up as a deathbed confession and eliminate a bunch of people from suspicion over that Zuniga kid's death."

"What's the rap on Diego C de Baca?"

"Gene's finished with him. I delivered him to SCSO, and Roma Muñoz's claws are out for him. Since the Gondas declined to prosecute, not sure why. But she was rough on him."

"Probably pissed at us for finding the winery intruder before she did and is taking it out on Diego," I said.

"Whatever, she wrung him dry and put him in SCSO Detention Center on Montoya Road to hold for the feds. Not sure what's going to happen there. If I heard you right, we've got Natander's dying confession he killed the priest over in Iraq without Diego's or Pastis's knowledge. Diego's turning over the stolen artifact will also help."

"Do you think they'll return him to Iraq for trial?"

"I doubt it, since the Iraqis will get their treasure back and Natander's confessed to the murder. If they do anything, they'll do it over here. Aiding and abetting's a possibility since he mailed the artifact back to the States. Other than that, failure to report a crime is the most likely possibility."

"And Sergeant Pastis?"

"Not one of my concerns, but I understand Gene's holding him in the Bernalillo County Detention Center for the feds. They'll likely come down hard on him since he was AWOL, something Diego was not."

"Keep me posted, will you? What about Gonda's grandson?"

Del blew air through his lips. "You know Billy Jenkins?"

"I met him for the first time when I was down in Carlsbad the other day."

"Talk about a sharp lawyer hiding behind a country-bumpkin front. Normally I'd say it's pretty clear-cut. When there are no parents, grandparents stand next in line for custody."

"Is that what Gonda's asking for?"

"I don't think he knows what he wants at this point. He just wants to make sure he has a role in the child's life."

"I'm not sure custody is the right thing for the boy at the moment."

"I'm not either," Del replied. "Not until his father's shooting is solved. I assume you haven't ruled out someone inside the Gonda family."

"Not at this point. Do you think that's why Gonda doesn't know his own mind on this? He's acknowledged to me that he already decided to include the boy's father as a Gonda heir."

"Which probably got the kid killed."

"He claims no one knew, not even his wife or nephew."

"By now the whole clan knows of the blood tie, and they also know Ariel Gonda. You didn't have to tell me he'd decided to leave something for the Zuniga kid, and I've known him less than a month. Don't you think Margot and Marc knew?"

"At least suspected. So what are you doing for Gonda until he makes his mind up?"

"Talking to Bill Jenkins to establish the Gonda family's rights. Let him know Gonda wants to be involved. I won't press for custody but leave the issue open. By the way, Billy's already raising the issue of the child's safety, given the murderer of his father's not yet identified."

"What's Barbara Zuniga's position in all this?" I asked.

"I don't know. I don't represent her, but I understand she engaged an attorney in Las Cruces. Despite what Gonda decides to do, she might seek custody of her grandson."

"What does this do to the Forsyths' wish to adopt little David James?"

"Slow track. If Jenkins goes to court, he knows I'll put forth the Gonda claim, which should be superior to an aunt and uncle. Also trying to arrange for them to meet on neutral ground so the Gondas can see their grandchild. And, of course, Billy's having me jump through hoops validating Zuniga's paternity and the blood relationship between Zuniga and Gonda. That will take a little time to get done properly. Especially since most of it will have to be done by blood test."

"How are you going to do that? Zuniga's buried. Will you have to exhume?"

"Probably not. Gonda saved his son's bloodstained clothing, had it attested by the medical examiner. It's already at a local lab."

That caught my attention. "Why? He didn't know about the baby at that time."

"Gonda's a detail man. He might have had some question about Zuniga's patrimony in his own mind. Maybe he didn't accept Barbara Zuniga's claim he was the father and wanted it settled once and for all."

I shook my head. "He convinced me he'd accepted Bascomb Zuniga totally. And Margot reinforced that belief when she recognized the boy as her husband's son back when he was a child."

"When there's money like the Gondas have, a guy learns to protect his back. He may have figured he'd have to prove he and Zuniga were father and son someday. So what are you going to do now?"

"While Hazel and Charlie take another look into Katie Henderson's boyfriend's background, I'm going to take another crack at the Daytons."

"Another trip to Las Cruces, huh? Be sure and stop in at Coas Books. Best used bookstore in the state for my money."

"I remember them. They started in a little space down on North Main—"

"And kept adding space as other tenants moved out," Del finished for me. "Fascinating place full of nooks and crannies." He switched abruptly on me, as Del was wont to do. "What's Paul up to these days?"

"About finished with his master's. Plans on graduating at the end of the term."

"Is he going thesis or master's exams?"

"Thesis. But now I've told you everything I know."

"What's he going to do when he gets his degree?" Del asked.

"Thinks he can make a living off the internet. Right now he's sifting the listings on Mediabistro.com for publisher jobs and JournalismJobs. com for newspaper and magazine positions. He believes he can do freelance work from home."

"Man, how this world's changed since we first went looking for work," Del said with a sigh in his voice.

"Yeah. And I keep wondering if that's good or bad."

Chapter 24

I WAS reluctant to leave for Las Cruces the next morning. This was an important time in Paul's life. But we discussed the situation, and he said everything was under control. He'd opted to go for UNM's Plan 1, which was to write a thesis. He would, he assured me, have his required hours in 599/thesis, whatever the hell that was, and do his thesis defense. After that, he had ninety days to turn in the manuscript itself. Appropriately enough, the subject he'd chosen was to examine the effects of social media on journalism. The subject was more specific than that, but that was my take on it.

The last thing he needed at this point, he claimed, was me hanging around the house and distracting him from his research and writing. That might have been true or he might just be making it easier for me to do my job, but there had been an air of desperation about our lovemaking last night. He came across as one confident young man, but he possessed nerves like the rest of us, and they were plucking at him. All I could do was lend support.

So morning found me on the road to the City of Crosses once again, with my mind at least partially back at 5229 Post Oak Drive with the human being I loved more than all others on God's great earth.

With difficulty I dragged my attention back where I needed it at the moment. Yardley had given me the names of two individuals who claimed they'd seen Dayton Sr. at the bar called the Crippled Aggie. Sherree Rinds was a waitress there. The weird name of the establishment apparently came from the owner, a guy named Reggie Batt, who broke his leg while he was playing for the New Mexico State University Aggies. The weird spelling of Sherree, I'd leave alone.

The other individual was a Hal Silva, who Yardley said was an ex-Aggie pal of the bar owner who sold cars in the daytime and drank Scotch after the sun went down. Sold cars, huh. Any connection to the Forsyths?

Usually I enjoy travel. I can look at a flat expanse of desert and realize that forty miles over in that direction was an old archaeological dig or in the opposite direction was a place that served one of the best hamburgers in the state. Today, my mind wanted to go back to my partner at home. Eventually it ended up at the Crippled Aggie, appropriately enough not far from Coas, the bookstore Del mentioned.

Sherree hadn't come on duty yet, but I met all two hundred seventy pounds of Reggie Batt. He was my kind of bar owner. He answered all my questions readily and with a smile on his jowly face. Of course, I had no idea if he answered them honestly. According to him, James Dayton was in the bar that night with a woman, but contrary to Dayton's claim, she wasn't married. Hester Heigh was single and apparently available. Why would Dayton complicate his life by withholding her name from the police by claiming she was married? Hard to say. Some people just resented answering questions and told a lie when the truth would serve them better. That was pretty much my impression of James Dayton.

When asked how he could be so clear about events on a night almost four weeks ago, Batt acknowledged he hadn't until Lt. Ray Yardley of the NMSP contacted him. Then he went back over the calendar and bar receipts to fix the date. He was, however, unable to confirm how long the couple remained in the bar. That was left for Sherree to clear up when she came in later. Dayton and Hester left the bar around eight thirty the night in question, but Dayton reappeared alone in the Crippled Aggie about half an hour later. The waitress claimed Dayton remained until the bar closed, but Batt disagreed. The more they talked, the more I became convinced that Sherree was covering for Dayton, either by request or out of a sense of loyalty. On the other hand, Batt seemed to liberally partake of his own brews, which might cloud his recollection. Nonetheless, each espoused his or her position vehemently.

I left the bar and headed for the address Batt provided for Hester Heigh. She was, he explained, a lady of leisure by virtue of a penurious dead daddy. A thin but somehow semiattractive woman of fifty years or so opened the door to my knock. It was quickly apparent she was up for a good time. In fact, so pressing was she in the pursuit of a party, I told her I bounced the other way. She merely said she was confident she could put the bounce back on the appropriate trampoline if I'd just give her a chance.

Aside from confirming Sherree's version of the story that she and Dayton left the bar around ten, all I learned was that she considered "Jamie" to be a quite adequate performer—something I didn't need to know. Their conversation that evening had been limited to a rundown on the other patrons of the bar and intimate talk, which led to their early departure. According to Hester, there was no discussion of Baby David or any other member of the family. Nor was there a mention of the child's paternity. I accepted her view of things, since she appeared to be one of those people who would have delighted in creating a problem for someone else. Anyone else. She did contribute one solid fact. She told me where James Dayton habitually filled up his gas tank and said he hadn't done that while they were together that evening.

A swing by the Gas House revealed Dayton topped up the tank on the Continental about once a week, usually on a Friday night. But the attendant couldn't say whether or not Dayton altered his pattern a month ago.

WILLIE DAYTON, the eldest brother of the baby's dead mother, was openly hostile, bothered apparently in equal measure over questions about his whereabouts, the mention of Bascomb Zuniga's name, and most likely life in general. He mirrored his father in that attitude, so far as I could tell. He did give me, probably inadvertently, the youngest brother's—Patrick's—place of employment. He was a clerk at Spilled Ink, one of Coas Books' rivals farther up Main Street.

As soon as I introduced myself to the youngest of the Dayton clan and shook his hand, a few things fell into place for me. Slender, sandy-haired, gray-eyed, and attractive in an understated way, Patrick blipped on my gaydar. This effeminate young man undoubtedly worshiped the extremely good-looking Zuniga and longed for a sexual connection. Perhaps there had been one, and Zuniga's subsequent attraction to his sister cut two ways. An indirect, sympathetic connection was better than nothing, which would have bonded him to the young man even absent a physical relationship. Or jealousy of Zuniga's sexual contact with Pat's sister could have driven him crazy. The gentle soul I observed before me seemed more apt to hang on to whatever relationship was left to him than to take revenge.

He turned the cash register over to a female clerk and walked to a reading area with comfortable chairs grouped around a huge, square coffee table... except it was loaded with books, not coffee cups. He answered my questions without hesitation. The night was firmly fixed in his mind because of his trip to the Santa Ana Star to see a comedy show and, of course, by the death of his friend. Eventually I asked him a highly personal question.

"Pat, I don't want you to take offense at this next question, but it's something I need to know. Were you and Bas lovers?"

His head dropped and he went still for a moment before he spoke in a low voice. "No… not—"

I held up a hand. "Let me make something clear. The question wasn't designed to expose or embarrass you. I'm gay myself, so I don't view it as an odd question. But it might help me to understand your friend and give me another direction to go in my investigation."

He leaned forward in his chair and glanced around. We were alone in the area. "You're gay? You're not just leading me on, are you?" When I shook my head, he leaned back. "I wished we were lovers…. Bas and me, I mean. Even if he was taken away like he was, I'd have that to remember. I'll be honest. I loved Bas… like Lucia did. My sis and I looked a lot alike, and I fantasized that he did it with her because he could pretend it was me." The kid blushed with that admission and made an impatient gesture.

"It wasn't like that, but anyway…." He let a long moment of silence pass. "We talked about it. He knew how I felt. Sometimes I thought it was going to happen. I know he got aroused when we talked about it a couple of times. But it just never happened. Then when Lucia showed some interest in him, we stopped flirting and talking about it." Sadness thickened his voice at the end.

"Do you think he was active with other men?"

He shook his head. "We talked about that too. He started teasing me about this guy or that, you know, who appealed to me. So I'd do the same, ask if some guy or the other turned him on. But he said he'd never done it with a guy and—" Pat's voice died away, and I gave him a moment to recover. "—and that if he decided to give it a try, it would be with me."

"Did you believe him?"

Pat flared. "Yes! Not… not just because I wanted to believe it, but because Bas was so open and honest about everything. I miss him. S-so much."

I changed to questions of another nature to give him an opportunity to recover. "Pat, why did Zuniga show no interest in his new son?"

He drew in a sharp breath. "He did! He tried to see little Davy lots of times."

"When I spoke to your father, he said that wasn't true."

"Well, my father lied! He's a bully and a liar. Every time Bas came around trying to see Lucia and the baby, my dad always set my brothers on him. Even tried to shame me into taking Bas on. You know, for getting my sister pregnant."

"Why didn't he and Lucia meet elsewhere? At school. His room. Anywhere?"

Pat's features sagged. "She had a real hard time with the baby. After Davy was born, she was bedridden most of the time. And even on her good days, she didn't leave the house. So he had to come to her.

"I don't know how many times Bas went around with bruises and black eyes because of my dad and my brothers," Pat went on. "Finally he had enough and put up a fight. Defended himself from Bart and Willie with a baseball bat. Got him in trouble and run outa town."

"The assault charge was dismissed. No reason for him to leave."

"That's what happened officially. But my old man's friends with some of the cops. Plays poker with them. They hassled Bas every day, so he just took off and started working the vegetable fields."

Pat's complexion darkened. "That's why Lucia did… what she did. She wanted to see Bas. Needed to see him, but they wouldn't let her. Chased him away and took her cell phone. I used to lend her mine so she could talk to Bas every once in a while. But she seemed sadder after she got off the phone than she was before she talked to him."

Pat sat back and straightened his spine. "Even after she was gone, Bas slipped back into town a couple of times. My dad caught him once in the house with me, looking at the baby. Dad called the cops. Bas had to take off."

So Dayton got Zuniga run out of town by his buddies down at the police station. Why didn't the boy go to his mother? She might have straightened things out for him. The answer to that one was easy. He didn't want to bring trouble down on her head.

"Pat, were you aware that Bas's mother didn't even know he fathered a son?"

He ran a hand over his face. "Yeah. He was ashamed." Pat's hand fluttered. "Not ashamed of the baby. Ashamed of the way he'd done it. His mom's a big churchgoer. I kept telling him she was entitled to know she was a grandmother, but he kept putting it off."

"Didn't Mrs. Zuniga know what was going on? If he had all those bruises and black eyes you spoke of, wouldn't she have demanded to know about them?"

"You gotta remember, Bas lived on campus. He wouldn't go near her when he was beat up. He was awful protective of his mom."

Perhaps he *was* ashamed of fathering a child without the benefit of marriage. Our background checks confirmed what Pat said. Barbara Zuniga was a churchgoer. If only that tragic young man had known the circumstances of his own birth, he might have reacted differently. And lived.

After digesting that, I asked Pat if he knew Zuniga was standing guard on the winery the night he died. He claimed he hadn't.

I learned nothing more of interest from that interview other than the fact the two young men had remained in contact. They talked about once a week via cell phone, which meant Zuniga *did* have a private phone. When I dialed the number Pat provided, it went straight to voicemail.

Although Bart Dayton was in jail the night Zuniga died, I took the trouble to look him up at NMSU, where he was a sometime student. His attitude was less hostile than his father's and older brother's, but he wasn't interested in adding to my store of useful knowledge.

I COULDN'T leave town without having another go at the old man. James Dayton was no "old man" in the strictest sense. I judged him to be in his mid- to late forties. His occupation as a water-well driller kept him in fit physical condition. The scarcity of work likely put a perpetual burr under his saddle, as my father would have said.

When I knocked on the door, he came charging out of the house with the obvious intent of bodily harm. I backed to the edge of the broad front porch.

"Mr. Dayton, I'm—"

"I know who you are, you nosy son of a bitch. Been asking questions about me all day. Well, I got a right to my privacy, and you got no right to be standing here on my porch!"

He managed to get those words out before he lunged. I stepped aside and clipped him on the back of the head as he passed, sending the man stumbling down the steps and tumbling on the concrete walkway. I followed him down and planted my feet on his front lawn, conveniently out of reach of the big man. He got to his knees and lunged for me again. He anticipated my sidestep, but chose the wrong direction. His arms closed on thin air. I shoved his face in the lawn with my foot.

"You bastard! Attacking me on my own property!" he sputtered through a mouth full of grass.

A sharp, shrill voice startled me. "James Dayton, you started this fight. Now get up and act like an adult, not like one of your sons!" Wilma Brandini, the neighbor who helped me on my last trip, stood on the sidewalk with a bag of groceries in her arms. "I saw it all, and I'll tell it like it was to anyone who asks."

"Nosy old bitch," Dayton muttered beneath his breath. "Just a misunderstanding, Wilma. Nothing to be concerned about."

"Not if you'll behave," I said. "I just want to know—"

"You just wanna know if I killed that randy son of a bitch who knocked up my little girl. Well, I didn't. Ask anybody."

I removed my boot and moved out of the way. He staggered to his feet while muttering beneath his breath. Apparently everyone in James Dayton's world was a son of a bitch, a bastard, or a nosy old bitch. What a sad world to live in. Did a fancy new Continental compensate for that?

"I'm asking you first, Mr. Dayton. Then I'll ask everyone else. And just so you know, attacking me makes me want to dig a little deeper into your life. As does claiming you were with a married lady you couldn't name the night Bas Zuniga died. It took about ten minutes to learn her name and that she wasn't married."

"Dig all you want. I didn't kill nobody." He swayed a moment before catching his balance. Drunk or three-quarters there, I suspected.

Mrs. Brandini went on down the sidewalk toward her home, but the fight was gone out of Dayton. He sat on his front steps and grudgingly answered my questions. My last hope of pinning the death of Bascomb Zuniga pretty well disappeared when he reluctantly admitted he'd been in a late-night poker game after he left the Crippled Aggie that night. Apparently it was a high-stakes game everybody in town knew about.

Before heading for Albuquerque, I confirmed his story of a late night of gambling with two of the other players, the fire chief and a police captain. They told me Dayton lost $500 he couldn't afford that night before they broke up sometime after midnight.

As long as I was in town, I looked up Hal Silva at the Biggest Little Car Dealership in New Mexico. No kidding. That was the name.

Silva was a car salesman to the core. He kept trying to trade me out of my Impala into a late-model Caddy he was obviously having trouble moving. In between, he said he really had no idea what time Dayton left the Crippled Aggie on the night of June 16. He just knew Dayton was there sometime that night. I also satisfied myself he had no connections to the Forsyths over in Carlsbad. And that he was pissed at James Dayton for getting his Continental from over there rather than from him.

I drove home that evening reasonably well convinced no one in the Dayton family could have killed Bascomb Zuniga. Of course, the youngest brother was in love with him, and lovers have killed one another for millennia. In addition, Pat was clearly frustrated by what I could only consider Zuniga's teasing behavior. Maybe Zuniga didn't intend it that way. Perhaps he only wanted to let Pat down easy, but from my perspective, the way Zuniga handled things would strengthen Pat's hope that something might develop between the two of them. Nonetheless, my gut told me the killer was someone closer to the Pines, either within the Gonda family or near it.

Of course, there were still the Forsyths. Could they have killed Bas because he objected to their adoption of his son? That was worthy of some additional scrutiny. And we hadn't yet fully looked into the C de Baca family.

Chapter 25

FRIDAY MORNING, after turning over my voice recorder for transcription and answering her questions, I asked Hazel to phone Sgt. Roma Muñoz and give her Zuniga's cell number to see if we could learn anything by checking the phone records.

Once that item was tucked away in her notes, Hazel let me know she'd broadened her search for Miles Lotharson and turned up a record in Odessa, Texas. Nothing serious, meaning nothing beyond underage drinking, drunk and disorderly, fighting, and being a delinquent in general. She talked to a police officer at OPD who remembered him well, even though Lotharson left the Odessa area about four years ago, when he was seventeen. The Texas cop's take on the kid had been that he was headed for a bigger and better criminal jacket, given time. Anger would be what would trip up the kid—at least in his opinion. I'd run into a little of that hostility when I took a run at him. That made him worth another look.

A swing by Childer's Motorcycle Repair in Bernalillo revealed Lotharson took the morning off. He wasn't due to report to work until later. I decided not to waste a trip north and headed west to the Pines. As I pulled into a parking lot holding more cars than usual, I noticed a Harley Davidson Hardtail and wondered if I hadn't located Miles Lotharson after all. He was visiting his girl, apparently on an especially busy day for her.

Heléne Benoir greeted me at the chocolatier's kiosk in the foyer with a big smile and said she'd let Ariel know I was here.

"Don't bother right now," I said. "I'll poke around downstairs for a bit first. Judging from the automobiles outside, it appears to be a busy day. Anything special going on?"

"We placed a notice in the *Albuquerque Journal* about our wine tasting, and that brought traffic to the front door."

After excusing myself, I made straight for the Bistro. The place was busy, but there was no sign of the waitress, Katie Henderson. Or her boyfriend. Margot was moving through the room, apparently handling their guests' needs. She came over when she spotted me in the doorway.

"BJ, how nice to see you. Do you want a table, or are you looking for Ariel?"

"I wanted a word with your waitress."

"Katie? She's on her break right now. Her boyfriend showed up, so she went out back to speak to him a moment. If you'll take those french doors right over there, they'll lead you to the garden."

I thanked her and headed outside. Other than some patrons sitting at a couple of tables on the patio, no one was around. I found the pair I was searching for just beyond the corner of the building. Katie stood against the wall while Lotharson leaned in close. But I sensed they were talking rather than spooning… as my mother used to call it.

Upon catching sight of me, Miles stepped back from Katie and planted his feet. "What you doing here?" His voice held a threat of violence.

"Miles," Katie cautioned.

"Shut up." He turned his attention back to me. "Answer my question."

"I will, since you asked so nicely." Sarcasm was wasted on this guy. "I'm doing a job for Mr. Gonda. But I was actually looking for you."

"You get outa my life and leave me alone, you hear?"

I took in the twenty-one-year-old bundle of hostile energy rippling with corded muscles and decided it would be better to de-escalate the situation. But I couldn't just walk away from him.

"Miles, Mr. Gonda asked me to do something for him, and I am going to do it to the best of my ability. That means I need to talk to people, see what they know, piece together things to come to a conclusion. You happen to have known Bascomb Zuniga, so that means I need to talk to you. We cool?"

"We ain't. You asked me about everything the other day. I don't have nothing to add. And you been snooping around in my affairs. Guy at the place I live told me you been asking questions."

I lifted my hands, palms up. "Wasn't me." I didn't lie outright. It was Charlie who'd called around on my behalf.

Talking man-to-man wasn't Miles Lotharson's thing. In his bully's mind, he was being bullied, and he wasn't going to put up with it. Maybe a little of the attitude was because Katie was present, and he wanted her to see he was a man. Whatever, this wasn't going to end well.

His hands folded into fists. "Walk away, man. Right now."

"Can't do that. I need to talk to Katie too."

Red meat to a hungry carnivore. His face flushed. "You leave her outa this. Off limits!"

"We can either talk here or talk down at the county sheriff's office."

Wrong thing to say. He flushed even darker and danced a little, shifting from foot to foot. "Yeah. You talk to me one day, and the next, a county deputy comes calling. Damned near cost me my job."

He came for me then. Not like a boxer but like a wrestler. I sidestepped his grappling lunge and caught him on the ear with a right that should have rung his bell. He turned to face me again, even madder and less lucid than before. When he lunged this time, I went into a squat and evaded his outstretched hands. Then I stood straight and hoisted him into the air. He went over my back and landed flat on his. He lay motionless for a moment with the wind knocked out of him, but he'd have to try for me again because his girl was watching.

When I grasped Katie's elbow to return to the Bistro before anything else happened, I saw Marc Juisson not thirty feet away. He'd obviously witnessed the entire affair.

"Break's over, Katie. Time to go to work," I said.

"But he's—"

"He's all right. Nothing's hurt except his pride." I pulled her around the corner and into the Bistro as Miles staggered to his feet.

Margot agreed to give me a few minutes with Katie at a table in the corner. After she delivered a couple of coffees, I started asking my questions.

My most lasting impression of the college girl was that her eyes were as startlingly blue as Lotharson's were. She appeared to be intelligent—other than in her choice of boyfriends—and forthright. She had liked Bas Zuniga and understood he was interested in her. When she told him she had a boyfriend, Zuniga backed off but remained friends. She even made an effort to build a friendship between the two men, but it didn't take. She didn't perceive hostility, but there was no bonding between the two. She confirmed that Lotharson helped Zuniga fix a problem with his bike, but beyond that, there was nothing.

All during the interview, her eyes continued to flick to the french doors and back to me, so I surmised Lotharson was standing there watching our tête-à-tête. As I thanked her and made ready to go, she reached out and touched my arm.

"Do you have to report… you know?"

"No, but Mr. Gonda's nephew was standing nearby and saw everything."

"Marc doesn't always tell everything he knows."

"What do you mean by that?"

She flushed. "Nothing really. Just that he doesn't always tell the boss when someone makes a mistake."

"If Mr. Gonda learns of the incident, it won't be from me."

Miles Lotharson was nowhere in sight when I got up and made my way to the main area of the chateau. Gonda stood at the chocolatier's kiosk talking to Mrs. Benoir when I walked up.

"Ah, BJ. I heard you were on the premises. Any progress?"

"I came to give you a verbal report," I said.

"*Gut.* Shall we go to my office? For a little privacy, no?"

As soon as we were seated opposite one another at a small table in the corner of his office, I told him about my trip to Las Cruces and the conclusions I reached. "The reason I am giving you this report verbally at the moment is that there is one development I think should be revealed, but I'll leave to your discretion as to whether it will appear in the written report."

I had his attention. He leaned forward over the table, his hands grasping his forearms.

"As I said, I'm convinced that neither the Dayton father nor two of his older sons killed your son."

He straightened. "I was of the opinion there were three Dayton sons."

"Yes. The youngest is Patrick."

"But he was Bas's friend. The only friend in that family."

"And that is why we're talking about it instead of you reading it. Pat was quite taken with Bas."

"Taken with?" Gonda started. "Do you mean he had designs on him? He lusted after him?"

"Essentially, that is what I'm saying. Patrick would have liked a liaison with Bas. Bas was aware of his desires. They discussed it."

"Did they…?"

"I don't believe so. But Bas told him that if he ever decided to go that way, it would be with Patrick. That could have been honesty, or it could have been your son's way of letting someone he considered a friend down easy."

"I see. Does it mean this Patrick could not be the killer?"

"Not necessarily. Frustrated love can drive people to do both wonderful and terrible things. In all honesty, I don't think Patrick is the killer, but that said, he deserves another look. He was, however, in contact with Bas. He provided me with Bas's cell phone number, which simply goes to voicemail. I gave Sergeant Muñoz the number and asked if she can provide us with any information as to its present status. She hasn't had time to respond yet."

"Is that important? His having a cell phone, I mean?"

"Not unless someone answers it one of these days. But the question I want to put to you is important. Do you want that information about Pat and Bas included in the report? It should be disclosed—and I have just done that—but it doesn't necessarily need to be in the written report."

"Thank you. I am not sensitive to the discussion of personal relationships, but I see no reason to include it."

Margot's voice startled me. I turned to find her at the door with Marc hovering at her shoulder. "BJ, Marc told me you were here. Are we interrupting anything?"

"No, my dear," Gonda said. "BJ was just filling me in on what he's learned."

"What I've eliminated is more like it."

"Just so. But that is the process, is it not? Eliminate everything until you get down to the kernel."

The two entered the room and took seats at our table. Gonda then proceeded to summarize my report as virtually eliminating the Dayton family as Bas's killer. He did not mention Patrick's desires.

"So where does that leave us?" Marc asked.

"BJ found a number for Bas's cell phone and turned it over to the police. Perhaps they can learn something from that."

"Is it still working?" Margot asked.

"It goes to voicemail. It's the standard prerecorded voice. Not Bas's."

Marc leaned forward in his chair. "You say the Dayton family's out? How about the brother who was up here at the Santa Ana Star Casino that night? Have they traced his steps?"

"I've talked to the two friends who were with him, and they claim they weren't separated except for a bathroom trip or two. Certainly not enough time for Patrick to sneak off and meet Bas."

"Can you believe them?"

"Let me put it this way. There's no reason to disbelieve them at this point. That would make them coconspirators in a murder. Not many people would do that out of friendship."

Marc pursed his lips and grunted. Then he spoke again. "What about the people who are trying to adopt the baby? Maybe they were afraid Bas would claim custody."

"A possibility," I acknowledged. "But they're reputable business people. I doubt they'd put that business at risk. Nonetheless we're still looking into them."

"Then where does that leave us?" Margot asked.

"Still searching. But the field has narrowed."

"Narrowed to what?" she asked.

Marc spoke up. "Narrowed to right around here. Maybe one of his coworkers."

"I-I cannot believe that!" Gonda sputtered.

"Or maybe Katie's boyfriend," Marc said. "I saw your dustup with him a few minutes ago."

So I was forced to inform the Gondas of my run-in with Miles Lotharson.

"I will ban him from the property!" Gonda exclaimed when I finished.

"Has he caused any other trouble?" I asked.

"Not to my knowledge. Margot? Marc?"

Both shook their heads in the negative.

"Then there's no reason for that on my account. He'll likely keep his distance and sulk."

"Unless he killed Bas," Marc said.

"That's true. But if he comes at me again, that tells us something too."

When Gonda insisted on treating me to lunch at the Bistro, Margot and Marc went about their business. Between bites, I answered all Gonda's questions about my investigation, most of which had been covered before… and likely would be again.

As we finished and parted, I decided to visit SCSO to see if Roma learned anything. I sat in the Impala for a moment puzzling over what to make of Lotharson's aggressive hostility. It could mean he had something to hide, but not necessarily Zuniga's murder. There might be something else the young man didn't want revealed. Or he could have been grandstanding for Katie. Probably bitched to her about my questioning him the other day and wanted to show he knew how to deal with the problem. Didn't work out that way, but if he'd gotten his hands on me, things would likely have turned out different. He had twenty pounds on me while I had sixteen years on him.

The Impala's engine hummed with perfect precision when I ground the ignition. Backing out of the parking space presented no problem, but when I stopped before pulling out onto the road, the brakes felt mushy. Maybe the old girl required some attention. I'm usually pretty good about maintaining my vehicles, but I'd been out of town more than usual lately, so the car was overdue for service. I'd have them check the brakes for me.

I turned right onto State Road 165 and started the long downhill trip into Bernalillo. As I approached Placitas, I tapped the brake to slow down while going through the community. Nothing happened. I pressed the pedal more firmly this time. Still mushy. And it didn't slow me down any. I pressed again. The pedal went all the way to the floor. The car picked up some speed while I fruitlessly stomped on the brake. I shifted into second gear before the car picked up too much speed. She slowed a little, but not enough. I pulled it all the way into low and thought the gears were stripping before the motor growled and the car slowed a little more. I wasn't going to wreck or go off the road for the next few miles, but after that the decline increased sharply, and if I went barreling into Highway 550, there would be a terrible wreck, probably with fatalities.

I put my foot on the emergency brake but held off while I calculated a few things. This was a gravel road with houses or a few places of business in the near proximity. At my present speed, I would likely go off the road when the emergency brake took hold. There was a spot on the other side of Placitas that leveled out a bit with nothing but mailboxes on the side of the road to take out. I gritted my teeth and waited. I rounded the curve, and the road stretched out straight for a distance. But the level area looked a little more pitched than I'd remembered. Oh well, it was now or never.

I pressed slowly but steadily on the emergency brake pedal. The Impala started slowing, but I apparently overdid the thing. Her wheels locked up, and she went into a skid. There wasn't anything I could do but ride it out. She flirted with the ditch but decided to do a roundabout instead. I came to a dead stop in a cloud of dust on the wrong side of the road, looking back in the direction I'd just traveled. A screech of tires and a blaring horn behind me told me someone didn't like me blocking his lane.

I got out of the car as a big, beefy man with an orange baseball cap with "Woof" stitched in white letters climbed out of a black Ram pickup. Two big hounds barking in the truck bed confirmed he was a dog man.

"Sorry about that. But my brakes failed."

"Had to go to the emergency, huh?" At my nod, he continued. "Lucky you didn't end up in a ditch… standing on your head. Well hell, fella. Let's get you outa the road 'fore somebody drives up your tailpipe."

I was lucky a second time. Once I released the emergency brake, the wheels freed up. I was afraid to drive the vehicle since I didn't know if the transmission had suffered damage when I downshifted, but between the two of us, we managed to get the car onto a flat space at the side of the road. Then, without my asking, he flopped down on his back and poked his head under the car. A moment later he reappeared.

"Who'd you piss off? Some jasper cut your brake line right clear in two. Wasn't no break. It was cut clean."

Might as well make light of it. "I'm a private investigator, so I couldn't begin to tell you which one of my clients I ticked off."

He laughed and offered me a ride to town. I declined, electing to remain with the car until I could get a tow service.

After I placed a call for help, I reported in to the office. Charlie wanted to come get me, but we decided to wait until I knew what time I'd arrive at the tow service's office. He'd meet me there.

After that I called Ariel Gonda, told him what happened, and asked him to post someone in the parking lot to inquire whether anyone saw someone working on a white Chevy Impala. Then I dialed the Sandoval County Sheriff's Office to report the incident and still had plenty of time to lean against the car and play things back over in my mind. Miles Lotharson was a mechanic. He resented me looking into his background. I'd humiliated him in front of Katie. And, if I remembered correctly, his motorcycle was gone when I left the Pines. It wasn't proof, but he was a logical candidate.

Roma Muñoz showed up before the tow truck arrived. She crawled out of her county cruiser giving me the fish eye. "Crime statistics sure go up whenever you're in my jurisdiction."

"That's a fine greeting. But yes, I'm all right. Not hurt. Pissed but not hurt."

She planted her diminutive feminine form—made a little less so by uniform, boots, and equipment belt holding a holstered pistol—right in front of me. "All right, let's have it."

After I dictated a statement into both of our voice recorders, her attitude eased. "You figure this Lotharson character clipped your line?"

My recorder was still going, as was hers, I'm sure. "Possible, but others witnessed our dustup and might have decided to take advantage of a situation."

"Like who?"

"I'm certain the entire staff knew of our confrontation before I left the Pines. Katie Henderson, the Gondas, and Marc Juisson knew about it for sure."

"Then you're right. Everyone knew. Say, cowboy, you figure that little stunt was because you're poking around in my murder case or just because you're a general pain in the ass?"

"Hmm," I mused. "I hadn't thought of it that way. Where were you around eleven o'clock this morning?"

That earned a smile. "Not that the thought hadn't entered my mind, but it wasn't me. On a serious note, you know what this means, don't you?" she asked.

"Bascomb Zuniga's killer is someone at or near to the Pines. Unless you can put Pat Dayton or one of the Forsyths on the premises this morning, that's likely what it means."

Me and my big mouth. After that remark, I had to provide a briefing on my trips to Las Cruces and Carlsbad, specifically how I'd got Zuniga's phone number Hazel had asked her to check out.

"Turnabout's fair play," I finished. "Do you have anything to share with me?"

I took her dead-in-the-eye stare as a refusal, but she gave me a tidbit. "You can count the Forsyths out unless they hired a hit man. Carlsbad PD confirmed they were both in Carlsbad the night Zuniga died. In fact, it's pretty clear the Daytons hadn't shared the name of the baby's father, so they likely didn't know about Bascomb Zuniga at that point. Las Cruces PD sat on Patrick Dayton's two travel companions. They're sticking to the story they remained together the whole night watching the show and gambling at the Santa Ana Star."

"Same for me, and they didn't tell it in the same way. I'm inclined to believe them. What about Zuniga's cell? That tell you anything?"

"Found he called or received a call from Pat Dayton's cell about once a week. They were in contact. Other than that, nothing. I suspect the phone's lying in a ditch somewhere near the Pines. When the service runs out, it'll go dead."

The tow truck, followed by another car, showed up at that moment. She glanced at them before turning back to me. "I'll have your statement transcribed and forwarded to you as a PDF document. You look it over and sign it if it looks okay."

The second car was Charlie. He started off by apologizing for ignoring my instructions and explaining he'd given in to Hazel's harping that he go make sure I was all right. Neither one of us was going to touch that one.

Roma halted the wrecker driver when he had the Impala's nose lifted for the haul up onto the adjustable platform on the rear of his truck. We needed more headroom, but even from this angle, it was clear the brake line was cleanly clipped. Satisfied, we let him go about his business. Roma took off down the hill while Charlie and I decided it was just as well Hazel sent him. We'd take the opportunity to look up Mr. Miles Lotharson and see what he had to say for himself.

Upon pulling to Childer's Motorcycle Repair's parking area, we found Roma beat us to Lotharson. She stood before his towering figure shaking a stern fist in his face. Rather than angry, Lotharson looked to be pouting. That changed when we got out of Charlie's car.

"Couldn't handle it like a man. Had to bring backup, huh?" he groused.

"Handle what?" Charlie demanded. "You think he's on the side of a road somewhere after you cut his brake line?"

"After I what? Don't know what you're talking about."

Roma demanded his attention again. "Seems like he handled it just fine. Put you on your backside, I hear. Without you laying a glove on him." She backed up a pace, probably so she could see his face instead of his beefy shoulders. "But that's not what we're talking about. I wanna see all the tools you carry in your bike's saddlebags."

"Huh?"

"Do I have to get a warrant, or are you going to cooperate?"

I nearly laughed aloud at the sight of this tiny woman bullying the big biker. Charlie's face held a smile as well.

"Don't need no warrant. Go ahead. Take a look." Then he squinted down at her. "What you looking for, anyway?"

"Just take me over to your bike. You two can tag along if you want."

We followed Lotharson over to his Hardtail, where Roma brushed him aside and started fishing around in the bags. Eventually she held up a pair of shears that would have done the job very well.

"Okay, you're going with me down to the station," she told Lotharson.

He blinked and swallowed a couple of times. "Am I under arrest?"

"Not yet, but you might be if you refuse to do an interview."

"All right, but I'm gonna take my own wheels."

"Better not run, buddy boy. Every cop in the state will be on your back if you do."

I didn't know about Lotharson, but *I* wouldn't have run. That woman could have intimidated a charging bull elephant.

Chapter 26

ROMA BANNED Charlie and me from her interview with Lotharson, so we returned to Albuquerque to rent a car while mine was being repaired. What did I get? A white Impala was my inclination, but I went for a blue Ford Taurus this time. Made it harder to identify my vehicle in case someone was bent on mischief.

Before Charlie, Hazel, and I gathered around my table to discuss the sabotage of my Impala, I placed a call to Ariel Gonda, who told me he put Marc Juisson and James Bledsong in the parking lot as soon as I alerted him of my near wreck. They asked the occupants of each departing car if anyone was seen near my Impala. That brought no positive results. However, some cars had departed before I called.

The first task my team and I addressed was to ascertain where all the players had been in the hours before noon today. And that meant *all* the players, even if we'd eliminated them for other reasons. To help out, I phoned a Las Cruces PI I'd known over the years by the name of Chandler Godsby. He agreed to check the Daytons and Forsyths. That was undertaken out of an abundance of caution.

Then the three of us tackled the more likely prospects: the people at the Pines and their familiars, such as Lotharson. Charlie agreed to contact Roma to see if she would share her interview with the biker. Next we turned to the people on the winery property. After examining each for a possible motivation to kill Bas Zuniga, we discussed the possibility that the severing of my brake line had nothing to do with the murder. That did not seem likely, even though I'd made my share of enemies after fifteen or so years of poking into other people's affairs, either as a city cop or a confidential investigator.

Although it was impossible to know the internal dynamics among and between eight staff members plus the management team at the Pines, nothing we uncovered so far pointed toward any animosity beyond the normal everyday things that made a man puckish. But my mind kept coming back to one thing. Bascomb Zuniga was a spectacularly handsome young man. In addition, he was sexy—which was not the same thing. More than one individual in our earlier interviews had expressed doubt about his sexuality.

I was wading in quicksand here. I was gay, so my mind naturally looked for things like that. So could I be intuiting something that wasn't there? Or was I so conscious of those things that I picked up something important? I opened the question up to the other two.

"I been wondering about that too," Charlie said. "But both Natander and Pastis witnessed the attack and didn't say anything about an attempted... uh, rape, I guess you'd call it."

"No, but they said Zuniga and the attacker spoke for a few minutes," Hazel said. "Enough so somebody might have been turned down."

I clicked my ballpoint pen a couple of times and threw it down. "Maybe if there'd been previous attempts, the attacker might have held out hope Zuniga would change his mind. When he said no a final time, that was too much, and the guy lost it."

"I didn't get any gay vibes from the other staff," Charlie said. "Did you?"

"I can tell you from experience, straight guys sometimes make approaches."

Hazel gave a subdued snort but kept her mouth shut. She really didn't like discussing matters like this aloud. She loved Paul as much as she did me, but if we started showing open affection, she'd run for the hills.

"I guess you oughta know," Charlie said. "But do they go nuts when they're turned down?"

"Certain men do. Believe it or not, it's an affront to their masculinity. Gay guys—fags, as they'd consider them—oughta be slobbering all over them. When they're turned down, some get really nasty."

"Guess some people figure a gay guy goes for anybody with a—" He interrupted himself and slid a look at Hazel. "—with the right kind of equipment." Charlie stretched his legs under the table. "Garcia was living with him. I know he's got a wife and kids down in Juarez. Maybe he was frustrated."

"I talked to Garcia. He's the one who threw cold water on the idea Zuniga was gay."

"Maybe it was for cover?"

I lifted my shoulders in frustration. "Could be. But I didn't get that feeling when I spoke to him."

"Maybe we should go back and talk to all of them again." Charlie wrinkled his nose. "Although I'm not anxious to go around asking them if they got it on with Zuniga. Especially that vineyard worker Tso. He's one big Indian."

I chuckled. "Parson Jones might get a little upset too. Yeah, we need to talk to them again, but maybe we can take the temperature without asking the question. Do you remember who relieved Zuniga that night?"

"Winfield Tso," Hazel answered. "That's what your notes say, if I remember right."

"Natander didn't give me a description of the killer, but what did Pastis say?"

"Enough to know it wasn't Tso," Charlie said. "I recollect he claimed the guy was ordinary-sized. About the same as Zuniga."

"Zuniga was five ten. You're right, it wasn't Tso."

"Coulda been any of the others." Charlie continued on down the road. "Which ones you want me to tackle?"

"All of them. I'll start in on the family."

"The Gonda family?" Hazel asked.

"By that, you mean the nephew. Juisson," Charlie said.

"Do we know for sure the killer was a man? After all, it was night."

"Margot? You don't honestly believe she was the killer." Hazel's comment came out as a flat statement, making it clear where she stood.

"Why not? Zuniga was taking money out of her son's pocket. Or potentially would have."

"Isn't there enough for all of them?" she asked. "I understand there's also family money in Switzerland."

Charlie covered that one. "There's never enough money for some of them. And the bigger the pot, the bigger the fight to keep it. But it does seem a stretch that she'd be the killer."

"Why? Because she's attractive, likeable?"

Charlie scratched his head, indicating I was backing him into a corner. "She seems like a very secure woman. Hell, she knew about Zuniga for years but kept her trap shut. Never let on she knew."

"But Zuniga wasn't on the scene then. He wasn't a factor in Gonda's life. All of a sudden he was."

"Glad you're going to handle them instead of me. Think I'll head out for the winery now. Take them by surprise."

"Lean on them hard, Charlie. Because—"

He raised his hands in protest. "I know. I know. Because if it isn't one of the workers, then it's one of the family. And if it's one of the family—"

"Oh good Lord!" Hazel straightened in her chair. "The baby. The baby might be in danger."

Charlie paused in the act of leaving. "You know, that puts a new light on things. Maybe you oughta get some protection for the Forsyths since they have the little boy now."

AFTER CHARLIE and Hazel left my office, I sat at my desk and dithered over whether to call Sgt. Roma Muñoz or Lt. Ray Yardley. I lifted the receiver and dialed Yardley. The state police had a longer reach. Besides, I should have been running all over Roma and her people on this, but that hadn't been the case. Was she relying on the state police to do it for her? Of course, Yardley hadn't exactly been on the scene either. Maybe they were relying on me to solve it.

Yardley, when I managed to run him down by phone and get his attention, let me know that his involvement in the affair ended when we caught the intruder... intruders, if you included Natander and Pastis. The murder of Bascomb Zuniga was a separate case altogether, which belonged to the county, at least since we eliminated any of the intruders from suspicion.

After hearing my concern for the Dayton child, Ray got Roma on the phone in a three-way conference call. I regretted involving him because of the way he poked at Roma, almost accusing her of not pursuing the case, but he salvaged the situation—and put some of the heat on me—when he described the possible threat to a child in Carlsbad and asked if she needed his help in covering that base.

"How come you didn't bring this to me, Vinson?"

"Because he knew I had people in that area." Ray headed off the attack.

"And I have kept you up-to-date on my findings, Sergeant. What's your feeling about Lotharson? Did he admit to cutting my brake line? And do you see a connection between that and the murder case?"

"I told Charlie Weeks what I thought a few minutes ago. Lotharson's a dimwit. Capable of doing it, but I'm not sure he has the imagination—

or initiative. Forensics didn't tell us anything useful about the cutter I took from his saddlebags. No evidence of brake fluid."

She switched gears. "Anyway, Lieutenant, I'd appreciate it very much if you'd cover the Carlsbad end for me."

"Not sure I can do more than have a trooper swing by and make the Forsyths aware of the situation."

"Carlsbad PD would probably put a hand in if you ask them," Roma said. "What are you going to do, BJ?"

BJ. I guess that meant she was over her pique... for the moment. "I'm going out this afternoon and talk to Ariel Gonda. Make sure he understands there may be a threat."

"Be sure you don't stir up a viper."

MARGOT JOINED Ariel and me in his office—at his request. After declining an offer of either wine or coffee, I studied the two. They projected the air of people who believed things were beginning to come to a head. I wished I shared that feeling. Margot, in particular, seemed affected. She was her usual friendly self, but there were lines around her mouth I hadn't noticed before. Concerned about someone taking to my car again, perhaps.

"Don't worry, Margot. I'm in a rental until my car's repaired. And this time I got something besides an Impala."

She frowned at me across the small table where we sat. "I didn't know it showed. I would feel very responsible if something happened to you, BJ."

"Thank you, but I know the risks of my job, and they are accepted voluntarily."

Margot sank back in her chair and seemed to relax. "In other words, you're a big boy, so don't fret over you."

"Bluntly put, but that's the general idea."

"It is not a trivial matter, BJ," Gonda said. "I did not realize I put your safety at risk when I asked you to look into this matter. Perhaps we should reconsider."

"More importantly, we should get down to business," I said. "I need to warn you of two things. You can expect Sgt. Roma Muñoz and some of her deputies to come around. I believe she's going to take a more proactive approach to your son's murder than she has to this point."

"I see," Ariel said. "Is that a good thing?"

"Definitely. She has more manpower than I have, and she'll approach things differently, so that's good. And my associate Charlie Weeks will be questioning each of your employees again."

Gonda nodded. "Yes. He arrived earlier and is at the winery right now, talking to Hakamora and Jones."

"This is going to be a little tougher questioning than before."

Margot sighed. "I suppose this means you've narrowed the killer down to someone at the Pines."

"Not exclusively. But everything points to that probability." I drummed my fingers as I considered sharing something I hadn't revealed to them before. "The night Bas was killed, Natander and Pastis were across the street in the woods, keeping watch. They reached the conclusion that Diego C de Baca moved after dark, so they set up night surveillance. They thought they'd struck gold when Bas came walking out of the Pines parking lot. We've remarked on how much the two men resembled one another, not just in features, but in stature. Natander was certain it was Diego, but Pastis didn't think the man walked like their quarry. At any rate, they waited before moving so Pastis could get a better look through the sniper's scope he carried. While they waited, someone stepped out of the trees at the edge of your property and stopped Bas. They talked a moment before Bas moved on. Then the other man pulled out a pistol and shot him."

Gonda drew a sharp breath. "So they saw who shot my son?"

At this point, I indulged in some fantasy. "It was dark, and unfortunately Pastis didn't have night-vision equipment. However, he gave a general description of the killer. Enough so we have a pretty good idea of *how* to look for the man." Purely by instinct, I added, "Or woman," while watching Margot. All I saw was surprise.

"Woman?" Gonda blinked. "A woman shot my son?"

"Can't rule it out until I run down a couple of things." Time to ease up a bit. "Charlie's tackling the workers. My job is to handle management. Might as well start with Marc. Is he around?"

"I'm sorry, but he left not long ago for a trip back to California. He has a meeting with the CFO of Halversack Wine Distributors in Los Angeles. They are signing with us to carry the Lovely Pines brand." Gonda frowned. "I doubt he has reached the airport as yet. Do you want me to ring his cell phone and call him back?"

"No, I imagine that's an important meeting for you."

"Very important," Margot said. "It will bring us into the black ahead of schedule."

"If you'd give me his cell phone number, I can ask him a few preliminary questions."

"Certainly," Gonda said.

Margot spoke up. "He has a new cell but hasn't changed it to the old number. I have the new number in my office. You can stop by and pick it up when you leave, BJ. If you will excuse me, I've got to go make some phone calls to put final details on the meeting Marc's headed to."

She rose and left the room. I watched her go. Something about our meeting upset her. I turned back to Gonda and found him studying me.

"What are you not telling me, BJ?"

"Before I answer that, may I ask what your intentions are with the Dayton child?"

"By all rights, it should be the Zuniga child." Bitterness hid in his voice, but he cleared it away before answering. "Uncertain at this point. I would like to claim the child and bring him into my household. Raise him and let him, along with Marc, take over the business someday. I'm afraid our son Auguste has no interest in wines."

"What's stopping you?"

I read indecision on his face. "There is such animosity among the Daytons against Bas that I fear they would fight me. As the elder Dayton—James, I believe it is—is likewise a grandparent, he has as great a claim on the child as I do. If he were retaining custody of the child, I would certainly fight him on the matter. But from what Del Dahlman tells me, the Forsyth family in Carlsbad would likely provide a good home for the boy." He arched an eyebrow, silently asking a question.

"I believe that to be true. They undoubtedly care for little David and have a prosperous, stable household."

Gonda placed both hands flat on the table. "Then, too, there is the mess we are in at the moment. I shall reserve my decision until we know who killed his father and why."

I looked him dead in the eye and agreed that was wise.

The meeting effectively over, I took my leave and stopped by Margot's desk, where she gave me Marc's new phone number. Except that it wasn't. When I dialed, I got a greengrocer on the south side of Albuquerque who had no knowledge of a Marc Juisson.

"Oh dear!" Margot's eyes went wide like quarters, giving her a flustered look. "I must have written it down wrong." She consulted a memo book on her desk and compared a number from there with the one she provided me. "I'm certain I wrote it down correctly, although we were hurried because he was leaving for the airport later than expected because of the excitement this morning."

"So this is a brand-new phone?"

"Yes. He got it yesterday afternoon in Albuquerque. He wanted the latest model. It's a monstrously big thing to carry around, but he can dictate notes to himself and do his email, and I don't know what else."

"How about the old number?"

She provided it without hesitation. When I dialed, the call went to voicemail. The voice was clearly Marc's. He hadn't terminated service on the old phone yet.

A sudden shiver ran down my back, alerting me to something. But I wasn't sure what. I asked Margot what flight Marc was on and took my leave, saying I'd begin questioning the others tomorrow.

I MADE it to the airport without incident, although I was surprised I wasn't pulled over during my race down I-25 all the way through Albuquerque to the Sunport. I parked in the short-term structure and ran up the stairs to the American Airlines counter to find the right gate. The TSA security post was near enough to the waiting area that I had a good view of the passengers already in the process of boarding the flight. None of those still visible was Marc Juisson.

The American Airlines ticketing desk couldn't or wouldn't tell me if Marc Juisson had boarded that particular aircraft, so I made the rounds of the parking structure looking for his red Miata. Eventually I located the car on the third level. He'd obviously caught a flight to… somewhere.

Surrendering to my churning gut, I thumbed through my pocket notebook and found the telephone number of Halversack Wine Distributors that Gonda had given me. When they answered, I worked my way up from the receptionist to the CEO's office to a secretary named Miss Penny who owned a nice contralto voice.

"My name is B. J. Vinson, and I need to speak to Mr. Marc Juisson of the Lovely Pines Winery. I can't reach him by his cell phone, but I know he has a meeting tomorrow with one of your vice presidents. Can you please let him know I'm trying to reach him?"

"I'm sorry, sir, but that meeting was rescheduled for the day after tomorrow. I will be happy—"

"Rescheduled? Can you tell me who rescheduled the meeting?"

"The Lovely Pines Winery."

"Who requested the delay?"

"I don't have that information. Who did you say you are?"

Rather than argue with her, I thanked her for her cooperation and terminated the call. The New Mexico Airlines counter was not only closed; it was also abandoned. Signs indicated there was only one flight to and from Carlsbad a day, and the departing plane took off about thirty minutes ago.

Jim Gray was in his office at the Double Eagle Airport and agreed to fly me down to Carlsbad. An ex-military pilot now running his own charter service, Jim said that rather than have me waste time driving across town, he'd pick me up at Cutter Flying Service on the west side of the Albuquerque Sunport. I'd just finished telling Hazel where I was heading and why when Jim's silver-and-cherry Cessna Skycatcher arrived. Within minutes we were aloft. As I stared down at Sandia Peak passing beneath our wings, I wondered what in the hell I was doing. Heading for the Cavern City Airport, that's what. Based on nothing except one rescheduled meeting and a strong feeling of unease.

Chapter 27

JIM ELECTED to remain at the airport when he chanced upon a mechanic buddy from the Vietnam War. I rented a car and headed straight for the Forsyth house. Although it was late in the afternoon, either Hadley or Jane—or both of them—might still be at the dealership, but the boy would be at home. And it was the boy I was concerned over.

My gut eased a bit when I saw a Carlsbad police unit in front of the house, but a blue Nissan parked behind it raised the hair on my neck. Relief turned to panic when I found an officer slumped in the driver's seat of the patrol car. He was unresponsive. I leaned in the open window, picked up his radio mike, and put in an "officer down" call. Pausing only long enough to identify myself and give the dispatcher the address, I dropped the mike on the seat and reached for the officer's holster. It was empty. His attacker took his sidearm. Marc had traveled here by passenger jet, so he wouldn't have been able to bring a weapon with him. I had elected not to put Jim's pilot's license at risk by bringing my 9mm semiautomatic. It still rested in the trunk of my car back at Cutter Flying Service.

The officer's shotgun was locked into place, and rather than search for the key, I snatched his baton before starting up the sidewalk. The front door was locked—at least Juisson had sense enough to lock things behind him. I took the quickest way inside by punching out a pane of glass with the officer's truncheon and reaching inside to release the deadbolt. The old gunshot wound in my right thigh began to burn as soon as I opened the door and slipped inside, moving out of the open doorway as quickly as possible.

No one was in the hallway or in the sitting room so far as I could see. Then I spotted a leg protruding from behind a sofa. I scuttled across the thick carpet, keeping my eyes peeled for the intruder. Jane Forsyth lay on her back out of sight of most of the room. I found a pulse. She was alive. The ugly gash on her forehead told me Marc struck her with something, probably the weapon he carried.

Then the sound of a childish "No!" from somewhere upstairs drew me to the stairway. Marble, not wood. The steps wouldn't creak and give me away. Nor would they betray Marc if he was on his way down.

"We're just going for an ice cream cone" came a male voice. Marc's voice? "You like ice cream, don't you?"

As I started to ascend, a scrap of paper on a table beside the stairway caught my attention. A note in crude, obviously disguised lettering said to bring $500,000 to the Bat Cave at 8:00 p.m. that night if they wanted their son back. Yeah, right. Forsyth would be left waiting at the Carlsbad National Park forever for the little boy who would never return.

But the note told me one useful thing. Marc intended to leave this house with the child, probably alive since he wouldn't want blood or body fluids to give away his game. That was why he'd dragged Mrs. Forsyth out of sight behind the sofa. He didn't want the boy to see her and panic. Even so, he seemed to be having trouble with the child. I was halfway up the stairs when Marc appeared at the top, his attention distracted by having to drag along a distressed two-year-old child. Except it wasn't Marc. That is, it was and it wasn't. The voice I'd heard before I saw him on the stairway seemed to be his, and this man resembled him… strongly. Yet there was something amiss about him.

The sound of multiple sirens caught the kidnapper's attention. He glanced down, his eyes going wide as he spotted me. I didn't even get a warning out of my mouth before he reacted. He jerked the little boy by the arm and slung him straight at me.

I managed to catch the squealing child, but little David's weight threw me off balance, sending me backward down the stairs. I heard a roar and understood the would-be-kidnapper had shot at me. Probably at both of us. By the time I bounced my way to the bottom of the stairs and regained my senses, he had disappeared. I heard cars screeching to a halt outside as I scrambled to my feet. Ignoring the pain of a wrenched right knee, I shoved the weeping boy toward the door—yelling for him to let the police into the house—and hobbled upstairs, using the banister to haul myself up each step.

The intruder was gone, of course. Nowhere in sight. He'd have made his way to the back stairs and escaped the house. But it wasn't something I could count on. I checked each room as I came to it until I heard a harsh voice.

"Freeze! Put down your weapon. On your knees."

I immediately obeyed the voice. One of their own was down, and the cops would be on the prod.

I waited until strong arms hoisted me roughly to my feet and steel bracelets circled my wrists before speaking. "My name is B. J. Vinson, and I'm the guy who radioed in the 'officer down' call. How is he, by the way?"

They turned me around so that I faced two uniformed officers. The younger one fished my wallet out of my pocket. "Yep. Vinson. Driver's license and a PI license."

Of course, that didn't mean I hadn't injured their buddy and then called it in to cover my tracks. If they reasoned that out, they'd wonder why I was still in the house if that were the case. But this wasn't the time for rational thought.

I nodded to the billy club lying on the floor. "That's your officer's weapon. I took it off him after I found him unconscious and called in to get him help. His sidearm was missing. Presumably the kidnapper has it."

The older officer gave me a blank stare. His breast tag read Roger Pillars. "How'd you find our officer?"

"I was on the way to the house because I feared a kidnapping was taking place. I'm the reason you had an officer on the premises. I called Lt. Ray Yardley at the state police and told him of my suspicions. He called your office and requested a guard. Is your officer okay?" I asked. "I only took time to make certain he was alive before I broke into the house to find Mrs. Forsyth unconscious behind the sofa and a kidnapping taking place. You'll find a note on the table at the bottom of the stairs asking for half a million dollars."

Pillars nodded to his partner, who headed back downstairs. Then he ignored my question for a second time. "Do you know who the kidnapper was?" he asked.

I hedged. A man doesn't accuse a member of a wealthy and prominent family of such a crime unless there's proof. And I didn't have any proof. Not yet, anyway. "He was familiar, but I can't identify him absolutely."

At Pillars' prompting, I gave a spot-on description of Marc. "Five ten, one seventy, dark brown hair, green eyes, athletic build. I traced him to the New Mexico Airlines flight that arrived here earlier today. That Nissan is a rental, probably in his name." I took the gamble. "His name might be Marc Juisson." Pillars asked me to spell both names.

As we went downstairs—me still in cuffs—a human dynamo burst through the front door. Hadley Forsyth was furious that despite clear warnings, the police allowed his wife to be bludgeoned and his son nearly stolen. I heard a different sort of siren that told me the injured officer, Mrs. Forsyth, and little David were on their way to the hospital. I didn't think the child suffered any injury when we fell down the stairs, but the police would want to make certain. Forsyth remained only long enough to get a sketchy idea of what happened before rushing out to go be with his family at the hospital.

Pillars released me from the handcuffs and settled in to hear the entire story. In the meantime, two other officers searched the house, returning later to indicate they'd found no one. After putting a guard on the place—and the rented Nissan—the sergeant invited me downtown to make a full report. I declined his offer of a ride and agreed to meet him at the station. Pausing beside my rental, I phoned the office and brought Hazel up-to-date on events.

"And you're okay?" she pressed.

"Wrenched my knee when I fell down the stairs, but it feels better already. I assume Charlie's out at the Pines questioning staff?"

"Yes. You're certain it was Marc Juisson?"

"I'm pretty sure it was. He'd added a fake beard and did something to make his face seem fatter, but it was him."

"Then I'll call Charlie back in."

"No, have him go to the chateau. Hang around the vicinity of the office. I want him to judge reactions when word reaches them of what's happened."

"Anyone in particular?"

"Everyone."

"So you're assuming the nephew is the killer but don't know if anyone else is involved."

I dug my notebook from a shirt pocket and gave her a number. "Hazel, ask Gene to call a Miss Penny in the CEO's office at Halversack Wine Distributers and ask who rescheduled Marc Juisson's meeting with their VP. A lieutenant from APD ought to be able to get that information from her. She was reluctant to give it to me."

"They're liable to check with the Lovely Pines about our inquiry," she warned.

"Good. Just make sure Charlie's at the chateau before Gene makes the California call. And tell Charlie not to say anything about what's happened down here in Carlsbad."

I closed the call and got into the driver's seat of my rental. I hadn't gone a block before something cold and hard and round pressed into the back of my head.

"Keep driving."

"I'm getting sloppy," I said, fighting to keep my leaping heart from clogging my throat. "I never thought to check the back floorboard of my car. Of course, I usually keep the car locked. Guess the excitement of the moment distracted me." Was I babbling out of fear or seeking to calm him down? I didn't know.

"Shut up. Take the next right and find a way out of town. No freeways. Just a quiet street that leads us to someplace private."

I pressed the accelerator slightly. "Don't think I want to do that."

He dug the gun barrel into my flesh. "Do it! And slow down."

"Don't think I want to do that either." I pressed the gas pedal harder and blew through a red traffic light, causing two cars to skid to a halt, horns blaring. "Next light's coming up in about six blocks. Hand over the gun, Marc. You're not cut out for this business."

"Slow down!" he yelled and whacked me in the head with the pistol hard enough to send my eyesight blurring.

The car went into a skid, heading for the curb on the opposite side of the street. I made no effort to correct it. I simply threw myself sideways as far as the shoulder restraint belt would permit and tried to relax. Easier said than done.

The vehicle hit the curb going virtually sideways and flipped. My head banged on the steering wheel, and I fought desperately to avoid losing consciousness. I know we rolled once and probably would have again if we hadn't broadsided a tree. That finished it for me. I went black.

I CAME semiawake at the sound of noises. Banging on metal. Excited voices. The thought of Marc Juisson brought me back from la-la land in a hurry. My head throbbed, but all my various parts seemed to work—except the knee I'd wrenched falling down the stairs. But I was constricted, unable to move freely. After a longer period of time than it should have taken, I figured out I was still strapped into the seat belt. I managed to hit the release button, which freed me to fall a few inches. The halt was painful. That's when I figured out the car was lying on its side. The sound that had brought me conscious was someone prying the front passenger's door open. Even as I slowly rounded on that fact, it came free with a screech of tortured metal. An indistinct face peered down at me, haloed like an angel by the bright light outside.

"You okay, fella?" a voice asked.

"Need some help getting out, but think I'm okay. But the other man in the car—back there somewhere, he's a criminal with a gun. Wait for police, but don't let him escape."

Ignoring me, the man disappeared for a moment. I heard the crash of glass as he punched out the window to the back door. A moment later, he reappeared and lowered himself into the front of the cabin.

"Don't worry about him. He ain't gonna give nobody no trouble. Shoulda wore a seat belt."

Epilogue

GENE ENRIQUEZ helped me out of the front seat of Charlie's car in the parking lot of the Lovely Pines late the next afternoon. Roma Muñoz and a deputy pulled in beside us and exited their vehicle. The four of them surrounded me as I slowly made my way to the front door of the chateau, aided by a walnut cane with a shiny brass duck's head as a knob. The verdict on my knee was still out—one specialist wanted to operate; another counseled waiting. I planned to go with the second opinion. Other than the knee, I was in decent shape. A knot on the head, glass cuts on a shoulder. Sore as hell all over. Nothing I couldn't handle. I was in a hell of a lot better shape than Marc Juisson, who was lying in the OMI's morgue with several broken bones… one of them being a vertebra in his neck.

As soon as we came through the door, Heléne Benoir slipped from behind the chocolatier's stand and rushed to meet us. After assuring herself I was fitter than I appeared, she ushered us into the sitting room, where the Gondas awaited our arrival. Both stood as we entered.

Gonda took an involuntary step toward us but caught himself. "BJ, are you all right?"

"Fine, thank you. Bum knee and a bruised forehead."

"And a cut or two where it doesn't show," Charlie volunteered.

"Sit down, sit down!" Gonda rushed to fill coffee cups from an urn set on a table at the end of the two facing couches.

I examined Margot as we greeted one another across the space of a broad coffee table. She was carefully made up, but signs of stress—or sorrow—leaked through.

Following a tussle with Roma, who clearly wanted this to be her show, we'd earlier agreed I would start the meeting by relating what happened in Carlsbad the day before. I did so in excruciating detail. Everyone listened to my narrative without interrupting, except for Gonda's question as to whether little David was all right after the rough treatment he received.

Once I was finished, the room fell silent. An old-fashioned French pendulum clock sitting on a sideboard at the end of the room provided the only sound.

Gonda broke the stillness. "So it is all finished now? It is over? Marc killed my son?"

Roma handled that one. "We believe so, Mr. Gonda."

"But why?" His question came out with a sob.

Roma hewed to the line we agreed to. "Because Juisson knew you well enough to understand you would acknowledge Zuniga. He would have become an heir."

"But there is enough for everyone. There is—" He stumbled over his words. "—enough for everyone."

"Apparently not."

"Thank God my grandson is safe."

"Is he?" Roma asked.

"Of course he is! Marc is dead." Ariel Gonda gasped. He flinched. "Are you saying someone else is involved?"

I walked all over Roma's territory at that point. "Margot, why did you change Marc's appointment with the wine distributor from today to tomorrow?"

Gonda's features grew mottled. He appeared to be holding his breath as he looked at his wife of twenty-odd years.

Margot seemed startled as well. "Because Marc asked me to."

"Did he give a reason why?"

She colored slightly. "He arranged to meet a woman he knew while he was there. Someone from Switzerland. He told me she had a scheduling conflict, so he wanted a delay of the meeting by twenty-four hours."

"Why didn't you tell me, my dear?"

She reached over and patted Gonda's hand. "Why? Halversack expressed no problem with the rescheduling. If they had, I would have told him to stick with the original timing."

Gonda sighed as if it came from his soul. "I see."

"We found the young lady's name and number in your nephew's diary. She confirms his story," Roma said.

I broke in again. "How were you to let Marc know if the change was unacceptable? Halversack says the change was made yesterday morning. In fact, just before we met." I nodded to Gene. "Lieutenant Enriquez confirmed that for us. That is why he is present this morning."

Margot now had the look of a careful adversary. I was rapidly making myself unwelcome in the Gonda home, I suspected. "By calling Marc on his cell phone, of course," she replied.

"But you didn't have his new cell number. It got me a grocery store in the South Valley."

"But I did not know this at the time. I did not realize I wrote it down wrong."

"His old cell phone still works, and that is the only cell we found on him. There was not a new one."

Gonda could no longer contain himself. "He apparently deliberately misinformed my wife. As a ruse to be out of touch—incommunicado until it suited him to return to the fold."

"What rational reason would he give her for such a mistake when it came to light?"

Gonda fluttered both hands before his face, which turned into the beard-smoothing gesture. "Must we consider Marc a rational man thinking reasonable thoughts? Killing my son and attempting to kidnap my grandson are not the acts of a rational man."

"Perhaps he would have gotten a new phone upon his return and provided me with that number, saying he made a mistake," Margot suggested. "After all, his plans were rushed. We only recently learned where the child was, you know."

"Possible," I said, although I wasn't so sure of that.

"Let us return to what is paramount in my mind," Gonda said. "You are certain Marc killed my son, Bascomb Zuniga?"

"I cannot tell you we could prove it to a jury," Roma said, "but the preponderance of evidence we have collected tells me he was the murderer."

"How is that possible?" Margot asked. "BJ told us he confirmed Marc's absence on another California sales trip on the night of Bas's death."

Gene spoke up. "It is not a crime to lie to a private investigator, Mrs. Gonda. But it is a different matter when you speak to a police authority. I rechecked Mr. Juisson's story. He was there, all right—with the same young lady, as a matter of fact. But upon questioning by Los Angeles city detectives, she acknowledged she remained alone in their hotel room one night while he left a day early to take care of some business, asking her to keep it confidential."

Gonda sucked air through his teeth. "And that was the night Bas died?"

"I'm afraid so," Gene concluded. "You will recall that he claimed to have arrived the day of the discovery of Mr. Zuniga's body. Actually, he arrived the night before."

"So it is likely he shot my son." Everyone waited as Gonda processed that information. "And tried to kidnap Bas's son." It was a statement, an acknowledgment.

"For ransom, you said," Margot added.

"In my opinion, the ransom note was misdirection," I said. "Marc would have taken the boy out on the desert and killed him. And by the time we finish gathering all the information, I believe we can prove it in a court of law."

"I will accept your verdict." Gonda rose, signaling the meeting was at an end.

As we broke up, he delayed me on the veranda of the chateau. "From your attitude, I can only gather you harbor further suspicions. You do not truly believe Margot was involved with my nephew in this madness, do you?"

"The questions had to be asked, Ariel. Unfortunately, it is you who will have to make a decision in that particular matter and then live with that decision."

I held his pale blue stare and read vacillation. He went off subject. "I am mortified that one of my own nearly caused an accident that could well have taken your life. I assume Marc cut your brake line."

"Yes. I believe that to be true. But you are not responsible for the actions of other people, Ariel. They are. Now you tell me something," I added. "What are your intentions about the Dayton child? Will you pursue custody of the boy?"

A look of infinite sadness washed his features. "I intend to instruct Del Dahlman to make certain I have the rights of a legitimate grandfather. Nothing more."

I limped back to Charlie's car convinced Gonda had as many questions about his wife's involvement in this mess as I did.

But at that moment, all I wanted was to have Charlie drop me by 5229 Post Oak Drive, where a handsome young man with a fascinating dragon tattoo on his left pec was waiting to ease my aches and pains... and perhaps a few other things, as well.

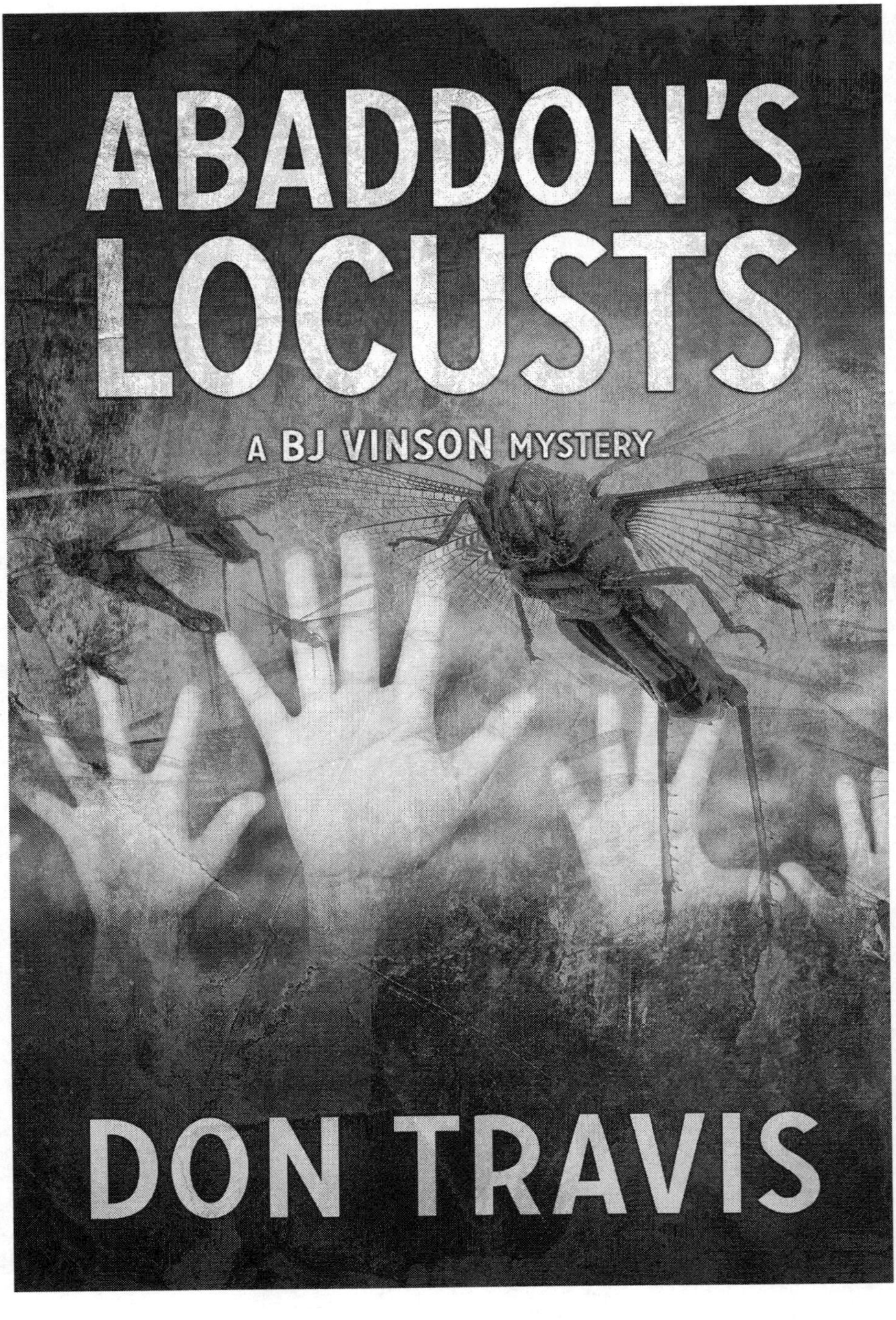
ABADDON'S
LOCUSTS
A BJ VINSON MYSTERY
DON TRAVIS

Turn the page
for an exclusive excerpt!

When B. J. Vinson, confidential investigator, learns his young friend, Jazz Penrod, has disappeared and has not been heard from in a month, he discovers some ominous emails. Jazz has been corresponding with a "Juan" through a dating site, and that single clue draws BJ and his significant other, Paul Barton, into the brutal but lucrative world of human trafficking.

Their trail leads to a mysterious Albuquerquean known only as Silver Wings, who protects the Bulgarian cartel that moves people—mostly the young and vulnerable—around the state to be sold into modern-day slavery, sexual and otherwise. Can BJ and Paul locate and expose Silver Wings without putting Jazz's life in jeopardy? Hell, can he do so without putting themselves at risk? People start dying as BJ, Paul, and Henry Secatero, Jazz's Navajo half-brother, get too close. To find the answer, bring down the ring, and save Jazz, they'll need to locate the place where human trafficking ties into the Navajo Nation and the gay underground.

Coming Soon to
www.dsppublications.com

Prologue

TWO MEN gazed down at the sleeping youth sprawled across the mattress. The older, his pleasant features blemished by a glint of cruelty in his hazel eyes, smoothed silver wings at his temples before handing over a number of hundred-dollar bills to a young Hispanic almost as handsome as the boy on the bed.

Now fully clothed, Silver Wings exuded the authority of a player, of someone who counted. "Fucking beautiful. How old did you say he is?"

"Eighteen. Barely. Know that's older'n you usually like. But he's a rare one, no? As *linda* as a woman and as macho as a man. He took care of you, huh?"

Silver Wings rubbed his eyes as if remembering the last hour. "Fantastic. Must have worn himself out. Does he usually go comatose?"

"Ah, that is the drug. He claims he gets a bigger bang by charging up. But you benefit as well, no?" He eyed his companion. "He is yours for $25,000."

Interest flickered and died. "Tempting. But my household isn't set up for that kind of arrangement. I prefer to call when I feel the need. Even if that means sharing him."

"You don't take him, then we move him south."

"South? To Mexico, you mean? Juarez?" That wouldn't be too bad. El Paso was a short hop, and Juarez lay just across the border.

"At first, but then we gonna trade him up."

Silver Wings understood the human trafficking language of trading up, but it was unusual to move members of the "family" out of country these days. "In Juarez? Sounds more like trading him down."

"¡Órale! There's some big money in Juarez. But a bigwig in the Middle East went apeshit over the kid's pics. He wants him. And for a lot more than twenty-five. I only give you that price to let you know how much we 'preciate your help."

"Middle East, huh?" Silver Wings licked his lips. "Put off that transfer while I see if I can work something out."

"Two days. Then I gotta move him. You know, easier to ship him overseas from Mexico than from the States."

Silver Wings' voice hardened. "You can do better than that. Give me a week to reorder my life. I'd like to visit him a couple of times. Usual fee, of course. That gives you reason enough to hold him here."

"Okay, but not no more'n a week. I got people to answer to, you know."

"I'd like him again tomorrow night, but it will have to be late. I have a dinner meeting."

Hispano lowered his head. "As you wish. All you gotta do is call me."

Silver Wings left the motel reluctantly. What would take place in that room now that they were alone? Just thinking about it raised a bead of sweat on his upper lip.

Chapter 1

I PARKED the Impala in front of my detached single-car garage and sat for a moment trying to figure out the cacophony on the radio. I'd failed to reset the station after Paul and I went for a rare game of weekend golf at the North Valley Country Club. Paul Barton was the sun in my sky, but I still struggled to understand my companion's taste in music. Now something called "Alejandro" by a gal proclaiming herself to be Lady Gaga committed assault on my classical-music-loving ears. As I switched off the noise and stepped from the car, a high, uncertain voice snagged my attention.

"Yoo-hoo, Mr. Vinson. BJ!"

Mrs. Gertrude Wardlow, the late-afternoon sun catching in wayward strands of her white hair, waved at me from the foot of her driveway. She had lived in the white brick across the street for as long as I could remember. Mrs. W. and her husband, Herb, were with the Drug Enforcement Administration from the time it was formed in 1973 until their retirement. Some ten years ago, Herb passed on to his reward—an urn on his widow's mantelpiece. I walked out to meet her in the middle of Post Oak Drive.

"I'm so glad I caught you." She fiddled with frilly lace at the neck of her lavender blouse. "A man on a Harley has been driving up and down the street. He stopped at your place twice. Rang the bell and then rode off."

No doubt she was recalling the time when two thugs on another motorcycle attempted to gun me down. When she'd yelled to distract their murderous attention, they shot up the front of her house, scattering her husband all over the carpet.

I touched her shoulder. "Don't worry, I'm not involved in any gang disputes at the moment. Not that I know of, anyway."

Her smile turned impish. "That was an interesting day, wasn't it? I just thought you should be aware someone was trying to contact you."

"Thank you, Mrs. W. I'll be on the lookout."

After exchanging pleasantries, we parted. I mounted the steps to my front porch and paused to enjoy the welcoming aroma of tea roses my late mother planted. No evidence of a note on the door or in the mailbox. That meant the mysterious biker would probably return. I went inside and forgot the matter as I removed one of Paul's casseroles from the fridge and got out a pan of rolls. I enjoyed their yeasty aroma almost as much as I liked their yeasty taste. Our household mantra was Paul Barton, freelance journalist, whips up gourmet meals; B. J. Vinson, former Marine and ex-cop turned confidential investigator, burns toast.

We planned to stay home tonight and watch an episode of a new gumshoe program on the tube called The Glades. Matt Passmore, the guy who played the detective, was a way-cool customer who Paul claimed should be my role model. I'd no sooner set the dishes to heating than a rumble on the street caught my attention. A moment later the doorbell rang.

I turned off the stove and opened the door to reveal a tall raven-haired Navajo with high cheekbones. It took a moment to recognize the good-looking guy. "Henry Secatero, as I live and breathe."

His deep voice came up out of his nether regions. "Wasn't sure you'd remember me."

"How could I forget the guys who helped me solve a case. Is Jazz with you?" His quick frown told me he was about to deliver bad news. "Come on in."

We settled in the den with a couple of jiggers of scotch. He laid what appeared to be a sleeve for a laptop computer on the floor beside the chair and took a sip before speaking. "Jazz is gone."

"Gone?" My hand tightened on the rocks glass halfway to my mouth. That free spirit was too young and lively to be… gone. "You mean—"

"Naw, not hit the dust. Just disappeared. Poof. And that ain't like Jazz."

Jasper Penrod, who dubbed himself Jazz as soon as he was old enough, was Henry's mixed-blood half-brother. The two helped me solve a case I mentally called the Bisti Business up in the Four Corners area three years ago.

I rubbed my chin, trying to recall what I knew of Jazz's situation. "Are you sure? Way I understand it, he spends some of his time on the Navajo Reservation and some in Farmington. Hard to keep track of him."

"Yeah, he bounces around, but he don't go outa touch for long. He calls me regular-like. If he can't reach me on my cell, he leaves a message at the chapter house. I didn't get worried until I saw his Uncle Riley in

Farmington and found out Jazz hadn't called him or his mother either. Been three… four weeks since anybody heard from him."

"Do you have any idea why?"

"Not sure, but this might have something to do with it." Henry leaned over and picked up the canvas case. He hesitated after pulling out an Acer laptop computer. "Man, I sure hate to show you this."

My raised eyebrows probably expressed my surprise better than my spoken "Why?"

"You'll see a Jazz you ain't seen before. Hell, I ain't seen before. You gotta understand. Jazz being like he is—you know, gay and all—it's not easy for him up in Farmington. When he was growing up, he didn't mind casual… affairs, I guess you'd say. Until he saw what you and Paul had together, he didn't believe nobody was out there for him. Permanent, I mean." Sweat formed on Henry's upper lip, attesting to how hard talking about his brother's homosexuality was.

I called to mind an image of the uncommonly handsome, unabashedly gay, and friendly-as-a-puppy-dog kid I'd come to admire. All his life he maneuvered successfully in an environment of miners and oil field workers normally hostile to his lifestyle, thanks in large part to the aggressive protection provided by Henry, their Navajo father Louie, and Jazz's Anglo Uncle Riley.

Henry drew a deep breath and let it out. "Anyway, he started looking for a steady. Someone he could build something with. And there wasn't nobody in Farmington. Nobody he could attach to, at any rate. Not on the rez neither. He'd try with this guy or that but didn't find what he was looking for." Henry gave an insincere laugh. "Jazz looking like he does, lotsa guys you wouldn't expect would go with him for a while. Some might even have stuck, but they wasn't what he was looking for." Henry's face twisted in perplexity. "You want the truth? I think he was looking for another you. He really dug you."

"There was never anything between—"

He waved a hand. "I know. He told me he offered, and you said you already had somebody. That really impressed him. That's what he was looking for. A guy who'd turn down an offer because they belonged to him." Henry ran an agitated hand through thick black hair. "Aw, I'm screwing this up. All I'm saying is he was looking for love. Just like I do, but on the other side of the bed."

"You're doing fine. Tell me something. What do you really think about your brother being gay? I know you won't stand for people picking on him, but how do you feel about it down deep?"

"I don't understand it. I look at a guy—hell, I look at you—and ask myself, what would Jazz see?" Henry shrugged. "He'd see mutton stew while I see butter squash. Sometimes I sorta understand when I remember that it's the same as me looking at a woman. At least to him, it is."

Despite just being called butter squash, I nodded. "Now show me what you came to show me."

He fired up the laptop and stared at the blank screen as the device went through its booting up process. "How'd you get his password?" I asked as we waited.

"It's taped on the back of the computer. Jazz was private... but not secretive, I guess you'd say. I felt like shit going through his stuff," he added in a low voice. "But I'm glad I did. I found these."

He handed over the machine. Jazz used AOL.com for his email, and Henry went to the Sent section to select a message. "That's the first one I found. After you read it, scroll up to the next one. Jeez, I need to go for a walk or something while you do that. Okay?"

"Leave the door unlocked. Just come in when you work it off."

Henry had selected the first email message where his brother responded to a contact from someone named Juan. They apparently connected through a site called nm.lonelyguys.com. Unwilling to switch back and forth between Jazz's Sent and Trash containers, I searched his My Folders until I spotted one labeled Juan. Upon opening that file, I found messages between the two stretching back about four months and ending five weeks ago, right after they exchanged Skype addresses. The pair started off using Aesopian language, but as time went one, they became more direct.

The first photograph in the email file was a bust shot of Juan showing an attractive, smiling Hispanic on the shy side of thirty with a white blaze in his dark hair. He wore a bright yellow polo shirt. Jazz responded with a photo of himself standing beside the old '91 Jeep Wrangler ragtop I'd helped him buy during the Bisti case. He wore a pair of walking shorts and a blue sleeveless pullover that clearly showed his six-pack.

Juan responded with a request for a head shot, a close-up to see if he was as "beautiful as he seemed to be." Jazz's next photo was a wowser, as I used to say when I was a kid. Jazz qualified as stunningly handsome, and the camera wallowed in it. The half-dozen messages led me right where I feared this was going. Juan's second photo was without a shirt. Jazz matched it. Long before I reached the modest naked and the stark-naked shots, I knew what had happened to Jazz Penrod. The internet swept him into a sex ring. Grateful his brother was out walking off his frustration, I considered my conclusion for a minute before acceptance came. The Jazz I knew was open and honest, and if you couldn't take him the way he was, he'd write you off. He wasn't venal. Money had its place, but it wasn't that important to him.

When Henry returned, I set aside the laptop

He balked at my conclusion. "No way! Jazz ain't... whata you call it? Promiscuous. He had sex with guys, but he didn't spread it all over the place. He wouldn't go to bed with nobody he didn't like."

"Which is why this Juan—probably not his real name—took his time. He reeled Jazz in like a deep-diving trout... playing him and teasing him until he landed him. As soon as Jazz sent him his first picture, Juan knew he had a winner. So he played him, feeding him more and more. That's what the pictures were all about. Getting Jazz to commit deeper and deeper to what he thought was a kindred soul."

Henry poked a finger at the Acer. "Some of them emails do tell me Jazz was getting to like the guy. When you get to the end of them, you can see where they talked about meeting here in Albuquerque. At someplace called Robinson Park."

"Then they went to Skype, and we don't know what they talked about after that because they were talking face-to-face with cameras and mikes," I said.

"Where's Robinson Park?"

"It's a city park in the southeast section. Lots of big trees. They could sit and talk without being bothered. It looks like he might have come to Albuquerque to meet the guy."

"That don't hold water. I'm worried, man. He wouldn't go this long without getting in touch with none of us."

I studied Henry. "You know what puzzles me? Jazz once said wasn't usually attracted to people who looked like him. You know, black hair, brown eyes."

"This Juan guy has a big white streak in his hair. Maybe that's enough to make him different."

"Maybe. But it's more likely the butterfly effect."

"Huh?"

"Small things leading to big changes. Juan devoted the time necessary to snag Jazz's attention. In some of those messages, they talked about what they liked and disliked. But if you noticed, Juan asked and Jazz answered.

And then, of course, Juan liked everything Jazz did. One small step led to another until Jazz finally took the bait and came to Albuquerque."

Henry bounced out of the chair and stalked the den stiff-legged. "But if it's what you say, if he's been tricked into a sex ring, why does he stay? He don't look all muscled up, but that boy can fight when he wants to. How come he don't just take to the road?"

He wasn't going to like my answer, but before I could deliver it, Paul came through the back door and yelled a greeting.

Don Travis is a man totally captivated by his adopted state of New Mexico. Each of his B. J. Vinson mystery novels features some region of the state as prominently as it does his protagonist, a gay ex-Marine, ex-cop turned confidential investigator. Don never made it to the Marines (three years in the Army was all he managed) and certainly didn't join the Albuquerque Police Department. He thought he was a paint artist for a while, but ditched that for writing a few years back. A loner, he fulfills his social needs by attending SouthWest Writers meetings and teaching a weekly writing class at an Albuquerque community center.

Facebook: Don Travis
Twitter: @dontravis3

THE
ZOZOBRA
INCIDENT

A BJ VINSON MYSTERY

DON TRAVIS

A BJ Vinson Mystery

B. J. Vinson is a former Marine and ex-Albuquerque PD detective turned confidential investigator. Against his better judgment, BJ agrees to find the gay gigolo who was responsible for his breakup with prominent Albuquerque lawyer Del Dahlman and recover some racy photographs from the handsome bastard. The assignment should be fast and simple.

But it quickly becomes clear the hustler isn't the one making the anonymous demands, and things turn deadly with a high-profile murder at the burning of Zozobra on the first night of the Santa Fe Fiesta. BJ's search takes him through virtually every stratum of Albuquerque and Santa Fe society, both straight and gay. Before it is over, BJ is uncertain whether Paul Barton, the young man quickly insinuating himself in BJ's life, is friend or foe. But he knows he's stepped into something much more serious than a modest blackmail scheme. With Paul and BJ next on the killer's list, BJ must find a way to put a stop to the death threats once and for all.

www.dsppublications.com

THE
BISTI
BUSINESS

A BJ VINSON MYSTERY

DON TRAVIS

A BJ Vinson Mystery

Although repulsed by his client, an overbearing, homophobic California wine mogul, confidential investigator B. J. Vinson agrees to search for Anthony Alfano's missing son, Lando, and his traveling companion—strictly for the benefit of the young men. As BJ chases an orange Porsche Boxster all over New Mexico, he soon becomes aware he is not the only one looking for the distinctive car. Every time BJ finds a clue, someone has been there before him. He arrives in Taos just in time to see the car plunge into the 650-foot-deep Rio Grande Gorge. Has he failed in his mission?

Lando's brother, Aggie, arrives to help with BJ's investigation, but BJ isn't sure he trusts Aggie's motives. He seems to hold power in his father's business and has a personal stake in his brother's fate that goes beyond familial bonds. Together they follow the clues scattered across the Bisti/De-Na-Zin Wilderness area and learn the bloodshed didn't end with the car crash. As they get closer to solving the mystery, BJ must decide whether finding Lando will rescue the young man or place him directly in the path of those who want to harm him.

www.dsppublications.com

![THE CITY OF ROCKS](A BJ VINSON MYSTERY)

THE CITY OF ROCKS

A BJ VINSON MYSTERY

DON TRAVIS

A BJ Vinson Mystery

Confidential investigator B. J. Vinson thinks it's a bad joke when Del Dahlman asks him to look into the theft of a duck… a duck named Quacky Quack the Second and insured for $250,000. It ceases to be funny when the young thief dies in a suspicious truck wreck. The search leads BJ and his lover, Paul Barton, to the sprawling Lazy M Ranch in the Bootheel country of southwestern New Mexico bordering the Mexican state of Chihuahua.

A deadly game unfolds when BJ and Paul are trapped in a weird rock formation known as the City of Rocks, an eerie array of frozen magma that is somehow at the center of the entire scheme. But does the theft of Quacky involve a quarter-million-dollar duck-racing bet between the ranch's owner and a Miami real estate developer, or someone attempting to force the sale of the Lazy M because of its proximity to an unfenced portion of the Mexican border? BJ and Paul go from the City of Rocks to the neon lights of Miami and back again in pursuit of the answer… death and danger tracking their every step.

www.dsppublications.com

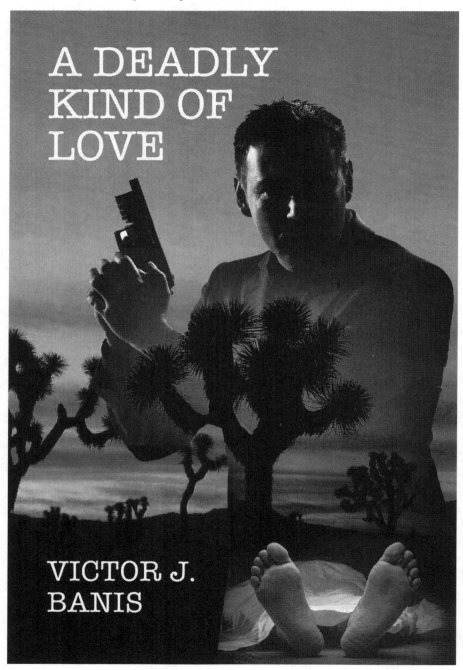

A DEADLY
KIND OF
LOVE

VICTOR J.
BANIS

A Tom and Stanley Mystery

Nothing bad is supposed to happen in Palm Springs.

At least that's what San Francisco private detective Tom Danzel and his partner Stanley Korski believe. But when their friend Chris finds a dead body in his hotel room bed, Tom and Stanley drive out to help the local police investigate.

What they discover is a rather nasty green snake and an elegant hotel that offers delicacies not usually found on a room service menu. As the body count increases, the two detectives are going to have to rely on their skills and each other if they're going to survive this very deadly kind of love.

www.dsppublications.com

SOUTHERNMOST
MURDER
C.S. POE

Aubrey Grant lives in the tropical paradise of Old Town, Key West, has a cute cottage, a sweet moped, and a great job managing the historical property of a former sea captain. With his soon-to-be-boyfriend, hotshot FBI agent Jun Tanaka, visiting for a little R&R, not even Aubrey's narcolepsy can put a damper on their vacation plans.

But a skeleton in a closet of the Smith Family Historical Home throws a wrench into the works. Despite Aubrey and Jun's attempts to enjoy some time together, the skeleton's identity drags them into a mystery with origins over a century in the past. They uncover a tale of long-lost treasure, the pirate king it belonged to, and a modern-day murderer who will stop at nothing to find the hidden riches. If a killer on the loose isn't enough to keep Aubrey out of the mess, it seems even the restless spirit of Captain Smith is warning him away.

The unlikely partnership of a special agent and historian may be exactly what it takes to crack this mystery wide-open and finally put an old Key West tragedy to rest. But while Aubrey tracks down the X that marks the spot, one wrong move could be his last.

www.dsppublications.com